HIDDEN WIVES

HIDDEN WIVES

Claire Avery

FORGE®

A TOM DOHERTY ASSOCIATES BOOK

New York

HIDDEN WIVES

Copyright © 2010 by Claire Avery

All rights reserved.

A Forge Book
Published by Tom Doherty Associates, LLC
175 Fifth Avenue
New York, NY 10010

www.tor-forge.com

Forge® is a registered trademark of Tom Doherty Associates, LLC.

ISBN 978-0-7653-2689-8

First Edition: June 2010

Printed in the United States of America

0 9 8 7 6 5 4 3 2 1

To all the victims of polygamy

Acknowledgments

We owe a huge debt of gratitude to our editor, Kristin Sevick. Her brilliant insights, enthusiasm, and unerring instincts have helped shape this book in so many ways. We'd also like to thank our amazing publisher, the legendary Tom Doherty. In addition, we could never have gotten here without the help of our friend and dream-maker, Bill Fawcett. His determination and candid advice were invaluable. We want to express our deepest thanks to our good friend, author Teresa Patterson, for opening that first critical door for us. Thanks to NaNá V. Stoelzle, who did a superb copyediting job. We'd also like to acknowledge the extraordinary marketing team at Forge for their faith in the book. We recognize that many people at Forge helped see the book through the publication process and beyond, and we are deeply grateful for all their help.

So many individuals were instrumental in helping us while we researched and wrote on the subject of polygamy. We are so grateful to author Andrea Moore-Emmett with Tapestry Against Polygamy for answering our many questions about polygamy. Author Irene Spencer deserves special mention for her kind words and her incredibly inspirational story. Thanks also to Elaine Tyler with the HOPE Organization for all the tireless work she does for victims of polygamy. We also want to acknowledge Vicky Prunty with Tapestry Against Polygamy for her bravery, her words of encouragement, and her devotion to the cause.

And finally, with deepest gratitude to each and every member of our family: their infinite understanding and support were essential during our writing journey. We love all of you so much.

HIDDEN WIVES

ONE

For as long as Sara could remember, she jolted awake every morning, startled to be alive. Whenever her father looked at her, she imagined him calculating the width of her neck and the degree of pressure he would have to exert in order to snap it. This preoccupation with her own demise had become a morbid distraction, preventing her from planning her life further ahead than minute by minute. Yet somehow those minutes had stacked up over the past fifteen years, propelling her to this day.

Waiting by her father's dilapidated truck, Sara shivered despite stagnant desert air that had choked the valley for months. Swallowing hard, she fixed her gaze on the temple with its starchy white bell tower etched across the burnt umber of the foothills. It stood in reverent splendor and jarring contrast to the chalky aluminum meeting hall where Prophet Silver would soon decide whom she would marry.

Sara eyed movement behind the dirty mesh of the screen door leading into their home. Rachel emerged from the house with a bounce to her step. "Ready?"

Sara nodded, overwhelmed by Rachel's beauty and excitement. If only she could borrow a little of both, then perhaps she wouldn't feel so doomed.

Their father surged through the back door, followed by a swarm of women and children. He pecked the cheeks of the four women and ruffled the heads of the toddlers. Approaching the truck, he actually smiled. It was a big, toothy grin that split his cheeks in two like a cracked egg. He flung open the passenger door and the two sisters piled in.

"You girls need to pray," he ordered, thrusting the truck into reverse and throwing an arm across the seat as he pivoted to look behind him. "Ready your hearts and minds to receive Prophet Silver's words with humility."

Sara closed her eyes to pray, but she was disturbed by her father's presence. He smelled like skewered beef and heavy grease, the stench originating from the goop he applied to his hair every morning. Despite the gel, the hair behind his ears flipped outward, reminding Sara of the headgear on a ram.

The car shot forward on the gravel road.

Sara's stomach pitched. This was *it*. She cast a glance toward her sister, who had immediately bowed her head and closed her eyes. Sara did the same, but not a single prayer came into her mind. It was rumored that the prophet could peer into a soul and pluck out the one thing a sinner was most intent on hiding. That alone should jump-start the prayers, but it didn't. Sara pressed her leg against Rachel's and was comforted by the reassuring pressure back. Maybe she wasn't praying either.

Planters filled with an assortment of spiky cacti, some as big as bathtubs, marked the entrance to the meeting hall. Thin, gun slit–shaped windows straddled the doorway of the metal building.

Sara followed Rachel and her father on wobbly legs. The foyer was deserted and their steps echoed in the empty building as they made their way to the prophet's office.

The prophet was an elderly man, yet he exuded a youthful energy and an intensity that seized Sara in the gut. Taller than her father's six feet, he loomed large with his lumpy nose and square jaw. Hard, gray eyes were crosshatched with seventy years' worth of wrinkles. She had never been this close to him. It felt both humbling and frightening. Sara wanted to bolt for the door.

"Good to see you again, Brother Abraham," Silver said, briskly shaking their father's hand.

"We're honored to be here."

Silver turned toward them. "It's not every day my office is graced with such lovely young ladies." Sara flushed at the moist palms she presented. His eyes barely brushed hers before moving to Rachel. Wrapping two massive hands around hers, he held them while soaking up her beauty. "You must be Rachel."

"Yes, sir." Rachel kept her head down. Sara watched in horror as the prophet wrenched her chin up with his forefinger, forcing her to maintain eye contact. He was the closest person to God that Sara had ever met, and yet all she wanted to do was shield Rachel from his penetrating gaze.

"You will look at me when I address you."

Sara held her breath. She knew what an effort it was for Rachel to maintain eye contact with any adult, much less the Chosen One.

"Yes, sir," Rachel whispered. She cleared her throat, and spoke louder. "I'm sorry, sir."

"Good girls submit and receive blessings. Willful girls rebel and are cursed," the prophet said. "Do you choose total submission over rebellion, blessings over curses, the Celestial Kingdom over hell? Will you submit to the divine authority deeded to me by the heavenly Father in the Law of Placing?"

"I do," said Rachel. He dropped his hands, turning to look at Sara.

She echoed Rachel's proclamation, but the words rang hollow in her ears. She didn't care who the prophet had chosen for her. Her future consisted of minute-by-minute survival, and that was all.

Still, a bubble of curiosity percolated in her chest.

"Good." The prophet smiled paternally. "Please take your seats."

Several maroon leather chairs were arranged in front of an enormous mahogany desk. Walking behind it, Prophet Silver took a seat and shuffled papers. Sara's upper lip went numb as it did when she was frightened.

The prophet cleared his throat, picked up a pair of glasses and settled them low on his nose. "Now to business."

He looked down at a sheet of paper on his desk, then back up, catching Sara and her sister under his penetrating stare. "The two of you will become the mothers of our future priesthood holders. Perhaps your own sons will be called to a position of great authority on the Ruling Council. That is an enormous responsibility, and one that I do not take lightly when placing girls in a blessed union. Normally, my role is straightforward. As a girl comes of age, a member of the community will come to me with a testimony asking for the hand of that girl. I then pray for guidance and will receive an answer from the Almighty."

Sara sensed her father's movement as he nodded in agreement with the prophet's words.

Prophet Silver continued, "Sometimes, the Lord speaks to me immediately, and the couple becomes sealed for all eternity within weeks of the initial testimony of marriage. Other times, the Lord has different plans that may take months or even years before divine inspiration is received."

Sara suppressed a nervous smile. She thought of a few of those girls whom no man had ever received a testimony to marry. There was Henny Reynolds, a woman well into her twenties, who had been born with a severe limb deformity that caused her arms to resemble two tiny chicken feet. Julia Walker, a friend of their mothers, had scaly skin that rose from the collar of her dress and wrapped around her neck like a reptilian choker. Several other girls came to mind, all suffering from some affliction or another and all of whom remained single.

Prophet Silver leaned back in his chair and plucked the glasses off his nose. Looking right at Rachel, he said, "You're approaching your sixteenth year and still have not been placed. Sara is several months younger than you, but she must wait until you make your endowment before she too can be married." The prophet stroked his chin. "However, a situation has developed that will further delay your endowment."

Sara darted a quick look at Rachel, whose bottom lip had begun to tremble. She wanted to reach out and grasp Rachel's hand to steady her.

"We've had sixteen testimonies from various members of the community." The prophet leaned back.

Sara thought she might be sick. She pressed her index finger against her upper lip, testing its obedience.

"You mean to tell me," Father said, "that sixteen men have received testimony for Rachel?"

"Correct," Prophet Silver said. "And to complicate matters, several of these revelations have come from very holy men that sit on the Council."

Father leaned forward. "Who are these brothers?"

"That is not your concern." The prophet picked up the pages and slid them into a folder. "The problem is that you waited until your daughters were fifteen before seeking my guidance. Most men consult with me when their girls reach the age of preparedness at thirteen."

"But the obligation only says I need to bring them no later than fifteen."

"True, but not when you have a daughter such as Rachel who is exceptionally blessed."

Dread settled in Sara's stomach. Sara was a little surprised at his use of the word "blessed" to describe her sister's beauty. Whenever a woman was called blessed, it was always in reference to her fertility.

Rachel's beauty had impacted her own family all her life. She had thick chestnut hair, sea green eyes that blazed gold in certain lights and a sweet nature that inspired love and rage in equal parts from those who lived with her. The children all adored her, but the mothers occasionally treated Rachel as a threat. It was her father's anger, however, that most concerned Sara. As Rachel's beauty grew, so did their father's rage.

Father cleared his throat. "What am I supposed to do?"

"The Lord has special plans for your daughter. I didn't realize it

until I saw her. I must pray about this before I make any decision."
Prophet Silver cleared his throat and turned to Rachel. "Obviously,
there is something about you that has caused these men to confuse
their desires for divine intercessions. Have you in some manner
enticed these men?"

Rachel shook her head in a slow, ambiguous way.

"That remains to be seen." Prophet Silver turned to their father.
"I need to see Rachel privately in my office to discuss this matter
further. Is this acceptable to you?"

"Of course." Her father's voice sounded defeated as he squirmed
in his seat. "What about my younger girl? Don't she have to wait
'til Rachel is placed?"

Sara held her breath. For the first time in weeks, she felt hope.
Perhaps she would have time to finish school before making her
marriage covenant.

"Walter Merrick has received the testimony for her hand. I
prayed about it and God ordained that Sara will belong to Brother
Walter."

Sara clenched her teeth to bite back a scream. Suddenly the room
seemed smaller and the air stingier. She grasped the arms of the
chair as though readying herself for flight. Only there was nowhere
to run.

"After Rachel is married, Sara will follow suit. In the meantime," Prophet Silver turned to Sara, "consider yourself engaged."

"But he's my . . ." Sara's heart pummeled against her chest. Her
tongue tangled before she could get the rest of her protest out.

"Do you dare question the will of the Lord?"

"No, sir, no . . ." Even though it had been an hour since she'd
eaten, Sara's lunch crawled back up her throat. She looked at Rachel,
whose features were clenched in a silent plea, imploring her not to
challenge him. Suddenly the words her mother gave her came to
her. "I . . . I'm filled with gratitude for my heavenly placement."

"Good. You will be blessed in this union."

She had no choice but to accept the dictates of the prophet. She would marry her father's half-brother. Even death would offer her no reprieve, because once she became sealed to her uncle in the temple, the bond survived the grave. She would become her uncle's wife for all eternity.

"Well," the prophet said, brushing the folder aside, "I think we've had a very fortuitous meeting." He seemed to be enjoying himself, as if destroying her life was entertainment. His head pivoted toward Rachel. "I'll be in touch." His eyes traveled from the tips of Rachel's feet all the way up to her face. His expression troubled Sara. He didn't seem concerned with her sister's salvation, but with something else. Sara wrapped her arms around her middle. An incredible sense of loss welled in her, bleak and suffocating. Their childhoods were over.

Her father held the door open for the girls, allowing them to exit ahead of him. The gesture, full of innocence, waved a red flag in Sara's brain. As they climbed into the truck, Sara pulled Rachel close to her side. Her entire body braced against the unspoken threat.

He closed the door, gently, and then spun around with hands that came out swinging. They connected with Rachel's tender face, and his words were sharp and stinging like the needle teeth of a piranha. "You filthy whore!" He grabbed a fistful of hair and jerked her head back. "How dare you throw yourself around this community like a slut? Even the most holy of men have been tempted by your ways!"

"I'm sorry . . ." Rachel held up her arms in a defensive posture. "I didn't mean anything."

"You never mean nothing." He released her hair, yanked the gearshift and threw the truck into reverse. It backed away from the parking spot, moving surprisingly slow considering all the rage flying around the interior of the cab. When they turned the corner, her father gunned the engine, causing the wheels to spin out and spit gravel. They shot down the road.

"I must look like a father who can't control his own daughter.

You've shamed this family, and dragged my good name through the filth!" He slammed a fist against the steering wheel.

Sara plastered herself against the door of the cab, pulling her sister as close to her as possible. She took both of Rachel's hands, feeling the tremors course through her body. Sara knew she should say something to defend her, but she couldn't. It was almost as though she was flying outside her body, riding shotgun with these two strange girls who were being screamed at. She pinched her arm hard, trying to bring herself back to the moment.

"You know what the prophet said back there?" His voice had that dangerous tone to it. The one that caused the air to settle around Sara's feet like a sullen mist. "He was saying that I don't have control over my hussy daughter who's out there tempting the most holy of men."

"Father, I'm sorry."

"Sorry? You'll be sorry when I finish with you."

THEY had arrived home to a festive dinner. An elaborate three-tier lemon cake that Sara's mother, Anna, no doubt had baked, presided triumphantly in the middle of the table. Anna loved to bake, and it was one of the few times Sara would see a genuine smile pierce her mother's thin lips. But there was no celebration. The mothers bustled about, their faces tightening with anxiety as Father refused to tell them anything about the meeting. They dared not press him. Pure torment gripped Sara as she waited for Rachel to reemerge from the whipping shed. It seemed incredible to her that life transpired within the household. Shouldn't alarms be ringing or prayers rushed to heaven while Rachel was being beaten? Instead, the home pulsed with the electrified chatter of her mothers, the whinnies of small voices trickling down from the boys' bedroom and the clatter of dishes that were shunted from table to sink where Sara worked.

Through Sara's little window, she watched the sickle-shaped moon brighten as the sun bled into the night. It enraged Sara that nobody, not even nature itself, cared what was happening to Rachel.

"Sara Anne, I am speaking to you!"

Sara jumped, nearly losing hold of a dish. She turned to look at Mother Marylee, her father's first wife, a broad-hipped, thick-lipped woman who birthed Rachel, along with Rowan, Russell and Rudy. Sara secretly called her the Queen since she threw her power around and actually considered herself to be the most blessed since she was his first wife. In Sara's eyes, the Queen had just married misery before the other three wives did.

"I'm sorry, I was just daydreaming."

"I know what you were doing." Mother Marylee nodded in the direction of the woodshed. "And you better stop doing it and pay attention to those dishes before you break something. Understand?" She planted another stack of dessert dishes on the counter.

"I'll be more careful."

Sara turned back toward the sink and immersed her hands in the oily water, but Mother Marylee stayed put. Her voice turned light and conversational. "So, what happened at the meeting?"

Sara could feel hot stares on her. Her back pinged as though assaulted by a thousand needle pricks. She pulled her shoulders together as though readying herself for a thump on the back of her head.

"It was all so strange," Mother Marylee continued. "Your father wouldn't even so much as look at the celebratory cake we made special. What did that girl do to get his ire up?"

That girl, Sara wanted to say, *is your daughter and she has a name.* Instead, Sara swallowed her anger and turned around to face Mother Marylee. "Nothing. Rachel did absolutely nothing."

"I don't believe that for a minute."

"It's true. It just all got mixed up." Sara turned back to the sink and dropped her hands into the oily water.

"What do you mean, mixed up?"

Sara blew air toward her eyes, trying to stop them from filling with tears.

"Answer me!"

"I'm . . . I belong to Uncle Walter." Sara glanced at Mother Marylee. For a split second, only a small comma-shaped curve at the corner of Marylee's mouth revealed her satisfaction.

She nodded. "He's a good man. You should be grateful. We'll plan an engagement party next year when he gets back from his mission."

Murmurs of congratulations came from behind her. Her stomach rollicked and the tears welled up. They smelled of salt. She batted them back. At least her *betrothed* was out of town for a while. Reality sank to her stomach. She would become a mother to her cousins and a wife to her uncle.

"And Rachel?" Marylee asked.

"The prophet doesn't know yet."

"What? You mean you're to marry before Rachel?"

"No. It's just that sixteen men have received testimonies for celestial marriage with Rachel."

Marylee's eyes brightened a notch, but her features remained impassive. Sara continued, "Prophet Silver said that he needs to pray about it."

"Sixteen?" Sara's birth mother asked.

Shaking her hands off, Sara grabbed the dish towel and turned around to face her birth mother. "Yes. And several of the testimonies were from apostles."

Mother Marylee plopped into a kitchen chair as though the weight of the situation had knocked her off her feet. "Oh my word."

Twenty-one-year-old Mother Jane hoisted baby Alice onto her lap. The baby shoved the end of her mother's thin brown braid into her mouth and chomped contentedly.

The newest mother, Esther, turned to Marylee and said, "What does this all mean?" Esther had been raised as a traditional Mormon. She was smart and funny but less attractive than the other mothers. She had told Sara that Father had been her "first love." Esther had been driving home from work at the nearby Wal-Mart when her car broke down. Sara's father helped fix her tire and within a month she was sealed in marriage to Abraham as his fourth wife.

Marylee paced the floor with beefy thighs that slapped together with each step. She stopped to rub both cheeks with the flats of her hands. "I don't know. I've never heard of such a thing."

"That's why Father's taken her to the shed. He says that she's being a whore."

Marylee stopped pacing. Sara couldn't make out her features because her back was to her. Sara continued, "It's not fair. Rachel is so quiet and shy."

"Do not question your father's authority!" Marylee spun around to face her. "She must have done something to get this beating."

"Nothing."

"It's because we kept them in that public school last year," Sara's mother said, propping her elbows out so that her hands were wedged on her waist. Anna was all bones and sharp angles, and her clipped voice mirrored her eaglelike appearance. She had also birthed Sara's younger brothers, Seth and Sammy. Rachel's full brothers were all given "R" names, and Mother Jane's kids' names started with "A." Father created that naming system to remember which kid belonged to which mother.

"Rachel must have received too much attention from the boys at school and has learned the sin of vanity," Marylee said. "And who knows what else from the godless."

Esther pivoted to face her. "Sister Marylee, you know that the school is at least a third full of Blood of the Lamb members. It's hardly godless."

Mother Esther had been the one responsible for cobbling together another year of high school for Rachel and Sara. "Besides, Rachel never calls attention to herself."

"I don't care if that school was populated one hundred percent by the community kids," Marylee continued. "School officials still would force them to park their beliefs at the door and learn about the history of the Gentiles."

"It's called separation of church and state. I'm not saying it's right, but they have to obey the law," Esther said.

"The only law our children have to obey is the Lord's." Marylee snuffled with righteousness.

"They do have to function in the real world, you know," Esther said.

Sara could have heard a pin drop in the kitchen. Turning back to the sink, she covered up the silence by rattling some silverware. She was grateful for Mother Esther's defense of public school, but by doing so she had made a bad situation worse.

Mother Esther didn't grow up a fundamentalist Mormon, and even though she converted, the other mothers never really trusted her. They had been taught all their lives that outsiders such as non-fundamentalist Mormons and Gentiles belonged to Satan.

Mother Marylee stood up. "How dare you! You're responsible for this mess to begin with."

"Responsible? How could I be responsible that men desire Rachel?" Esther sounded brave but had taken several steps away from Marylee.

"How dare you insult the intentions of these holy men!"

Esther snorted. "Holy? Horny is more like it."

Sara didn't know what "horny" meant. Mother Jane strode over to Mother Esther and slapped her solidly across the face. "How dare you!"

Mother Esther cupped her face, gaping at her sister-wives in shocked silence.

"Sara, get out of the kitchen now!" Mother Marylee screeched.

"But the dishes . . ."

"Now!"

Sara slapped her hands on the towel and rushed out the door.

Ignoring her brothers' pleas to come and play, Sara continued up the stairs that led to the room she shared with Rachel. The attic was dark, with only thin cracks of evening light spilling around the towel that hung over the small window. Sara crouched to her knees and pushed the towel aside. With a quick swipe from her sleeve, Sara removed the condensation that gauzed the attic window: a product of a swamp cooler that was overburdened in the August heat.

She scrutinized the whipping shed. Clusters of pine trees towered above it, and a gust of wind fanned the evergreens, moving their needles like streamers across the metal rooftop.

The roar from a lone car echoing off the foothills pierced the whir of the swamp cooler fan. Sara wished she were in that car. She didn't care with whom or where they were going, but it had to be better than here.

The condensation was filming the window again. As she lifted her sleeve to wipe it, she noticed the door to the shed had swung open. Sara released the towel, careful not to draw his attention up to her window.

Sara's ears pricked from the rasp of the door latch moving stealthily across its cradle. Soft steps climbed the stairs. Their eyes met briefly in the dark before Rachel eased herself onto the mattress.

"Are you okay? Can I get you something?"

Rachel buried her face in the mattress. Sara wanted to reach out and cradle her sister, but she was afraid to. Instead, she studied her, looking for any exposed flesh that would indicate the degree of hurt. Her long skirt was pulled down to the top of her feet, which were clad in thick gray stockings. One loafer was partially suspended from her foot, the other lay on the floor.

Sara couldn't find a single thing to say that would comfort her. A surge of anger quickened her pulse and curled her fingers into knotted fists. It was a sin to question the decisions of the priesthood holder in the family, but the way he treated Rachel didn't make sense.

She suddenly felt sorry for herself. "How come you get sixteen proposals, and I get Uncle Walter?"

Rachel sucked air, shaking her head. "I don't know . . ."

"Why couldn't I look like you?"

Rachel's head tilted in disbelief. "Why would you ever want to? You're much prettier than I am."

"Come on, I look like a horse."

Everything about Sara was too long including her legs, arms and face. Being razor-blade thin didn't exactly enhance her looks. She knew that she was not the beauty in the family, and even though she was grateful that she at least had a brain in good working order, she wished it was housed in a more attractive package.

She longed to be petite. Instead, she was only an inch shorter than her father and slid her feet into size-eleven shoes that clomped around, attracting unwanted attention. Although they made nearly all their own clothes, the community's dry goods store didn't stock women's shoes that large, and her family refused to patronize the town's Gentile-run shoe stores. Sara was forced to wear men's shoes. She cringed at the absurd combination of prairie dresses and black lace-up work boots.

Her sister, on the other hand, was put together with a symmetry that bordered on the divine.

Sara sighed. "Is today for real? Or is this all a dream?"

"It was all too real."

"I can't believe I have to marry Uncle Walter."

"You need to pray for acceptance," Rachel said automatically. "This is a divine order from God."

"So how do you explain the fact that there are currently sixteen divine orders from God, all of them contradicting the previous one, and all claiming a testimony for a celestial marriage to you?"

Rachel was silent for a moment. "I don't know."

"I do. Just watch. Prophet Silver will get his own revelation, and you'll end up his wife, which would make you a mother to hundreds before you even turn sixteen."

"That's not going to happen." Rachel's voice pitched with rising panic. "If I was to become his wife, it seems to me he would have received a testimony by now."

"He's never seen you before today."

"What's that supposed to mean?"

Sara shrugged. "Nothing."

"Well, I'm keeping my heart open to the will of the Almighty."

Sara wished she could have the faith that Rachel had. "Well, let's hope God keeps quiet so we can have a chance to finish high school." Sara paced the room, trying to dislodge the dread that was pitching its tent in her gut. "I'll die without school."

Rachel exhaled impatiently. "No, you won't. I'm actually looking forward to getting married and having babies." Rolling onto her stomach, Rachel tucked the pillow under her chin and looked thoughtful. "Maybe I'll be a first wife."

"Wanna bet?"

"Betting is a sin. Why not? Why can't I become a first wife?"

"Because some of the testimonies came from the apostles, several of whom are ancient relics from the Stone Age."

"The what?"

"Back before cutlery was invented."

Rachel stared blankly at her.

Sara shook her head. "Forget it. The point I'm trying to make is that the apostles always get the pick of the litter and that's you."

"That's not true. You're much smarter than me and—"

"Men don't want brains, they want . . ." Sara caught Rachel's eyes for a moment as fear passed behind them. She fumbled for the right words. "They want . . . spiritual purity. A wonderful helpmate here and in the afterlife."

"But that's you."

"No." It bothered Sara that the apostles and the wealthier members always married the most beautiful girls. If marriage was supposed to be divinely ordained, why did this happen? The sacred tenets of the true Mormon faith required a man to have three wives in order to attain the "fullness of exaltation in the afterlife." But they never seemed to stop there. The prophet had at least fifty wives. Sara chewed her lip saying a quick prayer of forgiveness. She needed to stop questioning the choices of the most righteous. Questioning them was no different from questioning God.

Sara glanced at her sister. Rachel looked as troubled as Sara felt. She cleared her throat. "Oh, who knows what kind of man the Lord has in mind for you. Maybe you'll be a first wife."

Rachel was slow to react. "You just said . . ."

"I know what I just said." Grabbing a hairbrush off her nightstand, Sara methodically brushed her hair. "I'm to be cleaved for all eternity to Uncle Walter. What do I call him now? Uncle? Wally? Walt?" She lowered her head, letting the hair tumble across her face. Her strokes became harsher, and the pulling and pinching on her scalp was strangely comforting. "Do you think he's mean like Father?"

"No, of course he's not as mean as Father." Rachel sucked in her breath as she realized what she had just admitted. "Father's not mean. It's just . . . he's got a lot of responsibility. Our salvation rests on his shoulders."

Sara couldn't believe her sister could defend their father after a beating. Whenever Sara returned from a trip to the whipping shed, she cursed him in her pillow. She pounded the bed with her fists, imagining it was his face. Of course, she always prayed for forgiveness afterward. It endangered her soul to harbor such hateful thoughts toward her father.

Rachel wrapped her arms around her middle as though trying to keep herself from splitting in two. Sara swallowed the guilty knot that suddenly fisted in her throat. "Maybe your husband will be good looking and young."

"Really?"

Sara averted her gaze as she lied. "Uh-huh. Think of the benefits of being the first wife. He'll adore you and your children more than the other wives and kids. You can give thumbs-up or down to your husband's future wife choices." She hesitated, knowing the "Right of Sarah" was really more fiction than fact. It created the illusion that the first wife had a say in who would become a sister-wife, but to Sara's knowledge, no wife had ever challenged her husband's testimony. "And you'll get to take his last name, which will keep you safe from any prosecution."

Rachel flushed.

Never far from anyone's mind was the thought that the authorities might finally catch up with the families and their unlawful practices. When Sara was very young she had once told her mother, "I want to be the first wife when I grow up." Her mother had slapped her across the mouth hard. Anna told her that harboring those thoughts was selfish and wicked. She warned her that if she didn't watch it, God would punish her by placing her in the worst possible marriage: a union maligned with poverty and too many sister-wives. At first Anna's reaction had stunned her, but eventually she suspected that her mother's anger had to do with not being the first wife.

Rachel sat up. "Prayer time. We need to head downstairs for that."

"Sometimes I hate prayer time."

"Please don't talk like that."

Sara rocked on the milk crate. "It's just . . . everything's so confusing."

Rachel shook her head. "You know this is our trial."

"I know. It's just that sometimes it doesn't seem worth it." The crate slipped away and Sara slammed hard on the floor. The sharp stab at the base of her tailbone was satisfying.

"What's not worth it?"

"Going to the Celestial Kingdom, where all the wives will still live together, and you know what that means." Sara lifted herself off the floor and walked to the swamp cooler and stood in front of it. "Endless fights."

"There'll be no strife in the Celestial Kingdom. You know that, Sara."

"Do you sometimes wish we could pick our own husbands?"

"Why would I want that burden? What if I didn't understand God's intentions and made the wrong choice?"

Sara almost asked: what made Uncle Walter better qualified to know what God wanted for her life? But she bit back her words. She had no choice but to obey.

———

SARA woke up, scrubbing the sleep from her eyes. Her head was heavy with the weight of bad dreams. She cracked her lids and glanced toward the attic window where sunlight gilded the edges of the towel. She was alone. Rachel must have dressed and slipped downstairs without waking her.

Her future had been handed off torchlike from father to prophet at the meeting yesterday. Her conscious mind had not allowed her to grasp the fact that she would be marrying Uncle Walter; she just couldn't bear to think about it.

Uncle Walter possessed powerful hands that were similar to her father's. Her father's hands terrified her. The thought of those hands jolted her awake many nights, causing her to claw at the air as though it was some elusive substance that she had to catch. She didn't know if these dreams were premonitions or paranoia. Maybe it had been Uncle Walter's hands around her neck all those nights. She rolled out of bed, trying to remember how many wives her fiancé had. Three or four. It didn't matter.

She was the girl with no future.

Downstairs, Mother Esther was at the sink sniffling and Mother Marylee stormed about the kitchen as though the devil himself were nipping at her heels.

"Good morning," Sara said. "I'm sorry I wasn't here to help with breakfast."

No one acknowledged her. Sara pulled a chair out as Rudy spilled his milk. She lunged for some napkins to stop the spillage from leaking onto the floor. Mother Marylee yanked Rudy from his chair and shook him so hard that his head snapped back and forth like a marionette puppet.

"You clumsy idiot!" Marylee screamed.

"Leave him alone!" Esther said. "It was an accident."

Sara sopped up the milk with a thin, ineffective napkin. Rachel jumped up, snatched a dishrag from the sink and returned to help.

"You! You have no business interfering with the way I discipline my child!" Marylee propelled Rudy away from the table before releasing him.

"Go! Get out of here." Mother Marylee pushed his left shoulder. "All you kids go!"

Jane jumped up to usher her own children away. Sara knew she removed them to shield them from Marylee's hands, rather than the situation. She was the most protective of the mothers. Unfortunately, that protection only extended to her biological children.

Chairs scraped the linoleum as children darted from the room.

"It was not your night last night, yet you took it anyway," Marylee said to Esther.

Sara carried the soaked napkin to the trash. After depositing it, she turned to leave.

"It wasn't my idea, you know," Esther said.

Mother Marylee shot a look of pure hatred at Esther. "You're lying!"

Sara sucked in a gasp, glancing at Rachel. With a dripping dishrag in her fist, Rachel stood transfixed. Marylee no longer seemed to notice they were there, and if she didn't move a muscle, maybe she and Rachel would remain undetected.

Esther shrugged. "Just ask him." The slightest hint of a smile threatened her show of ambivalence.

"It was my night," Marylee said, spitting the words out like a bad taste.

Sara's mother stepped into the hornet's nest. "Sister Esther, I know you're still new here. But you just can't go taking another wife's night with Abraham."

"I know what the rules are, Anna. Maybe you should save the lesson for Abe."

For the second time in two days, Esther had challenged her sister-wives. Sara was astonished by her newfound brazenness. Over the months, her other mothers had whittled the newest wife down to a mere shadow of her former self. Esther had once been outspoken, and she had even worn heavy makeup, probably to cover the pockmarks that dotted her face. She initially resisted wearing the ugly dresses, even appearing in pants to the first family dinner after she and Father were sealed. Eventually, Esther gave up her makeup and the clothes of a "wanton woman" and became quiet.

Anna raised her eyebrows in her scolding way. "Oh, I'll give him a lesson all right. And it will be all about what *you* are really like." She wagged her finger in front of Esther. "You haven't fooled me one bit."

Esther's shoulders began to sag under wavering confidence. Sara stifled the urge to cheer Esther on, surprised at the total absence of loyalty toward her own mother.

"What the heck are you good for anyway?" said Mother Jane. "It's been a year, and you're still not pregnant." She rubbed her soft abdomen proudly. "I was with child by the end of our honeymoon."

Esther's face brightened. "Abe invited me to his room last night. If you girls have a problem with that then you need to take it up with him."

Mother Marylee shook a frying pan at Esther. "You listen here." Sara's heart raced. Was she really going to hurt her? "I don't believe for a minute that Abe invited you to the room. Sunday nights have always been mine. It's the holiest day of the week, and it's reserved for the first wife."

"Looks like he cancelled holy day," Esther said.

Sara watched helplessly as Marylee lunged at Esther, the frying pan swinging within inches of her head. In a split second, Anna darted behind Marylee, yanking the raised weapon out of Marylee's fist. The force of Anna's tug in the opposite direction sent the frying pan helicopter-like through the air. It crash-landed onto the massive oak table. A loose windowpane rattled in protest.

"Sister Marylee, we need to be sensible here," Anna said, as if she were reminding her to slow cook the roast, instead of reprimanding her for attempted murder.

Mother Marylee exhaled explosively. The women settled into the kind of stunned silence that came with the realization that a major catastrophe was narrowly averted.

"What's goin' on down there?" Father bellowed, his voice snaking through the air ducts.

Mother Marylee tilted her head in the direction of the stairs, listening for Father's descent. Anger lapped her features as she stepped near Esther. "If you ever pull a stunt like that again, I'll have you thrown out of *my* home. Is that clear?"

"Crystal," Esther answered, squeezing past Mother Marylee's ponderous hips. Tossing the broom and dustpan into the wedge between the fridge and countertop, she made a beeline for the adjoining living room.

"Whoa, easy there," Father said, rounding the corner into the kitchen as Esther raced out. He took a quick survey of the tension in the room, bracketing Mother Esther to him until he decided what to do next.

Sara pulled herself, chameleonlike, into the paneling, hoping he would ignore her.

"What's goin' on here?" He nudged Esther back into the kitchen.

Marylee hooked her forearm through his and pulled him toward the kitchen table. Esther slipped from his grasp and hung back in the doorway.

Anna grabbed the basket of her fresh-baked biscuits that only he would be allowed to eat. She stood there holding them out, waiting, no doubt, for the moment she could announce her gift.

"Abraham, come sit with us and have breakfast," Marylee said, in that silky voice that was reserved only for him. She stroked his black hair with one hand, while sliding a plate of eggs, scrambled with fresh tomatoes from her personal garden, in front of him. Sara thought she would vomit.

"What was all that commotion I heard down here?" He looked at each of the wives before settling on Esther. Sara could tell her mother wanted to talk about the biscuits, but now was not the right time. Anna clutched them to her chest and remained silent.

"We were so busy feeding the kids that I dropped a frying pan," Mother Marylee said.

"Is that right?" Father's eyes never left Esther's face. Esther gave him a lopsided smile that resembled a stroke victim. He seemed satisfied by it though.

Sara wanted to shake her and scream, *You almost got killed!*

He dissolved into his chair looking exhausted before he even started his workday. He closed his eyes and cracked his neck first on one side and then the other.

Stealing a glance at Rachel, Sara mouthed the words, "Let's go."

Rachel nodded, and as they inched their way nearer to the family room, Esther looked directly at them, saying, "Wait, girls."

Sara's heart sank. They had almost gotten out of there without anyone really taking notice of their presence.

Grabbing an empty juice glass from the counter and clanking it with a spoon, Mother Esther said, "I have an announcement to make."

Sara inched next to Rachel, not sure what to expect.

"I'm pregnant!"

Sara was certain Esther expected at least a token kind word, if not exactly jubilation. What she got instead was dead silence. Her smile wavered before completely dropping off her face. All eyes turned to Father. His eyes bulged and red traveled from his neck to his forehead.

"Esther! You . . . I . . . This was not the place!" Father stood up, bolted past everyone and wrenched the back door open. His steps hammered down the stairs. He was gone.

"What? Wait!" Esther wrung her hands, tears pooling in her eyes. "I don't understand." She turned to follow him and then spun back to the table where the sister-wives glowered at her.

"Congratulations," Rachel whispered.

With that one word, Rachel had placed her neck on the chopping block. Sara wished she was that brave, but her own lips had dissolved into numbness.

Esther looked around the room then burst into tears. She pushed past them, stumbling out of the kitchen.

Sara quaked with fear. Esther had no idea that she just violated the Law of Chastity. The law forbade sexual acts while expecting. Father knew of course, but that didn't stop him. Not to mention that the patriarch always announces the pending arrival of a new child.

This was war, only Esther didn't know it.

TWO

The community had outgrown their meeting hall a couple of years ago, as everyone had dutifully followed Prophet Silver's edict to create more saints. Hundreds of people crammed the hall. Some rows were populated entirely by a single family. Each family had several sister-wives, lots of kids and a lone male seated on the far right of them. Rachel's family sat at the rear of the temple, relegated there by her father's lack of prestige.

A gnarly wreath of twigs adorned the lectern, reminding Rachel of Christ's crown of thorns. As she squeezed her way into the pew, she gazed at the massive pine cross suspended from the ceiling above the lectern. It shimmered in the breeze of the air conditioner. The cross soothed her. Everything would be all right. God had a plan for her. She just had to trust Him more.

The twelve council members were seated on the elevated platform to the left of Prophet Silver. Families shuffled in as the prophet approached the podium. "Brothers and sisters, it's time to start our meeting." He nodded toward the organist to begin the opening song.

After the hymn concluded, Brother Jebediah, one of the apostles, approached the lectern. Clearing his throat, he said, "The Lord promised Abraham, Isaac, Jacob and all men who live the Principle that their seed would outnumber the stars. Husbands, if you are *true* to the Principle, your seed will populate whole worlds where you will one day rule as a god. Wives, imagine your body as an acre for a man to sow his seed. Your duty is to bear the fruit of your husband's seed."

Sara scribbled something in a pocket-sized notebook. She told her father she was taking notes on the various sermons and testimonies. Rachel knew it was her journal. Sara needed this outlet for her own peace of mind, and Rachel believed God would understand, even if their father wouldn't. Rachel picked at her cuticle, chastising herself for letting her thoughts wander.

Then she saw him. He was walking to the rear of the building near the bathrooms. Even at that distance, she saw the color of his eyes: a startling royal blue. His mouth was full and bow shaped, and it sat in sharp contrast to his high cheekbones and strong jawline. He was the most handsome boy she had ever seen.

He turned in her direction, and his eyes locked on hers. For a moment, she forgot to breathe. He stared hard at her, and just as she was about to drop her head, she caught a subtle smile curling his lips. The heat of shyness scalded her face as she fixed her gaze on the hands folded in her lap.

The assortment of testimonies following Brother Jebediah's talk merged into a blur. Rachel replayed her brief exchange with the boy. Somehow he had found her in this crowd of nearly a thousand and met her gaze. Was this a sign from God?

Prophet Silver's booming voice shattered her thoughts. Her head snapped up, just as the mysterious boy ducked into his seat . . . in the front row! "My brothers and sisters, it is my great pleasure to introduce the newest members of the Blood of the Lamb community, Brother Robert Wilkinson, his wife Elaina, and their son, Luke." Rachel wondered where the other wives and children were.

The family stood up, turning to face the crowd. "Brother Wilkinson has moved his family from Salt Lake City to be with us. We're blessed to have them join our community. He has generously offered to finance a new, state-of-the-art meeting hall." The crowd erupted in applause. The prophet raised his right hand to quiet them. "And he is relocating his construction business here to provide jobs to everyone who needs one." The crowd buzzed with excitement.

Rachel felt the enthusiasm around her as everyone—except for Sara, who still hadn't looked up from her journal—craned to get a better look at this new family. Brother Robert had an air about him of someone important. Rachel was sufficiently awed. Brother Robert smiled, waving to the congregation.

"We have all prayed such a long time for a new place to congregate, share and worship together. Now, through Brother Wilkinson's gracious gift, we will have a meeting hall befitting the Blood of the Lamb community. As you know, my brothers and sisters," his voice rippled with significance, "we are the *only* community that holds the true priesthood keys to the Celestial Kingdom."

Rachel clung to that reassurance whenever her own soul seemed in jeopardy. As long as she followed the teachings of Prophet Silver, she was assured a place in heaven.

"Of course . . ." he continued, his baritone lowering even further, "there are false prophets out there. Those with blackened hearts who will try to lead you astray." Rachel's stomach knotted. "I'm sure Brother Wilkinson has met a few of them." Brother Wilkinson nodded, mouthing a yes. "But there is no need to fear, or doubt or question anything, my brothers and sisters. For it is I who hold all the keys to the heavenly authority, and I will *never* lead you astray."

Rachel's stomach relaxed. She joined in the thunderous applause.

A shard of sunlight stabbed her eyes, as drops of sweat trickled down the nape of her neck. The crowd had bottlenecked outside the front door of the meeting hall, and Abraham maneuvered the family farther from the group and closer to their cars.

Mother Jane, in her efforts to corral Adam and Aaron, who were crawling on the ground pretending to be puppies, had put Alice down for a moment. Rachel scooped her up to keep her from being trampled.

"Ray, Ray," Alice said, burying her face in her big sister's chest. Rachel inhaled her milky baby smell. Sara's blond braid swayed with determination as she walked a good hundred feet in front of them, trying to avoid the usual, after-church small talk. In that way, Sara was like their father. They both were restless: always wanting to escape from whatever social situation arose.

Rachel listened as her mothers discussed the new job prospects, while Father Abraham tried to track down the older boys. She rearranged Alice onto her hip before she felt *his* eyes on her. She knew it was him. She didn't have to look to know that. The high collar of her dress threatened to strangle her. She had a horrible urge to rip the entire thing off. She began to pray; little snippets of prayers rattled in her mind at a frantic pace. *Please God, help me not make a fool out of myself, please don't let me blush, please, please, please!*

"Okay, let's go." Father planted a hand on each of her brothers' backs, prodding them forward. Rachel expelled the breath she was apparently holding again. If she kept forgetting to breathe, she was going to end up with brain damage. She turned to her right. There he was, standing next to his father and looking directly at her. Luke's father pointed in her direction and said something to him. They began to walk toward her family. Rachel's hair was plastered onto her forehead with sweat. *Oh please God, don't let them come over here!*

"Brother Abraham, don't leave quite yet," Prophet Silver's voice boomed over the chitchat. Her entire family froze in midflight.

Out of the corner of her eye she saw Luke and his father retreating. Rachel shuddered with relief.

"I'm sorry to bother you, as you clearly had more pressing matters to attend to." He reached the family, who stood ramrod straight in their discomfort.

"It was no bother, no bother at all." Mother Marylee showed an impressive set of strong white teeth.

The prophet's eyes remained on Father Abraham. Rachel realized that her father hadn't responded to the prophet's comment.

"Nothing more pressin' than the Lord's work," he finally said.

"Amen to that." The prophet ran a hand through his thick salt-and-pepper hair. "I need to borrow your daughter Rachel for a few minutes."

Rachel's stomach lurched. Had he seen her looking at Luke? That was impossible. Then again, he did receive direct messages from God.

Her father's face hardened.

"Why of course you can *borrow* Rachel," Mother Marylee said. She scooped up Alice then nudged Rachel toward the prophet.

As Rachel was led back to the meeting hall, she was aware of the crowd parting like the Red Sea to allow them to pass. She heard her name woven into the murmurs of the group and felt the stares piercing her back as the doors to the emptied building closed behind them.

The prophet offered Rachel a seat in his office, yet he remained standing. She sat primly with her knees pressed together so hard that her legs felt bruised from the effort. Perspiration oozed from every pore in her body. She blotted her drenched hands on her dress.

"Where have you been hiding all this time?" he said. Rachel was confused. She had always lived here. He spun her chair around to face him. "Look at me when I address you." She pulled her head up, dizzy with fear, and fixed her gaze on a brown mole on his forehead. A tendril of hair escaped her braid and covered the right side of her face. He pushed the hair out of her eye with sandpaper fingers. Her cheek stung like it had been scratched.

"Look at *me*."

She forced her eyes to meet his. He was a man of God. She was furious with herself for being so afraid of him.

"You are different from the other girls."

He smelled like maple syrup. Rachel's stomach heaved.

"I believe God has a purpose for you, a *very* important purpose."

It was torturous to look directly at him. She already knew what her purpose was in life. Why did he feel the need to tell her?

"The reason so many men believed they had testimonies of marriage was because they sense your importance to this community. Because of the aura you possess, many *holy* men can be drawn to you in a way that leads them to believe they have received a celestial testimony directly from God."

Rachel wondered what "aura" meant. She would have to ask Sara later on.

"But you listen to me." He cupped his hand under her chin for emphasis.

Rachel gulped down the lump rising in her throat that threatened to cut off her airway. She prayed. *Please help me to accept his message, please help me not to scream, please help me not to throw up.*

"I am the *only* mortal who is infallible. You know what infallible means, don't you?"

Rachel squeaked out a barely audible yes.

"When there are conflicting messages, *Satan* is involved, *tearing* our unity down, and *confusing* us with his lies." She'd heard this singsong voice many times when he preached to their group. "There are many men out there, even *righteous* ones, who are misled by *Satan* and his false promises." He stepped away from her, his eyes never leaving her face as he moved behind his desk. He began pacing back and forth. "*Satan* is trying to tempt these men, using the aura *you* possess like a spell."

Rachel's breakfast clawed at her stomach, wanting out. Satan was using her to corrupt good men.

"*Confuse* them," he continued, his voice reaching a feverish pitch, "*darken* their hearts.

"Listen to *me,* trust only *me,* or you could be led astray." He snapped his fingers in front of her. "That's how quickly you can lose your soul."

Lifting his eyes upward he said, "I am the only one who can care for your soul. You must pray and purify your heart and mind to accept God's will." He stopped pacing and moved toward the blinds. He snapped them shut.

"You trust me, don't you, Rachel?"

His sweet maple scent clung to the air between them. She shuddered in a spasm of revulsion. Immediately, waves of guilt washed over her. How could she be so upset when she was near a man of God? Actually, God Himself was here with them, speaking through Prophet Silver, and all she could think about was how to keep from vomiting. It must be Satan. It had to be. The Prince of Darkness was determined that she harden her heart to the word of God.

Get thee behind me, Satan, she repeated in her head over and over.

"What did you say?"

Oh sweet Jesus, he could hear her thoughts. "N-nothing." The word felt like the blade of a knife cutting her throat. She could not believe she had just lied to him.

"I asked you if you trusted me, and you mumbled something about Satan."

It's true! He did know what she was thinking.

"I . . . I meant . . . I was trying to . . ."

"What were you implying?"

What did he want her to say? Her thoughts were webbed in confusion. Her tongue sat thick and useless in her mouth.

He lifted her chin with that sandpapery hand again. "Look at me," he said, after her gaze had returned to the mole.

Mother Marylee had always said the eyes were the window to the soul. "I'm so sorry," she said. "I'm just so confused."

His face relaxed. He sighed, a long and stretchy sound, but not an angry one. "Of course you are." He patted her shoulder. "It's difficult sometimes to articulate a destiny greater than oneself. If I am just beginning to understand the magnitude of what God has in store for you, how can I expect you to fully comprehend the significance of what is yet to come?"

She was more confused than ever, but at least he wasn't mad at her.

"If you follow God's commands, as they are revealed to me, you will be exalted in heaven. If you reject God's plan for your life, I can *guarantee* that you will spend eternity suffering in the bowels of *hell*."

Rachel felt her bottom lip begin to tremble.

"I think you need some time to grow comfortable with the idea that your life is meant for a much higher purpose than what you had aspired to have for yourself."

"Okay."

Her rigid posture collapsed under the weight of his words. Her heart felt heavy with *purpose*. She didn't recognize the girl he was describing.

The trembling in her lip had now spread like a wildfire to every inch of her body. "Come here." He took her elbow and coaxed her out of her chair. He wrapped his arms around her and squeezed hard and tight until Rachel swam in dizziness. She choked back a tidal wave of nausea.

"As long as you trust me, you'll have nothing to fear," he whispered. His arms loosened before releasing her.

As he cleared his throat, his furrowed brow sat atop eyes that scanned the length of her body, no doubt to determine her commitment to her faith. Precisely the thing she lacked right at that moment. If God could just help her hide her doubts *just this once*, she would transform herself. She would work on the transformation every moment of every waking hour until she could be a purified vessel for the Lord, ready to receive whatever He and Prophet Silver wanted from her.

"I think we've had enough for one day."

"Thank you, Prophet Silver." As she turned to leave, he grabbed her sweat-slicked hand.

"What I have told you today is to go no further than this room." She nodded vigorously. "Yes."

"Good. Then we understand each other."

Fighting the urge to sprint to the door, she kept her arms at her sides, determined not to speed up her pace of departure. As the doors closed behind her, she gulped mouthfuls of muggy air as if she were drowning.

THREE

The tension was as thick as the butter that Sara spread on her piece of toast. The smaller children had already been fed and had cleared out of the kitchen while the school-age kids took their turns at the trough. It was going to be a sweltering day and Sara was already perspiring in her long dress. She always lost her appetite on the first day of school. She knew they would endure the usual stares for their clothing, but Sara didn't care. In less than an hour, she would be free of this house and be able to escape into the world of books.

Her stomach heaved at the sight of so much food on the table. A spoon perched, handle up, in a mound of watery eggs. Little rounded grooves pockmarked the soupy eggs, like an old excavation site. Sara skipped them and took a bite of toast instead.

Mother Marylee returned to the kitchen alone. Sara sensed something was wrong. She tried to push her discomfort aside. It was probably just another lecture about not socializing with Gentiles. Sara glanced at the clock. If she didn't hurry and get it over with, they would miss the school bus.

"I have an announcement to make," Mother Marylee said.

"Yes, Mama, you have our attention." Rachel wiped her lips and placed the napkin on her lap.

"You've probably noticed a lot of activity occurring near the meeting hall lately."

They nodded. Four double-wide mobile homes had been placed in a quadrangle about five hundred feet behind the meeting hall.

"Well," continued Marylee, "you'll be attending the new school there. It's called 'the Blood of the Lamb Academy.'"

Sara returned the toast to her plate, suddenly sick with despair.

"But what about Centennial? I've already met my new second-grade teacher. Her name is Mrs. Mackerel," said Seth. "Like the fish."

"The prophet has received a revelation." Marylee's words effectively ended all dissent. "Now don't be upset about the facilities. The school will be relocating to the old meeting hall once they finish construction on the new one. In the meantime, these temporaries are quite sufficient."

"I don't understand why we can't go to Centennial," Sara said. She pushed the chunk of bread into the corner of her cheek.

"The Lord has instructed Prophet Silver to forbid the children from starting this year. If some families can't or won't homeschool their children, then the community will provide the Academy as an alternative."

"But today's the first day and it's my sophomore year and what about my job at the library after school? Miss Wiley is expecting me," Sara said.

"It's sounds to me as though you're questioning the will of the Lord," Marylee said, giving her an icy stare.

"No, ma'am." Sara dropped her head, batting her eyes furiously to shore up the tears. If she started to cry, she wasn't sure she could stop. Ever.

"Well I'm glad to hear that. Now I want you to finish up. School starts at nine."

"Today?" Sara clasped her bottom lip between her teeth, giving it a punishing bite for letting a question pass through.

"It's the first day of school, isn't it?"

"Yes, ma'am."

"Well then, hurry up and eat." Marylee picked up the pitcher of milk and carried it to the refrigerator. "Oh and Seth, you'll like this: you may not have a teacher who's named after a fish, but your very own mother is going to teach your class."

"Hooray!" Seth bounced in his chair. For reasons unfathomable to Sara, the boys seemed genuinely excited about this.

Sara glanced at Rachel, but she had her head lowered, studying each bite of egg.

Sara's biggest nightmare had morphed into a dream come true for her mother. Anna was a tall, spindly brunette who looked like an artist but had never pursued anything creative. She had no qualifications to teach, except that she actually finished her sophomore year. Anyone around here with more than a ninth-grade education came from other communities where they placed more value on education.

Sara managed to swallow the piece of toast. The congealed butter sitting on top of her toast nearly caused her to gag. She couldn't throw it out because nothing was ever wasted in their home. Every bite had to be finished, and anything disposable was used over and over. During the school year, plastic sandwich bags were clipped to clotheslines suspended over the sink. They were scrubbed nightly of peanut butter or mayonnaise and reused the next morning.

"Why are you kids dillydallying? I want breakfast finished, dishes cleared and all of you outside sitting on the stoop waiting for Mother Anna. She'll be taking you to the school today."

Mother Marylee opened the door to the fridge and buried her head in it, shuffling food around. Sara saw an opportunity and slipped out the back door.

She sat on the back step, feeling the tears fill behind her eyes. She blinked hard, refusing them freedom. Perched on top of the scarecrow Father Abraham had built for Marylee's garden, a crow stared straight at her. For a moment, she understood the crow and envied its empty heart. It hurt too much to care. She should pray, but her mind was blank. Rebellion served no purpose. She could only do what she had been taught all her life to do. Obey.

THEIR teacher, Mrs. Gladys, an ancient relic of a woman with enormous jowls and an even bigger behind, sat at the front of the classroom. All the interior walls had been removed, except for the bathroom, leaving one large room lined with rows of brand-new desks. Without air-conditioning the windows were open, allowing an army of flies to come in and out. Strands of stickyfly paper coiled from the ceiling. Sara decided that the demise of the flies would probably be more entertaining than the lectures.

Sara took a seat in the far back corner of the classroom. Much to Sara's dismay, Rachel had planted herself in the first row. Sara's only neighbors were the stove and refrigerator, which had not yet been removed. The refrigerator would periodically sputter on, huffing and puffing before shutting off in a final gasp. When it was on, she wouldn't be able to hear a word Mrs. Gladys said.

The fridge cut off and Mrs. Gladys' voice pricked at her ears. "Now I know everyone knows the story of Joseph Smith's beginnings, so we're just going to touch on it before moving onto the journey from Nauvoo to Salt Lake City. From there, we'll discuss how the Mormon Church fell into a state of apostasy by failing to uphold the Principle."

Sara couldn't believe they were going to rehash the founding of Christ's one true church. Every kid in there could recite that story.

"Who can tell me how the Book of Mormon was found?"

A cluster of hands shot up. Mrs. Gladys peered around the room. She pointed to a boy of about thirteen with beaver teeth covering his bottom lip. Sara thought she recognized those teeth. He was an apostle's son.

"Please stand up and tell the class your name so that we can all get to know each other."

"Noah Jenkins, ma'am." He stood. "The angel Moroni appeared to Joseph when he was seventeen. He told him that he had been sent by God to locate sacred gold plates where the word of God was written." He sat back down.

Mrs. Gladys pointed to the girl everyone thought cursed because of a cleft palate. She stood. "I'm Mary Miller," she lisped. "Joseph visited the hill every year but always returned empty-handed. Finally, during one of his visits, the angel Moroni said that Joseph would have only one more chance to get them."

Mrs. Gladys nodded to the boy next to Mary. He stood. "Aaron Taylor. Let's see. He didn't know why he hadn't been allowed to get the golden plates. Joseph used to find buried gold and stuff when he looked at these stones called seer stones. One day he was looking at the seer stones, and he saw that the only way he would get the sacred plates would be if he married a girl, Emma Hale, and that she would have to go with him to the Hill Cumorah." He plopped down hard in his chair.

The next boy stood. "Joseph brought Emma with him when he dug the golden plates from the ground." He scowled and sat back down.

"And your name was?" Mrs. Gladys asked.

"Adam Silver."

Mrs. Gladys beamed. He was one of the prophet's sons. "Well done. And I might add I am so pleased to have you in my class. Give your father my regards."

Adam grunted and put his head on his desk.

The next boy stood and said, "David Silver."

"Well now, how many Silvers do we have in here?"

Half the class raised their hands.

Mrs. Gladys would not stop smiling.

Since the prophet had no brothers in the community, all these boys must be his sons. Sara was envious that they could all take their father's last name. Even the ones who were not from his first wife. The prophet could do whatever he wanted, and he had decided that all his children would bear his name.

David began, "Joseph couldn't read the book because it was written in Egyptian. So, the angel Moroni gave him glasses called interpreters, and when he wore them, he could read the plates. Joseph wrote and wrote, but then something happened and then the book was lost or maybe thrown out. Joseph was upset."

"Excellent. Next student, please."

A boy Sara didn't recognize stood up. "Benjamin Heinemann. So, Joseph prayed and the angel Moroni returned the plates in 1928." There were a handful of snickers from the classroom. "I mean 1828. But this time the angel didn't give him the interpreters, so Joseph wasn't sure how to read them. Finally, he used his stones that he had called Urim and Thummim. He placed the seer stones in a hat, buried his face in it and told Emma what to write."

"And what is this book called today?"

"The Book of Mormon."

The fridge kicked on and began its death rattle. Sara laid her head down on her desk. She noticed that there were packed leaves and twigs in the small space between the fridge and stove where mice probably nested. She closed her eyes and prayed for unconsciousness.

When Mrs. Gladys dismissed them for a fifteen-minute break, Sara used the restroom. The bathroom had a huge hole gouged in the floor in front of the toilet. Weeds thrust up into the opening. She sat on the rust-stained bowl and stared into the hole while she urinated. She finished. The water surged upward, threatening to spill over the top before swirling downward. Exiting the small room, Sara noticed Rachel speaking with some boy she didn't recognize. Sara was stunned. Rachel never spoke with boys unless they were relatives.

This boy was very tall, well over six feet. He was extremely good looking with flashy white teeth and wavy black hair that grazed his shoulders. It was much longer than that of any of the other boys in the community. Sara swallowed her shock when she noticed his bare forearms. How was that possible? No one in the community exposed their bare arms. How could they when they needed to conceal their sacred undergarments from the outside world? This was not just scandalous, this was sacrilegious. And he wore the clothes of the Gentiles: a black T-shirt and jeans. All the men and boys in Blood of the Lamb wore the same wool pants and long-sleeved button-down shirts, even in the oppressive heat. She had no idea how he managed to pull that off without being driven from the community. His father must be a very important man.

"Oh, Sara." Rachel spun around. Her cheeks were flushed. "I'd like you to meet Luke. He's new to the community."

He held out his hand. The sensation sent a jolt through her. "Nice to meet you, Sara."

"Same here."

Luke smiled briefly at her before returning his eyes to Rachel. Never before had Sara felt so jealous of her sister's beauty. "So, what brought you here?" Sara asked.

"My father began investigating the Principle about a year ago."

"So, you're not even from another group?" Sara asked.

"No. We came from Salt Lake City."

"This must be really different for you," Rachel said.

Luke cleared his throat. "Yep. In fact, until a year or so ago, we didn't even go to meetings, church, nothing."

"How in the world did you end up here, then?" Sara asked.

"My dad started delving into his Mormon roots, and before I knew it, we were spending all our free time attending services back in Salt Lake."

"How did you find out about our community?" Rachel said.

"Well, Dad had sort of a midlife crisis and decided to look into some of the more fundamentalist groups. Initially, he checked out the True Saints community. Know them?"

Rachel nodded. "Definitely. They're the only other fundamentalist group besides us who have their own temple. They're also the largest, and they're located right on the Utah, Arizona border."

Sara was stunned that Rachel could speak this much with a complete stranger.

Luke grinned, revealing a dimple on his left cheek that Sara hadn't noticed before. "You sound like a tour guide."

Rachel turned crimson. "Well, they're sort of . . . I guess you could call them our rivals."

"So, how come your family didn't join them?" Sara asked.

"They're almost twice as big as us. They've got a following of like ten thousand people."

"Don't know. But after a little prophet shopping, here we are."

Rachel gasped and looked around to make sure no one had heard his irreverent remark.

"We had to leave Salt Lake City anyway. Once the mainstream church leadership got wind that my dad was seeking to dump his family into an existence where everyone seemed to be trapped in a pioneer house of horrors, they excommunicated him," Luke said. "They're not too happy about polygamy these days."

Rachel launched into a lecture about how the mainstream Mormon Church had gone astray when they abandoned the Principle and how great it was that his father had returned to the one true faith. Sara just swallowed a forbidden laugh. She'd never heard anyone that brazen. His boldness gave her courage. "Were you as surprised as we were about school?"

"Not really," Luke said. "I overheard my parents talking. They weren't happy. We thought I'd be attending the public schools when we moved. But my father really believes in the *divine righteousness* of the prophet, so here I am."

Even Sara felt off balance at his obvious hostility. She lowered her voice to barely a whisper. "Why'd they wait 'til today to tell us? Did they think the children of the Blood of the Lamb would rise up and revolt?"

Luke grinned. "It was probably part of the operating instructions from the Almighty: 'Behold, I commandeth that you not informeth the children until the day of reckoning dawns.'"

Sara covered her mouth to keep from laughing. "What grade are you in?"

"I don't think it matters since there doesn't seem to be any distinction between grades at the *Blood of the Lamb Academy*." Luke marched the name across his lips. "I would have been a senior though."

"We're sophomores," Rachel said.

"Take your seats, please." Mrs. Gladys clapped her hands together. "We're going to continue our discussion of the Great Shakedown."

Everyone shuffled to their seats. Sara excused herself and walked to the rear of the classroom. She didn't want Rachel to get her hopes up, but something told her that it was already too late. Rachel was falling for this new boy, or maybe it was she herself who was falling.

She plopped into her seat, realizing that no one would ever look at her the way Luke looked at Rachel, least of all her future husband, Uncle Walter. Sara would never experience love, and she would never go to college. That kicked her in the gut.

"Who . . ." Mrs. Gladys' voice penetrated her consciousness. The fridge was momentarily silent, thereby forcing Sara to hear Mrs. Gladys say, ". . . wants to continue with our discussion of the Manifesto of 1890 that abolished plural marriage?"

Sara sank into her chair. Mrs. Gladys' voice needled her brain.

She rested her face on her hands and discreetly inserted her fingers in her ears. What about math, science, language arts and social studies? Tears filled her eyes. She allowed them to slide onto the blank page of her notebook. She spent the rest of the period that way, swallowing her sobs and trying to make it through to the next second, minute and hour.

Sara and Rachel met outside at lunch. Rachel gripped Sara's arm. "Let's go somewhere to talk."

"How about over there?" Sara pointed to an abandoned car a few hundred feet away. They walked toward the rusted, 1950s Chevy whose overturned hubcaps served as a hatchery for mosquitoes. Sara kicked them over as she encountered each one.

"This is far enough away," Rachel said. The seat from the automobile had been removed and was wedged against the rusty frame of the passenger-side door. They settled on the cratered vinyl, avoiding the larger gash, which expelled fetid brown foam from its core. The parched weeds and creeping vines tickled their legs.

"Oh my gosh, he's coming this way," Rachel whispered.

Sara knew the only reason they had extracted themselves from the crowd was to talk about *him*.

They sat in silence as he approached. "Okay if I sit with you guys?"

"Sure," Sara said.

Rachel scooted to the far end of the seat, forcing Sara to sit on the foam in the middle. She tucked her legs tightly against the back of the seat, hoping that he wouldn't notice her man-shoes. Luke plopped down next to her, dropping his sack lunch between his feet. Sara could feel heat coming from his leg. Her lip began its tickle, threatening to turn numb.

"Thanks." Luke stretched his legs out in front of him. "You two are the only people even remotely close to my age who'll talk to me."

"I'm sorry," Rachel said. "Sometimes they're just afraid of people from outside the faith."

"They're worse at the priesthood meetings."

"They'll come around," Sara said.

Luke shrugged. "No worries. I'm just ticking off the minutes."

Rachel sucked in a big mouthful of air, and Sara laughed nervously. "For what?"

"For my life to begin."

"And when's that?" Sara touched her upper lip. Although numb, it hadn't disappeared. Her teeth were covered.

Luke met Sara's eyes. "The second I get away from here."

Sara was amazed at the freedom with which he spoke. "Aren't you worried about your soul?"

"I'll take my chances." Luke opened his lunch sack and pulled out a bag of Doritos. "I was never a good Mormon to begin with. We were practically ex-mos before my dad found religion. Now, I'm supposed to become a good fundamentalist?"

Ex-mos? Sara had no idea how to respond. She frantically searched her mind for something intelligible to say. Thankfully, Luke spoke up.

"Is it just me or is this weird?"

Rachel leaned across Sara to look at Luke. "Weird?"

Luke gestured toward the younger children who made up all four of the remaining classrooms. "There's like young kids everywhere. And how come there are no girls our age here?"

Sara scratched her ankle. Sweat beaded in the thick mesh of her stockings. "They're already married."

"That's lame."

Lame?

"And these clothes . . . I feel like I'm trapped on a really bad rerun of *Little House on the Prairie* only everyone drives cars instead of covered wagons."

Sara didn't know what "little house" he referred to, but she did know that her clothes were ridiculous. If he could see her man-boat-shoes, he would definitely find her repulsive. She pressed her lower limbs even tighter against the seat.

"You'll get used to it and realize how righteous this life is," Rachel said.

"I'm sorry. I can't seem to stop saying things that piss people off."

"It's going to take a while to adjust. This is all we know, and sometimes it's hard for us too," Rachel said. "Please feel free to say anything you want."

"Thanks." Luke held out the bag of Doritos.

Sara was tempted to take one, but both she and her sister politely declined.

Luke popped a few in his mouth, turned the bag over and appeared to be reading the label. "Anyway, it's official." He swiped his fingers down his pant leg, leaving an orange streak. "My father is getting married on Saturday."

Rachel smiled. "Have you met your new mother?"

Luke blanched. He appeared to have difficulty swallowing his chip. "This girl . . . she's like two years younger than me. My father is getting married to a *fifteen-year-old*! It's so fu . . ." His eyes met Rachel's face. He looked back at his chips and popped one in his mouth. He chewed slowly.

"What's her name?" Sara said. "Maybe we know her."

He swallowed. "Beulah. I don't know her last name."

Rachel looked at Sara. "That must be Brother Jebediah's daughter. He's one of the twelve apostles."

Luke cracked a half-smile. "So you know her?"

"Sort of," Rachel answered. "She didn't attend the public school, so we never became close."

"My mother is really tripping. She cries most of the time, except in front of Dad." Luke batted at a fly. "I guess he's punishing her 'cause she can't have any more kids. Bad news for a Mormon, especially a fundamentalist. It sucks."

Sara mentally rolled that word around in her head. *Sucks. Sucks.* She angled her eyes toward her sister, hoping she wasn't taking offense.

Rachel looked flustered as she opened her sack and removed a sandwich. "Will she live with you?"

"God, no. My mom put her foot down on that one. My dad bought a trailer. Beulah will live there while they start construction on a set of four duplexes. I guess he's planning for the future expansion of his wife collection."

Sara cleared her throat. "That's not so bad. It will make everyone's life a little easier. Not having to share the same house and everything."

"If you say so." Luke darted his hand out, trapping the fly. He held it in his hand. Sara could hear a slight buzz coming from beneath his fist. "So, how many . . . mothers do you two have?"

"Four. And we share one home."

"That sucks."

There was that word again. *Sucks.* Sara glanced at her sister.

"It's not so bad," Rachel said. "Having so many mothers around, I mean."

"With four mothers you must have a lot of brothers and sisters."

"Only two sisters and seven brothers."

Luke whistled. "Sounds like your dad did it backward. I think the goal here is to have lots of girls to supply their buddies with brides."

Rachel gasped and had Sara eaten something, she probably would have choked.

"It's not that way," Sara said.

"Then why aren't there more guys my age around? There are plenty of little boys, but then they hit puberty and just seem to disappear."

"Sometimes they leave," Rachel said.

"That's convenient."

Sara blanched. She thought of her own little brothers. Her father had no status. She tried not to dwell on their fate, but she worried that they'd be driven out. If her father had something to offer either of more daughters or money, they'd have a fighting chance of getting them into leadership so they could stay.

Luke stood up, walked over to a large pine about fifty feet away and opened his fist. He returned, wiping his hand on his jeans. "Hopefully, it won't come back."

Never before had Sara seen somebody catch a fly only to release it. Luke was different from anyone she'd ever met.

As he took his seat, Luke's leg bumped against hers for a moment. The touch was electric. Sara bit on her lip to keep from gasping out loud. Instead, she pressed closer to Rachel. He didn't seem to notice or care. Scooping up his bag of chips, he began to crunch on them.

Luke scrutinized the clumps of students lining the trailer. "See? Only four guys around my age. All of them I've seen in the leadership. Where do the others go?"

Rachel rummaged around in her sack lunch. "Maybe they're learning a trade and will return?"

"Doubt it. I think they're being forced out. Kill the competition. More brides for the old guys."

"That's very disrespectful," Rachel said softly.

Luke peered around Sara to make eye contact with Rachel. "I'm sorry. You're right. I stepped over the line."

"It's okay." Rachel smiled. Sara knew the impact Rachel's smile had on someone. If he wasn't in love with her at first sight, he would be now. She could change the course of a river, alter the spin of the earth on its axis and drive away all darkness from the deep recesses of space with one quick smile. Sara was certain he was hooked.

No point in trying to win his affection. The depression had arrived, locked and loaded. She surrendered to the sensation as the weight of sadness wilted her spine and idled her heart.

FOUR

S ara watched the dust swirl in a wedge of morning sunlight. She wanted to be one of those dust particles, floating randomly in a life that was simple and without pain.

Rachel stirred and threw an arm over her head. Her sister's beauty never failed to startle Sara. With her eyes closed and thick, tangled lashes feathering her cheeks, her delicate features made Sara's heart swell with protectiveness. "It's going to be okay," she said aloud.

Rachel sighed and rolled away from her. Sara longed to hurl herself down the stairs and run far away. But she would never leave Rachel. For a split second, she wished that she didn't have a sister. Then she wouldn't feel so much of everything: worry, love and most especially, fear.

Deciding not to wake her, Sara rolled out of bed and pulled on the thickest, ugliest dress she could find. Anxiety tweaked her nerves, strumming the promise of pending disaster as she entered the kitchen. Her mother stirred an enormous pot of oatmeal. Alice played under the kitchen table with the lids. Adam and Aaron slithered beneath the chairs hissing at one another. They were having too much fun for Father to be around. Sara let out a deep breath.

"Good morning, Sara." Her mother's face was bright and inviting.

She felt a surge of something resembling love, or maybe she was just content to get a kind word from her mother. She dropped to her knees and scooped Alice up, planting a kiss on the toddler's soft cheek.

"Morning. Can I help with anything?" Sara said.

Alice wrapped chubby baby arms around her neck and bounced up and down, gurgling with delight. Sara peppered the soft folds of her neck with kisses.

"I don't think Mother Esther's feeling well." Anna's tone was jubilant. "Your father was in here asking about her, but he stepped outside before I had a chance to answer. You probably ought to go check on her."

"Okay." Sara's joy flapped away on borrowed wings at the mention of her father lurking nearby. Sara detached Alice from her body, redirecting the baby's attention to the pots and pans. "Where is she?"

"In the basement."

Sara opened the door leading off the kitchen and headed downstairs. The basement was a hatchery of laundry lines. Clothes, in various stages of drying, were randomly clipped across them. Esther stood trembling with arms full of dripping-wet laundry. Greenish froth puddled at her feet. Her teeth rattled, and her eyes squinted as though she had been peeling an onion.

"Are you okay?" Sara rushed the rest of the way down the stairs. Behind her, the heavy tread of her father's feet resounded followed by Mother Marylee's slower plodding. Sara snatched the clothes from Esther's arms. Another spasm of nausea ripped across her features. Sara jumped back as an arc of bile escaped her lips. Her own stomach heaved.

"Not again?" Her father's voice wasn't an accusation, more a statement of fact.

Mother Esther started to reply, "I'm . . ." A trail of saliva dribbled from her lips. Her shoulders racked and she vomited again.

Sara's own mouth pooled with warm water.

"I'm sorry."

"Don't be sorry. It's your first baby. It happens. Here, come sit."

Father led her to a threadbare sofa with mashed pillows. Esther collapsed onto the sofa. A plume of dusty sand shivered upward, causing another spasm of gagging. Father fanned the air in a futile gesture. Sara hoped that he felt like an idiot for sitting her on the "dirty clothes couch."

"Marylee, give the laundry duties to someone else," he said when the dust settled. "I don't want her straining herself like this no more."

Mother Marylee peeled a shirt from the pile that Sara clutched. She unfurled it with an angry snap before piercing it to the line with a clothespin. "Unless the girls stay home from school, I don't see how any one of us can handle more chores since Sister Esther's pregnancy."

"Do what you gotta do. She's having a hard time carrying this baby."

"We've all been pregnant, and not one of us had trouble."

"Well, she's starting a lot later than you girls. I think the younger ones handle it better." His other wives were all pregnant by seventeen, whereas Mother Esther was giving birth for the first time at nearly twenty-five. "Look, I don't care what you gotta do. Take the girls out of school. Just get these chores done."

"No. Don't make the girls stay home." Mother Esther's voice was raspy. "I can handle it." She started to lift herself from the couch. Father pushed her back down in a gentle but firm gesture.

"You're not doin' this laundry no more. That's final."

"But the girls need to go to school."

"They're going to quit school anyways. Once they get sealed."

"They need to go to school as long as they can. I'll do the laundry."

Sara held her breath. The Blood of the Lamb Academy, in and of itself, was one kind of torture, but being housebound with nothing but endless chores and no interaction outside of a houseful of bickering women was a death sentence. At least at "BLA," as Luke referred to the school, the three of them got to talk.

"I'm telling you, no more laundry." His voice had that "no argu-ment" quality to it.

Marylee took another shirt from Sara's arms. With an aggressive tug, she turned and clipped it to the line.

"I suppose Mother Jane can pick up this chore," Mother Marylee said. "Her workload is less since all she does is look after them babies."

"There. It's settled," Father said. "The girls can stay in school." He pivoted on his heel and helped Mother Esther off the couch. "Let's get you into bed." Esther leaned on Abraham, and he half-carried her up the stairs.

"I can't believe the way he coddles that girl." Mother Marylee's angry words matched the action of her wrists as she peeled more clothing off Sara's arms. "I recall your mother being sick a time or two. Did he lighten her workload? No." *Snap.* "Why's he letting you girls stay in school?" *Snap.* "A girl don't need more than a sixth-grade education to raise up children right in the Principle."

Sara swallowed the knot in her throat. "Yes, ma'am."

"*Outsider.* She's not going to last in this family. Mark my words, Sara. Mark my words."

SARA wasn't used to the grocery store's shiny floor filled with feet all clattering different rhythms across it, or the black skid marks of shopping carts that peeled across its surface, or even the disembod-ied chatter that floated between the aisles. She was used to the somber tones of the Blood of the Lamb Outpost with its muted col-ors, homegrown vegetables and paltry selection of canned goods. When Mother Jane had summoned her, Sara shifted impatiently from foot to foot as Jane, with tongue secured in the corner of her mouth, began chicken-scratching a shopping list. It was slow and tedious. Her poor spelling and blocky, childish letters were almost too painful for Sara to witness. But she wouldn't dare point out to Jane that she could remember the items. Her freedom was a fragile gift, not to be rushed or taken advantage of.

She practically ran the entire mile and a half to the Gentile-run grocery store before deciding to pace herself as she approached the town of Centennial. It was more satisfying to savor the freedom.

When Mother Jane assumed the laundry duties, she complained for three days solid. Then she attempted to convince Father Abraham to remove one or both of the girls from school. With an eye on Esther, he refused.

"It's the straw breaking my back, Abraham," Mother Jane complained. The laundry loads were enormous, but the diapers, they were the thorn in her craw. She needed some type of relief.

Surprisingly, he suggested using disposables for a while. Since the Blood of the Lamb Outpost did not carry disposable diapers, Sara could go purchase them as needed with the welfare money.

As Sara steered the cart toward aisle #12, marked BABY ITEMS, her eyes immediately landed on the books. She hadn't seen books, other than religious ones, since the start of the summer. Delicious words flowed in front of her eyes. She wanted to devour them, wrap her arms around the entire selection and get lost. If only the town had a library. If only she was still a student at the *real* high school. She picked up a book and turned it over in her hands.

What if she "borrowed" it?

She could return her borrowed book on the next diaper excursion. Was that a sin? Maybe Jesus would understand. He was a scholar himself. Sara recalled the story about His three-day disappearance to the temple where He bandied scripture with the most educated of men. His mother was frantic with worry, but the Savior was lost to intellectual discussion. If Christ could make such a mistake, surely He would understand her thirst for literature.

Besides, she would only be borrowing.

Her eyes glazed with fear at the prospect of taking it. The titles swam together like alphabet soup. Without looking down, Sara snapped open Mother Jane's purse and propped it on its side in the cart. Her heartbeat clanged like cymbals, tears streaming down her face.

Borrowing wasn't a sin. Jesus would have done the same thing. Yes, the more she thought about it, the more convinced she became that Jesus would borrow books too. Absolutely.

The thick, compact book slid effortlessly into the purse. Sara snapped it closed and continued toward the baby aisle. Her hands shook. Wobbly legs somehow propelled her to the diapers. She should know how to breathe, having mastered it years ago. Yet her lungs rebelled. Blackness threatened. *Oh Lord, help me.* They would find her passed out with a stolen book in her purse.

With a sharp intake, she sucked air. Immediately, the darkness scattered. Breath shot through her nose easily. After several deep ones, her legs steadied and vision cleared. She stood there savoring these breaths, trying to focus on her task. Find the cheapest, largest bag of diapers and purchase them. She did that and proceeded to the checkout counter.

Several ladies scanned items. No one paid any attention to her. She chose the checker who looked bored and inattentive. The girl was of high school age with hair that matched the color of a stop sign. She pushed the cart to the checkout before realizing she hadn't removed the wallet. Another woman pulled behind her, blocking her exit.

There was no way to reverse course now. Sara took a deep breath hoping to steady her frayed nerves. She reached inside the purse for the wallet. The book seemed larger than life. It was everywhere her fingers explored. Finally, she touched the vinyl wallet and managed to inchworm it up the side of the purse. Sara glanced up. The checker was studying her fingernails. They were long and pink with little silver glitter balls glued on them.

She removed the wallet. "Nice nails."

The checker smiled, revealing slightly bucked teeth. "Thanks. I did them myself. I'm thinking about going to school to get a license. May as well get paid for it."

"Great idea. Where would you go?" Sara couldn't believe she was conversing while a stolen book blazed like firecrackers in

Mother Jane's purse. The girl launched into a tale about nail schools, and Sara somehow managed to make all the appropriate responses, smile at her most graciously and leave the store without bells and whistles revealing her crime.

The exhilaration was beyond belief. The fact that she hadn't been caught confirmed that she was carrying on in the tradition of Christ. He inspired her to get creative with her intellectual needs. He went to the temple, and she went to the IGA. And now she was in temporary possession of a real book.

Sara rushed past an island of concrete where low, plain-looking clapboard stores were anchored. The smokestack from the only industry in town comprised the skyline. The Blood of the Lamb community owned it. The factory chugged clouds of cottony white into the empty blue sky. Her father would be toiling away on an assembly line somewhere in that building.

Silver Enterprises produced highly specialized bolts that were used by their "archenemy," the federal government, in production for military aircraft. The fact that the company's biggest customer was the U.S. government struck her as ironic. The community leaders never tried to hide this irony either. They encouraged everyone in the community to "bleed the Beast." The benefits collected from welfare, Medicaid or food stamps were all part of the Saint's plan to bleed the Beast.

Without the federal government's dollars flowing into Silver Enterprises, the company wouldn't be able to pay its employees in "Blood of the Lamb Bucks." Families used these bucks to pay rent on their homes, which were built on Blood of the Lamb properties. They purchased food at the Blood of the Lamb Outpost and pumped gas at the Blood of the Lamb gas station. Their community claimed to be the most pure adherents of the United Order: saints must care for one another and share everything.

Sara tried not to dwell on the inequities. Like how some of the families received more of everything: bigger homes, bigger cars and expensive trips. Some even went on trips to Mormon holy sites.

One of her classmates, Jessica Quille, had visited Hill Cumorah in New York, where Joseph Smith received the gold plates. Her father was an apostle.

She pushed those thoughts away as she approached their driveway. What should she do with the book? She paused at the clump of pines that marked their road, knelt down and tucked the tome at the base of the thickest tree, arranging dried pine needles across it. She stepped back. It was completely invisible to the naked eye. The book would be safe until she could return for it later in the night. Her step was a little lighter as she hurried to the house, slinging the bag of diapers. Tonight, she would read.

FIVE

The smoldering heat on those waning days of August had wilted Rachel's concentration and sapped her energy. Slumping in her chair, she blotted the droplets of perspiration beading her forehead. Her gaze traveled lazily outside the window, where it caught a tangle of morning glories; their petals were sealed in anticipation of the sun's relentless assault.

She had never truly desired anything for herself until Luke entered her life. She didn't even know he existed a week ago. Now everything that she did revolved around him. She marveled at the strangeness of her new emotions: they both terrified and thrilled her.

Rachel had this intense longing to be near him, but whenever she was, she became paralyzed with self-consciousness. Sara always had a thoughtful question to ask him or an insightful comment to make, while Rachel sat there like the stupid younger sister who bothered them on a date. The only thing she could manage to utter was an occasional criticism about an improper remark he made. She made her thirteenth vow of the week: *stop being so judgmental*.

"Rachel, I'm speaking to you!" Mrs. Gladys smacked her hand down on Rachel's desk. With a spasm of surprise, Rachel fell back in her chair. She flayed about like a circus clown, barely catching herself before she reached the floor. There was a smattering of laughter.

"I'm so sorry," she said. Her voice was raspy, like she hadn't used it in months. She untangled herself from her desk, rearranging her body to fit on the small seat again. "What did you say?"

"I've asked you the same question three times and you just sit there like an *idiot*."

Yes, she was an idiot. There was no doubt about that. "I'm very sorry. I'm not feeling well."

"Do you need to go home?"

"No, ma'am." Going home would be much worse than the embarrassment she suffered here. And she wouldn't be able to see Luke if she left. But then again, maybe she didn't want to see him after this.

"Well then, you can answer my question." Mrs. Gladys turned her back and began walking to the front of the class. "Who . . . ?"

All she heard was the first word of Mrs. Gladys' question; the rest of the words ran together like a foreign language. Instead of racking her brain to interpret the question, she looked in Luke's direction. He winked at her. Was he making fun of her? Her heart sank.

Mrs. Gladys had returned to her desk and drummed her fingers on it. "Rachel?"

"Yes . . . um . . . aaah," she sputtered. Her new vocabulary had been reduced to a series of vowel sounds.

"Brigham Young," Sara whispered urgently.

"Brigham Young," Rachel managed to say aloud in her new, raspy voice. Thank goodness, Sara had finally decided to sit at the front of the class with her.

"Correct," Gladys said. "So, did Brigham Young think there was any redemption for the Negro?"

Rachel was so happy that she knew an answer. "No. Cain was one of the sons of Adam, and he killed his brother, Abel. Instead of killing Cain and ending that evil line of the human race, God cursed him with black skin."

"Excellent." Mrs. Gladys smiled. "I think we should take a lunch break."

Rachel made yet another vow: *pay more attention in school and get smarter. Somehow.* Why couldn't she be more like Sara? Her sister managed to write in her journal the entire class period, and it didn't matter when she was asked a question, she always knew the answer.

Most of the class, Luke included, shot out the door with crumpled lunch bags in tow. Mrs. Gladys followed like a snowplow pushing them all out of the room. Only Sara and Rachel remained. Sara pulled her lunch bag out of the desk.

"How did you know that answer?"

"When in doubt say Brigham Young or Joseph Smith."

"I don't know what's wrong with me. I made such a fool out of myself," Rachel told her, laying her head on her desk and wallowing in self-pity.

"It's okay." Sara patted her back. "Luke's waiting for us outside, but I need to run to the bathroom first."

"I'm too embarrassed to go."

Sara stood up. "Why? He's crazy about you."

"No, it's you he's crazy about." Rachel shrugged off the tears.

"What makes you think that?"

"Because you two have a connection, a bond. You understand him. And you are *so* smart, just like he is." The more Rachel spoke about it, the more truth there seemed to be to it.

Sara shook her head as though trying to shake the idea out of her mind. "Rachel, I've seen him watch you."

"Yes, he watches me make a fool out of myself." Rachel started picking at her cuticle.

"No, he doesn't. We'll talk about this when I get back."

Rachel opened the top of her desk and pulled her lunch bag out. If Sara and Luke were supposed to be together, why did Prophet Silver confirm Uncle Walter's testimony of marriage to her sister? Prophet Silver said himself that his judgment was infallible. It must be God's will that Sara and Uncle Walter get married. Luke and Sara couldn't be together even if they wanted to be!

Calmness, like a gentle breeze, glided over her. But a sting of guilt punctured her tranquillity. She was appalled that she felt relief at the prospect of Sara already being betrothed to her own uncle.

She was going to have to step up the number of prayers she said for weeks, if not months, to rid herself of such terrible thoughts.

Luke opened the door. Her eyes darted around all corners of the classroom for anyone else that may have been there that she somehow hadn't noticed before. Rachel couldn't possibly be alone with him!

"Hey, how's it goin'?"

"Uh, hi." Her verbal skills were now officially at one-year-old Alice's level. Something resembling terror caused her body to bolt out of her seat and jut her hand out to shake his. *You've already met him, you idiot!*

He gave her a strange smile. She dropped her arm to her side in profound embarrassment. At that moment, she wanted the earth to swallow her.

"I didn't see you outside, so I figured you'd still be in the class-room." He brushed a tuft of coal black hair out of his eye.

"Sara's not here right now."

"That's okay. I wanted to talk to you."

"Me?"

"Actually, I had a question for you."

He slid down into the desk in front of her, sitting backward to look at her while straddling his seat.

"We haven't had much time to talk." He searched her face for something. What did he mean by that comment? They'd talked to him so much that she lived in constant fear that someone would tell her father how they spent their entire lunch hour with him every day.

"Sara and I have talked to you more in the past few days than we have with anyone else in months." She bit her lip, realizing she sounded accusatory.

"I meant alone."

Could he really mean what she thought he did? Her mind galloped with possibilities. But she sat quietly, distrusting her response.

He shifted in his seat and sat up a little straighter. "I thought if you wanted to, maybe you and I could hang out after school today."

Rachel's heart soared. "That would be great."

His smile returned, and his posture relaxed. The words had tumbled out of her mouth with absolutely no thought as to how she would arrange for this to happen. All she knew was that somehow she had to be with him today. He must like her and more than just as a friend. Maybe more than he liked Sara. Oh no, she had forgotten about Sara. What would she tell her?

"So, what's there to do around here?"

"Um. We could go to the water hole."

"Is that like a coffee shop or something?"

"Of course not. We're Mormons! The water hole is a man-made lake."

"Sounds fun. I'll meet you after school then."

Sara returned. She took a step back when she saw Luke, then she recovered from her surprise and walked in the room.

"Oh, hi."

"Hey, Sara, what's up?"

"Nothing."

"Here's your lunch." Rachel handed the wrinkled bag to her. Sara took it and headed for the door.

Rachel slipped out of the seat behind Luke. As they went outside, Luke whispered in her ear. "Are we still on for today?" His warm breath sent a shiver down her spine.

She nodded her head, but as soon as her feet hit the steps, panic set in. Of course she couldn't meet with him! It was completely impossible. She'd never be able to obtain permission. She would have to sneak off, risking getting in huge trouble. Plus, she'd be setting a terrible example for her sister. That settled it. She'd have to tell Luke she couldn't go. She was shocked she had even considered it.

THE afternoon dragged. Rachel said a quick prayer for strength to resist Luke's considerable charm. She looked at the clock, and it seemed to stand still. One more hour.

"Okay," Mrs. Gladys said, slamming the book closed with the finality that only the end of the school day brings. "I talked with the other teachers, and we decided over lunch today that we would give you children a special treat for making the first week at Blood of the Lamb Academy such a huge success.

"Soooo." She stretched the "O" out like a piece of taffy. Rachel assumed it was to create suspense. "We are ending the day early and letting you all go to the watering hole for some fun."

Rachel's head swam in relief. She could still spend time with Luke after school today, and he would never have to know that she was about to cancel their *date*, or whatever he considered it to be.

She glanced at Luke, who now wore a scowl, but when he caught her eye, he shrugged and smiled. She was pleased that she didn't have to let him down.

The pencil gray clouds were swollen with rain as they sagged in the sky, threatening to interrupt the afternoon swim. Overgrown wheatgrass, checkered with sunflowers, outlined the dirt path the students followed on their way to the water hole. Mother Anna led the parade of small children, while Mrs. Gladys brought up the rear. She and Sara sandwiched Luke. Periodically, his swaying left arm grazed hers, causing her breath to lock in her throat. He didn't seem to notice.

Luke and Sara were engaged in an animated discussion of *The Lord of the Rings,* a series of books that Sara had borrowed from the school library back when they attended Centennial. He explained to them that his father was holding his entire book collection hostage until he "got with the program." Maybe she should read one or two of the books Sara brought home, then she would have something to contribute to the conversation. At the very least, she would be a more interesting person. She never knew she was so boring until now.

The air thickened with humidity. Her hair was pasted to her face, damp and kinky. A smattering of gnats had tried to park themselves on her forehead, and as soon as she shooed them off, a new batch appeared. But Luke was too busy with Sara to notice. *Please God, forgive me for my jealousy, and if you could stop me from sweating, just this once, I would be so grateful.* Seth and Sammy had run so far ahead, she could no longer see them, but she bit her tongue rather than voice concern for their well-being. She didn't want to interrupt the flow of their conversation to sound like a mother hen. A really boring mother hen.

Since they were only allowed to remove their shoes and socks, it didn't take long for all the younger kids to jump into the water in a splashing frenzy. The humidity had acted like a lubricant, loosening Rachel's braid until her curls cascaded out of it. Her dress, now bathed in perspiration, clung to her body in an immodest way that made her feel naked.

"Let's go in," Sara suggested.

Rachel had stopped swimming in the water hole years ago. She hated the weight of her wet clothes, threatening her like an undertow. Sara knew that. Rachel would dip her feet and ankles in the water to cool off, but the extent of her swimming was monitoring the boys to make sure they didn't drown.

"Sure." Luke raised his arms over his head and removed his shirt. Rachel gasped, immediately dropping her gaze to the ground. She had never seen a man's unclothed body. Her face blazed with embarrassment.

"What's wrong?" he asked, looking in her direction.

"Um . . ." How could she explain to him that his immodesty was a sin without sounding judgmental? "We aren't allowed to swim unless we keep all of our clothes on." At least that didn't sound like it was her idea.

"What kind of bullshit is that?" He made no move to cover himself.

The girls gasped.

Rachel's heart ached for him. He understood so little about their way of life. She knew mainstream Mormons wore modified sacred undergarments, allowing them to wear more contemporary clothing, but he didn't even have that on. He needed her guidance and her patience.

"It's okay," Rachel said, shocking herself by touching his forearm to comfort him. His eyes found hers, and she felt his rock-hard arm unknot. "Prophet Silver teaches that our bodies are temples of God. We should keep them covered at all times in public. If we expose our skin, allowing others to look at it in a carnal way, then we invite lust . . ." She paused, the shame at using the word "lust" threatened to choke off her message. ". . . in the hearts of others."

He put his shirt back on. "Sorry."

"You didn't know," Rachel reassured him.

"I meant for the language."

"Oh."

"Don't worry about it." Sara kicked off her shoes and stockings. "Let's go swimming." She jumped in.

Luke hung back. "Are you going in?"

"No. I usually don't swim. Wearing wet clothes somehow takes the fun out of it."

"Yeah, I had the same thought."

Sara had plunged in, looking expectantly in their direction.

"Do you want to take a walk?" His eyes looked so deeply into hers that she literally felt weak in the knees. They were startling in their sadness.

She just wanted to make everything right for him. What could she possibly do to take away that unhappiness? *Please God, give me an answer.* And then she knew. In spite of the heat, she shivered with the gravity of her purpose.

"Yes."

She waved Sara toward the shore. "Luke wants to go for a walk with me. Can you watch the boys?"

There was a very real possibility that one of the boys would drown if Sara were put in charge, but Rachel decided she needed to put her trust in God that He would protect all of them while she was ministering to Luke.

Sara took an unsteady step back, as if she had been slapped in the face. Guilt poured over Rachel, sticking to her like honey. "I just thought 'cause you wanted to swim . . ."

Sara glanced in Luke's direction. He stood at a safe distance, waiting patiently for the details to be worked out.

"It's okay," Sara said with a false brightness in her voice.

Rachel held on to her answer like a life preserver. "Thank you so much."

She pinpointed Anna's location. She and Mrs. Gladys were engrossed in conversation with the other teachers. They would never notice her absence. She made one final tally of bobbing sibling heads before she slipped into the forested cover.

Rachel knew she had to be careful. Others in the community wouldn't understand her justification for spending time alone with Luke. Her purpose in life was to bring Luke back to the fold. *He's so unhappy because he doesn't know how to live a life that would glorify God and ensure him a place in the highest level of the Celestial Kingdom.* Through her words and example, she could show him the truth, and she would save his soul.

Maybe that's what Prophet Silver meant when he said she was no ordinary girl. After all, saving the souls of the unbelievers and the apostates is usually reserved for priesthood holders and the church leaders. She was just a girl. She couldn't even get into the Celestial Kingdom without her father or a husband pulling her through the gates.

When they came to a narrow creek that scissored through a grove of aspens, he slid his arm under hers, cradling her elbow.

"If I had known we were going to take this detour, I would have stuffed a blanket in my backpack."

"We can keep walking."

"I have an idea."

He placed his backpack on top of a mound of rust-colored dirt. "Sit on this." He crouched down next to it.

She did, her dress billowing over the makeshift seat.

"I have a question for you."

"Okay."

"Tell me something that matters to you that no one else knows you care about."

She could hardly focus on what he was saying when he was sitting so close to her. She tried not to look at his naked arms. His fingertips grazed her knee. She wanted to jump out of her skin, but she sat motionless, pretending not to notice the feathery touch.

"I've always cared about children, but it's the troubled ones that really touch my heart. The kids who need to be protected," she paused, "so they won't break from the hardness in this world." Her eyes brimmed. He must've thought she was incredibly weak. She hung her head, and as her hair covered her embarrassment, she realized for the first time that it was no longer braided. She would definitely get sent to the whipping shed for that.

"You just care about people. That's nothing to be ashamed of." He took his thumb, first to one eye and then the other and dried her tears. "So, do you want to be like a kid psychologist or something?"

"Well, I'd have to go to college for that."

"Yeah," he said, clearly not understanding what the problem was.

One more thing he hadn't been told. "The girls in Blood of the Lamb don't go to college."

She could see anger mantling in his face. "Why the hell . . ." He stopped, took a cavernous breath and started over. "Why not?"

"Because we have a higher calling," she said, struggling to find the words that could have maximum impact. She had to remember that she was there to teach him.

"A higher calling than educating yourself?"

"A woman's purpose or calling is to be a fertile ground for her husband's seed, creating a multitude of saints on earth."

He looked sick. Maybe he didn't like children.

"And to be a strong helpmate to her husband." Surely that would appeal to him.

"It sounds like it sucks to be a girl in the cult these days."

"We're not a cult. We're a big family."

"A big family that has sex with one another."

She had no idea what he was talking about. It took a moment for her to realize he was speaking about relatives marrying each other. She didn't like that either, but sometimes that was what God intended for a couple.

"So you're going to give up your dreams of helping kids to be a servant to some guy who's old enough to be your grandfather and already has eight other wives?"

He had a knack for making everything to do with living the Principle sound awful. "First of all this isn't about giving up your dreams, it's about changing them—"

"Or ignoring them."

She disregarded his comment, and continued, ". . . to fit God's plan for your life. Secondly, I would be serving God when I meet my husband's needs." She paused to see if anything she said sunk in. He shook his head ever so slightly. Not a good sign. "Besides, I actually might be someone's *first* wife."

"Yeah right."

"No, it's true. If a young man, who has never been married before, has a celestial testimony for me, and Prophet Silver confirms it's authentic, I might be the first wife." She hoped that didn't sound like a hint.

"So that's how it works. A man wants to marry you, and then he asks Prophet Silver for permission to do it?"

"Well, it's not really about wanting to marry *me*. It's based on a divine order from God."

"No, it's *all* about wanting to marry you."

Panic skirted around her mind, but she refused to invite it in to stay. If he couldn't come to accept the Principle, he would lose his soul. She felt crushed under her new responsibility to convert him. She was just a girl, a stupid girl who never had the right words.

"I bet there are guys lining up at Silver's office as we speak, to fight over who will get you."

How could he know about those other men?

"What makes you say that?" She had to know what he had found out.

"My God, Rachel, just look in the mirror!"

What was he talking about? She sat there racking her brain trying to determine what he knew, what he meant by his comment and what she should say in response. Once again, words failed her.

"You really don't know, do you?"

"No."

"You are so . . ."

"So what?"

He rubbed his hands together. "You're a pretty girl. Very pretty."

Rachel felt the color rise in her cheeks. "No, not really. Not like those girls in town."

He stared at her, eyebrows raised.

"But, thank you, anyway," she added, not wanting to be rude. He said she was pretty! "But even if I was pretty," she continued, "that would have nothing to do with a man receiving a message from God."

"It would just make it a lot easier to hear it."

"So you think that these men made up testimonies of marriage to me just because they think I'm pretty?"

"Of course. And by the way, I was speaking hypothetically."

She felt her brow knit in confusion. He was always two steps ahead of her.

"So there have been men already asking to marry you."

Rachel's stomach dropped to her knees. How could she have been so stupid! "I really don't want to talk about it."

"Well, I do."

"I really can't talk about it, so please don't ask me anymore."

He took both her hands and held them. She bit her lip to still the shiver she felt moving through her body from his touch.

"I just want to know if this incredible girl, who I really like, is going to be getting married next week, or what."

He said he *really* liked her. For a brief moment, she wondered if it was a sin to be flattered by all his attention. She would add it to her nightly confession, just for good measure.

"No, nothing's been decided. I'm not getting married anytime soon."

He exhaled, as his face loosened. "That's the best news I've heard in a very long time."

She felt a smile tug at the corners of her mouth. Maybe he's *the one.* Maybe that's why Prophet Silver hadn't made his decision. Luke hadn't received a celestial testimony, and unless he did, the prophet would have no way of evaluating whether or not it was a divine revelation from God. But then again, if Luke didn't believe in the Principle, he wouldn't receive a celestial testimony in the first place.

"What's wrong?" he said.

"Oh, nothing."

"Do you want to go back?"

"No. Never."

He picked up her right hand and kissed it softly, letting the fullness of his mouth linger on it. This was the happiest day of her life.

SIX

Never before had Luke challenged his father so directly. Even making this bullshit move here didn't cause Luke to confront his father so vehemently. But enough was enough. His dad had screwed with his life just one too many times.

"I'm not going."

Robert paced back and forth in front of empty bookshelves lined with cardboard boxes awaiting someone to empty them. They had lived there two months and his mother was too depressed to do anything. So they tripped over moving boxes and pretended they hadn't sold their home and moved to Polygamyville.

"I will not allow you to embarrass me in front of Prophet Silver." His father crossed the space in two strides, placing his hands on a sofa table. "You will attend the wedding, and that's final."

"I can't believe you can do this to Mom." Something passed across his father's face. Luke hoped it was guilt. "Or to me."

"Your mother's accepted this decision because she knows what's good for her soul. You better get with the program or . . ."

"Or what? I'm going to burn in hell? Too late. I'm already there. Don't you see what this is doing to Mom? Are you blind?" Luke wanted to add, *And stupid too?*

"How dare you talk to me like that! I am the priesthood holder in this family. I make the decisions and my decisions are final. Do you understand?"

"No. I don't." He stood up, not wanting to give his father the height advantage. "I'm not going."

Their eyes locked. The vein in his father's neck pulsed. The last time he'd seen that, Luke had been smacked in the back of the head.

Robert dropped his gaze. "Look, what can I do to make it easier for you to attend my wedding?"

Luke didn't enjoy this small victory as much as he thought he would. Maybe it was because things weren't as bad here as they could have been. He had met Rachel. Just the thought of her steadied his nerves and sent a warm rush to his gut. "Let my friends attend."

His father looked confused. "What friends?"

"Rachel and Sara."

"Aaah yes, Brother Abraham's daughters. You're friends with Rachel?"

"Both of them actually. I want them to come."

"Absolutely not. They're nothing in this community." His father made a dismissive gesture. "We don't even know if they're eligible for entry to the temple."

"Then count me out."

His father cleared his throat. "I'd have to invite the girls' parents and get permission from Prophet Silver. They'd need a temple recommend."

"If you make it happen, I'll go." Luke turned to leave. He didn't want to give his father any more time to change his mind. His father would make it happen. Money talked and people listened, especially Prophet Silver.

LUKE had never been in the temple. Although it had looked all right from the outside, he wasn't expecting it to be decent on the inside.

Frail columns supported walls that were painted a pale gold. Although there weren't any windows, the place was filled with bright white light. He craned his neck upward, seeking the source, before slamming hard against an entry table. He snatched a huge arrangement of flowers as it headed south. He took a stick in the face for his efforts.

"Watch where you're going," his father said.

Luke steadied the vase, opening his mouth to reply, when the prophet swept into the room. Tiny hairs on the back of his neck pricked a warning. Every time he laid eyes on this crazy dude, his body responded this way. It really pissed him off.

"Brother Robert, Sister Elaina, welcome to the Lord's house. Come in, come in." He approached Luke's dad with a hand shoved straight at him. They shook like they were long-lost brothers. The prophet then embraced his mother. Luke was surprised to see her face lift in greeting. This had to be hardest day of her life, yet she managed to act the part of happy helpmate.

"Thanks so much for your personal welcome," she said. "And of course you remember our son, Luke."

Luke felt his mother's nails pierce his back as she pushed him forward to shake hands with the fruitcake.

"Glad you could make it, son."

Luke nodded. Thankfully, he didn't stop and try to chat him up. An elderly temple worker, with protruding teeth that barely fit under her lips, handed him a bundle of clothes. He shoved it under his arm and followed his family.

Gritting his teeth and balling his fists up, he took a few deep breaths as he followed his father and the self-proclaimed prophet toward the men's area. The men in the dressing room greeted his father, making corny remarks about what a special day this was for him and how he was now on the path toward righteous living.

Luke tuned them out. He walked to the farthest corner of the room and sat on a bench in front of a locker where he could hang his real clothes. Luke undressed, quickly pulling on the white shirt, pants, tie (thankfully a clip-on) and socks. He tried on the white cloth moccasins. They were too short and tight. At least he didn't have to put them on now. He almost cracked up at the chef's hat and the green silk apron with nine fig leaves sewn on. Gathering the ceremonial wraps and white moccasins, he headed out.

A small crowd gathered outside the Creation Room. Luke

scanned the faces before seeing Sara. Their eyes met. Sara smiled. She looked pretty in the white outfit and for a brief moment, her gawkiness disappeared. But then his eyes found Rachel, and everything else around him paled.

The group moved into the room. He lost sight of Rachel and was forced to take in the sights. Murals depicting the creation of the earth dominated the walls. Meadows, teeming with grazing animals, were backed against horizons splayed with the colors of dawn. Luke almost expected a Disney melody to twitter from the loudspeakers and for little mechanized birds and squirrels to start chattering.

Sara's height towered above the other women, drawing his attention back to where they stood. Luke zeroed in on Rachel. They moved to take their places within the chapel, sliding into pews that were on the left side. The men were on the right. At the front of the chapel was a curtain. It rippled, and a man appeared from behind it. He was dressed in some type of white, pajama-looking thing. He was almost completely bald except for a handful of long hair that had been brushed over to one side. For a guy playing God, the comb-over struck Luke as pretty vain. Luke glanced at Rachel. Her face beamed up at the actor on the stage. It bothered him that she embraced this experience.

The actor cupped his hand to his left ear, tilting his head. "You will now hear three voices. The voices of Elohim, Jehovah and Michael."

Luke was taught that they were the three creators of earth. Elohim was the name of God, Jehovah was born into the world as Jesus and the archangel Michael was born as Adam. At the mention of these names, Luke was reminded of a virulent argument that he got into at camp one summer. His debate partner, Stephen, was a Catholic from Chicago, smart mouthed and funny. They were roommates and spent many nights talking. Somehow the conversation turned to religion. Stephen had never met a Mormon and shot him question after question. Their conversation had degraded into an argument when Luke told him that the Mormons believed that any man could become a god in his own universe in the afterlife as long as he was a good Mormon on earth.

Stephen told him that he was a polytheist. That accusation hit Luke in the gut. He had never considered that possibility. The discussion cooled the friendship and when he left the camp, Luke had a seed of doubt planted in his brain that eventually grew to complete rejection of his faith.

God finished his speech and retreated behind the curtain where three voices arose, apparently from a distance. "Jehovah! Michael! See, there is matter unorganized. Let us go down and form a world like unto other worlds which we have formed, where the spirits awaiting bodies may tabernacle."

Luke watched as the two actors playing Jehovah and Michael walked around saying things like, "We will go down," and after each day, they uttered, "It is well." On day five, someone flicked on the chandelier to represent the creation of light. Luke took that opportunity to seek out Rachel. She sat on the edge of her chair, and Luke couldn't see her face. He settled farther back into his own and watched until the seven days were finished.

Jehovah spoke first, his tone wooden and his voice completely devoid of inflection. "See the earth which we have formed, but there is not a man to till the ground." Luke rolled his eyes. Jehovah was pretty unenthusiastic for having just patched together an entire universe in seven days.

Elohim continued, "We will make man in our own image." Elohim and Jehovah began making passes over Michael with their hands. Then they breathed on him, making Michael go to sleep. Luke wished he could join Michael for a nap.

Elohim faced the audience. "This man who is now being operated upon is Michael who helped form the world. When he awakens, he will have forgotten everything and will have become as a little child and will be known as Adam."

Elohim turned back to Michael. "Adam, awake!"

Michael/Adam snapped awake. He flailed his arms and legs in this dramatic amoebalike performance. Jehovah and Elohim discussed Adam's need to have a partner on this new earth, while Adam walked around looking awestruck and uncoordinated.

After much discussion Elohim snapped his fingers, and an old woman walked onstage. She was dressed like one of the many geriatric temple workers that populated the premises. For a moment, Luke thought there had been a mistake. Surely she wasn't supposed to be Eve? But when she spoke to Adam and recited some Eve-type lines, he realized this was no mistake.

"Eve" looked like Adam's grandmother. Luke looked around, hoping someone else found the situation hilarious. He suspected Sara did, but when he glanced at the pair, he could only see their backs. Rachel sat so far forward in her seat that Luke worried she was starstruck by Adam's spastic performance.

Adding to the hilarity of Grandma Eve, Lucifer decided to take this moment to show up. And although he was dressed like a gentleman in a black suit, silk hat and cane, he acted like a rabid dog that stomped and snarled. The entire effect was made even stranger by Satan's own Martha Stewart apron cinched politely at his waist. Lucifer made eye contact with him, giving Luke an extra-special snarl.

Luke glanced at Rachel. Their eyes met for a moment. It was obvious he had been laughing. Her gaze sobered him immediately. Rachel's face softened, and she smiled at him. Then she turned her attention to Lucifer, while he climbed on the stage, stalking back and forth in front of the massive curtain that was supposed to be the Garden of Eden.

Lucifer turned to Adam. "Adam, you have a nice new world here. It is patterned after the world where we used to live."

Adam denied any knowledge of this other world. Lucifer plucked an invisible apple from an invisible tree and began taunting Adam to partake of the fruit of knowledge. After failing to entice him to take a bite, he turned to Grandma. "Ye shall not surely die but ye shall be as the gods."

Apparently, this interested Grandma, and she decided to partake of the invisible apple after all.

Grandma Eve taunted a reluctant Adam. "Our Father commanded us to be fruitful and multiply and replenish the earth. Now I have partaken of the forbidden fruit and shall be cast out, while you will remain a lone man in the Garden."

Luke swallowed his laughter, trying to suppress the vision of Grandma Eve and her menopausal delusion that she could reproduce.

Adam was not as amused as Luke and decided he had no choice but to eat the fruit. After all, it was a tall order to populate the entire planet and an impossible one without a woman, even one pushing eighty years. Adam bit into the apple. The two were partaking away when Elohim arrived on the scene. He was pissed and suddenly Adam and Grandma decided they were embarrassed to be nude in front of God. They tied their fig leaf aprons on, and the audience followed their example.

Settling back in his seat, Luke watched Elohim chastise Adam and Eve. Then he addressed the audience and told the women to obey their husbands in everything, so long as the husbands obeyed God. After the Law of Obedience, he asked the participants to take the Law of Sacrifice, where they were covenanted to give up all they possessed, including their lives, if necessary, to defend the church.

"You will now arise, push back the seats, put on your caps and moccasins and receive the first token of the Aaronic priesthood," Adam said. "And you will not forget that the utmost secrecy is to be observed with respect to these proceedings."

Luke put on the squashed chef's hat and fiddled with the ribbon intended to keep the holy hat on his head. Elohim had other ideas and began to instruct them in how and when to perform the special handshake.

"We covenant and promise that we will not reveal any of the secrets of the first token of the Aaronic priesthood, with its accompanying name, sign or penalty. Should we do so, we agree that our throats will be cut from ear to ear and our tongues torn out by their roots."

Everyone passed their thumbs across their jugulars, while pledging to give their lives up just as casually as if they were stifling a yawn. Apparently, their lives were less important than protecting some secret handshake.

A somber mood settled over the participants.

Adam pointed to a curtained door. "The brethren will now follow Adam and the sisters will follow Eve into the room representing the Lone and Desolate World."

He silently wished his mother luck before falling in step behind the prophet and his troupe of merry men.

The Lone and Desolate World was an antidote to the peaceful Creation Room. Whereas that room had murals depicting gently flowing rivers, the Desolate World showed craggy, turbulent waters. Where vegetation abounded in the Creation Room, this room was full of vines that twisted and entwined to choke out the sunlight. Animals were locked in ferocious combat, while wild-eyed birds circled overhead. Luke found it a thousand times more interesting.

Several temple workers emerged to help the participants learn their tokens and penalties. His dad made eye contact with him at one point, and Luke gave him a small smile. He got nothing in return.

Finally, some kid he recognized from BLA approached him. "So, this is your dad's big day, huh?"

Luke looked at the pimply-faced kid. "I guess."

"Man, he must be important."

"Why do you say that?"

"Because nobody gets their own endowment ceremony except for Prophet Silver. I've attended a couple of my father's weddings, and there were at least ten to twenty other couples doing the exact same thing." The kid scratched his head before adjusting his hat. "And my dad is an apostle."

"Maybe it's a slow time of year."

"Nope. There's a group one tomorrow." The kid yawned. "You know we'll be cousins after this."

"Really?"

"Your father is marrying my sister."

"Doesn't that make you my uncle?"

"Whatever. Hey, you want to go over the penalties with me?"

Before Luke could answer no, the kid pantomimed cutting out his heart. Then he made a low, slashing gesture across his abdomen to disembowel himself. Luke couldn't believe how casual the kid was about all this.

After a few practice runs, Luke felt compelled to make a joke. "So, if I have this uncontrollable urge to blurt out the temple secrets, does it mean somebody will kill me or would I have to do all this to myself?"

"No, someone will do it for you."

"Oh, glad to have that cleared up."

"Why don't you sit next to me? The good part's coming up."

Luke felt he had no choice but to agree to the settlement offer. He didn't want to look like an asshole. The men were instructed to move back into the main room. Unfortunately, he was out of Rachel range and now seated next to a man who chugged air instead of actually breathing. He also dripped sweat, flinging it every now and then. Not that he blamed the heavy guy for sweating. They were all swaddled like newborns in their sheet sets. He watched as the women were veiled so the men could gather in a prayer circle around the altar and receive the true order of prayers and see how they were given. Luke remained in his seat and so did his new cousin.

He tuned out Silver's lecture until the curtains lifted, revealing an enormous white sheet that temple workers were pulling apart and lengthening. It had deep slits stretching about six feet in height. The workers slid their arms through the slits and waited while the guy who played Peter explained what their presence signified. The area behind the veil represented the "afterlife," while the temple workers represented "God."

Luke dreaded this moment. He would have to embrace these workers, or God, and give them the correct tokens and penalties. His father would take the "God" position behind the veil to usher his mother and his new wife, Beulah, into the "afterlife." Since Luke was male, he got the *honor* of having God usher him in.

Luke took his place in line. Several hands pushed him forward until he stood behind his father. He knew Rachel and Sara were somewhere behind him in the line. He dared not turn around and look. He also kept his eyes down, not wanting to see his father with his new almost-wife or his mother's face as Dad brought Beulah through the veil.

After Dad completed being lord over his women, it was Luke's turn. He approached the veil. A temple worker stood behind him and told him to embrace "God." He did, feeling bile rise in his throat.

God quizzed him about penalties and tokens before clearing his throat and saying, "Power in the priesthood be upon me for generations and throughout eternity." God placed Luke's hand in one of the secret grips, pulling him through the slits and into the Celestial Room.

His father was on his knees alongside Beulah. Several feet away from the supplicant couple, his mother sat primly in an opulent chair.

"You okay, Mom?" Luke said, barely above a whisper.

"He wants us to pray," his mother said, nodding toward the kneeling couple. "As a family."

"Oh." Nobody made an effort to move. "He's not married yet," Luke added, as if the sealing ceremony wasn't going to happen as soon as everyone present passed through the veil. He immediately regretted saying anything because of the look that passed behind his mother's eyes.

He took a seat on another overstuffed number watching the stream of people coming through the veil.

Rachel had barely passed through the veil when Sara followed close behind. Luke got up and motioned for them to follow him over to a vacant corner. Rachel's eyes were glittery with excitement. Luke's throat knotted as he took in her beauty.

"That was the most incredible thing I've ever witnessed," she said.

"What was the story with Eve?" Sara asked.

Luke's head swung in Sara's direction as he realized he had been gawking at Rachel. "I know. Man, I thought I was the only one who was wondering that." Luke and Sara discussed their reaction to Grandma Eve while Rachel peered around the room.

Finally, she hopped into the conversation. "It's gorgeous in here."

Luke bit his tongue to keep from blurting out, *You're the gorgeous one.*

"Of course it is," Sara said. "The Celestial Room is supposed to be an ecstasy of delicate and luxurious color. I read that somewhere."

"I liked the Lone and Desolate Room myself," Luke said.

Rachel turned toward Luke, and he felt his stomach do a flip-flop. "Thanks for inviting us. I can't tell you how much it meant to me."

Luke's pulse quickened. *My god . . . she is so beautiful.* And even her stupid prairie dress couldn't hide the outline of an incredible body that Luke periodically stole glimpses of. She was hands-down the most beautiful girl he had ever seen, on the streets, in magazines, or even in the movies. "No problem," he managed to eke out.

SARA stared at her second piece of wedding cake, surprised to find tears puckering the sugary surface. Piles of stacked chairs circled her, creating a cagelike atmosphere. What seemed like the perfect place to hide moments earlier, now felt desolate and claustrophobic without Rachel and Luke. Had they ditched her and sought out a better hideout where they could be alone? Sara didn't just feel like a third wheel, she was more of a third appendage.

She put the plate down on the righted chair that Luke had sat on minutes earlier and moved toward the front of the storage room. As she neared, male voices cut across the racket coming from the reception.

She recognized Apostle Orlin's voice immediately. If the prophet wasn't on hand, Orlin often assumed the role of coordinator. He ran many meetings, tossing fiery speeches that condemned the evil nonbelievers. Who Orlin was talking to was a complete mystery though.

"I agree with you, Brother Norwood," Orlin said. "The service today was most spiritually gratifying. Now, what is it that you wanted to discuss with me privately? I'm most intrigued." Norwood. Sara frowned. The name didn't ring a bell either.

"I have an idea that you might want to hear," this Norwood person said. "You know how the other day when you saw my girl for the first time? You told me she was a pretty thing."

"Um-hmm."

"I'm offering my girl's hand to you in marriage."

"And why would I be interested in that?" Orlin said.

Sara held her breath.

"You said she was pretty and all."

"I think the Lord did right when he created womankind. I think they're all pretty in their own way," Orlin said. "Doesn't mean I want to marry them all."

"Well." Norwood cleared his throat. "My daughter says that you have a girl named Martha. I hear she's twenty-five or -six, and just between me and you, getting a little long in the teeth."

"Brother," Orlin said after a lengthy pause, "I hardly think a twenty-six-year-old is 'long in the teeth.' Still, I'm not so sure that's a fair deal. You'd be moving up in status and prestige by marrying Martha. What would I get out of it?"

"My daughter is a fine-looking gal, but Martha, she's . . . well, she seems like a very nice girl."

"What are you suggesting?"

"I'm just saying she's probably getting antsy to have babies. Don't you think?"

"Even if I was intrigued by your deal, how can you support her? You can barely feed the family you've got."

"I thought maybe . . ."

"You thought maybe your position would improve by allowing you to earn more at Silver Enterprises? Perhaps we would build another home for your burgeoning clan. Am I correct?"

"Yeah," Norwood said. "No disrespect to Martha or nothing. I'd do right by her."

"So, I'd get your daughter, who I will admit, is quite pleasant to look at. And you'd take Martha as a wife."

"Uh, well . . . well, I just think it'd be a pretty fair deal."

"Tell me about your daughter," Orlin said. "What's her name?"

"Joan Lynn. She's devoted to the Principle. She minds well. I made sure of that myself."

Sara braced herself against a stack of chairs. Joan Lynn. She knew the girl and suddenly Norwood's identity became clear. He was a dreadful person. This couldn't possibly be happening. She pinched her arm to make sure it wasn't a dream.

"I have several very attractive wives already. Why would I want another one?" Orlin said. "The Lord hasn't even begun whispering in my ear that it is time to take another."

"She's young."

"How young?"

"Only just turned thirteen."

"Hmm. I see," Orlin said.

"You wouldn't have to worry no more about Martha."

"Well, it might be an interesting exchange. I tell you what, I will pray about it, and if the Lord gives me confirmation, I'll set the wheels in motion."

They moved out of earshot. Sara's knees buckled, slamming against the concrete floor. The pain shot up her legs, exploding in her brain. She ignored it and crawled to the nearest wall. Pulling herself against it, she tucked her throbbing knees tight against her chest.

This didn't just happen. It couldn't have. Her eyes ached to cry, but they were dry. She knew both those girls, and pity swelled in her throat. To have such awful fathers like that . . .

The accordion doors rattled. Sara held her breath. She'd been discovered.

"Sara," Luke whispered.

"What's wrong?" Rachel took one look at her huddled against the wall and then handed Luke her plate of cake and pushed past him.

"I . . . I . . ." The tears started, choking Sara's words off.

"We couldn't come earlier because some brothers were standing right outside the entry. What's wrong?"

Sara needed to buy time and think about whether or not she should even tell Rachel. "I thought I'd been discovered."

"But you weren't."

"I know . . ."

What if Luke's father made some type of deal to marry Beulah?

Rachel leaned over and hugged her, saying reassuring things that Sara couldn't process. Suddenly everything was suspect. Questions about her engagement swirled in her mind. Maybe that was why the prettiest girls always ended up with the powerful council members. Look what was happening to Rachel. Maybe Sara's own father had been afraid nobody would want his freakishly tall, horse-faced daughter and asked his brother to unload her. She wanted to scream.

What would her father get in exchange for giving up his cash cow, Rachel? What if she married someone like Brother Orlin who just gave Martha away? She'd never survive in Norwood's home.

Sobs racked Sara's shoulders. Rachel shushed and comforted, but Sara's control spiraled away.

"Come on, Sara. It's not like you were caught. And even if you were, what's the big deal?" Luke said after a few moments.

Sara snuffled. "They would have accused me of spying on them."

"That kind of thing wouldn't be looked upon favorably," Rachel said to Luke. "Maybe we should get out of here. Maybe the Lord was trying to tell us that."

"I think He has other things to do," Luke said.

"You're probably right, but still we had a close call. Maybe it's time we returned to the party," Rachel said, her eyes darting to the door.

"I can't go. Not yet." Sara grabbed her sister's hands and squeezed.

"Okay. But you need to take a few deep breaths."

Rachel demonstrated for her as though Sara had never breathed before a day in her life. It suddenly struck her as funny. Not just funny, hilarious. Absolutely the most hysterical thing she had ever seen. It was forbidden to laugh, but she couldn't stop. Her sides ached and tears continued to flow.

"Sara. Sara. What's going on with you?" Nervous amusement marked Rachel's words.

Luke began laughing with Sara and soon the three of them were hunched on their knees, holding their stomachs and guffawing. Nobody knew what was so funny, and that made it funnier, even though they'd be beaten within an inch of their lives if they were caught laughing.

"This . . . is . . . crazy." Luke swiped his eyes. "What . . . is so funny?"

"I don't know," Sara said. They roared louder.

He stood, held out a hand to Sara and pulled her to her feet.

He then reached for Rachel, practically lifting her off the floor. "This day has been so strange. Did you see that weirdo staring at you during the sealing ceremony?"

Rachel shook her head.

"He actually mouthed the vows while staring you down. It was creepy."

Sara had noticed that as well and had been disturbed. He was a fairly prominent apostle.

"Guess he had the delusion he was marrying Rachel."

Sara laughed. "Yeah, well, Farley needs to get in line with the other sixteen guys all vying for Rachel's hand."

"Wha . . . what did you say?" Luke shook his head.

Sara glanced at Rachel, who looked deathly white. How could she have been so stupid?

Luke came to Rachel in the dead of night. Had she not been awake already, her heart torn by Sara and Luke's collective misery, she might never have heard the rap of the pebbles as they hit the attic window. Peeling the towel back, she saw him framed in the abundance of moonlight, looking expectantly up at her room. She pried the window open, splintering the palm of her hand.

"What are you doing?" Sara said.

"Ssssh," she hissed. "It's Luke."

"What!" Sara jumped up.

"I have to talk to you," Luke said.

"Now?"

"Right now."

She raised her finger at him, motioning for him to wait. "Hold on."

"Luke needs us."

"Luke needs you," Sara corrected her.

"But—"

"Rachel, he wants to talk to you. He didn't ask for me."

"What should I do?"

"Go to him."

"I don't know."

"You want to be with him, don't you?"

"Uh, yes."

"Then you've answered your own question. I'll cover for you."

"What about you?"

"Just go. Don't worry about me."

Rachel returned to the window and nodded her answer, afraid to use any more words. She began to twist her hair into a braid.

"Rachel, you have to go. Now!"

"But I don't have stockings on and my hair . . . it's not braided."

"Now, Rachel!"

She let her waist-length hair fall in untamed waves down her back. Hugging Sara tightly she said, "Thank you."

She tiptoed along the edge of the stairs, clutching her shoes to her chest, not realizing, until she slipped through the back door off the kitchen, that she was wearing only her thin cotton nightgown. He was still standing under the attic window when she found him.

"Rachel," he said, his eyes widening.

Her name sounded melodic on his lips. She wondered what he could possibly be thinking. He acted like he had never seen her before or like she was some sort of ghost. He must be so upset about the sixteen testimonies.

"Are you okay?"

"No. Not at all." He put his hand on the small of her back, nudging her away from the dangerous nearness of the house and its occupants. "Come on. Let's get out of here."

The silvery moon hung polished and gleaming, illuminating their way to the edge of the woods. They slipped into the lush blackness of the forest, its shadows promising concealment from the unforgiving fullness of the moon.

Pulling out a flashlight from his pocket, he flicked it on. "Let's go farther in," he said.

The beams of light, sliced into jagged edges by the soaring pine trees, danced like skeletons across their path. Strange indeterminate sounds swirled around them, as if the forest was haunted. Rachel shivered.

Luke stopped walking. "Are you cold?"

"No." The night air was still warm, like the dying embers remaining after a raging fire. "It's just the noises," she added. She was embarrassed for being so afraid.

He turned around to face her. Slipping his arms around her waist, he pulled her close. She felt the muscles of his torso press into the softness of her chest. The harder she clung to him, the safer she felt. He suddenly released her.

"We better go," he said hoarsely.

Rachel was stung by his abruptness. "Go where?"

"Just a little farther. Near the creek."

"Okay."

She was amazed that he could navigate the wooded sea of darkness as if it were a playground from his childhood. She heard the flow of the creek, thinned and slow moving from the summer's drought. A large rock, shaped in the form of a tabletop, tipped ever so slightly toward the creek bed.

"How about we sit on this?"

"That's perfect."

"This time I came prepared."

Pulling a rolled-up blanket out of his backpack, he unfurled it over the rock like a tablecloth. He extinguished the flashlight, setting it down on the blanket. They no longer needed it. The rock was drenched in moonlight.

They sat in silence for a few minutes. The rippling sound from the creek balmed her frayed nerves. She was taking a huge risk sneaking out with him. Her father would never understand that God had designed all of this so that she could help save Luke's soul.

He raked a hand through his hair. "So, when were you going to tell me about all these other guys?"

Rachel had agonized all day over it. She was so humiliated by the sixteen testimonies of marriage. He would think she was a whore, just like her father did.

"I'm so sorry . . . I just . . ."

"Ssssh," he said, putting a finger to her lips. "You have nothing to be sorry for."

"But—"

"Rachel, don't you understand? It's not your fault."

Please God, just don't let me cry. She blew air up into her eyes, and they refocused.

"See, this is what I get so angry about!"

What had she done?

"These people are deluded. Or evil. Or both."

Who was he talking about?

"I mean, how can I compete with Messiah Silver and his twelve apostles? They hold the truth, right?"

"Right."

He shook his head, tugging a handful of hair out of his eyes. "They've got you and my father and everyone else here brain-washed."

Rachel didn't understand what he meant by that.

"These guys all want one thing and that's you. They all claim to have had some message from God, but if there is a God, he'd sure as hell get it right the first time."

If there is a God? She really had a lot of work to do.

She bit her tongue, swallowing the explanation Prophet Silver had given her to explain this apparent inconsistency. Now was not the time. He was too angry. He needed to get all that anger out before it consumed him.

The words rushed out as if a dam had been broken. "How many of these sixteen guys even know you, anyway?"

"Uh . . ."

"How many?"

"I don't really know who they are . . ."

"What! You weren't even given their names?"

She shook her head. She had never considered that odd before now.

"I get it." He slid off the side of the rock, part of the blanket following him. He picked up a rock, hurling it at a tree. The forest came alive with the sound of startled creatures. "You have absolutely no say in who you marry. They spring it on you, before you have any chance to react. A guy you don't even know sees you at church, wakes up the next morning and says, 'I've been ordered by God to have this girl in my bed every night.' Definitely divine inspiration."

"Luke, it's not like that at all."

"That's exactly what it's like." He paced along the banks of the creek, and all she wanted to do was hug him and tell him it was okay. But it didn't feel okay, and she didn't know what to say.

He moved toward her again. "I'm so sick of all of it. Silver is going to order you to marry, probably some member of the Council whom he owes a favor to, and before you can even blink, you'll be with Grandpa, I mean your husband, and I'll never see you again."

"Maybe . . ." She stopped.

"What?"

"Oh, nothing." She was appalled at herself. She had almost told him that he should pray for a testimony of his own. Now she was playing God too!

"This is all so screwed up."

"If it was an easy path for the righteous, then there would be no reward at the end of our lives." She could see the fierce anger in his face melt into melancholy. He stood at the edge of the rock she was still perched on top of.

"The only true thing I know is how I feel about you."

She held her breath, the beauty of his words washing over her. "That's so beautiful."

"You're so beautiful." He ran his finger along her cheek. "So beautiful it hurts."

He called her beautiful! Much better than pretty.

His mouth came so close to hers that she could feel his shallow breath on her face. Suddenly, he backed away, as if she was dangerous. Maybe when he got a close-up look at her, he didn't think she was so beautiful anymore.

"How do you feel about sharing your husband with several other women?"

"Well . . ." she said, cautiously. She hoped he wasn't laying his trap. She was no good at this verbal sparring. "I would pray to God to give me patience and love for my new sister-wives."

"Yes, but how would you feel if, say, you were really in love with the guy?"

In love? She had never considered actually falling in love with her husband. When she thought about him, he was always a ghost-like stranger, not someone real, whom she could touch and kiss . . . like Luke.

"That would be much harder. I guess I would have to put my selfishness aside and—"

"Don't you mean your self-esteem?"

Words failed her.

"I would *never* share my wife with another man, so what right would I have to expect her to share me with other women?"

She had never heard any man voice concern over how the wife would feel.

"It just seems so unfair," he continued. "I mean, my mother is so . . ." He stood with an unnatural stiffness, so different from his casual posture that it looked like he had borrowed someone else's body for the night

Her heart swelled with love for him. Sliding off the rock, she moved behind him and put a tentative hand between his shoulder blades. The flesh over the entire expanse of his back felt taut and knotted. "I'm so sorry . . ." She held her hand there as his back began to unlock.

Then she heard it.

"What was that?" she gasped. They both stood perfectly still. It was the unmistakable sound of human feet and the crunch of dead pine needles and withered bracken under the weight of the intruder's shoes. Luke flashed beams of light, slingshot style, into the shadow of the surrounding trees. They could hear retreating footsteps.

Her father! Could it be her father? The tightness in her chest left her no room to breathe.

"Wait here."

"No! Don't leave me!"

He curled her into him. Her heart thundered in her ears.

"It's okay." He stroked the back of her hair. "Whatever it was is gone."

"My father—" Just saying his name aloud sucked the remaining air out of her windpipe.

"It wasn't your father."

"How . . . how do you know?"

"He would *never* have left you alone with me."

Hope threaded through the raw fear. The vise grip in her chest unlocked and she said, "You're right."

Now it was her turn to say, "We better go."

"Yeah."

The stillness of the house reassured her as she tiptoed up the stairs to the bathroom. Securely behind the locked door, she exhaled violently. "Please God," she begged, "please forgive me." She dropped panicky knees to the startlingly hard floor. Propping her elbows on the edge of the toilet, she clasped her hands so tightly together that they shook with the effort.

"Give me a sign. I need a sign, something, anything." She started sobbing, quiet, dry heaving sobs, peppered with hiccups. Her fear of her father hearing her guilt-laden cries forced her to bite down hard on a musty bath towel. The terry cloth muffled her grief nicely.

She woke with a start on the cold tile of the bathroom floor. Fragments of her dream slowly formed into a solid memory. As the magnitude of its meaning settled over her, she trembled with euphoria. In the dream, God told her it was Luke. God had ordained that he was to be her husband. They would be sealed together for time and eternity.

EIGHT

Clusters of pine trees hugged the curves of the road Rachel trudged down, sagging under the burden of last night's December snow. It was her sixteenth birthday today, and even though they rarely celebrated birthdays in her home, her mother did allow her to visit her childhood friend, Ruth Ann Pierce, for the birth of her first baby.

Rachel was touched that Ruth Ann wanted her there to share such an important event. They had been inseparable in elementary school. She left after the sixth grade. Rachel still loved Ruthie despite the fact she rarely saw her. Marrying her first cousin, Bryce Hogan, right after sixth grade, Ruth retreated into a dilapidated double-wide mobile home on the outskirts of town. It housed Bryce, his three wives and their ten children.

He was a short, muscle-bound man in his late fifties who had lost his right arm, at the shoulder, in Vietnam. He had an unnerving tendency to talk to himself, repelling potential brides and their fathers. Finally, the prophet told him that his soul was in jeopardy if he didn't start accumulating some wives and children. He took two wives within a year, and then he hit, as Sara called it, "a dry spell."

Rachel was about halfway there when she spotted the trailer with the sign WILKINSON CONSTRUCTION in front of it. Luke had mentioned that he worked there on weekends. Craning her neck to see around the blue spruce that obscured the entrance to the trailer, she noticed that Luke was outside with two men. With his back turned to her, he was pointing in the direction of the new meeting hall that was still under construction. It was a massive structure, sitting on a concrete throne, dwarfing the trailer in front of it.

He stood so tall and broad shouldered, with his flannel shirt flapping in the wind, while his black hair jostled around his head. Tears sprang in her eyes. Longing, greater than any she had ever felt, an actual ache in her chest, tore at her. She didn't think God would give her such a yearning for him if she were to be sealed with another man. He wouldn't be that cruel.

It had been months since she and Luke were together in the woods, but they had not been alone since then. Although he had asked her several times to meet him there, she always declined. Someone had been in the woods that night, and she couldn't risk it. But each day she and Sara spent every free moment at school with him, and every night she prayed for his conversion and the strength to set a good example for him. And even though she was falling deeply in love with him, she carefully avoided asking God for divine intervention to give Luke a testimony. He had to receive that on his own.

She heard Ruth's screams as she rounded the corner of the Hogans' driveway. She had never been present at the birth of a baby before. They tended to keep the unmarried girls away from those events. Hearing Ruth's anguished cries, she now knew why.

Ruth's mother, Melinda, answered the door, her face flooding with relief when she saw Rachel. "Thank the Lord you're here. The midwife said the baby is breech, no one can find Bryce, and I've got all these kids running around that need tending to."

"Where are Ruth's sister-wives?"

"Both of them are holed up in the back bedroom with the flu. She'd been taking care of them herself for the past two days. She finally called me when the pains got too bad."

"I'm so sorry. What can I do to help?"

A high screech reverberated through the cramped home. "She's been asking for you." Rachel was still confused about why Ruth would want her there rather than some others closer to her.

"What about Bryce?"

"You're a calming influence, Rachel." She started moving in the direction of the scream, waving Rachel to follow her. "Bryce is not.

"I gotta check on those kids. She's in there." Melinda pointed to the last door on the left.

"Thank you." Rachel heard soft moans coming through the door. She knocked softly.

"Come in," said a harried voice.

"Rachel, you came," said Ruth. Patterns of purple and red mottled her face. Her eyes were ash gray, bloodshot and watery.

"Of course."

She nodded at Leona, the community midwife who had assisted in thousands of births. Leona began to examine Ruth Ann down there. Rachel immediately turned her attention back to Ruth's head. She didn't want her to be embarrassed. Leona finished her exam, giving Rachel an appreciative smile. "You can help her with her breathing."

In between contractions, they talked as if they'd never been apart. Ruth told Rachel that she was hoping for a girl. When Leona left the room for some more water, Ruth confided that she wanted her daughter to be tough and independent, like she used to be. Her eyes filled with regret.

Rachel sat stroking her friend's hand as another contraction hit.

Tears trickled down Ruth's cheeks. Rachel took a tissue and dried them. "No more worries. Today is the happiest day of your life."

Ruth leaned back in the pillows.

Melinda popped her head in occasionally, satisfied that everything was under control. She seemed relieved not to have to witness her daughter's physical pain. Leona had managed to get the baby turned into the head-down position, telling the girls that it wouldn't be much longer. Once the baby had been turned, Ruth had dilated to eight centimeters quickly.

Ruth seemed to have a surge of energy. "I can't wait to see her."

"Or him . . ." Rachel reminded her.

"No, it's a girl."

Ruth Ann huffed and moaned and pushed, while Rachel alternated between putting cool compresses on her forehead and squeezing her hand.

"The baby's head is crowning," Leona said. "Rachel, get Sister Melinda."

Rachel bolted to the other side of the mobile home. "It's time," she told Melinda, who sat on the floor surrounded by tiny children.

"You're in charge," she told a wide-eyed girl of about eight.

"Yes, ma'am."

The baby's shoulders were being eased out of the birth canal when Rachel and Melinda made it back to the room.

"Ruthie, the baby has a full head of hair!" Rachel said. She had forgotten to go back up to the girl's head. She was witnessing a miracle.

"Oh God!" Leona said. Her tone was filled with shock.

"What's wrong?" Ruth asked, her voice unnaturally high.

The baby had piles of ropey-looking flesh towered on her belly. It took Rachel a moment to realize they were intestines. A gaping hole in the baby's tummy housed this tangle of flesh. Leona moved the intestines to the side and cut the umbilical cord.

"It's a girl," said Rachel, wanting desperately to give Ruth something joyous to hold on to.

"A girl!" Ruth said in awe. "What does she look like?"

The room was choked with silent dismay.

Rachel moved up to Ruth's head. She smoothed the stringy hair out of her eyes. "She's beautiful."

The door flew open. Bryce stood at the edge of the room, taking all of it in. Then he saw the baby. The infant squirmed and mewled on top of a receiving blanket between Ruth's open legs.

"What the hell!" Bryce said, staring at the hole.

"What's wrong with my baby?" Ruth said, hysteria rising in her voice. "I want my baaaaby!"

"It's okay," Rachel said. She had just told the biggest lie of her life.

"Get *it* out of here," he ordered Leona.

Ruth Ann convulsed with sobs. "What's wrong?"

Melinda stood in the corner paralyzed with shock. Leona cleaned the baby off, carefully avoiding the hole which spilled intestines that looked far too large and thick to ever be placed back into the baby's tiny belly.

"My baby, my baby . . ." Ruth said, rocking in the bed.

"I'm getting your baby ready for you," Leona said.

"I don't want her holding that thing," Bryce said.

Leona leveled her eyes at him. "Get out. Now."

To Rachel's immense relief, he backed out of the room, his face twisted in revulsion.

Leona piled the intestines on the baby's tummy and then swaddled her. She handed her to the girl. Ruth searched the baby's features for something hideous. Finding nothing, she kissed the infant's forehead and looked around her in confusion. "She's perfect?" Ruth asked.

"The baby's insides aren't right. Something happened when she was forming in you, and her intestines are outside of her body," Leona said.

"What!" Her face had fallen. "Can't you put them back in?"

"No. They're far too swollen to fit in her little tummy. I'm sorry. We're just going to try and make her as comfortable as possible and let nature take its course."

Nature take its course. The words echoed in Rachel's head. Sara had used those same words when describing what the other polygamous groups did when a baby had a problem. "No! Can't they fix this at the hospital?" The words were out of Rachel's mouth before she had time to think.

Ruth Ann rocked the baby, kissing her forehead and shushing her, even though the infant made no noise.

"The baby isn't right. It's the will of the Lord." Leona's voice was ripe with conviction.

"No, *this* isn't right. We have to take her in. We have to try and save her. Please!" Rachel said.

Ruth continued her rocking, now humming a lullaby to the quiet baby.

Melinda snapped into the conversation. "We don't need the law breathing down our necks."

"That doesn't matter right now, please, all that matters is her life!" Rachel wanted to grab the baby and her organs and run for help herself. She was trying so hard to push the frenzy out of her brain and stay calm.

"Rachel, I've seen this before. It's not uncommon to have something go wrong, especially when the parents are kin," said Leona.

"What?" A vision of Sara having Uncle Walter's deformed baby exploded in her head. She shook it off.

"We can't talk about that right now," said Melinda. "We just need to be here for Ruth Ann and her little one."

Rachel gasped. "Please, there must be something . . ."

"There is something *you* can do," said Melinda.

"Anything."

"Leave."

Rachel reeled backward as if she had been slapped. "I don't understand."

"We appreciate your help and all, but I know what's best for my daughter."

But what about your granddaughter!

Melinda proceeded to wrap up the bloodied sheets that were strewn all over the bed. Ruth's eyes were glazed over, and she continued to rock the baby girl.

Bryce returned, holding in his remaining left arm a shovel and a black lawn and leaf bag. "Did it die yet?"

She had never felt so much anger toward another person in her entire life. Time was running out. She had one last idea. "Can I take her to the hospital? I'll tell them she's mine, so you all won't get in trouble."

Melinda said, "Rachel, this is a private matter. They'd know you're Blood of the Lamb, and we don't need the government sticking their noses in our business. Bryce, would you see that Rachel is escorted out?"

"Let's get a move on." Bryce capped her elbow and pushed her through the bedroom door. Ruth's lullaby lingered in her ears, breaking her heart in every place.

A surge of biting arctic air stung Rachel's cheeks as she left Ruth Ann's house. Spiny brush, stripped naked from winter's assault, dotted the landscape. Everything looked cold and lifeless.

Each time she closed her eyes against the pellets of ice pinging her face, she saw the baby's intestines, purple and shiny and lying useless, a small mound spilling over the gaping hole. Her eyelids popped back open. She walked faster, her shoes soaking up all the slush on the ground like a sponge. Despite her best efforts, bits of conversation kept popping back into her brain. *When the parents are kin . . .* Luke would know if the birth defect rate was higher for Sara if she had a baby with Uncle Walter. But how could she discuss it without Sara around?

She didn't hear him approaching. When he touched her shoulder, her body jerked in a spasm of surprise.

"Oh, I'm sorry. I didn't mean to frighten you."

She forced her eyes to his face. It was Brother Duane Farley. He was the youngest apostle on the Council of Twelve, which meant he was still in his mid-forties, older than her father by several years.

"Oh, it's okay."

"I've never had the pleasure of meeting the lovely Rachel Shaw personally." He smiled.

How did he know her name?

"Nice to meet you," she said. She picked up her pace. "I don't mean to be rude, but I really have to go."

His stride matched hers, a heavy, urgent tread. It was all she could do to stop from breaking into a sprint.

"I'm meeting friends," she added. "In fact, I'm already late, and they're waiting on me." All the lies . . . her soul was always in jeopardy.

"That's good. That you have friends to see, I mean."

"Well, I really have to go." She was incapable of making small talk today.

"I just wanted to make sure you were okay. A beautiful young girl like you . . . it's not safe at this time of night to be out alone."

What was he talking about? It was four in the afternoon.

"Oh, I know, but I'm not really alone . . . they're expecting me . . . my friends are."

"Okay, great. I'll be on my way then. Have a good evening."

"You too," she said, waves of relief flooding her. She paused in her unease, looking behind her. Brother Farley hung a sharp left, turning away from her, and heading in the opposite direction.

The new meeting hall came into view. There were no longer any trucks there, as there had been on her way to Ruth Ann's house.

"Wait . . . before you go," Brother Farley called after her, swooping in from behind in a matter of seconds.

Not again. "Yes?"

"It was rude of me not to offer you a ride, to your friend's house. My car's parked just about fifty yards up the road."

What was he doing out here anyway?

"No thanks. I like the fresh air."

"But you're late, and they're expecting you."

"Really, thanks, but I just want to walk."

"Oh, come on. It'll save you some time."

"No . . . thanks anyway." Was it a sin to say no to an apostle?

His eyes darkened to round pools of oil. "You haven't even given me a chance." The big teeth were gone.

"I'm sorry. I truly am, but I really have a lot on my mind, and I'd just like to be alone."

"Sorry to have bothered you." He turned on his heel and walked away.

Why was he so persistent? Did she do something to encourage

him? Her father said she acted like a slut around the men in the community. Maybe what she considered polite behavior was actually a way of flirting and inviting unwanted attention.

The decision was made for her. She'd have to stop by the construction office. She didn't expect Luke to be there, but she decided to at least give the appearance of having someone to meet, in case Brother Farley was still lurking about.

She gave a tentative tap on the door, and Luke swung it open. "Rachel? What are you . . . what's wrong?"

It was a combination of the baby, Brother Farley and Ruth Ann, or all of it, but suddenly it was too much. She fell into his arms, crumbling at the tenderness and concern in his voice. "It's Ruth Ann."

"Your old friend?"

She nodded furiously, wanting the awful news to be out and over with, but she didn't have the strength to say it. "They're going to let her . . ." A sharp cramp cinched her stomach. She almost doubled over.

"What?"

She could not get the word "baby" out of her mouth.

"They're going to let the . . ."

"It's okay. I'm here." He was smoothing her hair.

". . . the baby die," she sputtered.

He held her tighter as if to protect her from the news she had just given him. He was about to speak, when they heard footsteps on the porch. "It's my father."

"Oh no!" She pulled away from him.

"My dad won't care."

"I have to talk to you," she whispered, as the steps got closer. "Tonight."

"I'll be there."

"One o'clock?"

"Yes." His father swung open the metal door, ushering in a blast of frigid air.

He looked as shocked as Luke had been just moments before. He recovered immediately and gave her a wide welcoming smile. "You must be Rachel."

"Yes, sir." Her cheeks flamed. What would he think of her being here alone with his son?

Brother Wilkinson was close to his son's height, with the same thick black hair that Luke had, and those dimples that would keep him forever boyish.

"So what brings you to this part of town?"

"I was visiting a friend, and I thought I'd stop in and say hi on my way home." That was mostly true.

"Well, we're glad you did, aren't we, son?"

Luke nodded warily.

"You're always welcome here. In fact, it would be nice to have you over for dinner some night. Luke never brings any friends over. I can arrange it with Elaina."

"Thank you."

"Would you like to take a tour of the new meeting hall?"

"Dad, she has to get home."

"All right. I'll give you a ride back. The time you'll save by not walking, we can use to take a tour of the site. It's still a work in progress." He herded them out the door.

The framing had been done, and all the wiring had been finished, but it was hard for Rachel to imagine how it would look completed. His father went into long exhausting details about the plumbing fixtures, the lighting and the layout of the building in general. She felt Luke's arm tighten as it brushed against hers.

Finally they piled into the pickup. The seats were soft leather. She didn't even know they had leather seats in cars, much less a computer. When Brother Robert saw her gaping at it, he said it was a "GPS." Then he proceeded to tell her what it did. She had so many realizations that day, and another one had just hit her: the enormous gap between their families' wealth. And for the first time ever, she felt like maybe she didn't belong in Luke's world.

Rachel was sandwiched between them, praying fervently that her father would still be at work. Luke didn't say a word on the entire way home, while his father chatted about the weather. As they pulled up, she could see that her father's typical parking spot was empty. She said a quick prayer of thanks under her breath.

Luke let her slide out the passenger side, holding her hand briefly to help her step out of the truck. She squeezed it ever so slightly, and he squeezed back. She thanked both of them and made her way to the back door. As she slipped behind the screen, she saw them still sitting there, not saying a word to each other, just watching her disappear into the house.

THE house lay in monastic silence as Rachel slipped down the stairs, pulling her boots and coat on and inching open the back door. The porch light flickered in protest. She turned it off, shrouding herself in the blackest iron of the night.

Her eyes were still adjusting to the shadows when Luke moved behind her, wrapping his arms around her waist, and whispering, "I'm here." She leaned the back of her head into his chest. They stood together for several quiet minutes.

She loathed shattering the calmness, but her concern for Sara loomed large and threatening. "Let's go somewhere, anywhere but here."

"I found a place."

"Where?"

"You'll see."

They stopped at a run-down fishing cabin, chasing the banks of Angler Creek. It was padlocked, but Luke just shrugged, undeterred. He went to the rear of the shanty, pried open the back window with his pocketknife and hoisted her inside.

The air was stuffy and filled with dust, but it locked the chill out of their lungs. He shined his light into every dank corner of the room, checking for anything unwelcome. Satisfied that it was safe, he pulled a blanket out of his backpack. This time he rolled it out slowly, trying to keep to a minimum the disruption of the dust that had layered every square inch of the room. Standing the flashlight on its end, he placed it on top of the blanket, bathing the room in a soft amber glow. He eased his long legs down to the floor and reached for her hand.

"This is perfect." She joined him on the blanket, curling her legs underneath the length of her coat.

"Thank you for coming with me tonight. I've wanted to be alone with you ever since that night last September."

"Don't thank me. I'm the one who asked you this time."

"Tell me what happened today."

She explained the birth and delivery, describing the shock and horror that descended on them after it was clear that the baby had something terribly wrong with her. "Then I asked Leona if we could take her to the hospital, and she said to let nature take its course."

"Maybe there was no hope."

"The baby was moving and breathing on her own."

"Hmm. I don't know."

"Couldn't they have put the organs back in and sewed her back up?"

Luke's silence was thoughtful. Finally he said, "It seems like they might have been able to do something like that at a hospital."

"They didn't take her because they didn't want to risk discovery."

"Are you sure? I mean, maybe they just thought it wouldn't do any good."

"I'm sure. I offered to take her myself, and they wouldn't let me." She started shaking. "They didn't even give her a chance."

He pulled her to his chest, and she could feel the thumping of his heart.

"I told them I'd take care of her if they didn't want her."

He hugged her tighter.

Big heaving sobs were just below the surface of her control. She didn't know how much longer she could hold them off. But she had to.

"Leona said something about how she saw a lot of defects in babies whose parents were kin."

"Was Ruth Ann related to her husband?"

"They were cousins."

"First cousins?"

"Yeah."

"That explains why the baby had something wrong with her."

"Why?"

"The closer the parents are in the gene pool, the more likely they are to pass defects on to their kids."

Rachel didn't want him to see her panic. "Sara had told me that the Nelson clan has a lot of babies with defects. I thought she was exaggerating."

"They have extensive inbreeding. It's really sick."

It's really sick. She felt light-headed and suddenly very warm.

"There's something you're not telling me."

There were so many things she couldn't tell him.

"What is it? You're not getting married to your cousin . . . are you?" She could feel his heart thumping harder against his ribs.

She exhaled deeply.

"Are you?" Anxiety weaved its way into his voice.

"Sara is engaged to be married to our uncle. My father's brother."

"That is bullshit! She can't do it." He lifted away from her. His rage filled every inch of the shack.

She knew he would never hurt her, but his anger reminded her too much of her father's uncontrollable rage. When he noticed she was crying, he looked horrified. He knelt on the blanket, taking both of her hands in his, and said, "I'm so sorry, baby. It'll be okay. I promise I'll figure things out for your sister."

They discussed Sara's predicament well into the night. *High rate of birth defects, risk to Sara's children, it's just sick.* Luke's words simmered in her brain.

"You're so quiet," he said, mercifully interrupting her tortured thoughts about deformed babies. "Are you okay?"

"I think so . . . yes." How could she explain to him that even with everything that had happened earlier that day, she was remarkably peaceful because she was in his arms? Easing her head off his chest, she looked into his eyes. "There's something else I want you to know. Remember what you said earlier, about wanting us to be alone?"

"Yes."

"I've wanted to be alone with you too. Every time I've told you no, I've wanted to be with you. I just couldn't. My father—"

He put his finger on her lips. "No talk about your father tonight."

"But I just want you to understand."

"You don't have to explain anymore. I'm just relieved that you want to be with me."

"I always want to be with you."

Everything about his face softened at that moment. "Rachel . . ." He stroked her cheek with his hand. He would not take his eyes off her face. Then he moved his mouth near hers, and she tilted her head up to meet his. She closed her eyes and parted her lips. At first they barely touched, his lips grazing hers, gently, sweetly until she found herself pressing her lips eagerly onto his soft, full mouth. Putting his hand on the back of her neck, he kissed her slowly and deeply.

NINE

S ara's shoplifting spree took on a new kind of urgency. She read more and more each evening, clicking the minutes away into the wee hours of the morning. Sara felt starved, barely able to assuage the hunger that nibbled at the corner of her mind. She read each book several times between weekly diaper excursions. She read carefully to preserve the spines of the books so that they appeared new when she returned them.

These books were different from the ones she had read at school. They were adult books, generally best-sellers, chock-full of sex and violence. The books educated her, opening up a world that Sara didn't even know existed.

Mrs. Gladys' interest in teaching declined. She actually fell asleep in class daily. Her arms would drip over the ends of her chair like wet diapers, and then her head would bob and nod. She was out cold within thirty minutes.

With snores marking Mrs. Gladys' exit, Luke, Rachel and Sara would hightail it to the back of the classroom and talk. For the first time in her life, Sara had a friend other than Rachel. But her looming marriage prevented her from enjoying it fully. Soon she would disappear into her uncle's house to become a brood mare. She prayed desperately for grace to accept this, but in the back of her head she heard Norwood's and Orlin's voices.

Winter had settled in with blustery winds and hiccups of sleet. The power lines behind the school hummed in radioactive harmony with the wind. Sara sensed a cellular change occurring within her body. Her upper lip went numb whenever someone even looked in her direction. She slept less and less. Her book demand outweighed the supply, and as Christmas approached, she stole two books at each visit, instead of one. She sensed the end looming near.

The evening was cold, but the sights along the street leading to the IGA distracted Sara from the chill. Gaudy strings of color were looped around trees and icicles of light dripped from the eaves of the houses. A chubby, red Santa waved rhythmically.

The parking lot of the IGA was thick with dirty slush. It wasn't as crowded as she would have expected on Christmas Eve night. She toted her return items in the purse, along with a short list of stuff that they needed for dinner tomorrow.

Sara selected the items before moving to the book section. At first glance, there was nothing left that she hadn't already read. Disappointment twisted her gut. She'd hoped a new best-seller had arrived. Then she found one hidden behind a romance novel. Sara picked it up and scanned the aisle for people. Feeling confident no one watched, she removed the two books and returned them to the shelf. Sara slipped the new one into her purse. Only one book this time, but that was okay.

"Merry Christmas," Sara said to Miranda, the redheaded checker. They had developed something of a friendship over the months that she'd been buying diapers.

"Merry Christmas," she mumbled, scarcely lifting her eyes. Fear stabbed at her stomach. Miranda always was friendly and conversational. Sara looked around, trying to appear casual. Nobody was paying attention to her.

She relaxed a notch and paid the amount indicated on the register. Maybe Miranda was having a hard day. She'd read that holidays depressed some people. Sara thanked her, wished her a happy holiday again and turned to leave.

The hand was heavy on her shoulder. A man spoke, "I need you to come with me."

Sara's stomach dropped. The moment she fully expected had

arrived. Sara was as good as dead. It occurred to her that maybe that was her intention all along. Dead people didn't have to get married.

A large, burly man with trim salt-and-pepper hair and a bright red nose held her shoulder. His name tag read, KYLE WALKER, STORE MANAGER. She nodded mutely and followed him up the narrow stairs into an elevated box that stood front and center in the store. He motioned for her to take a seat next to his desk. Sara sat, clutching the grocery bags and purse to her chest.

"Open your purse, please." Sara slid the bags from her wrists and unclasped the purse. A knot lodged in her throat, threatening to choke the breath from her body. She removed the book and placed it between them. He thumbed the pages and placed it to the left side of his desk.

"I can call the police or your parents. Which do you prefer?"

Sara cleared her throat and croaked, "The police."

He looked stunned, taking his time to lean back in his chair. He drummed his fingers on the desk before abruptly sitting upright. "Nope, I changed my mind. I'd hate to drag the police out on Christmas Eve for a shoplifting call. What's your name and number?"

Sara closed her eyes and rubbed numb lips. "Could you give me a break, since it's Christmas Eve?"

"Nope. Too much merchandise has been walking out the door."

"I was planning on returning the book."

He leaned back in his chair and sneered, "Yeah, and I'm Santa Claus. Give me your name and number, or I'll call the police *and* your parents."

He looked too pleased with himself to ever change his mind. She gave him the information.

"Ask for Anna."

Sara's mother arrived alone, giving Sara a withering look before discussing the situation with the manager. Following her mother out to the van, Sara couldn't keep her limbs from twitching. Every step she took was uncoordinated and off-balance. Somehow she managed to pull her limbs into the van. They drove home in silence.

Through shivery teeth and numb lips, Sara faced her mother. "Does anyone else know?"

"No."

"Are you going to tell him?"

"Of course." Her voice was flat.

"*Oh please, no.* He'll kill me." Sara's bladder shivered as though she might lose control of it. "I'm so scared, please, Mama. I'm begging you."

"Well, Sara, you should have thought about that before you stole from that store."

"Please don't tell him." Tears scrolled her cheeks. "I'll do extra chores, anything. Please."

She parked the car and cut the ignition. "I'll think about it."

Sara leaned over to hug her, but Anna flung open the door and climbed out. A thousand prayers traipsed through her mind. Maybe her mother would protect her. She felt almost giddy with hope.

FATHER Abraham wakened Sara from a deep sleep. His hands were fisted in her hair and jolted her upright.

Rachel jumped out of bed. "What's going on?"

"Get back in bed!" His voice was a snarly whisper.

Sara didn't make a sound as he pushed her toward the stairs. Her stocking feet slid along the hardwood floor, but his hold on her hair propelled her forward. The hall was deserted and deathly silent on the second floor. Sara reached back to grab his hands, but he tightened his grip on her hair and jerked her head back until she could only see the ceiling. Somehow her feet found their way down the steps onto the main floor. He hustled her into the kitchen, releasing her hair with an almighty shove.

"Get your coat, gloves and boots on. Now!"

Her coat was hanging on a rack near the back door. Sara removed it and slid it over her nightgown. She pulled her boots on and slipped gloves over shaky fingers.

Her father retrieved a thermos from beside the sink. "Out."

Outside, Sara headed in the direction of the whipping shed.

"To the garage. And get the shovel." She didn't dare question him. Opening the door, she took a moment to adjust to the darkness. *Why did he want a shovel?*

Fear welled inside her, heightening her senses. The snowflakes hitting the roof echoed like a sledgehammer. A warning clawed at the corner of her mind, but she couldn't hear it through her own panic.

Sara could almost feel his impatience outside the door as she retrieved the shovel. He led her to the edge of the tree line where an enormous spruce canopied the ground.

He settled himself against the trunk of the tree and opened his thermos to take a long drink. "Dig."

"Why?" Her teeth clattered in her mouth.

"I said dig." He twisted the lid closed on his thermos and slammed it on the ground. His eyes were steeped in shadows. Through black hollowed orbs, he returned her gaze. Reality dawned like a nightmare. He couldn't mean . . .

"*No!*"

He shot off the ground and wrapped his gloved hands around her fingers. The hard metal of the handle cut into her hand. She pleaded with him silently. His eyes were as dead as the needles and leaves underfoot. A slow tear leaked from her right eye. His hands became more insistent until she heard a snap and felt a needle of pain shoot up her hand.

"Dig!" He ground out the word between clenched teeth. With a final squeeze, he released her hands. Her left index finger was no longer throbbing. It had become completely numb.

Sara began digging. The ground was hardpacked and frozen. It seemed like hours, but perhaps only minutes passed before a small hole appeared.

"Wider," he commanded periodically. Sara dug, shaping her own grave. Flecks of icy snow dribbled from her bare head, cooling the sweat that heated her entire body due to the exertion.

"You're a strange girl." He was sitting on the ground with his back to the trunk of the pine next to where she worked. "You don't belong in the family." He yawned. "My father told me that you can't force a square peg into a round hole. He's wrong." He paused, threading his hands behind his head. "If you make the round hole big enough, you can fit anything in it. Keep digging."

The blade of her shovel cut into the ground. It was much more compliant the deeper she dug. Even facing death, she still couldn't stand up to him.

She stopped and hung on her shovel. She didn't know what to do. Maybe she should run, but this community was nothing more than a den of vipers. If she made it to the woods she could hide. When it was safe to come out, she could make it into town. Luke would help her.

He stood up and walked to her hole. She put her head down and piled another mound of dirt onto her shovel. As soon as the idea entered her head, her body was in motion. She hurled the dirt at his face, and scrambled out of her hole. She had perhaps a few seconds' lead, as he sputtered and cleared his eyes. The surprise element may have added a few more precious seconds.

She hitched her nightgown up and flew across the field. A series of curse words punctuated the night. She heard him move, a hunter and his prey. The gravel road was so close and across it was the dark shield of the forest. It was her only chance. Fear batted around her chest like the wings of a frightened bird. His breath was at her neck. Sara strained harder. His hands and body engulfed her. She slammed to the ground.

For a moment, the only sound was the rasping of their breath. An owl hooted overhead. The wind kicked up, rattling the trees. The fear was gone. In its place was numb resignation. She always knew her life would end at his hands.

With the right side of her face smashed against the earth, Sara waited. She peered, one eye out at the world, drinking in the sights for the last time, waiting for the sound of her neck snapping. She didn't even know if she was sad.

Finally, he reared back, grabbed her hair and rubbed her face into the snow. He stood up, taking her exhausted body with him, and shoved her ahead. Sara's limbs obeyed his silent command. They were now detached from her own will and completely under his control.

It wasn't until they had returned to the hole that he spoke. "Try that again and your sister will join you."

Nodding mutely, she picked up the shovel. She had only wanted to read.

She thought of how much she would miss Rachel. She would never look out at the mountains again or hold another baby and breathe in the soft, powdery smell of newborn skin. She would never lie next to Rachel at night talking about Luke. She would never read again.

Sara took a ragged breath and plunged the shovel into the earth, again and again.

"Look at me, girl."

Sara looked around, confused. His voice came from everywhere and nowhere. Time had stopped. She was standing in her grave.

Her eyes traveled upward to his face. It loomed inches from her own. His breath was sour and stank of stale tea, and his eyes were glazed with excitement.

"Now, I want you to be a good little girl and lie down."

He held out his hands. She obediently handed him the shovel. She couldn't think of the words to plead for her own life. Her bladder loosened. Warm urine streamed down her legs. She lay down. Fear coiled her heart and squeezed as dirt thudded against her body.

Pressure from the mounting soil increased. The dirt cocooned her body, crept around her head and slid off the planes of her face until eventually even that was covered. Sara slumbered in the arms of death, lulled by its seductive whispers. She surrendered, succumbing to the blackness, letting it fill her nose, mouth and soul like the sticky strands of a dark, dark web.

TEN

L ight returned, buoyant and weightless. Sara glided along its
fragile edges. Sound was next, announcing its presence in a
chorus of raindrops. Sara sank back into the darkness for a moment
and then fought to open her eyes. The light was blinding and confusing. She closed them again. Slowly, so as not to shock her eggshell-
fragile head, she moved. First, she lifted up one arm and then the
other. Hoisting herself up from her reclining position, Sara nestled
her head against the cooling edges of the bathtub.

Sensations charged her. It wasn't rain, but water that streamed
onto the top of her head and thudded dully against the flannel of her
nightgown. Sara's nose was packed with the mealy smell of earth.
She sucked air greedily through her lips. Blowing hard, Sara cleared
each nostril with a loud snort and opened her eyes.

She was alone in the bathroom. Her father had dumped her fully
clothed into the tub, turned on the shower and left. Sara's nightgown was bunched above her knees and made rivers of mud that
streamed toward the drain. Dirt was everywhere. An astonished
giggle burst from her, packed with relief and nervous energy. Sara
looked up as light edged through the narrow window above the
bath, ushering in Christmas morning.

SARA woke up in her bed sometime late in the afternoon to
Rachel's gentle touch. "You must be starved," she said. Rachel's
face swam into focus. A rock of pain lay behind her right eyeball,
but she forced herself to keep her eyes open. On the nightstand was

a dented tray that displayed a plateful of mashed potatoes and a turkey sandwich. Next to that was a glass of milk. Her throat felt nubbly and raw. Bits of grit were wedged between her teeth. Sara picked up the milk and drank gratefully, swirling her last mouthful in an attempt to clear the dirt from it.

"What happened to you?"

Sara's voice was raspy. "I died but then was resurrected. You missed the funeral, though."

Rachel furrowed her brow. "What do you mean?"

"I don't know what I mean."

"There was mud everywhere, and your nightgown was lying in the middle of the floor. It was soaked and filthy."

Rachel's skin was the color of parchment. Lines of worry sprang from nowhere and etched themselves along the corners of her eyes. Rachel's concern overwhelmed her, and Sara began to cry in great big, air-choking sobs.

Rachel grabbed a pillow, glancing toward the door at the bottom of their stairs. Her sister didn't need to tell her to stifle it. Sara took the pillow and buried her face. All the fury, terror and betrayal blasted into her pillow. The screams ebbed into sobs and then collapsed into whimpers. She was spent.

"Tell me."

Sara looked up. Rachel's face was plastered in wetness. She'd been crying along with her.

"He tried to kill me last night."

Rachel stared at her with fear-shaped eyes.

"I got caught stealing a book."

"But God . . ."

"God had nothing to do with this. I was using Him to justify it."

Rachel's face sagged. "What did Father do to you?"

Father. He no longer deserved that title. He was her tormentor, her abuser, her enemy. "He made me dig my own grave, and then he buried me."

Rachel held both hands over her mouth and shook her head. "That's not true."

"It's true." Rachel pulled her into her arms, and they both sobbed until Sara could no longer ignore the throbbing pain in her finger. She pulled back and examined it. Her index finger had swollen to twice its normal size.

"How did that happen?"

"I refused to dig, and he pressed my hand against the shovel until it snapped."

Rachel examined it. "Do you want me to get some ice?"

"No. Don't leave me."

"I won't."

Sara leaned back against the pillows. Rachel crawled in after her. They remained silent while each tried to make sense of everything.

"I can't believe I'm alive."

"Do you think he was just trying to scare you?"

"No, something changed his mind."

"I think he only wanted to scare you."

"I was digging my own grave. He didn't have to lift one finger to kill me. He only had to tell me to lie down, and I did."

SARA'S chest filled with fluid. It was heavy and thick like black molasses. At first she was terrified, shaking with cold and the panicky intake of her breath. She was drowning in the muck that clogged her lungs. Sara's dreams led her back to her grave. The cold alternated with tremendous heat: great, stoking flames that consumed her. The grave in which she dreamt became a pyre that roasted her body. Sara woke from these feverish dreams to violent coughs seizing her body until she believed her heart had stopped, and she would never take another breath.

Sara's mother came and stood over her, but Anna's face dissolved into millions of drops of water. Entranced, she watched her mother turn from solid to liquid to solid again. Imagining her mother's melting face, not as water, but as tears of regret, caused Sara to laugh out loud.

Rachel bathed her body with a cool rag. If she became too cold, Rachel bundled her in the quilt and held her like a baby. She helped Sara onto a bedpan, cleaning her if she messed. Sara believed her sister was an angel.

Everything that had been buried so deeply rose to the surface of her consciousness. A pageantry of doubts marched before her eyes, waving banners that bore the questions she'd been so intent on hiding. Examining each question, Sara turned it over and over in her hands to study it from all angles. It was sinful and dangerous to indulge these questions, but the fever toppled her inhibitions. She knew if she walked away from her faith, she would be damning her soul for all eternity. The worst sin was to apostasise: to leave the faith. She would be cast into the deepest level of hell where Satan and the other apostates were condemned.

Still, she would rather suffer eternal damnation than believe. Hell couldn't be worse than what she was experiencing now. Her father, who charted a course and set the sails to the Celestial Kingdom, had tried to kill her. He did everything the faith commanded of him. As the priesthood holder in the family, he would be rewarded in the afterlife no matter what he did to them.

She wanted nothing more to do with it.

Time passed and the air no longer shimmied in a sick haze. Her cough diminished to an irritant. Hunger gnawed her body. She tried to get up and make her way downstairs to the kitchen. After a few steps, her legs folded. She crawled back to bed.

Her ears prickled with anticipation when she finally heard her sister's soft steps. She told her that she needed to eat, and Rachel immediately disappeared back down the stairs. Her mother returned with a tray. On it was a bowl of soup and a Christmas present. It was a small wrapped rectangle that made her think of a book.

Anna put her hand on her forehead. If Sara hadn't been lying flat on her back, she would have pulled away. "You're as cool as a cucumber."

Sara had nothing to say to this Judas, so she just stared at her.

"Look, I'm really . . . I'm sorry you got sick."

Sara sensed her mother was flustered. That sent a jolt of pleasure through her body. Her mother had never apologized to her before.

Anna continued prattling on in the face of her stony silence. "I know you've probably had enough of soup, however, I don't want to shock your system."

She busied herself with the spoon, stirring the soup and blowing into the bowl. "You haven't eaten anything solid in almost two weeks."

Sara recoiled at the news. How had she managed to lose two weeks of her life? Still, it was two weeks more than she had expected to live.

Her stomach growled at the aroma that wafted up as her mother stirred. Sara had no recollection of eating anything during that time, much less soup. Her mother placed the tray on Sara's lap and handed her the spoon. She eased up in bed and began slopping spoonful after spoonful into her mouth.

"Slow down, it's not going to get up and walk away." Anna laughed nervously.

Sara ignored the scorch to her tongue, along with her mother's advice. When she finished, she drained the glass of orange juice. Pushing it away, she said the only word she believed her mother deserved to hear. "More."

"I don't think you should overdo it."

"More."

"Why don't you open your present?" Anna tentatively smiled and held out the present to her.

Sara pushed it away. "More." If she had had the energy, she would have stood up on the bed, stomped her feet and screamed.

Her mother's smile wavered. Anna picked up the tray, put it

back down and then picked it up again. "I guess you're just really hungry. I'll see what I can do."

She watched her mother's back, sending mental daggers flying after it. She wasn't sure how she felt about this new anger, but it sure beat the alternative, which was bone-penetrating hopelessness.

Sara studied her finger while she waited for food. It was still swollen, but she could bend it slightly. It no longer hurt. She didn't think it was broken, but she wasn't sure. Sara practiced flexing it until Rachel returned with a tray.

Sara smiled gratefully and bit into the peanut butter and jelly sandwich. She ate it in four bites, chasing it with a small glass of milk while listening to Rachel effuse about her recovery.

"I have chores to do." Rachel lifted the tray off her legs. "I'll be back as soon as I finish. I'm so glad you're okay."

"Thank you." Sara settled back into the covers. The Christmas present lay on the nightstand. She stared at it for a few minutes before picking it up. Too light for a book. In a way, Sara was relieved. She was not interested in any more of their ideas. Everything her family told her would be suspect from now on. She finally opened it. It was a hanky set with beautiful embroidered flowers along the edges. Somebody had put a lot of effort into making these.

"How appropriate," Sara said aloud. She could fill the delicate hankies with her snot and tears. Once they were saturated, she could wring them out and begin again. Sara opened the box, withdrew one and blew her nose.

"Merry Christmas."

SARA felt better but was told to stay in bed for the weekend. That was fine with her. She wasn't emotionally prepared to go downstairs and see her father, the Grim Reaper. Rachel sat on the floor while Sara braided her sister's hair, preparing her to go to Sunday Sacrament meeting with the family.

After Rachel left, the house echoed with emptiness. Sara took off her nightgown and examined her body. Shock charged along her veins as she stared at the skeleton in the mirror. She couldn't be more than a hundred pounds wet, and with her extreme height it was horrifying. She turned away in disgust.

The impact of her survival hit her with full force. She pulled her nightgown back on and crawled into her bed. She didn't think she had any tears left, but they poured down her cheeks, soaking her nightgown.

The *plink, plink* of pebbles against the attic window shook Sara from her self-pity. Luke should know Rachel wouldn't be here. She tried lifting the window but was so weak that she managed only a few inches.

Sara squatted down and placed her mouth near the narrow opening. "Rachel's not here."

"I know. I came to see you when I knew everyone would be gone."

Taking a few seconds to compose herself, Sara yelled out the window, "The back door is unlocked, come up to the second floor and I'll be at the landing."

"Okay."

She met him at the bottom of her stairs.

He hugged her. "You're a bag of bones."

A cough rattled in Sara's chest.

"That doesn't sound good."

"It's a lot better actually." Sara stepped onto the landing, and turned to watch Luke's face as he surveyed their room.

He looked around. "Yep, it's an attic."

"At least it's private."

"I'll give you that. Here, I brought you a Christmas present."

Sara felt her soul shimmy at the sight of the book that he removed from his coat pocket. "You got me a book?"

"Yeah. I've started working for my father's construction company."

"Rachel told me. But you can't buy books at the Outpost."

"I wouldn't work for him if I got paid in Blood Bucks."

They both laughed. Sara looked at the book. It was *The Eye of the World* by Robert Jordan.

"I thought you'd really like it."

"I know I will. Thank you so much. I've never gotten a real present before."

"You're kidding?"

"Just homemade stuff. Yuck."

"That sucks."

Sara motioned him toward the rocker while she sat on the bed.

"You've lost a lot of weight."

"It's my new diet. I call it the Dead Zone."

Luke laughed uneasily. "Rachel said you were really sick."

Sara's bravado crumpled. She began to cry. Luke moved toward her, but she held up a hand to keep him back. "I'm sorry," she said, snuffling. "I've become amazingly gifted at crying lately."

"Rachel only told me you had some bronchial thing. I think something else happened."

"It doesn't matter. Look, I need you to do me a favor."

"Anything."

"We've got to get out of here. All three of us. Out."

His face sagged with relief. "I can't tell you how glad I am to hear you say that. I thought maybe you believed this bullshit."

"Not anymore." Sara took a deep breath. "I think the prophet wants Rachel for himself."

Luke grabbed the arms of the rocking chair. His face drained of all color. "What?"

"Otherwise, he would have picked his favorite apostle, and she'd be sealed already."

"She won't go for it. No way."

"Like she has a choice? Besides, we can't just tell her the guy's a false prophet, and everything's a gigantic lie. They own her soul. Reason is not going to work. It didn't work for me until . . ."

"Until what?"

"Until, well, I got buried in the truth."

"What do we do?"

"Rachel thinks she's received a testimony to be your wife."

Luke's eyes softened. "Wow. Why hasn't she told me this?"

"Because she's praying that you'll receive a testimony to marry her. She can't tell you because she wants it to come from God."

"Consider it done. I'll pick up a ring immediately. I'll get married in this hellhole if that's what it takes to keep her safe."

"Not so simple. Everyone wants her."

"Yeah, but doesn't she get some say in who she marries?"

"Are you kidding?" Sara laughed bitterly. "But . . . she thinks if *both* of you receive testimonies, the prophet will take that as a sign from God and allow you to be married."

"Could that happen?"

"Doubtful. But Silver would have to at least *pretend* to pray about your testimonies. That would buy us critical time to work on Rachel . . . especially if you ask your dad to help out."

Luke sighed. "I don't know if he'll help me. I haven't exactly been the model polygamist son."

"True. But you could tell your father that by marrying Rachel, you'd be willing to give the Principle a chance."

"That might just work." Luke smiled. "Maybe Silver will let us get married. Problem solved."

"No. I'm a hundred percent convinced that he wants Rachel for himself."

Balling his right fist up, Luke smashed it into the palm of his left hand. He was a powder keg, and Sara had just lit the fuse.

"We've got to leave. Now!"

"Wait, calm down." Sara held up her hands to placate him. "We can't just kidnap Rachel. Even if we did manage to physically remove her from this place, she's brainwashed. We need to soften her up so that she *wants* to leave on her own."

Luke groaned. "Ahhh, this is making me crazy!"

"You and me both. I was going to let these people marry me off to my uncle just a few weeks ago! That's the kind of hold they have on you here."

He sighed. "Okay, you're right. Until then, I'll save every penny so that we'll have something to live on when we take off. Oh. And you *have* to get ahold of your birth certificates. We need them to start a new life."

Sara worried her lip between her teeth. She didn't even know if they existed, much less where they were. She didn't want to burden him with that though. He had enough to deal with.

"What about your family?" Sara said. "Grandparents, aunts, uncles?"

"Believe me, if I had family to go to, I wouldn't have come here in the first place." Luke frowned.

"So, there's no one?"

"Not really."

"Oh." Hope fizzled in her chest.

"No worries, we're still out of here."

"Lay it on thick for Rachel. We've got to back her out of this place slowly and methodically."

"Consider it done."

Sara glanced at the alarm clock perched on her nightstand. "You'd better go. They could come home early." She walked Luke to the stairs. "Thank you for the present."

"I'll get you the next one in the series." Luke nodded at the book still clutched in her hand.

"No way. Save every penny you earn. I need to leave this place much more than I need to read."

ABRAHAM sat at the breakfast table when Sara walked into the kitchen. Any sliver of control flew out the window. Physically he looked no different, with his black lacquered hair and puffy lips which deflated when he smiled. His teeth were a gallery of grays and yellows, displaying two incisors that splayed outward like badly hung paintings. His razor-thin nose and feminine mouth were presided over by eyes the shape and color of two ripe olives. He directed those eyes at Sara and something inside her shriveled.

"I see you're up and about this morning, Sara."

She nodded while her breath bottlenecked in her throat. Her mouth filled with the taste of dirt. She willed herself invisible, but everyone's eyes seemed to be tracking her movements as she took a seat. Her father pushed away from the table. Sara jumped at the screech from his chair. He made his rounds, kissing the wives. God Himself couldn't elicit such jittery adoration in these women. Thankfully, he left.

Jane pressed a reassuring hand on Sara's shoulder. Breath caught in her throat at the tender gesture. "I'm glad you're better."

At school, they arrived right at the bell. Sara only had a moment to nod at Luke before taking her assigned seat.

As she went through the motions of morning devotional, she obsessed over how to obtain her next book. Apparently, nearly dying hadn't doused the flames of passion. She finally latched on to an idea. It was risky, but brashness had settled in her bones. Her near-death episode could buy her forgiveness should she get caught. Even her stupid father wouldn't risk killing her again . . . yet.

Mrs. Gladys began the bob-and-nod routine as a student read aloud from the Book of Mormon. Now or never. Sara walked to the front of the class. The student stopped reading. Sara sensed all eyes on her backside. She gently touched her arm. "Mrs. Gladys?"

The woman's head snapped to attention. She blinked at Sara in confusion. "What is it, Sara?"

"I'm sorry to bother you, but I still feel under the weather. I think I may be getting my fever back. I would hate to contaminate anyone." Sara faked a cough, which fortunately became a real one.

Mrs. Gladys leaned away from her and nodded. "You shouldn't have come in the first place. Go on. I'll tell your mother I sent you home."

She heaved her thanks out, doing her best to convey illness and despondency.

"Take care of that cough now."

Sara nodded, flashing a bone-weary smile. As soon as she was out of sight of the school, Sara took off jogging. She wanted to get to the public school, talk to Miss Wiley, the librarian, and return home before too much time had elapsed. Her legs were noodles, but steely determination drove her. The cold wind nipped her lungs. She felt more air hungry than she'd ever been in her life.

Arriving in town, Sara stayed to the back alleys and narrow, potholed streets to avoid Silver Enterprises. Her heart swelled at the sight of her old school. She stopped, taking huge swallows of air. She thought about resting but worried if she sat down, she wouldn't be able to get back up.

Miss Wiley sat at her desk with her back to Sara, labeling the spines of books. One other student walked the aisles. Sara did a double take. He was a tall boy in his mid-teens. And he was *dark skinned.* He had a stack of books in his arms and appeared to be reshelving. Sara couldn't help but stare. She did it longer than was polite, never having seen a black person before.

She tried to ignore the lessons telling her that the blacks were the children of Satan. God had taken away Satan's power to procreate the children of righteousness. He went to Cain, who showed him how to place his seed into the animals. The black race was born. *Stop it. You don't believe. He's just as much a human being as you are.*

She realized suddenly that she was cradling her arms. She averted her eyes from the black boy and sought out the librarian.

Miss Wiley had been the librarian for as long as the school had been in existence. Sara felt as though she'd known her a lifetime, rather than three years. They'd shared a passion. They were two women on opposite sides of the time divide, yet they were bridged together by their mutual love of the written word. Her graying yellowish hair piled extravagantly on her head looked like a crown.

Miss Wiley smiled when she saw Sara. She stood up, draped an arm around her shoulder and gave her a reassuring squeeze before leading her to a stack of books. "I thought of you when these arrived."

"I have a problem, Miss Wiley."

The black boy echoed her words. "I have a problem, Miss Wiley."

Sara spun around, but the boy neither looked her way, nor appeared to take possession of his words. Sara frowned slightly, wondering if he mocked her.

"And what is that, dear?"

"Dear," echoed from somewhere behind her.

Sara willed herself not to look. "I really want to read a book, but the problem is that I'm not enrolled as a student. I can't check it out."

"Can't check it out," said the boy.

Sara spun around. The black boy was a full aisle away and had his back to Sara. The echo clearly came from him. Once again, he seemed oblivious to his words, reading the spine of the book before sailing away to find its appropriate place. She turned back around to say something to Miss Wiley, who didn't mind the boy's rude behavior. Maybe she was having some type of auditory hallucination brought on by her lack of oxygen during the run.

"Anyway." She paused a moment, waiting for the boy to mock her. He made no sound. She continued, "I'm having a hard time obtaining any reading material. I was wondering if you would let me borrow some books from time to time."

"Borrow some books from time to time."

Sara gasped and spun around. Why was this boy tormenting her?

"Don't let him bother you. He can't help it. He repeats things," Miss Wiley said.

"He repeats things," echoed the boy. He scurried away, disappearing down an aisle and out of sight.

"Oh." Sara felt relieved that at least she wasn't crazy.

"That is a problem, my dear." She stuck a label on the spine of a book before placing it on the stack. She steepled her hands and re-garded Sara. "School policy states that the books are for students only."

Frustration flooded her cheeks. She darted her eyes to the boy, mumbling her thanks to Miss Wiley before heading for the door.

"Wait."

"Wait." Apparently, the boy didn't have a problem with his hearing.

Those hated tears had filled her eyes. Sara stood with her back to Miss Wiley, batting furiously to stop the waterworks.

"I'm allowed to check out books," she said.

Sara waited for the boy to echo Miss Wiley. He didn't. She swiped at her eyes with the sleeve of her coat and turned around.

"How about I check out a book for you, and you return it when you're finished."

"You would do that for me?"

"What they don't know can't hurt them."

"Can't hurt them," echoed the boy.

Sara smiled at both the boy and Miss Wiley. He returned her smile with a blaze of toothy whiteness.

Miss Wiley picked up a book lying next to her. "This is an excel-lent book. I think you'll love it."

"Thank you so much." Sara took the book titled *The Good Earth* from her outstretched hands and pressed it to her chest. "I'll return it as soon as I can; unfortunately, I can't tell you when that will be."

"Kind of hard to get into town?"

"Into town," echoed from an indistinct location.

"Yes."

Miss Wiley nodded. "There's no rush."

"No rush."

"Thank you so very, very much. I'll take excellent care of it."

"I'm sure you will, dear."

Sara practically floated out the door, strolling along the outside corridor that led from the library to the cafeteria. At the intersection of the two, she cut to the right and began up a small hill that led toward the road. Sara felt a hand on her arm. She spun around, panicked for a moment that it was the principal. It was the boy. Her heart continued its panicked flight. A black boy just *touched* her.

He said nothing as he handed her a notebook opened to a well-worn page. Sara took it from him and read the following: I'M SO SORRY IF I OFFENDED YOU. I HAVE A CONDITION CALLED ECHOLALIA. IT'S AN UNCONTROLLABLE IMPULSE TO REPEAT THINGS THAT I HEAR. I APOLOGIZE.

She handed the notebook back to him. "That's okay. Why didn't you just tell me that?"

"Just tell me that," he repeated before plucking a pen from the outside pocket of his backpack and scrawling on a separate sheet, I'M A MUTE. I CAN'T SPONTANEOUSLY CONVERSE. I CAN ONLY ECHO BACK WHAT I HEAR.

"Oh."

"Oh." He smiled shyly and began writing again. MY NAME IS IRVIN.

He handed Sara the notebook. She read his comment, which was followed by a drawing of a smiley face. "I'm Sara."

"I'm Sara."

They both laughed at that. He retrieved the notebook from her and his hand flew across the page. I COULDN'T HELP BUT OVERHEAR YOUR CONVERSATION. DO YOU BELONG TO THE BLOOD OF THE LAMB?

"Yep. I'm a bloody lamber."

"I'm a bloody lamber," Irvin repeated.

They laughed again. She watched as he continued writing. MY MOTHER AND I DON'T LIVE VERY FAR FROM YOUR CHURCH. WE'RE RENTING OUT THE OLD PHILMORE PROPERTY. DO YOU KNOW WHERE THAT IS?

"Oh yes, that's just a half-mile down the road from us. We live off of Tucker in the house with the broken weather vane."

"Broken weather vane." He nodded furiously and began writing. I KNOW THE PLACE!!! WHILE YOU WERE TALKING TO

MISS WILEY I WAS THINKING MAYBE I COULD HELP YOU. BRING YOU BOOKS AND STUFF.

Instantly suspicious, Sara wanted to kick herself for her overactive paranoia. "Why do you want to help me?"

"Why do you want to help me?" he echoed back. I'M NEW HERE. DON'T HAVE ANY FRIENDS, WHICH COMES AS A HUGE SHOCK SINCE I'M SO MUCH FUN TO BE WITH.

He flipped his notebook toward her, and she burst out laughing. They looked at one another. She couldn't believe how handsome he was. He had serious brown eyes trimmed in sadness. She could see by his face that his own life had its share of afflictions. He must have sensed that in her too. Maybe that's why she decided to trust him.

"The problem with being my friend is that I'm not allowed to have any."

"I'm not allowed to have any." He shrugged and wrote, WHO SAYS ANYONE HAS TO KNOW?

"But how would we see one another?"

He echoed her statement and scratched away at his pad. WE LIVE CLOSE. CAN YOU SNEAK OUT AT NIGHT? OR MAYBE ON WEEKENDS. WE COULD MEET IN THE WOODS?

"How about this weekend?" She couldn't believe she was saying this to a *black person*. "I can usually get out of the house Saturday afternoon somewhere around four. Do you know the creek that runs through the woods?"

He nodded eagerly while echoing her question. I'LL FOLLOW IT TOWARD YOUR PLACE. I'LL BRING YOU SOME BOOKS!!

Sara grinned. "It's a deal. If I don't make it by five, I couldn't swing it."

"I couldn't swing it." He returned her smile. As she handed him back his notebook, their hands touched briefly. She didn't mind it this time.

ELEVEN

Sara walked along a creek squeezed between serpentine crevices, with massive outcroppings of pine sloping over the water's edge. It was an unseasonably warm January day. The water was thick with the runoff of melted snow, and the aspen trees shed the ice on their branches like water from a faucet.

She made her way along the bank, spotting Irvin sitting on a boulder in a clearing. The sunlight ignited it, guiding her to him like a beacon. He waved. She hustled over, grinning.

"Hi."

"Hi." He pulled out his notebook and wrote, YOU MANAGED TO GET AWAY.

"Escaped is more accurate."

"More accurate," he parroted. He motioned for her to have a seat. Irvin had brought a thick blue plastic tarp that he spread over the rock. Sara shrugged her backpack off and took a seat. She felt shy and a little nervous about speaking. "How's school?"

"How's school?" He immediately began writing.

Sara waited, admiring the beauty of the creek and the novelty of sitting next to a friend other than Rachel or Luke. Finally, Irvin handed her the notebook.

IT WOULD BE AWFUL IF IT WASN'T FOR MISS WILEY. SHE TOLD ME ABOUT YOU. HOW YOU WANT TO LEARN EVERYTHING. SHE SAID YOU WERE WISE BEYOND YOUR YEARS.

"Is that good or bad?"

"Good or bad?" GOOD!! I THINK THERE'S ALL THIS WIS-
DOM INSIDE YOU THAT SETS YOU APART FROM EVERY-
BODY. MAYBE THAT'S WHY I THOUGHT YOU COULD
ACCEPT ME, ESPECIALLY SINCE I'M BLACK IN LILY-WHITE
UTAH AND REPEAT THINGS. TALK ABOUT A DEADLY
COMBINATION.

"I don't care about you being black. And repeating things is no
big deal." At least half of what she said was true.

"No big deal."

"Isn't there something they can do to treat your echolalia?" Sara
felt so profoundly relieved to have found something to say.

"Treat your echolalia?" He was already writing as the echo
passed his lips.

YOU'RE SEEING THE RESULT OF TREATMENT. I'M BET-
TER THAN I USED TO BE. I CAN USUALLY LIMIT THE REPI-
TION TO THE LAST FEW WORDS. BESIDES, WE MOVE TOO
MUCH, AND MY MOM DOESN'T USUALLY WORK IN JOBS
THAT OFFER INSURANCE, SO IT'S BASICALLY WHATEVER
THE SCHOOL DISTRICT AT THE TIME CAN DO FOR ME.

"How come you move so much?" A trickle of anxiety coursed
through her. She didn't like that feeling. She'd known him for such
a short time. Already she didn't want to lose him.

"Move so much?" He wrote, WE GO THE WAY OF THE
BOYFRIEND. WE MOVE WHEREVER THEY FIND WORK.

"Keep her away from the men in my community. She'd not only
have more than her share of boyfriends, but a whole pile of sister-
wives."

"A whole pile of sister-wives." He laughed. SOUNDS ALMOST
AS CRAZY AS MY LIFE. MISS WILEY TOLD ME YOUR
FAMILY IS POLYGAMIST. SOUNDS LIKE IT SUCKS.

"It's like hell on earth."

"Hell on earth." He searched her face. She knew he wanted her
to say more, but she felt knotted up. "I wish I could tell you, but

maybe another day." She blew upward on her eyes, trying to dry them out before the tears started. Sara turned away to hide her face.

"Maybe another day." Sadness weighed down his words.

He began writing. I UNDERSTAND IF YOU CAN'T TALK ABOUT STUFF, BUT I'M HERE IF YOU WANT TO.

"Thanks. So, tell me about your family." Sara rushed the words again. "Does your father live nearby?"

"Father live nearby?"

Sara winced at the ending she left for him to echo back to her. It almost seemed as though he had turned the question back on her, which of course was not true. Sara played with the strings on her coat as he wrote in the notebook.

He smiled gently and handed her the notebook.

MY FATHER WAS A TRUCK DRIVER. HE ALSO WAS A POET. MY MOTHER TOLD ME HE HAD A PASSION FOR WORDS (IRONIC THAT HE HAD A MUTE SON, HUH?) AND THE OPEN ROAD. DIDN'T TAKE LONG FOR HIS WANDERER'S LUST TO RETURN. HE LEFT. I THINK IN SOME WAY MY MOTHER HAS NEVER STOPPED BLAMING ME FOR BEING BORN—FOR TYING HER DOWN AND GETTING SADDLED WITH A BLACK KID. SHE'S WHITE.

"Wow, what a story." She handed him back the notebook. "Do you remember him at all?"

"Remember him at all?" He shook his head while leaning over the pad. I HAVE A PICTURE OF HIM HOLDING ME. I MUST HAVE BEEN ABOUT A YEAR OLD. DO YOU HAVE A LOT OF BROTHERS AND SISTERS?

Sara began telling him about her life. He laughed when she would say "mothers" or refer to them as sister-wives. Sara kept up a steady prattle to keep him from having to repeat everything she said. When she ran out of steam, she asked him questions.

The sun disappeared behind towered piles of cloud, and the dimness reminded her of the passage of time. She looked at his watch and was startled that two hours had passed. "It's getting late. I probably should be heading back."

"Heading back." He nodded, flexed his fingers as though they were stiff and closed his notebook.

"Oh. I brought back the book that I borrowed from Miss Wiley. Could you make sure she gets it?"

He nodded enthusiastically, repeated her statement while holding up one finger to indicate she should wait a minute. Picking up his own backpack, he removed a stack of three. Without a word he gave them to her.

She pressed them to her chest, blinking back tears. "Thank you so much. I can't tell you how much this means to me." Her voice shook. "Same time next week?"

"Same time next week." He nodded his head.

She placed the books in her backpack before shouldering it. For the past hour or so she'd completely forgotten that he was black. There was hope for her yet.

RACHEL had tucked her pillow against her chest when Sara finally slid under the covers. A steady hum of conversation crept through the floorboards. She fluffed her own pillow around her head to cut off the sound of her father's voice.

"Luke has something important to tell me. He wants to meet tomorrow night."

Sara hoped Luke had picked up the ring and would be popping the question. She hid a smile. "Be careful."

"I wonder what it could be."

"Don't know." She wished she could share her feelings about Irvin, but Rachel wouldn't be able to handle his blackness. She was a true believer in the church's teachings.

"Luke is so handsome."

"Yep." Maybe she could tell Rachel and just leave out the fact he was black. She took a breath. "I . . . I met a boy. At Centennial High."

"What? Sara, you can't!"

Sara was tired of hiding her thoughts and feelings. She launched into an explanation about his echolalia, and how she initially thought he was mocking her. She couldn't seem to shut up. "He's very good looking. Not like Luke, but in an unusual way."

"What do you mean unusual?"

"He's . . . black."

Rachel's body went still with shock. Her voice sounded high-pitched and squeaky. "You can't see him. Please, Sara, it's a terrible sin."

"I no longer believe in any of this anyway, so it doesn't matter."

"What do you mean?" Hurt and disappointment couched Rachel's question.

"I think everything about this religion is a lie."

Rachel gasped, her eyelashes fluttering rapidly. She sat up in bed. "Everything? Do you still believe in God?"

"I do. But not in the sense that the family does." Sara felt uncomfortable with Rachel staring at her in wide-eyed panic. She sat up too.

"What do you mean?"

"I don't believe God was once a man like *our father*."

Sara let that thought stir the answering silence. "Let's just suppose that our father lives all the covenants. He gets exalted to God status, complete with his own universe."

Rachel sniffled.

"And our father creates people in his image, and these people worship him."

Still no answer. "This *all-loving and merciful* God is the same man who tried to kill me." Sara stared directly into Rachel's discomfort.

"Sara, that's blasphemy."

"Answer me, Rachel, who made our God?"

"That's simple. It's the doctrine of eternal progression. Our father has a father, as his father had a father for ever and ever. There is no beginning and no end."

"Yes. Each father-god has a heavenly wife, and together they beget many millions of male and female spirits, who when they are born can earn the right to become a god of their own universe if they live righteously. But guess what? I was reading the Bible and somewhere in Isaiah . . . Isaiah 43 . . . it says that 'before me there was no God formed, neither shall there be after me.' Our religion contradicts that."

"You know the Bible is incomplete. Besides, the prophet's words override all biblical scripture because of his infallibility. The Bible was written by men who made mistakes. When the prophet receives a new testimony it eliminates everything in the past."

"And what makes him infallible?"

Rachel's bottom lip trembled violently.

Sara couldn't seem to stop. "The foundation of our religion is flawed. We aren't gods, never will be. And quite frankly, I don't want to be."

"You won't be. You'll be the wife of a god."

"Wow, lucky for me. I can't wait to get to the Celestial Kingdom and start cranking out those spirit babies, so my husband, *Uncle Walter*, can populate his own universe and play God."

"Please stop. You're scaring me." She began to cry. "Our faith . . . my faith . . . it's all I have to hang on to."

"You have me. You have Luke. Hang on to us."

TWELVE

The more Rachel contemplated her situation, the more optimistic she felt. Each day that passed with no announcement from the prophet about her placing, Rachel felt more certain of her own celestial testimony to marry Luke. God had a plan, and it was on His timetable. He wouldn't allow Prophet Silver to announce her engagement because the one man God had chosen for her still hadn't received the testimony.

During Sara's illness, Rachel had spent many lunch hours with Luke, discussing their views on the church and religion in general. He couldn't answer her when she told him that faith involved suspending disbelief and maybe even ignoring logic. His heart seemed to be opening to God's plan. And he told her that he had something very important to tell her tonight. Her mind raced with the possibilities.

Sara, on the other hand, was another matter. She had become angry and cynical. Last night, she had told Rachel that she didn't believe in any part of her religion anymore, and to make matters even worse, she had a black boyfriend! Rachel's initial shock had threatened to turn into profound despair. She prayed all night for God to reveal what it was that she was supposed to do to save her sister's soul. The thought of Sara spending eternity burning in hell was unbearable. Rachel fought the undertow of depression that threatened to suffocate her with its bleakness.

Then she had what could only be considered an epiphany. Self-sacrifice: that was the key! If Rachel could in some small way experience suffering, then she could offer her own pain or discomfort up for Sara's salvation. Surely God would hear her prayers and touch Sara's heart and mind with the truth.

A DEEP threatening silence lingered in the night. Rachel felt the danger before she met its embrace: a shift in the air and a foreboding that she chose to shake off. Luke was late. Winter's icy fingers ran down her spine, sending her teeth clattering together. The opaque sky was thick with low-hanging clouds that choked off any brightness.

Danger sensations skipped on the border of her consciousness, when she felt a powerful arm lock around her waist. A hand slapped her mouth shut before she could open it to scream. He lifted her off her feet, the tips of her boots dragging in the snow, but not slowing him down.

The panic came in torrents. Her breathing short and spasmodic. He dragged her toward the woods, the inky black sky his co-conspirator. He was going to hurt her, maybe kill her. *Why? What have I done? God, please help me, please. Luke! Luke, where are you!*

She tried to slow down her breathing and think. Her knotted thoughts started to untangle themselves. His breath was hot on her neck. She ignored it. *Fight him.*

She started kicking. Her heels found his shins. He slowed down. "Do that again, and you die."

She'd heard that voice before, but she couldn't remember where. With every bit of strength she possessed she flung her hands backward, hoping they'd find her target. Her hands slapped both sides of his face. Her nails pierced flesh. She clawed his face. He yelped. His forearm unlocked from her waist. Her feet hit solid ground.

She swung her body around and bolted back toward the house. Her lungs burned with every surge forward. Then she heard him behind her, vaulting after her like a racehorse clearing hurdles.

The heat from his breath was back on her neck: hot, urgent and vile. Looping his forearm around her waist, he threw her to the ground. Her back felt like it had shattered into pieces. He straddled her torso. His knees pinned her arms to the ground. A punch, thrown with the impact of a cement block, slammed her cheek. Pain knifed through her head.

He turned his black gaze on her. Brother Farley's features were greased in sweat. He slapped his hand over her mouth again. The devil must have possessed this man of God.

"Let's get something straight. You scream, and I'll slit your throat right now. If you come quietly, I'll let you live." He moved his face within inches of hers. "It's your choice."

Cold fear gripped her throat. He yanked her to her feet. Spasms rocked her back. Her knees buckled. He caught her under the arms, picking her up and throwing her over his shoulder.

He carried her effortlessly. In a few alarmingly short minutes, they were absorbed into the blanket of dark trees. Her body screamed in pain with each step he took. They were going deep into the woods. How could Luke hear her? How could he find her? She couldn't run anymore. Spasms, like shards of glass, galloped up and down her spine.

"My friend is coming to meet me tonight." The words were panic ridden, but at least they were out of her mouth. Maybe talking about Luke would scare him off.

"I know all about your *friend*."

How could he?

"He'll be looking for me."

"He's not coming for you tonight."

He had been watching her! Even in the woods months ago . . . on the walk home from Ruth's house . . . then tonight. He was everywhere. Her heart thundered so hard, she no longer trusted it to keep up its frantic pace. It could stop, exhausted, at any moment. She tried to orient herself. But the creek was silent from the frigid artic air, and in the moonless night, it was impossible.

"Yes, he will." She wondered if she said that more for her benefit than his. At the very least, it might slow him down, even if it was just for a few precious seconds.

"Do you have a death wish?"

"No. But maybe you do." She could not believe what she had just said.

"Shut up!" He seemed agitated, a little less in control.

"You won't get away with this."

They stopped at the slanted rock. He flipped her off his shoulder like a rag doll. She stood on wobbly knees.

"Watch me." He pulled his fist back and plowed it into her left cheek. Her short scream spiraled upward. She crumpled to the ground.

Her eyelids, heavy from the effort to stay alive, threatened to close. Her thoughts treaded upward, desperate to reach the surface of clarity.

"You little slut," he hissed. "I told you not to scream."

Fresh despair consumed her. He will kill her now. Luke will come for her, but it will be too late.

His lips peeled away from his teeth. Frothy saliva bubbled up in the sides of his mouth. Spit sprayed in her face. "I could have given you everything." He climbed on top of her. "You thought you were too good for me, didn't you?"

"Please," she croaked, "no."

"Shut up. It's too late now."

She felt her panties and stockings being yanked down, and with a quick jerk of his knee, he spread her thighs apart. His solid bulk had crushed her body against the cold slab of rock. Her limbs were fixed as if they were encased in cement.

I am so sorry, Luke and Sara. I wasn't strong enough.

THIRTEEN

With his right hand fisted around the man's coat, Luke yanked him off of Rachel, while his left hand plowed into his abdomen. Luke hurled him into a tree. The man's head hit the trunk with a satisfying thud. For a moment, time stopped, and then a vague awareness of Rachel crying out his name slipped into his ears. His head turned from the man, to Rachel trembling on the rock, awkwardly trying to cover her thighs, back to the man, with his pants down at his knees, slumped against the tree. A primal rage raced through his veins, and he knew then that he would kill him.

He lunged toward the man, pulling him up by the collar to see his face, and then screaming, "WHAT DID YOU DO TO HER?" The man's eyes were well deep and hollow, his features rubbery, moving from surprise to fear to disdain in seconds. Luke shook him until his head lolled helplessly around a thickly knotted neck. "WHAT DID YOU DO TO HER?" Rachel's soft cries cut his heart, loosening his grip on the man's shoulders. The man tumbled backward, the tree breaking his fall.

"Nothing she didn't want . . . the little whore."

Luke flew at him, hammering his face with both fists. The man's taunting voice rang in his ears, smothering Rachel's pleas. He could feel the bones crunch and shatter under his knuckles. He was crazy with fury. He wanted the man to scream and wail and beg for mercy before he snapped the life out of him.

She pulled on his arm, begging him to stop. He smelled the

blood on his hands as his right fist cleaved the man's bottom lip. He raised it again, aiming for the hollowed-out eyes.

Rachel's scream was shrill and panicked. "Luke, no! Don't kill him!"

His arm stood in midflight.

"Please, please don't . . ."

He would do anything she asked, anything at all, even giving her violator one last life-saving show of restraint.

She touched him again, stroking his arm as if he were the one who had been beaten. "You're not like him."

He couldn't look at her yet. His heartbeat thundered in his ears, and his breath was choppy and open mouthed. Pulling his flashlight out of his left pocket, he snapped it on, and spread the light over her tormentor. His lips were shiny and moistened with blood. The close-cropped, spiky hair, remnants of angularity still residing in his swollen face, the eyes deeper set than any place where sight could still remain. He knew this man. He was an apostle, one of the "chosen." His name escaped Luke's memory, but those soulless eyes did not.

"You'll . . . never . . . get . . . away . . . with this," the man said in ragged breaths. Raw hate swelled new and fierce in Luke's chest. His body quaked with the effort to maintain self-control.

She laced her hand in his, pulling him away from the man who had stolen her innocence. The man coughed and choked. Luke hoped he would drown in his own blood.

With each step she took, her face crinkled in pain. She limped, with stiff determination, away from her attacker.

"They'll never believe you," the bastard called after them.

She shuffled forward, even when Luke stopped. "If you *ever* go near her again, I'll kill you."

When they were out of the man's hearing, Luke moved the light nearer to her. He swallowed the horror that shot through his body when he finally allowed his eyes to rest on hers. Her swollen face was shaded in bruises. Blood streamed from her swollen mouth.

Her right cheekbone was puffy and oversized. Black, icy grief replaced the anger.

He had failed her. His throat cinched tight with emotion. He didn't trust himself to speak.

She must have seen the stark anguish in his eyes. "He didn't hurt me."

His mouth gaped open, starting to form words of protest.

"Not in the way that you think," she continued. "Not in that way . . ."

"He didn't . . ."

"No. You came for me. You came in time."

A thrill of relief startled him out of his grief. She wasn't raped! *Thank God, thank you God, thank you . . .* he said, over and over in his head, until he remembered he no longer believed in God. There was still some fairness left in this bleak place. Guilt twisted his gut. How could he explain to Rachel that he was late because his mother didn't know how to be a polygamist's wife? He had been in his bedroom that night until precisely 12:30 A.M., when he pocketed the ring and made his way downstairs. His mother was hunched over the kitchen table, crying in the dark. His father, the man whom she had loved since she was Rachel's age, the only man she had ever loved, was with his other wife. He spent the next twenty minutes consoling her, telling her the softest of lies, promising her he would make things right again.

He sprinted all the way to Rachel's house. She was gone. His gut told him she had been taken, but he still sprayed the pebbles onto the attic window. When Sara said she wasn't in their room, his body surged with adrenaline. He ran as if his life depended on it, straight into the woods.

When he heard the short scream, it echoed in his ears over and over, orienting him toward her. It throbbed in his head then moved into his bones.

He knew she would forgive him. But how could he ever forgive himself for not getting there sooner? He couldn't protect her. Someone was always there . . . always there . . . waiting to hurt her.

She stumbled. He tentatively put his hand around her waist. She curled her entire body into his. He kissed the top of her hair, then her forehead and finally the hollow of her neck. He avoided her face, terrified that even the softest brush of his lips against her bruises could cause her pain. "I'm so sorry . . . so sorry. Oh God, I'm so sorry. Oh baby . . ." He couldn't go on. The wetness on his face startled him. He hadn't cried in probably ten years.

"It's okay. You're here now. That's all that matters."

He buried his head in her neck, hiding the shameful tears. She looped her arms over his shoulders, and he circled the small of her back with his hands. He pressed her waist into his stomach, crushing her chest against his.

"I can't go back to my father's house. I think he would kill me."

"I know."

He begged her then, like a dying man pleading for his last wish, to run away. Right then, with just the clothes on their backs. He would come back for Sara, as soon as he could get Rachel to safety.

"I can't . . . I can't, Luke."

"Why not? Oh God, Rachel, please come with me!"

Her silence was deafening. Then it hit him. Her faith tethered her to this world. He had to convince her that he possessed those same convictions. He would tell a lie with the best of intentions: to get her away from the evil that circled overhead. Then she could feel that it would be all right to leave with him. But first the truth.

"Rachel, I have something . . . I . . ." He stumbled on his words, feeling incredibly unsure of himself. She might say no. Like the arrogant jerk that he was, he had never considered that possibility before. Unclasping his arms from her waist, he leaned back and looked into her eyes.

"I love you." Three simple words, which he had never spoken aloud before to anyone.

Rachel started crying again. "Luke . . ."

He dug in his pocket for the ring. He coiled his left fist around it. Then, taking her hand, he knelt down on one knee. "I received the marriage testimony." He heard her sharp intake of breath. "I want to . . . God wants us to be sealed together. Rachel, please . . . will . . . will you marry me?"

"Yes, oh yes!" She cried even harder, while he slid the ring on her left finger. He was filled with gratitude that seemed to reach the very core of his soul. She would leave this place with him, and they could carve a new life out for themselves. He didn't care if it was impractical, or that she was barely sixteen, or that he had only $65 in his pocket. He didn't even care that he hadn't finished high school yet. The only thing he knew to be true was his love for this girl.

"I love you too."

They were the sweetest words he had ever heard.

When she finally stopped trembling, she said, "I received the same celestial testimony. It must be God's will."

He wanted to stay there, holding her forever. But there was no time. "We need to get out of here." They had to leave before daybreak.

"Should we go to your house?"

"My house?"

"Just until we talk to the prophet."

"But I thought—"

"Prophet Silver is the only true keeper of the faith. He's really the keeper of our souls. We need to have his confirmation . . . you know . . . before we are sealed."

"Rachel, we can't go back! They would never believe us. The bastard who hurt you was an apostle."

"Yes, he's Brother Farley."

"Are you sure?"

"Yes."

"So you know him?"

"Not really." She started inhaling in short, erratic breaths. "But . . ."

"What, baby, please tell me?"

She told him in short, clipped sentences how Farley had been watching her for months. Luke felt as if he had just fallen through an ice hole.

"And my father . . . he'll think I did something . . . to make Brother Farley attack me."

"Rachel, that's the least of our worries. He couldn't possibly think—"

"Yes . . . yes, he will. It was my fault . . . I mean, he'll say it's my fault."

"That doesn't make sense."

"The apostle, he called me a slut. That's what my father thinks too."

He ground his teeth and took a steadying breath. "No way."

"Yes."

How could anyone who knew Rachel think that? He wanted to smash her father's face in. Kill him along with Farley. And Silver too.

"You need to listen to me." She would not look at him. "None of this was your fault. I don't know why the hell he says the things he does, but your father doesn't believe them. And Farley . . . Farley's just a piece of shit that . . ."

He had to watch what he said. The anger oozed from his pores. He could frighten her.

She still kept her head down.

"It was *all* my fault. I was late. I should have never risked your safety or even risked your father discovering us together. I asked you to meet me because I was selfish and wanted to be alone with you."

She kept shaking her head. "No, no . . ."

The guilt torqued his stomach. His throat squeezed with regret as he told her about his mother.

"You were taking care of your mother. She needed you."

"But . . . I should have known the danger you were in, I should have—"

". . . been with her." She raised her hand to touch his cheek.

"You did the right thing. It was the only thing you could do . . . because of who you are."

He felt like a fraud. If she discovered the real Luke, the man with hate festering inside him that was strong enough to kill someone with his bare hands, she would hate him.

"You're the best person I know."

Even if he wasn't that person, he could become the man she thought he already was.

But right now, he still hadn't convinced her to leave with him. He had to try something else. "They'll probably think I was the one attacking you, and Farley came to your rescue. That's how twisted everyone's thinking is around here."

"Your father can help us. He could even talk to my father."

"Rachel, I don't know that. Besides, he'll know we snuck out to be together. We can't explain that."

"We can tell him the truth. You had the testimony, and you wanted to tell me, before we went together to tell the prophet."

He shook off the rising panic that filled his chest, leaving no room to breathe. "Even if my dad did help us, Silver could say no, and order you to marry someone . . . whom he finds more . . . suitable."

"More suitable? Luke, God has found you to be more than suitable for me. Prophet Silver will see that. Especially since I have received the same testimony." She stroked his face with her icy fingers. "I don't think that happens very often."

"I'm sure it doesn't." He carefully extracted the sarcasm from his voice. "I still don't understand why we have to get the prophet's okay. Especially now that we've both had the testimony."

"Prophet Silver is the *only* one who knows what God's will is for us. If we don't get his permission, we're violating the Law of Placing that God created."

"I think God will understand."

"Not if we violate the laws. It's a huge sin not to submit to the will of the prophet. He's the only one who has the authority to seal us for time and eternity."

If she didn't leave now, after everything this church leader did to her, then she may never leave.

"Luke, all we have to do is follow the rules. Everything else will fall into place. God wouldn't have given both of us the testimony if it weren't true."

When that psycho prophet rejected their request to marry, it would turn her world upside down. Maybe she would end up facing in the direction of the truth. Then he and Sara could talk her into leaving with them.

"Don't worry. Your dad will help us. He's a man of great compassion. And he's been so generous to the entire community. That's where you get your goodness."

Like blows to the head, Luke absorbed both the shame and revulsion her words brought to him: shame, because he was far from a good person, Rachel just didn't know it yet; and revulsion, because the thought of being anything like his father sickened him.

"I'll agree to ask my father for help, if you'll agree that I may have to tell him some lies to explain how we both ended up out here tonight."

"I guess that's okay."

"We don't have a choice."

"What do we do about the apostle?"

What he wanted to say was, *Let him freeze to death.* Instead he said, "I don't care."

"We can't just leave him here. He might die."

Her empathy for the bastard was nothing short of extraordinary.

"I didn't mean that." His ability to lie was also extraordinary. "I'm sure my father will help me get him back to his house tonight."

HIS mother jumped out of bed, exactly like she had when he was a little boy and woke her up when he had a bad dream. She was disoriented for a moment, and then her maternal instincts kicked in, giving her bleary eyes lucidity.

"Luke, what's wrong?"

"It's Rachel."

"Who?"

"My friend from school." The word "friend" seemed ridiculous.

"Oh yes. Is she okay?"

"No, not at all. She's been attacked."

"What!"

"She's downstairs."

She threw her terry cloth bathrobe on and cinched the waist. She followed him down the stairs, coming to a halt when she saw Rachel sitting on the couch.

"Oh my Lord! You poor thing." She raced to her side and began inspecting Rachel's face with the thoroughness of a doctor. She sent Luke scurrying for hot water bottles that she instructed him to fill with ice water instead. She helped ease Rachel out of her coat, and then she fluffed the couch pillows up, moving her head onto them.

"Thank you. Thank you so much," Rachel said, with a tone of surprised gratitude that tore at Luke's heart.

"Who did this to you?"

Rachel's lips trembled.

"Mom, we need to call Dad." His mother looked at him, registering understanding in her clear green eyes.

She patted Rachel's hand. "You just stay put, honey. And don't worry about a thing."

She was on the phone in an instant. "Robert, you need to come home. Right away. Yes, it's an emergency. No, I won't tell you now. And hurry."

Beulah's trailer was only a football field's length away, so he was at the front door in minutes. His hair was rumpled, and he wore his favorite red flannel drawstring pajama pants and a white undershirt. It reminded Luke of that fact that he slept in another woman's bed tonight, instead of with his mother.

When Robert saw Rachel crumpled on the couch, he flashed a glare of contempt at Luke. He was at Rachel's side even quicker than his mother had been.

"What the hell happened here?" He looked from Rachel to Elaina and then up to Luke, where he rested his gaze. The ice blue in his eyes had darkened to a navy so deep it was almost black.

"I was going out to check on Silver's property—"

"At four in the morning?"

It was four already. Farley may be dead by now. "No. It was around one."

His dad's brows were raised.

Luke chose his next words with surgeonlike precision. "Remember you told me to check on Silver's place for you yesterday, because you had all the plumbers coming to the meeting hall site?"

"Yes, get to the point."

Luke was stuck by the disdain in his father's eyes. He felt his steady lie start to lose its footing. "Well . . . I . . . didn't get a chance to after school. I was too busy . . . and I couldn't sleep . . . and . . . I started worrying about it . . . so I went to check on things . . . and . . . I heard Rachel scream . . . in the woods . . . near the site."

He turned his black stare on Rachel, but his tone was softer. "What were you doing out in the woods in the middle of the night?"

Rachel's bottom lip trembled violently.

Luke had reminded her to take off her ring right as they arrived at his house, and now she stared at her hands, stroking her naked ring finger with her right thumb as if the ring were still on it.

"Robert, I don't think Rachel is in any condition to answer questions right now," Elaina said, rearranging the cold packs on both sides of Rachel's cheeks. "Why don't you and Luke go into the study and discuss this?" She spread a wool blanket over Rachel, tucking her feet under it.

"Why don't we do that," his father said.

They walked into the study. His father's books were piled high in stacks running along the baseboards and covering most of the floor aside from the large mahogany desk and a black leather captain's chair that were planted in the middle of the room.

"There's a folding chair in the closet. Pull it out."

Luke had to move three stacks of books out of the way in order to unfold the chair. His father leveled his eyes at him, pupils masking all but a narrow outline of blue. "What were you doing out there with her?"

"Dad, I told you—"

"Cut the bullshit."

Now, that sounded like his old father. He hadn't heard his dad swear since he "converted." This wasn't working. He had to approach it differently.

"Rachel hasn't been sleeping. For days. You can call her father right now and ask him yourself."

"Go on."

"She decided to take a walk, and that's when this asshole, Farley, grabbed her and dragged her into the woods."

"Brother Farley on the Council?"

"Yeah."

Robert leaned forward in his chair. His face was difficult to read, but Luke thought he recognized concern on it.

"Where were you during all of this?"

"I told you, I was checking on Silver's house, when I heard her scream for help."

His eyes narrowed. "So what happened after you heard the scream?"

"I took off running until I found them." The image of Farley on top of Rachel blazed hot in his memory. He swallowed his revulsion and said, "I pulled him off of her . . . and . . . I . . ."

"You what?"

"I hit him . . . a couple times . . . I think."

His father's stony face had the subtlest glimmer of approval in it. Luke's shoulders loosened.

"Did he violate her?"

"As you can see, he beat her up pretty badly."

"That's not what I asked you."

"I got there in time."

"You're sure?"

"I'm positive."

He nodded his head, accepting that part of his story. "What did you do with Farley?"

"I didn't really know what to do, so I left him there."

"That was stupid. He could take off and be sitting in the prophet's office as we speak telling him . . . well, who knows what he would tell him . . . maybe that you hurt Rachel, and he was trying to save her."

"He's not going anywhere. I made sure of that."

"Well, that's a positive."

"And besides, Rachel would tell Silver that it was him."

"Rachel can barely say two words for herself. Farley is clever. He could say that you wore a mask, and that Rachel was just trying to protect you because you were her friend, and she couldn't imagine you doing this to her."

"Dad, how do you get that?"

"How do you get the extraordinary coincidence of you being out in the woods in the dead of night at the same time Rachel is out sleepwalking—"

"She couldn't sleep, that was the problem."

"It was awfully fortuitous that you were out there to come to her rescue at exactly the right moment."

What did he want from him? Couldn't he even pretend to believe him? His lies were the harmless ones. It shouldn't matter that much to his father that he was going to meet Rachel tonight. As long as he was able to save her, get to her in time, that was all that should matter.

If he couldn't get his own father to support his version of the events, to back him against Farley and Rachel's father, then it was all over. Things could go from bad to worse very quickly. He was going to have to give it up.

"Okay," he said. "I haven't been entirely truthful with you."

"Oh, really."

"I'm sorry about that. I just didn't want to get Rachel in trouble with her father. We were supposed to meet tonight."

"Why?"

In that instant, something in his eyes made Luke pull back from the truth. "We just wanted to talk."

"And you can't do that at school?"

"I like her. A lot. And I just wanted to spend a little time alone with her to—"

"To fuck her?"

Luke almost fell off his chair. He started to say something, but he had no idea what it would be, so he clamped his mouth shut.

"You've had her."

"No, Dad . . . I would never . . ."

"More bullshit."

"Dad, I swear to you, I've never laid a hand on her."

"Luke, I was a teenage boy once too. I know what you're like."

"Look, I'm not saying I didn't want to . . . I'm just saying I didn't. She's not like that. She's not like any girl I've ever met."

"Why should I believe anything that comes out of your mouth?"

"I would never hurt her. She means . . ."

"Yes?"

"I just . . . Dad, please. I swear I've never laid a hand on her."

"You're lying."

"I swear to you . . . on Mom's life . . . I've never touched her."

He looked at his dad with the strength of conviction. He saw Robert's face soften in acceptance, and something else . . . Luke couldn't put his finger on it. Whatever it was, it hit Luke in the gut, churning and twisting his insides. Maybe it was the realization that his father didn't love him anymore. He could accept that, as long as Robert would help them. But then why would he help them if he no longer loved his son? Luke felt off-balance. Something wasn't right.

"All right." Robert scratched his stubble for what seemed like hours. "Here's what we'll do."

He proceeded to lay out a plan, which included the lies Luke already told, but later retracted. His dad obviously thought he could do a better job pulling them off than Luke had.

"No one's to know that you had planned to meet Rachel tonight."

"Okay. Her father would hurt her if he ever thought she was out—"

"Exactly. We need to get Farley and take him back home."

"What if he starts lying about—"

"I'll take care of it." He made everything seem so simple.

"What about Rachel?"

"She can spend what's left of the night here, and your mother will take her home as soon as she feels up to it."

Home. He had dreaded sending her back to that place. To her father.

"Her father's very strict."

"I'll handle her father."

His dad was being so kind, so helpful. He regretted the thoughts he'd had just moments before. He started to think maybe, just maybe, things would turn out okay.

"We need to get moving. Let me call the prophet and Rachel's father, and then we'll go get Farley."

"Thanks, Dad. I really appreciate it." His father stood, putting up his hand to stop the flow of gratitude. Luke started folding the chair up. "I'm just going to go check on Rachel, and I'll be ready to go whenever you get finished."

"Oh, Luke, one more thing."

"Sure."

"You need to stay away from her."

"What . . . but Dad—"

"How would it look if you were seen together after this?"

"I'll be careful. I don't want to put her in any jeopardy."

"You already have, haven't you?"

"I never wanted her to get hurt."

"But that's exactly what would happen again by going anywhere near her after tonight."

He felt the rising tide of panic. "I need to be with her," he blurted out, trying to pull the words back as soon as they escaped from his lips.

"You need to stay away from her. Just tell her that whatever little thing you had going is over."

Luke was once again stunned into silence. His father's tone was mocking and dismissive. He obviously couldn't ask his dad to help him with the whole testimony thing.

His father stared him down, daring Luke to challenge him. Luke wanted to tell his dad to cut the alpha male crap. He wasn't going to take it anymore. He was sick to death of his father telling him what to do, especially since everything he wanted Luke to do was wrong. His father waited, his arms crossed, legs splayed apart, for him to back down. Luke's mind raced. Though he was smart, his dad had always been smarter. Not anymore. He'd play the game. He just had to make sure that he'd win.

"Okay. I'll tell her it's over."

His dad smiled. He was a smug, arrogant asshole, but Luke needed him just a little bit longer.

"You made the right choice."

You have so underestimated me.

His father sank bank into his chair and rifled through his Rolodex. He picked up the phone, cradling it under his chin, and began to dial. Luke had been dismissed.

Rachel sat on the couch sipping hot tea through a straw. When she saw him, her face broke out in a crooked smile.

His mother stood up, wringing her hands, and asked him, "Is everything okay?"

"Dad's taking care of it."

"Oh." She wilted in relief. "Thank goodness your father was here."

"Yep."

He turned toward Rachel. "Don't you think we need to take you to the doctor?"

"Oh no . . . we can't do that . . . my father . . ."

"Luke, I've checked her out." She lowered her voice and spoke as if Rachel were no longer in the room. "She looks awful, but nothing's broken. She'll be okay."

"Rachel, we need to get you looked at. You may have a concussion." He was so sick of the cover-up. And he wasn't going to let Rachel's health be put at risk because everyone was so worried about the government ending their little polygamist orgy.

"I'm really fine. I promise . . ."

"Let me check with your father about what we should do here," Elaina said.

"You do that."

As soon as she was out of his line of vision, he scooted next to Rachel, curled his hand into hers and whispered, "I'm going to meet with Prophet Silver on Monday and tell him about the testimony."

"Are you sure we should do it so soon?"

"Yes. You need to come with me. We need to tell him together."

"But how? I can't get away."

"Go to school, and at ten tell Mrs. Gladys you don't feel well. Meet me at the foot of the first gravel road around the bend."

"Is your father going to help us?"

"Yes."

Her rigid posture softened. "Okay. I'll be there. Just don't make me go to the doctor or my father will make sure I can't go anywhere on Monday."

He hated agreeing to that, but now that he thought about it, his father would probably nix the doctor visit anyway. It was too much of a threat to his lifestyle. "All right. But if you feel dizzy or sick to your stomach or anything, you have to tell my mother. And you can't go to sleep, not for a while. I'll make sure my mom knows all of this."

"Are you leaving me?"

It cut like a knife in his heart to hear her say those words. "I have to go with my father to take care of Farley." Checking the door, he squeezed her hand, and then raised it to his lips. "We'll be together soon."

FOURTEEN

Rachel arrived home at dawn. Sara had been chilled to the core upon hearing about what happened to her sister. She fought the impulse to tell Luke it was time to just kidnap Rachel and leave. They had stayed huddled in bed together for the past two hours, listening to the muffled pitches of the mothers. Shouting began to rise from downstairs. Sara nestled deeper into the cocoon of blankets as the fighting escalated.

"Maybe we should get up," said Rachel.

"You're not going anywhere in your condition."

A tortured wail soared two stories and lifted Sara from the bed. She flew down the steps before logical thought made its connection to her limbs. Loosely aware of her bare feet on the floor, and the slap of her hand on the railing, she arrived at the landing in no time flat. She had a vague awareness of telling Rachel to "stay."

Blood was everywhere. Sara lost her balance and careened into the room. Her feet skidded across the thick slather. As she arched to the left to keep from falling on Esther, she landed hard on her hip.

Esther lay curled in a fetal position grasping her midriff. "It hurts!"

Children's cries joined Esther's.

"Get them outside," Marylee said to Anna, who snatched at arms and shoulders to steer the children from the room.

Esther screamed again. "The baby, the baby . . . oh God, it hurts!"

"What happened?" Sara's voice hinged on hysteria.

"I don't know." Jane moved toward the phone, stopped and wrung her hands.

Esther continued keening. When Sara looked at her face all she could see were the whites of her eyes. "My baby . . . do something!"

Sara patted her shoulder, knowing it was a pathetic gesture. The kitchen door opened and closed, bringing with it a blast of outside air. Heavy steps rushed toward them.

"What happened?" Abraham shoved Sara aside and knelt next to Esther. She grabbed his shirt, pulling him toward her.

"Help me!"

"We were . . . having a discussion," Marylee said, "when she fell to her knees. All this blood!"

"You did this to me!" Esther screamed at Marylee, grabbing her belly.

"Call the midwife," Abe ordered.

"She needs a hospital." Sara couldn't believe the words were coming out of her mouth. Her father turned an icy stare on her. "I mean, maybe we should call an ambulance?"

"My baby, my baby . . ." Esther moaned. "Help me, Abraham, help me."

He didn't reply for a moment. "Marylee, get the van. I want *you* to take her to the hospital."

"NO! Not that witch!" Esther curled tighter on herself. "You take me, Abe."

"You know I can't go with you."

"Should I call for an ambulance?" Sara said.

"No," he ground out between his teeth. "It would be faster to drive. Anna, you take her to the hospital."

"She did this to me!"

"Nobody did this to you." Her father didn't look convinced.

"I don't want them near me. Please, Abe . . ."

"Anna will just drop you off. I'll send Sara to stay with you instead. Okay?"

Esther looked at Abraham. "Promise you won't let those women near me."

"I promise. Only Sara. Now, calm down. I can't come to the hospital with you, not right this minute. You and the baby need me at home and not in jail."

Esther started crying again.

"Get dressed," he snapped in Sara's direction. She hopped up and ran to the stairs, wiping bloody hands on her nightgown. Jittery with fear, she stumbled several times on the steps, peeling off her nightgown when she hit the attic.

"What happened?" Rachel's face was swollen beyond recognition. Sara averted her eyes.

"It's Esther. There's a lot of blood. We're taking her to the hospital."

"Oh no! My dream!"

"What dream?" Sara grabbed clothes and began throwing them on.

"Oh, poor Esther!" Rachel struggled to her feet. "The baby's not going to make it! I need to pray."

"You have to stay in bed." Sara hopped on one foot over to the bed. The other was trapped in the thick stocking. "Lie down. Please!"

Rachel eased down.

Sara rammed the trapped leg through the stocking. Shaping it to contour to her foot, she said, "Listen, they're sending me. Everything will be fine. Just stay in bed and get better. Please!"

Rachel didn't answer. She continued to snuffle and mumble about her dream. Sara slid her feet into her shoes and started down the steps. She couldn't worry about Rachel right now.

Everyone had moved outside. The van was pulled up next to the back door. Esther was stretched across the middle seat on a blanket.

Her father turned to her. "Get back here and hold tight to her. Don't let her bounce around."

Sara climbed in and squatted on the floor near her head. She patted Esther's shoulder as Father leaned in and kissed her. "I will come up tonight. I'm only a friend of the family, got it?"

Esther nodded, tears scrolling down her cheeks. Sara couldn't believe he was sending her to the hospital all alone. His child could very well be dying. His cowardice sickened her. He kissed Esther again. "May God be with you and the baby."

He began closing the door. "Tell 'em you're her sister. Nothing more. Got it?"

Sara nodded. Satisfied, he closed the door.

At the hospital, everything moved at lightning speed. Sara stayed in the car while her mother ran inside for help. Six or seven people converged on them at once. Sara scooted out as a couple of men bent over Esther and transferred her to the gurney.

Anna pulled her aside, handing her Esther's purse. "You'll find her information inside." She jacked the driver's door open and climbed in.

"Aren't you going to stay for a while?"

"No. You're going to have to handle this."

"But—"

"Just say you're her sister. Don't say a thing about the father."

Anna pulled on the door to close it. Sara caught it and held it open. "Wait. I don't know anything. Do we have any parents?"

"What?"

"If I'm her sister, do we have parents?" Sara realized she knew next to nothing about Esther.

"Oh. Her mother's dead. She does have a father in Salt Lake somewhere. They don't talk."

She jerked the door from Sara's hands and slammed it closed.

Sara went inside. Esther disappeared between thick, wheezing doors. The reception area was stripped of personnel. An elderly woman sat in the waiting room flipping through a magazine. A thin girl with spiky blond hair pointedly ignored the baby that clawed at her knees. The child, dressed in filthy-footed banana-colored pajamas, had mucus smeared across her cheeks, giving her face a glazed-donut look. Sara didn't know where they had taken Esther.

"You the sister?" A woman with a sticky bob of black hair exited the automated doors and approached Sara. She nodded. The woman pointed to a chair opposite a desk and took a seat behind the computer monitor. She had droopy cheeks that were splattered with moles. Sara sat, listening to the woman's nails click along the keyboard.

The woman trotted out a long series of medical questions that Sara tried to answer. Finally, they were finished. She pointed back to the waiting room and told her to sit there. Sara gathered Esther's purse and backpack and started toward the closest chair.

The receptionist cleared her throat and Sara looked back. "Was that woman who drove her one of those sister-wives?" Her thin lips peeled back in a hateful grin.

"I don't know what you're talking about." Sara spun on her heel and went into the waiting room.

Sara took her seat and snapped up a magazine. A nurse appeared in the doorway after what seemed like hours. She stuck her foot, encased in a neon plastic blue clog, against the door to keep it open. "Are you Esther White's sister?"

Sara nodded. Her heart pounded its panic in her temples. "Yes. Is she okay?"

"She's in recovery. Come on, I'll take you there."

The nurse led her to the bank of elevators.

"Did she have the baby?"

"Yes. He's in critical condition though."

"It's a boy?"

"Uh-huh. Your sister had what is called placenta abruptia. In other words, the placenta pulled away from the uterine wall. Your little nephew was in distress. We had no choice but to deliver him."

The elevator pinged open. Sara followed her down the corridor. She pressed the metallic circle etched with the handicap logo. Automated doors slung open. They entered a room where curtained beds lined two walls. Esther lay on the farthest bed with her eyes closed. An oxygen mask covered her face. Another nurse hovered over her, observing the various monitors that were suspended above the bed.

They approached the beds and the nurse placed a hand on Esther's arm. "Miss White? I've got your sister here."

Esther's eyes cracked open. She tried to remove her oxygen mask, but the nurse pressed it back on. "You need to keep that on. You've just had surgery. You had a little boy. Everything's fine."

Esther mumbled something in her mask before her eyes fluttered closed.

The nurse turned to Sara. "She'll probably sleep for about an hour. The waiting room for recovery is the second door on the left." She motioned out the two doors they had just passed through. "Someone will take you to her room once it's ready. Okay?"

Sara nodded.

The blood-pressure cuff automatically kicked on. The nurse turned her attention to it. Sara glanced a final time at Esther before leaving the room.

ESTHER was asleep on one of the two beds when Sara was finally allowed to be with her. Sara was relieved the other bed was not occupied.

She must have fallen asleep for she snapped upright as the door opened. The curtain was bluntly shoved aside. Two physicians moved to the edge of Esther's bed. They seemed to swallow the room. Sara knew they came with bad news.

Esther stirred and fluttered her lashes. She moaned, struggling to sit up. The older man was bald except for a patch of white hair that grew along the rim of his ear. He put his hands on Esther's shoulder, gently pressing downward.

"Don't sit up," he said. "You've had major abdominal surgery, and it's going to be quite tender. I'm Dr. Pierce and this is my colleague Dr. Rhinehart." Dr. Pierce walked to her IV, removed a syringe from his pocket and injected something into a small port. "Just a little morphine to help you with the discomfort."

"My baby?" Esther's voice was raspy and painful sounding.

"Your son has been flown to Primary Children's Medical Center in Salt Lake City. He's in very serious condition."

Esther's breath caught in her throat. "How serious?"

"He weighs only two pounds. Still, babies have been known to survive at twenty-six weeks. It's just too early to tell. One day at a time."

"When can I see him?"

"We need to get you better first. You lost a lot of blood and we had to . . ." Pierce looked at his colleague before continuing. "We had to remove your uterus. I'm so sorry."

"I want to see William." Her words were suffused with tears. "Somebody needs to be with him."

"I'm going to keep you here at least another three days, and then we'll see about making arrangements for you to get to Salt Lake City," said Pierce.

"Any questions?" Rhinehart asked.

Esther stared at him uncomprehendingly; her eyes were glassy and vacant. When Esther dozed again, Sara stood up and went to the bathroom. She leaned against the wall and listened to the rush of water coursing through the hospital pipes. A string dangled over an engraved plastic sign with the words PULL IN CASE OF EMERGENCY. This was an emergency, but who would come and what would she say? Suddenly, she wanted to weep. Cry for the brother she may never know. William. Esther had named him William.

Sara thought about praying for him, but felt too hypocritical, too unclean to qualify for prayer. Her prayers might even hurt him more than help. "Hang in there, little guy." If he could survive this early battle maybe he could survive his father. Sara flushed the toilet, even though she hadn't gone, and went back into the room to sit with Esther.

Marylee came up with Abe sometime in the early evening. Esther had been sleeping all afternoon, not even waking when the nurses took vitals, checked her incision, emptied her urine bag and changed the IV bags. It took a few minutes for Esther to register their presence. Abraham had pulled up a chair and stroked her arm.

This action fascinated Sara. His hand seemed so harmless, even tender. Sara had always been frightened of his hands. She'd envisioned them as talons, clawing at bodies and scooping out souls. Here they moved with care. Strange.

"How's she doing?" Abe looked at her straight on.

"She's been asleep all day."

"They told me the baby has been sent to Salt Lake City. They wouldn't tell me anything else."

"We don't know much more than that."

"Is he okay?"

"They said to take it one day at a time."

"Well, the boy's a Shaw. And Shaw children are fighters, aren't they, Sara?"

There was something in his eyes that she didn't like, but for Esther's sake she smiled and nodded vigorously. "Oh yes, he's a fighter."

He nodded, pleased with her answer. "Marylee, why don't you take Sara to the cafeteria and get her some dinner."

"Of course."

The dining room had already closed for the evening, but a few desserts and prepackaged sandwiches were for sale. They each selected a piece of chocolate cake, and Sara took a turkey sandwich and a Sprite. They sat down across from each other, saying nothing.

Sara broke the silence. "How's Rachel?"

"Oh, she's fine. She came downstairs at around noon ready to help."

Sara nodded. "They had to remove her uterus." She hoped that made her feel guilty for treating Esther like crap.

"Oh my word, I did not know that!"

Marylee's body pinged with energy. Sara hoped it originated from feelings of distress rather than excitement. She might actually be happy about her sister-wife's condition. Without a uterus, Esther would be of little value to her husband.

"It was awful. They only had minutes to deliver him."

"The poor little thing."

"And then they couldn't stop her bleeding. She almost died."

Marylee stopped in midbite. She brought the fork back down to her plate and placed both hands on the table as though to steady herself. "That's terrible."

"I can't believe he left her to deal with this alone." Sara picked up her sandwich and took a bite, never dropping her eyes. Marylee squirmed. Sara enjoyed her discomfort and sunk her teeth into the sandwich with more force.

"You know how many problems this could cause the family."

"She *is* family and so is that little boy lying alone in Salt Lake City. Someone has to go up there. I think it should be him."

"No one asked you what you thought."

"Why? Nobody in this state gives a shit about polygamists."

Marylee gasped. Sara knew she'd made a mistake. Marylee might have done something to help Esther, but Sara had to curse. She blew it.

"I'll not have you speaking to me that way. I'm sure your father would not appreciate your rudeness." She straightened the bib collar on her dress and arched her brows.

"I'm sorry. It's just been a very stressful day and I'm worried about William."

"Who's William?"

"That's the name Esther gave the baby."

"We usually come together to discuss the baby's name."

"Maybe it was spur of the moment. I mean, Esther certainly wasn't planning on giving birth at twenty-six weeks."

"Now she's going to have to name all her other children names that start with a 'W.' That's dreadful."

"She's not going to have any more children. They removed her uterus."

"Oh dear, that's right." Marylee picked up her fork and severed a piece of the chocolate cake. She rammed it into her mouth and chewed quickly.

"I could go with William." Sara kept her head down and voice neutral.

"Don't be silly. You're too young."

Hope deflated in her chest. They finished their food in silence and wandered down the hall. Passing the gift shop, Sara stared at the brilliant assortment of balloons trumpeting GET WELL, and IT'S A BOY. She wondered if they had one that said, HELP! They strolled past the shop and waited for the elevator.

When they returned a nurse was checking Esther's vitals. She eyed Abe suspiciously before leaving. He cleared his throat and spoke a little too loudly. "Guess we'll be heading out." He turned to Sara, handed her a twenty-dollar bill still warm from his wallet, "For food." She took it from him, careful not to touch his hand in the process. He kissed Esther, whispered something in her ear and left.

Esther was too numb with morphine to react one way or another. She merely closed her eyes and drifted off to sleep.

Sara wrote in her journal about her fears for Esther, the baby and Rachel for at least an hour. A nurse came in and helped her with the chair, converting it into a bed. She brought sheets and a pillow for her before handing Sara the bed controls for the television. Flicking it on, the nurse showed her how to change channels and adjust the volume.

Stunned with the kindness the nurse had shown her, Sara held the contraption, feeling a jolt of pleasure. She scrolled through channels with a goofy smile on her face. She knew Esther would never tell her father that she'd been watching television. Esther probably grew up with TV. Prophet Silver had forbidden that. He wanted them to remain on the fringes of society.

Sara settled comfortably in her chair bed, tucking the covers under her chin. Though they shared few words, Sara thought she would appreciate her quiet presence. Sara was the reminder that Esther belonged, for better or for worse, to their family.

FIFTEEN

It had been three nights since Luke slept. He paced and plotted and beat his fists into the pillow. The memory of Rachel's battered face haunted him. Guilt racked him in the gut, bludgeoning him with his own inadequacy in protecting her.

He kicked the tire, climbed back into the cab and watched the road where Rachel would soon emerge. It took every fiber of his being not to kidnap her. The threats were so numerous and looming that they hung thick and toxic in the air, cutting off her capacity to reason.

He checked the time on the dash of his father's truck. She should be here any minute. Kidnapping fantasies tantalized him again, but he would never force Rachel to do something against her will.

As she rounded the corner of the road, her steps were tentative and unsteady. The contrast of untouched skin on her forehead only made the color under her eyes and cheeks a deeper and angrier blue-black. His chest contracted in such a vise grip that for a moment he couldn't suck in a single mouthful of air. It finally loosened, allowing him to climb out of the truck to meet her.

"Hi," she said shyly.

"Hi. Feeling any better?"

She touched her cheek self-consciously, as though she was somehow responsible for the damage. "Much better."

He held out his hand to help her into the truck before walking around to the driver's side. Closing the door, he turned to her. "I missed you," he said, a little too quickly, afraid he would lose control. He turned away from her, throttling the running engine.

"I missed you too." Her voice sounded watery. "But . . . something horrible happened Saturday."

"What?" he forced himself to ask. *I'm going to kill her father.*

"Esther . . ." Her breathing was choppy. "Esther . . . she began bleeding. They had to deliver the baby . . . he's very critical. He's only two pounds. They don't know if he'll make it!"

Rachel's sweetness drained the anger out of the air. Guilty relief settled over him. Her father hadn't hurt her. "I'm really sorry."

Leaning over, he swallowed her with his arms. Though they were exposed, he couldn't bring himself to drive off in search of some hiding place. Still, while she cried into his chest, he kept his eyes peeled on the road for the slightest stirring of dust that would warn of a vehicle.

Her crying tapered off. "I'm sorry. I can't seem to control my emotions anymore."

His nostrils filled with the scent of her skin. Without thinking, he touched his lips to the curve of her neck. She shivered. He pulled away, furious with himself for his lack of control. When she looked at him, her eyes were soft, and her lips were parted. Leaning in to kiss her, he stopped just inches away from her mouth. He was afraid he would hurt her. Exhaling, he moved away as her eyes clouded with doubt. She had no idea how much he wanted her.

"I love you, Rachel," he blurted out, feeling like a jerk, and wondering if she believed him.

Opening her mouth to say something, she stopped, listening to the rattle of an old engine and the backfiring of a car.

Shit! "Someone's coming." He twisted the wheel sharply to the left; the truck swept along the curve of the road and then spun out of the short driveway. Tires crunched the gravel while rocks sprayed the undercarriage. He shifted into low gear for the steep incline of a hill. In his rearview mirror he could see the plume of graveled dust kicking up behind them, but no visible car yet. They crested the hill. He hung a sharp right, while the tires hugged the road. Once around the corner, he rammed his foot into the pedal. The brakes absorbed his anxiety, squealing in protest.

The car came to a screeching halt. They both looked at each other in startled relief. Fear of discovery had become their constant companion. He didn't know how much longer he could handle being in this place.

Rachel touched his right hand, which was fisted around the steering wheel. "It'll be okay."

He was embarrassed by his show of weakness. "Yeah." He shrugged. "We better get going." He looked at the digital clock. "Silver's expecting us in five minutes."

Her face darkened at the mention of his name. For someone who extolled the virtues of this *holy man*, she sure seemed uncomfortable with the idea of being around him. That made him feel better. He would have an opening, admittedly a small one, through which to reach her.

Silver's black Lexus was parked along the primitive road that they had clear-cut for all the construction vehicles.

"Ready?"

"Yes."

Opening the car door for her, he kept his hand clasped tightly over hers. It would no longer matter if the prophet saw them together. Actually, he wanted Silver to see them holding hands.

When they entered through the makeshift doorway, Silver had his back to them. His shoulders were rounded with the gravitational pull of age. It gave Luke a small measure of confidence. He cleared his throat.

Silver spun around wearing a practiced smile that dropped as soon as he saw his visitors. He noticed Rachel first. For a split second, Luke saw no recognition in his eyes. Rachel's hand quivered. He squeezed it. Silver's eyes caught the subtle gesture, following the touch back to its original source. He trained his gaze on Luke. He tightened his narrow lips into a slash of pink.

"Rachel . . ." He moved toward her and swept her hand out of Luke's. "I'm so sorry for what happened to you."

Luke's body coiled up like a snake ready to strike.

"Thank you . . . for . . . your concern." Her chin dropped.

"I'm so glad you stopped by so I could personally tell you the news. Only the Council members know, so please keep it to yourself until I make my formal announcement." Silver lifted her chin up. "But under the circumstances, I think you should be the first to know."

Luke watched as a gulp of fear traveled down the length of her smooth neck.

"Apostle Farley has been kicked out of Blood of the Lamb. He'll be formally excommunicated in a few weeks."

His dad had pulled it off. A sliver of guilt wormed its way into his conscience, while a simultaneous surge of satisfaction coursed through his veins.

She nodded. "I'm . . . so . . . glad."

"Thank you." Luke forced the words out.

"Well, it had to be done." Silver didn't take his eyes off of Rachel, but he finally removed his hand from her chin. "Luke, let's give Rachel a tour of the house, and you can give me a status report."

Silver looped his arm around Rachel's waist. "You're shaking. It's no wonder after the ordeal you've been through. Let me help you."

Luke's throat was thick with frustration. With sheer determination he forced himself not to rip Silver's arm off of Rachel. Her posture was ironing-board straight. She avoided looking in Luke's direction. If she had given him even the slightest signal, he would have lunged at Silver, snatched her out of his grasp and carried her out of there.

Silver had managed to take over the entire conversation and never once bothered to ask what Rachel was doing here. Luke was never given an opportunity to bring it up. Silver filled the air with comments about the house, peppering his conversation with the occasional question about the time frame. By the end of the "tour," Luke's fists were clenched so tightly that his fingers were numb.

"So . . ." he turned to Luke, his arm still locked around Rachel's waist, ". . . when will it be finished?"

"My dad said in another month or so. Right around the time that the meeting hall is completed."

"Excellent."

It was now or never. "Um . . . Prophet . . . we . . . have something we wanted to talk to you about."

"Well, you can call my secretary and set up a meeting." He pulled Rachel a little tighter toward him. "Maybe late next week."

Rachel blinked rapidly. Luke felt cold desperation, as sharp and threatening as a knife, trace the ladder of his spine. "We really needed to speak with you today. It's important."

"Can't it wait?"

"No . . . no . . . it can't," Rachel said, her eyes soaked with fear. The prophet unraveled his arm from her waist.

"Well, what is it then?"

Luke was about to jump in when she said, "I've received a celestial testimony."

"You?"

"Yes . . . sir."

Turning to Luke, he said, "Well, this is quite unprecedented." The whites of his eyes looked eggy. "Let me guess . . . you've had one too?"

"Yes. I've received the celestial testimony of marriage to Rachel." Luke didn't blink. "We would like to request that you seal us for time and all eternity in the temple."

"Are you aware that there are seventeen other men who *claim* to have received the same testimony of marriage to this girl?"

Seventeen? "I knew there were others."

"You weren't supposed to know that," he snapped, scarlet anger creeping up his neck, into his cheeks and across the fist of his nose. "I have had many men in the community, very devout men, including four apostles—well, now three—that have claimed to receive the testimony for Rachel. Why should I even bother praying about whether or not you are to be sealed to her? You are hardly devout. I understand you don't attend the priesthood meetings."

"It seems to me that receiving the truth about something isn't correlated with your level of devotion. If it were, all these *holy* men wouldn't have contradictory revelations. Would they?"

Silver shifted his weight, straightened his spine and scowled. "Even Joseph Smith said that he experienced revelations that were later found not to be from God. Some are from God, some are from man and his desires and some are from Satan."

"Then how does anyone know the truth?" Luke couldn't seem to shut up. He stole a glance at Rachel. Her eyes darted between them. But she listened, and that was a good thing.

"As prophet of the church, I am a *seer* and a *revelator*. God speaks directly to me. Consequently, my revelations are infallible."

"But Joseph Smith was a prophet, seer and revelator too. Apparently, he still got things wrong. So, what's up with that?"

The prophet steepled his fingers together, and then bowed his head as if in prayer. Luke assumed he was buying time to answer. Rachel shot Luke a sideways glance, her eyes pleading with him to stop.

He knew he should back away from this confrontation with Silver, but he couldn't help himself.

Silver lifted his head, finding Luke's face. He glared at him with naked contempt.

Rachel apparently noticed, because she took a step toward the old man and placed her hand on his arm. "Prophet Silver . . . sir . . . doesn't the fact that I have received the testimony for Luke mean something?"

It must have taken every ounce of courage she had to ask him that question.

Silver's deeply carved face softened. She just had that effect on men.

"It could mean something."

Rachel's face lit up, and in spite of the bruises, she looked beautiful. Silver's eyes danced under his bushy salt-and-pepper brows. On some level, maybe it was unconscious, he wanted to please her. This could be very good for Luke.

"And Luke was the one who found me . . . he helped me in the woods that night."

"Yes, that's all true." He turned back to Luke. The ice returned to his eyes, giving them a metallic shine. "But there are other factors to consider as well. It's been brought to my attention that you don't agree in the righteousness of living the Principle."

Luke knew his father must have told Silver that. At least the prophet had let Luke's last challenge drop. He had to back down, for Rachel's sake.

Silver turned his eyes back to Rachel.

"If I were to agree to seal the two of you, not only would your soul be in jeopardy if you rejected the Principle, but Rachel, an innocent, would also be in danger of not reaching the Celestial Kingdom."

Luke watched Rachel's features crumple into worry.

"I would never do anything that would put Rachel's soul in danger. I'll do whatever it takes to keep that from happening."

"This whole situation has gotten completely out of hand. The only conclusion I have reached is that the issue of Rachel's marriage has far-reaching implications. I need time for careful deliberation."

"Please, just give me . . . give us . . . some consideration," she said.

The prophet's face was stony. "I'll pray about it."

Silver took Rachel's right hand in both of his. He lowered his voice as if he were revealing a crime he had committed. "I've had a terrible time with this. I had to stop taking names after the seventeenth man came to me. I only agreed to consider his testimony because he is such an outstanding member of the community."

"I'm so sorry for all the trouble," Rachel said.

Luke felt the anger rise and start to settle in his head. A drum began its slow beat in his temples.

"No, it's not your fault, my dear."

If it had been anywhere else, Luke could have watched their interaction and thought it was a loving grandfather dispensing comforting advice to his granddaughter.

"It's like I've said, the desires of men get convoluted and confused with the will of God."

Anywhere else . . . but here. He still had her hand locked in his gnarled grip.

"It will all be made clear soon."

Rachel bobbed her head in assent, but her eyes were glazed with doubt. Luke slid over to her side. He had jumped through all the hoops, and now all that they had left was to wait on his decision.

"I better get Rachel home. She needs to rest."

"Oh yes."

"Thank you . . . for . . . taking the time with us," Rachel said.

"Yeah. Thanks," Luke said. "I'll let my father know about the concern you had with the location of the kitchen island." He had almost forgotten that this entire meeting was originally planned to discuss the progress of Silver's house.

Silver held Rachel's hand hostage. It was really annoying him.

"Luke, would you give a message to your father for me?"

"Yeah."

"I think I have all the information I need now to make a fully informed decision, after considerable prayer, of course."

What is he talking about?

"Let him know that there will be a decision very soon regarding Rachel's betrothal."

It took Luke a few seconds to process the implication clinging to Silver's words. Then it hit him.

"My father had the testimony?"

"Oh . . . I just assumed he had told you, particularly since you're Rachel's friend."

He heard Rachel gasp, and he was vaguely aware of the slight smile traveling over the prophet's lips. Silver still held Rachel's hand. There was nothing for Luke to hold on to as he stepped into the shock.

He couldn't believe how stupid he had been. On that very first day that they had attended church, Luke's father had noticed Rachel, even making a quip: something about how it wouldn't be so bad living here with a girl like that around. He had suggested that they introduce themselves to Rachel and her family. Luke was stupid enough to think his father was doing him a favor by trying to help him get a girlfriend or a distraction or whatever it was.

He chose to believe that all of his dad's help with Farley was so that he could put Luke on the debtor's side of the favor. And when his father forbade him from seeing Rachel, he decided it was part of his dad's master plan to control him, dominate him, until he no longer could stand straight in his own convictions. The signs were all there. How could he have been so stupid?

Rachel managed to remove her hand from Silver's and sidled up to Luke. Placing her frigid hand on top of his balled-up fist, she said, "Maybe . . . there's some mistake . . ."

"There was no mistake."

"Let's go." Luke took her elbow and charged out the door. Cascading beams of sunlight streamed through the trees. The storm outside had passed, but the one inside him had gained momentum. He jerked the passenger door open and let her in. He threw himself into the truck, forcing the key into the ignition so hard that it almost broke in half. Gunning the engine, he peeled out of the construction driveway. On the way to his father's office, he hit the steering wheel, cursing with words he knew he would later regret using in front of Rachel. She didn't try to stop him.

They screeched up to the construction trailer. He threw the truck into park. The meeting hall soared behind it, edging the February sky. The building was palatial in scope and must have cost a fortune. It infuriated him that his father could give all his money to this cult. It was just a matter of time before Silver announced that Robert would be an apostle. His father would buy his way into the Blood of the Lamb leadership. And apparently, he had been trying to buy Rachel this entire time too. Maybe she was the reward for building a mansion for Silver and his harem. Just thinking about Rachel marrying his father made his chest hurt, as if someone had taken a knife to his heart and severed it, then turned him around and stabbed him in the back.

He couldn't take her into the trailer while he confronted his father, but he was afraid to leave her alone. He would just step outside to talk with his father. As they stood outside the trailer, enough control had finally settled over him to look at her. "This isn't right," he said. "I have to do something."

She nodded. She didn't say a word. She didn't have to. She would love him no matter what.

He pulled open the door, while his father remained hunched over some architectural plans that had been rolled across a long table. Its top corners were held in place by two pencil cups on either side of the top, and an unopened bottle of water anchored the bottom left corner. Robert glanced in the general direction of the door. "Just a second, Luke." He apparently didn't notice Rachel following behind.

"I need to talk to you."

"Uh-huh." Robert didn't see Luke motioning for Rachel to take a seat in one of the two cheap plastic chairs that were pushed against the back wall of the trailer.

"Now."

Robert had a slide rule out, crisscrossing it over the blueprints, marking them up in what appeared to be a haphazard manner. But like everything else his father had done in business, it was thoughtful and flawless in its logic. "I said in a minute."

Luke sat down next to Rachel and took her hand. His father was still too engrossed in his work to look up. After a minute or so, Luke said, "Come on, Rachel, let's go."

Just as Luke predicted, Robert's head jerked to attention. "Oh, I didn't realize we had company." He looked directly at her. "I'm sorry about the—" He stopped in midsentence once he saw Luke's face. His eyes fell to their entwined hands and then back up to Luke's eyes. "I take it you have something you want to say to me."

"Yes. But not in front of Rachel."

"All right. Let's step outside."

"I'll be right back." Luke followed his father out the door. As soon as he closed the door behind him Luke said, "How could you do this to me . . . to us?"

"Lower your voice, son. What are you talking about?"

"Don't pretend you don't know. The testimony!"

His features rested impassively in his face, which infuriated Luke even more. Robert rubbed his chin absently before saying, "Who told you?"

"Silver."

"What were you doing talking to the prophet?" A tightness pulled the corners of his father's mouth.

"You're the one that set up the meeting."

"To discuss the house."

"Silver brought it up. He wanted me to know."

"Well, that's beside the point. What are you doing with Rachel? I told you to stay away from her."

"You knew that I wanted to be with Rachel. You knew it when you went to Silver and told him that you had the testimony about her."

"How is that relevant?"

"How am I relevant . . . is that what you're saying?"

"What I'm saying is that when you are called by God to do something, you must follow that calling, regardless of how others might feel."

"Like your entire family." Luke rammed his index finger through the air, stopping just short of his father's chest. "*You* don't give a shit about anybody but yourself."

"Don't you dare speak to me that way!"

"You don't even know Rachel. You just want her because she's beautiful."

"And you don't?"

"I love her!"

"Spare me . . ."

"You've forgotten what love is."

"Love?" Robert sneered. "For God's sake, you're barely a man. I know what love is. And you're not in it."

"You have no idea how I feel."

"What you feel for her is lust."

"No, Dad." He spat each word out. "That's what you feel for her."

"The only difference between us is that I'm honest about it."

"I'm nothing like you."

"Don't fool yourself. You're exactly like me."

"I can't believe this! You're throwing money at Silver, hoping you can buy Rachel. It's like she's on the auction block and going to the highest bidder."

"At least I'm trying to live the Principle."

"Is that what they call statutory rape these days?"

Robert took a step toward him. "I've had it with you."

"The feeling is mutual."

"Give me the car keys."

Luke dug in his pocket, pulled out the keys and slammed them into his father's outstretched palm. "Here."

"You're to leave my house, leave my car and leave this community. If you so much as set foot on Blood of the Lamb property, I'll have you thrown in jail for trespassing."

"Fine. I'm just going to get Rachel, and I'll be out of your way."

"You're not taking the girl." Robert moved in front of the door.

Luke stood up straighter. He was ready to pounce. "Move out of the way."

"Get off my property."

"I'm not leaving Rachel here."

"You are no longer my son." His words burst with contempt. "Get off my property."

"I guess, since I'm no longer your son, I can beat the shit out of you."

His father narrowed his eyes. "You wouldn't dare."

"Wanna bet?"

"Leave, NOW!"

"I'm not leaving without Rachel."

"Luke?" Rachel's voice came through the door as the doorknob turned.

"Why don't you ask her what she wants . . . *Robert?*"

His father moved out of the way. Rachel stood in the open door. "Is everything all right?"

"Yes," Robert said.

"No, not at all."

"Rachel, why don't I give you a ride back home?" Robert asked, but his tone was a clipped command.

"No . . . let me just walk you home, okay?"

She glanced at Luke, then to Robert, and then back to Luke, her concerned gaze settling on his face. "I think . . . I'd prefer to walk home with Luke." Turning to Robert, she added, "But thank you."

She slipped his hand into hers, and they walked away from his life. When they reached the end of the driveway, she said, "I'm sorry things didn't go well."

"I didn't expect it to go any other way."

What was he going to do? His heart was pounding in his head, and he hadn't realized how anxious he was until now.

"Your father loves you." Her voice was gentle yet resolute. "That will never change. No matter what." Rachel's trusting nature, her willingness to always see the good in others, splintered his heart.

"And I *know* he never meant to hurt you," she added, pressing her hand into the small of his back, as if to prop him up.

Only the leaves underfoot, with their crisp winter coat of ice, made any noise as they skirted the tree line marking the entrance into the dense woods. Knowing he had no other option, he said, "I only have a short time . . . before I have to leave."

"No!" There was no surprise in her protest, just grief and the tight grip of desperation they shared.

"My father kicked me out of the house."

"Oh, Luke . . ."

"It's okay. Even though it doesn't seem like a good thing, it's really for the best."

He wasn't sure if the dull ache in his heart was from his father's rejection or the anticipation of leaving Rachel. He supposed there was always that small chance that the prophet would allow them to marry, if for no other reason than that Rachel wanted it, but then again, he ruined that possibility with his insistence on challenging the old man. That was brilliant. Silver was going to either give Rachel to Robert or keep her for himself. He had to convince her to come with him now or he might never get her out of there.

"Let's talk about it on the way to my house . . . I mean my father's house . . . I need to grab some money and some clothes and say good-bye to my mom. We'll take the shortcut so no one sees us."

"Okay." She bit her bottom lip, no longer seeming to notice the tender places. They walked in silence, lost in thought. As they rounded the bend, Luke could see the red brick peeking between the trees, and the dormers sitting as high and white as the snow-capped peaks behind them.

"Oh no! My father's at the house." Luke eyed the truck parked sloppily beside his mother's SUV. He pulled Rachel back into the shadows of the forest. Robert dared him to show his face, while feeding his mother lies about what went down between them. He would bet his life that Robert hadn't told Elaina anything about his own bullshit *testimony*.

"We've got to get out of here. I'll call my mother when we get into town. Maybe she can get me the money I've saved . . . it's not much, but it'll help us get by for a few weeks."

She turned to face him directly. "I can't go with you right now."

"We'll get Sara before we leave."

"It's not that. We have to have the prophet's blessing or we would be considered in apostasy."

"Rachel, we'll never get his blessing, he—"

"No, you're wrong. Didn't you hear what he said? He has all the information he needs *now*. That means *now* that we've come to him with our testimonies."

Luke exhaled. He couldn't believe how much they had brainwashed her. His biggest competition was a seventy-year-old man who claimed to be the voice of God.

"What if the prophet's wrong? What if he's mistaken, just this once, and he announces to everyone that you are to be married to someone else? What then?"

"He won't be wrong. Not this time. Our fate is designed by God. The prophet will know that."

"Please Rachel, I can't take the chance of losing you. Please come with me."

"You won't lose me. We'll be together very soon. The prophet said so."

"Rachel, I'm literally begging you . . . please come with me. I feel like I'm dying . . . the thought of losing you . . . I don't know if I can take it . . ." His chest filled with grief, and he struggled to suck in air.

She wrapped her arms around his neck, stood on the tips of her toes, pulled his face down to hers and began kissing him. She kissed his forehead, the damp lashes of his closed eyes, the stubble on his cheeks and then, when her lips reached his mouth, they pressed his open, and he returned her kiss, with enough longing to last a lifetime.

SIXTEEN

T he view from Esther's room was partially obscured by a giant pine still loaded with Christmas ornaments, even though it was late January. The predawn light streamed in, casting the room in mossy shadows. Sara shifted in her chair bed. The noise caused Esther to turn her head and look at her.

"Something's happened to William."

"Oh no, I'm sure he's fine. You're getting discharged tomorrow. I bet Father's already made arrangements to go to Salt Lake City."

She shook her head. Tears squeezed out of the corners of her eyes. "He's gone. I feel it." She pressed a hand against her heart. "In here."

Sara started to protest, but something heavy settled along her shoulders. Her scalp prickled. "Do you want me to call the nurse? We could ask her how he's doing."

"It's too—" A sob choked off her last word.

Sara climbed out of the chair and took her hand. "We don't know that, Esther." Sara pushed a loose strand of bang away from Esther's eyes.

"*I know.*"

"I'm going to get a nurse."

The three people at the nurses' station didn't look up when she arrived. Sara cleared her throat. A woman writing in a patient's chart reluctantly lifted her head to acknowledge her.

"Can I help you?"

"I'm Esther White's sister. She's wondering about her son, William White. He was transferred to Salt Lake City."

The other two stopped what they were doing and looked at her.

"I'll let her doctors know that she wants to speak with them. They should be here within a few minutes."

"Thank you." Sara's lips numbed with anxiety. She pushed open the door to Esther's room.

It seemed she'd barely settled into a chair when the two doctors who'd attended William's birth walked in, accompanied by a silver-haired woman wearing bifocals on a colorful chain and a rose-colored lab coat. "Miss White, this is Hannah Law, a grief counselor. I'm afraid we have some bad news about William," said Dr. Pierce.

Ester's face went the shade of spent charcoal. Sara reached out and took her hand. She squeezed it with all her might.

Dr. Pierce cleared his throat. "They tried everything, but in the end he gave up the fight. I am very sorry."

A cry tore from her chest. "I didn't even get to hold him."

"Miss White." The grief counselor approached. "I know this is . . ."

"Get out! You people sent him away and now I'll never hold him. Just leave me alone!"

"I understand your pain—"

"No, you don't! I am nothing without a child, nothing! Please, just leave me alone!" Esther struggled to sit up, tears making furious rivers down her face. Dr. Pierce removed a syringe from his pocket and injected something into a port.

"Get away from me!"

"This is just something to help calm you."

"Leave!" Snot and tears mixed together, spilling into her mouth. She sputtered and moaned. Her lids drooped and her cries settled into hiccupy sighs. Sara collapsed the hospital bed railing and sat next to her. She draped her forearm over Esther's chest. Esther's body began to lose the tension as she drifted away.

With Esther asleep, Sara finally released her own tears. She mourned for her brother but mostly for Esther.

When she finished with her tears, she left the room to call home. The phone rang twice before her mother picked up.

"The baby's dead." Sara had nothing more to say, so she hung up.

ESTHER no longer blinked. Sara noticed something else disturbing about her face. It was a perfect mask of ordinariness molded over grief. She went about her chores with little or nothing to say. When people addressed her, she looked through them. A tic pulsed in the upper arch of her left eye. She paced the yard aimlessly, lifting each limb in a stiff marching fashion as though she were a sentry patrolling the grounds. Sara felt sick with worry.

The mothers were careful around Esther. No one spoke critically. Abe went out of his way to spend extra time with her. Sara tried to ignore his kindness because she preferred to hate him and didn't like the discrepancy between her perception of him and his gentle behavior. The kindness didn't stop her from fantasizing about killing him. Something was definitely wrong with her. She wondered if she were the evil one and not him.

Within days after the family buried William, Sara began to lose her hair. When she brushed it, strands would spring from her scalp, covering her hairbrush and shoulders like petals from a wilting flower. Sara believed the ugliness inside seeped through her pores to the outside.

She spent an entire day contemplating whether to meet Irvin in the woods. He was bound to see her ugliness and reject her. Saturday morning dawned. Having finished her chores, she still hadn't decided what to do. At the last moment, she forced herself to go.

With feet cushioned in pulpy beds of pine needles and damp leaves, she found her way to the creek. Clouds of flying gnats congregated around her face and tickled her ears. Running water from an early spring thaw lapped at the stones.

Her heart swelled at the site of his knifelike shoulder blades edged around the trunk of a pine. She circled around the tree. His face lit up with a smile when he saw her. WHERE HAVE YOU BEEN? he wrote.

"Esther's baby died. We had his funeral."

"We had his funeral," Irvin echoed while writing. I'M SORRY. SHE WAS THE NICE ONE, RIGHT?

Sara told him what happened. "I shouldn't be here. I don't deserve this."

"Don't deserve this." They both ignored his repetition as he wrote, WHAT DON'T YOU DESERVE?

"Your kindness. You don't know what I'm like inside." Sara thumped a hand against her chest. "I'm so full of hate and anger, I feel like I'm going to explode. I can't keep it inside anymore. I'm even losing my hair."

"Losing my hair." After a few minutes, he pressed his notebook against her back and she turned around and took it. HE'S SELFISH AND A COWARD. HE'S DONE A LOT OF BAD SHIT, AND EVERYONE LETS HIM GET AWAY WITH IT.

Suddenly she could taste the dirt in her mouth and the crushing weight of earth on her chest. She'd begun questioning herself because Abraham showed tenderness toward one of his wives. Still, her desire to see him dead made Sara similar to him. She shuddered. "How do I let it go? I don't want this rage, but I don't know how to release it."

Sara handed him back his notebook as he echoed her words. His pen flew across the page. KEEP TELLING YOURSELF THAT HE'S NOTHING TO YOU. MAYBE THEN YOU CAN LET GO.

"You've given me more than I could ever give you in return. You probably saved my life."

He clamped his mouth shut, shaking his head vigorously. Picking up the pad, he scribbled on the page. WE NEED EACH OTHER! WE'RE A COUPLE OF OUTCASTS. I'VE NEVER HAD A FRIEND UNTIL I MET YOU. YOU MAKE IT POSSIBLE FOR ME TO EXIST.

"Really?"

He nodded vigorously. "Really."

He touched her hair. Sara felt the shimmer of loss as strands escaped into his hands. He gently tucked the hair back into her braid before lowering his head. This boy, a member of the *cursed black race and heir to Satan*, chased away the darkness inside her. No more doubts, she told herself. She wasn't evil any more than Irvin. It was time to gather strength from that knowledge.

The dusk cast a sepia tone over the grass and trees as Sara rushed through the woods to get home. Night sounds whispered at her back. She'd never been gone this long. Sara deposited her backpack, containing a new batch of books, in the shrubs at the back of the house. Inching open the back door, she listened to the flow of conversation emanating from the kitchen.

They were already eating!

A spring screamed as she pushed the door open. The conversation halted. In a rush of frigid air and dark shadows, she felt him before seeing him. He seized her, one hand locked in her hair, the other smashing across her face. "Where have you been, girl? Where have you been?" He slapped her again, but she dipped her face toward her shoulder. His hand crashed against her ear.

Blood oozed out the corners of her mouth. "I got lost. I was walking . . ."

He slapped her again, causing her teeth to slam together.

"Liar. You were meeting a boy, weren't you?"

"No . . . no." Silence reigned in the kitchen as all ears strained to hear each smack meet its mark.

"I'm gonna teach you . . ." He shoved her back out the door. Fear clawed her heart.

"I was just lost . . ."

He smacked the back of her head and shoved again. Her lower body was propelled out the door, but her hair was still locked in his fist as her head lurched back painfully.

"Wait!" It was Esther. His fist loosened its hold. "Please don't."

"You need to stay out of this." Though angry, he slackened his grip.

"It's just she helped me so much."

He didn't reply. It was as though her life hinged on his decision. Finally, his hand unlocked itself from the tangled remains of her braid. "Only this one time."

Esther answered, "Just this one time."

Copious amounts of hair loosened and fell away as he released his grip on her head. "I don't want to see your face."

Sensing his eyes on her back, she raced through the kitchen and living room. No one said a word. No one followed.

Sara stood in the mirror and looked at her face. With teeth syruped in blood, and the obvious emergence of a black eye, Sara should have felt pain. Instead exhilaration hopped along her veins. A mother had come to her rescue! Esther was their guardian angel. She'd been sent to protect them. With trembling hands, Sara cleaned herself up. This had been a day of miracles after all.

"THAT looks bad," Rachel said, as she squinted into Sara's face. Motes whirled in the thin strand of morning light that slashed across their bed. Sara gingerly touched her eye. It wasn't so much painful as numb.

"I guess I'll have to withdraw from the beauty pageant. Oh darn."

"Well, that makes two of us." Rachel laughed.

"Maybe things will change around here now that we have a defender."

Rachel rolled onto her back and held her hands up, moving them in and out of the light. "Why were you so late getting home last night?"

Sara pulled the comforter up to her chin. "I met Irvin."

"That's what I thought."

"I'm . . . falling for him."

Sputtering, Rachel sat up and spun around to look at Sara. "Oh no! You can't! He's . . . he's . . ."

"Black?"

"That's such a grievous sin! Negroes aren't even human."

A flash of anger stabbed Sara's gut. "I can assure you he's human."

A slow tear leaked from the corner of Rachel's eye. She turned away. "You're engaged to marry Walter."

"I'd rather stick a fork in my eye."

Rachel mumbled something under her breath.

Sara felt guilty and decided to change the subject. "I've been hearing cars all morning. It sounds like they're pulling down the driveway."

"I've heard it too." Rachel got off the bed, approached the window and hitched the towel back to look out. "There's a bunch of cars out there."

"Really?" Sara ran to the window.

"That's Prophet Silver's car." Rachel pointed to the black Lexus. "Maybe the Lord has given him revelation about Luke and I!"

"About Luke and me. It's an object, remember?"

"Luke and me," Rachel repeated, without taking her eyes off the action in the yard. "There are other apostles here too."

Sara glanced at the assortment of luxury vehicles filling the driveway. "Why?"

"I don't know. Oh my gosh, Luke's father is pulling in. This is it!" Rachel's face sparkled with delight.

Their presence here was not a good thing. Sara worried her numb lip with a finger.

Rachel raced to the milk crates and began pulling out dresses. "Watch his truck and see if Luke is with him. Maybe they've worked things out now . . . with the announcement and all. I better get dressed."

Sara let the towel drop back over the window. She pulled out the first dress her fingers grazed and slipped it over her head. Next came the ugly, gray stockings and man shoes.

"Oh my gosh, my face," Rachel said. She dropped her clothing on the bed and returned to the little hand mirror. "I forgot all about this."

"Don't worry. Everyone's seen your bruises. Mine are the new ones."

She squinted at Sara with eyes widening in alarm. "I don't want Brother Robert to think Father did that to you."

"Well, he did."

Rachel began braiding her hair with rapid-fire fingers.

"Don't worry, if he asks, I'll tell him I walked into the door."

"Lying is a sin."

Sara bit back an ugly remark, returning to the window instead. "That's weird."

Rachel had a bobby pin between her teeth when she answered, "What's weird?"

"The little kids are all being put into Sister Gramm's station wagon."

"What?" Rachel joined her at the window.

"Forget your hair. This isn't about your marriage. We better go down."

When they opened their door at the second-floor landing, several apostles huddled at the entrance of the bathroom. One of them pulled the bathroom door closed. The hairs on Sara's arm prickled. A horrible realization molded Sara's thoughts. She shook it away, telling herself not to jump to conclusions. They kept their eyes on the floor as they passed.

Prophet Silver sat at the dining room table next to Brother Wilkinson. Abraham was seated at the far end of the table. Butter, jelly and honey were laid out. The scent of fried eggs and yeast wafted from the kitchen. Three deserted cups marked the places of the men who had been at the entrance to the bathroom. The conversation halted at their arrival.

"Is everything okay?" Rachel said.

"Go help your mothers in the kitchen," Abe said.

They hustled into the kitchen. Marylee pulled biscuits from the oven. Jane scrambled eggs in the enormous iron skillet. Anna came in from the outside, hugging a flimsy sweater against her bones.

"What's going on?" Rachel's voice teetered on hysteria.

"I suppose you're old enough to know." Marylee pulled out a

chair for herself. She took an inordinate amount of time searching for the right words. Tears filled her eyes. "Mother Esther is dead."

Sara's heart lurched. The arteries in her neck thumped against her skin. "No." The word came from between her lips, but she had no sensation of moving them.

"I'm afraid so."

"How?" asked Rachel. Tears swam in her eyes.

Marylee struggled to get the words out. "She took her life."

"When?" Rachel said with tears gushing down her face.

Sara's stayed dry, but they felt dammed, held back by some force outside of her. She squeezed them shut.

"We're not sure exactly, sometime in the early morning hour."

"How?"

"In the bathtub. She slit her wrists."

Sara's vision filled with images of Esther lying in scarlet-colored water. The exact same place she had found herself on the morning of her resurrection.

"Oh my God!" Rachel held her stomach as she rocked forward.

"Rachel, do not take the Lord's name in vain. I don't care what the circumstances."

"I'm sorry," Rachel finally replied. "What are we going to do?"

"That's what they're discussing now." Anna scooped the eggs onto an enormous platter.

"They're going to figure out what to do with Mother Esther's body over eggs and biscuits?" Sara said.

Marylee shot her a look. "Watch yourself."

Sara clamped her mouth closed.

Her mother picked up the basket of biscuits, plates and utensils and disappeared into the dining room. Jane carried a pitcher of juice while Marylee stood and pulled a fresh pot of tea off the stovetop.

Rachel and Sara looked at each other. "What's happening to us?" Rachel's voice was barely above a whisper.

"Same thing that's always been happening, only now people are dying."

The remaining mothers returned before Rachel could reply.

Sara frowned. "The little kids don't know, right?" She had this horrible thought of one of them wandering into the bathroom and finding her there.

"Heavens, no. And we want to keep it that way," said Marylee.

Another thought occurred to Sara. "Have the police been called?"

Marylee gasped. "No, of course not!"

"Won't they have to investigate her death? Isn't that the law?"

"There's nothing to investigate. It was suicide, pure and simple."

"But there's a protocol . . ."

"Look here, Miss Smarty Pants, we can't bring the law in, not in our present state of persecution. The apostles are discussing alternatives right this very minute. Keep your trap closed or I'll close it for you."

Sara crunched her brow in feigned confusion. "I hadn't even thought of that. Of course we can't call the police."

Marylee raised her brows. "I'm glad you finally understand."

Anna poured herself a cup of tea and sat down next to Sara.

"I have to go to the bathroom." Rachel's eyes were wide with terror and confusion. They only had the one bathroom.

"Grab some napkins and a plastic bag to put the soiled paper in. Do your business behind the shed," Marylee said, in a voice completely devoid of emotion.

Rachel took a napkin from the dispenser on the table and pulled a bag off the clothesline. Sara felt a hysterical waft of laughter bubble inside her chest. She wanted to say, *Well, I guess we can't reuse that bag now, can we?* Ducking, Sara covered her mouth. Her shoulders shook with garbled choking noises.

Anna put her arm on Sara's back and rubbed. "There, there. Everything will be all right."

Sara laughed harder into her hand. Tears were flying down her face now, causing her swollen eye to throb. Sara couldn't seem to get control over this hysterical laughter. She prayed they wouldn't realize it was laughter and not tears. Finally, she managed to rein in the hysteria.

"Looks like it's going to rain," said Rachel upon her return. Her face was splotchy with tears.

Sara stood up with her own napkin and retrieved a bag. Her mouth twitched with mirth. She couldn't believe that the urge to laugh had returned. What was wrong with her? "I better go before it does."

Swift-moving scuds sped across the sky while wind rocketed the skirt around her legs. Flashes of light dappled the heavy rain clouds. Sara hustled to the whipping shed, pulled down her stockings and underwear and began urinating next to the wet circle left by Rachel. Drops of rain struck her head and arms. Finishing, Sara stood up and ran to the back door as the sky fissured and rain knocked against the crown of her head as though bringing bad tidings.

The mothers and Rachel sat quietly at the kitchen table when Sara entered.

"Shhh." Jane put her finger to her lips. "We're listening."

"Does she have any family?" Prophet Silver said.

"She has a father somewhere up in Salt Lake. They don't talk," Abraham said. "He don't know she's married."

"What about friends?"

"Not no more."

"So," another man spoke up, "what are we going to do with Esther's body?"

"It's simple," said Silver. "We bury her ourselves."

Sara caught her sister's eye. Rachel ducked her head, hiding her eyes behind a fringe of hair.

"She'd want to be next to her boy," Abraham said. "Is there room next to William?"

Sara was shocked at his sensitivity. Once again confusion clouded her mind. How could someone so evil have a compassionate side?

"Absolutely," Silver said. "And we need to give her a *proper* burial."

"But she committed suicide," the unidentified man said.

"What do you propose we do," Silver asked, "drive out to the desert and leave her there?"

"What do we do with the body while Brother Daly makes a coffin?" the man asked.

There was silence at both tables. The clock in the kitchen clacked as the big hand rotated a minute. Sara picked up a napkin and began making little tears in it.

"Drain the tub," said Silver. "Turn on the shower to rinse her off, wrap her in the plastic shower curtain and we move her."

"Where?" asked Jebediah.

"Does anyone have an old freezer?"

Sara audibly gasped at Silver's suggestion. Marylee put her finger to her lips and shot Sara a hateful look.

"I do," said Jebediah. "When we slaughter the pigs, we store the meat in several large freezers. We could keep her there."

Grief tightened her chest. Sara's stomach cramped with a sense of loss. *I'm so sorry, Esther.* Tears sprang to her eyes. She picked up the shredded napkin and pressed it to her face. "Maybe I should go outside," Sara whispered to her mother.

Anna nodded and Sara went out the back door. Rain pummeled the ground, tilting toward the earth at an extreme angle. Sara stepped into the rain, allowing it to mix with her tears. She moved away from the house and howled to the wind, finally unleashing her grief.

She didn't know Esther well. She was just learning to love her. Now she was gone. "I'm so sorry, Esther." Exhausted, Sara slid to the ground, curling her knees to her chest, and let the rain drench her.

When they brought Esther out, her body appeared filmy behind the opaque shower curtain. A towel must have been wrapped around her midriff and chest to afford her some bit of privacy. They maneuvered her into the back of the old gray van. Before the door of the van blocked her view, she noticed a smear of blood. Sara pressed a fist to her mouth to keep from screaming. So this is how it happens. A wife or daughter goes wrong and poof . . . she disappears. One thing was crystal clear to her: every last female was disposable. Every last one.

SEVENTEEN

Rachel wasn't sure how much longer she could go without sleep. Sacrificing didn't seem to be doing much good anyway. Sara still didn't believe. She'd lost Esther and Luke. It was only the certainty of Luke's love, and his promise to return, that kept her from falling into a bottomless chasm.

She could feel the tidal pull of his yearning when she lay in bed that night. It had been over a month since she had seen or heard from him. She could still feel his need scorch her heart. The guilt she swam in for not leaving with him threatened to drown her. He didn't seem to understand that she was making him wait in order to ensure the salvation of their souls.

When the pebbles pinged the window that first night in March, it didn't surprise her. She had been expecting him. Father had put a lock on their door. It could only be undone from outside the attic. Even though he never punished her for sneaking out to meet Luke the night of the attack, he seemed skeptical of the explanation Brother Robert offered.

"He's here," she said into the back of Sara's hair.

"What?"

"Luke. He's here. Help me get the window open."

The window was stuck again with a seal of disuse. When they finally pushed it open, it seemed to shake the entire floor. They waited for a moment, listening to the stillness of the house, before they both stuck their heads out the window. Seeing him standing in the moonlight, her breath caught in her throat. He was coatless and even in the muted light, she could see the outline of several days of stubble.

Thankfully, Sara spoke first. "Luke, how are you?"

"Okay. I'm sorry I couldn't come sooner. I have to see you. Both of you."

Rachel turned to Sara and whispered, "I can't get away."

"I know."

Turning back to Luke, Sara cupped her hands around her mouth, trying to give him every detail in a frantic whisper. "Saturday, follow the creek from our house. Four o'clock. It's the flat boulder on the east side of the creek."

"I'll be there."

"I don't think I can come," Rachel whispered into the night air, dreading his disappointment.

"Why not?" His voice was tight.

"Abraham watches her like a hawk."

Rachel could almost feel the stiffening of his body. "We'll be together soon," she said.

"Has Silver told you anything?"

"Nothing yet," Sara said.

"Soon." Rachel hoped to reassure him.

Someone flushed the toilet from the bathroom below. Rachel shot a look at Sara, each of them calculating the risk of discovery. "We have to go," Sara said.

"I love you, Luke." She managed to get the words around the lump in her throat.

"Oh God, Rachel . . . I just . . . I love you too . . ." He looked away as if she were standing off to the side instead of directly above him.

"Saturday," he said.

They watched him walk away, broad backed and thinner than Rachel had remembered.

THE long-awaited meeting hall was complete. Prophet Silver had planned a big event to celebrate its opening. Over the past week, the apostles contacted all Blood of the Lamb families to make sure that every priesthood holder in the community attended. Rumors flew that he would announce Apostle Farley's replacement.

The meeting hall stood nestled at the foot of the mountain range. The arched entranceway was tunneled with layered brickwork. Two massive wooden doors were hidden inside. The lanterns on each side of the entrance gave it a medieval feel.

Rachel heard her mother's sharp intake of breath as they moved into the expanse of the hall. Wooden beams made triangular peaks into the ceiling, and from each beam hung a long chain with a chandelier of candles. The rustic pews were drenched in prisms of color from the sunlight streaming through the stained-glass windows lining the sides of the building.

When Sara caught up to Rachel, she whispered into her back, "This place is incredible." Rachel understood why Luke's father was so excited about its completion.

In spite of its much larger size, the hall was already filled to capacity. Still, some late-arriving families straggled in. They were forced to line the walls of the room. The eleven remaining apostles filed in, moving onto a stage erected at the front. The prophet followed behind them, his hands folded in prayer. The congregation stood up, singing a hymn that Rachel had heard since childhood but couldn't seem to recall today.

After the song finished, Prophet Silver climbed a short curved staircase up to the lectern. It elevated him so he was able to look down on the entire congregation. A skylight had been built into the ceiling directly above the lectern. The prophet was bathed in a golden glow.

"Welcome, all of my brothers and sisters, to our new place of worship." Rachel clapped on cue, but all she could think about was how Luke and Mother Esther couldn't be there to share in all of the beauty. The prophet stayed on the subject of the new building for several minutes, pointing out numerous features and asking for a round of applause for Brother Robert.

When Luke's father stepped onto the stage, fresh grief rose inside her. Luke looked so much like him. As Rachel squinted, his features softened, blurring the line further between father and son. When the prophet said he had some news concerning Brother Robert, she had a panicky thought that maybe she was to be sealed for time and all eternity to father instead of son. *Quit that. That's stupid, Rachel.*

". . . our newest apostle, Robert Wilkinson," said Prophet Silver.

The crowd clapped again. Rachel sagged with relief. She wasn't to be sealed with him. He was their new apostle. Luke had predicted that. She really needed to work on trusting God more.

Sara nudged her. "He certainly earned his keep."

She shot her sister a disapproving look. The position of apostle was supposed to go to the man most spiritually deserving. Was he really the holiest choice the prophet could have made? After all, he disowned his son when Luke tried to point out the falseness of his father's testimony. Her conscience slapped her. How could she possibly question the prophet's decision?

She began her litany of fevered praying, begging forgiveness. Thank goodness she was fasting today. At least God would know she was trying.

Sara nudged her again. "Rachel," she hissed. Rachel's eyelids had been dropping under the weight of distraction. They flew open, wide with fear of what she had missed. "Listen," Sara ordered.

Rachel scanned the stage and saw that Luke's father was now sitting at the end of the line of apostles. Her head followed Prophet Silver's ebb and flow of words, until she rested on his crop of white hair.

". . . didn't realize this girl's significance. Satan gave many false prophesies to a number of our righteous men. We don't always understand the will of God, but it has all been made clear to me in an astounding revelation. As you all know, Joseph Smith was told that God will send 'the one mighty and strong' to save us from Satan and his minions. But, my brothers and sisters, I am *not* the one mighty and strong."

There were audible gasps in the crowd. Rachel perched near that chasm again. Why was he changing everything on them?

"I *am* your prophet, seer and revelator, just as Joseph Smith, Brigham Young and the other holy men who have preceded me were, but I am *not* the savior of the world."

The prophet stood tall in the lectern. The longer he spoke, the more enthusiastic he became. His voice was animated, his hands gesturing wildly. He had captured everyone's attention.

"This girl who is pure and obedient is holier than almost anyone in this room. Satan has tested her repeatedly, and she has been the focus of his interest because he knew her importance to all of us long before it was revealed to me. This girl is a vessel for my seed. From my seed will spring a new messiah, a saint to rival Jesus Christ. He will lift his Church out of the ashes and restore the true Mormon Church throughout the world."

Rachel heard the rumble of Sara's moist breath. She glanced over at her sister, who had droplets of sweat popping out from every pore on her face. What was wrong with her? Sara's eyes were trained straight ahead, looking at nothing in particular, yet she seemed to see everything.

"This girl is among us today, and God has ordained that we be sealed for time and all eternity in our temple three weeks from to-day."

Everyone looked around the room trying to figure out which girl would birth the new messiah. Rachel glanced down the row at Mother Marylee. She always knew all the community gossip, but her mother just sat in her seat reading her hymnal. Her father caught her eye, locking his gaze on her. He had a look of utter contempt on his face. What had she done? She snapped her head back to Prophet Silver.

"Allow me to introduce you to the future mother of our savior. Rachel Shaw, will you please come up here?" the prophet said, looking right at her in the crowd.

"It's okay," Sara said, her voice clotted with sympathy.

She heard Rowan's tiny voice ask Russell where their sister was going. "Rachel's going to be our savior's mama," he told him.

Iron bands of fear squeezed her chest. Acid flooded the recesses of her stomach, and the metallic taste in the back of her tongue returned. She heard her mother tell her to get up. A faceless, middle-aged man came to the end of their pew, motioning for her to come with him. Somehow she managed to climb over her family members, allowing the usher to take her elbow.

As she was helped up the steps to the stage by the anonymous usher, her eyes took flight to the newest apostle with the coal black hair and startling blue eyes that he shared with his son. Her own eyes were smeared with tears. When she looked at his face, he was Luke: the anger barely reined in, raw betrayal punctuating his features.

The prophet had descended from the lectern and opened his arms to receive her, but she stood where the usher had left her. The prophet strode toward her now, cutting the distance between them with terrifying speed. His crusty eyes and the canker sore perched atop his shaky smile swam into view.

A waft of syrup assaulted her nostrils. Her stomach heaved as this man of God touched her shoulder, thrusting her to center stage. His hand pressed into the crease of her spine. Maybe this was a test to see how much revulsion she could take before breaking down and abandoning her faith. If she could just keep from retching, crying or fainting, and could prove to everyone that she was a good and faithful servant, then she would pass the test and God and Prophet Silver would reward her with Luke: her real husband for time and all eternity.

Prophet Silver said some words that she no longer heard, and the crowd clapped over and over in frantic unison. The echo reverberated through her head long after the crowd quieted down. After standing until her legs were leaden from the effort, she was led to a seat next to Prophet Silver's vacant one and on the opposite side of the apostles. The rest of the service, Rachel sat in disbelief. Why would God give her and Luke the same testimony for marriage if it was false? Nothing made sense anymore.

When the prophet had finally finished speaking, the congregation stood for the final hymn. As the song started, Prophet Silver offered his sandpapery hand to her. She had no choice but to take it, allowing herself to be pulled out of the chair. Her hand felt like it was being scraped as it sat inside of his. He led her down the steps of the stage and through the center aisle of the room toward the front doors.

They stepped out of the building and into the sunshine. The prophet's arm looped in hers, as if they were already bride and groom on their wedding day. She looked up to the heavens. Clouds, like shredded cotton, streaked across the canvas of sky. *Where are you, God?* A wet breeze slipped off the foothills, drying the cold perspiration running down the knobs of her spine. She said a prayer for mercy under her breath, a prayer similar to what Christ said to his father in heaven before he was crucified. God didn't answer.

THE rest of the day was spent in the company of Prophet Silver and various clusters of wives, too numerous for Rachel to count. Slowly she realized, in bits and pieces, that this was not a dream, not a test, not a cruel joke. Prophet Silver had a revelation that she was to be sealed with him and give birth to the *one mighty and strong*.

And all day she asked God how He could have possibly let this happen.

The lights in the kitchen blazed with anticipation of her return. She thanked one of the prophet's wives for the ride home and walked to the back door. It was unlocked as usual, and as she entered, she was surprised and relieved to find it was empty. The countertops had been wiped clean of debris and the dishes were done. Everything was in order, but she could feel chaos darting around in her chest. She flipped the lights off and stepped into the living room. He was waiting. Alone.

"Where do you think you're goin'?"

She jerked away from him as if she had been slapped. "Oh, I'm sorry, Father . . . I didn't see you in here."

"You're comin' with me, girl." His voice sounded dangerous.

"I don't—"

"You don't what? You don't want to go?" He flipped the living room light on, and then cuffed her hands as she reached up to wipe away the tears trickling down her cheeks. He smelled like a mixture of sourness and spicy sweat. Anxiety twisted her throat, keeping her mute. She shook her head, trying to tell him she didn't mean to question him, but he seemed to interpret her gesture as open defiance.

"I'm the one who tells you what to do. When did you forget that?" He was busy looking into her eyes. Could he see her questioning authority, like she had with the prophet tonight?

"I . . . am . . . sorry . . ."

"You will be when I get through with you." He shoved her back into the kitchen then out the back door without allowing her to get her coat.

He clicked the flashlight on. It ricocheted off the trees in the backyard as he walked stiffly past her. The shed smelled moldy, and the dirt floor was covered with rotting leaves that had blown under the door. She walked toward the wooden horse over which they braced themselves when they were whipped. She might as well get this over with.

"I need that," he said, lifting the horse under his right arm and carrying it over to the door. He placed the light on the floor, and the walls of the shed were dappled with an oyster-shaded glow. But the light didn't hit every corner, and in some places the walls seemed to move and take shape, forming menacing faces.

The hinges squeaked as he closed the door and pulled the horse under its metal handle. He yanked it to make sure it kept the door securely closed. Anxiety coursed through her body. He'd never locked the door before.

He turned his eyes on her. In the shadowy light his face looked like a skull, all hollow angles and no flesh. She shuddered.

"Sixteen men, the Wilkinson boy, Farley, and God only knows how many others. Now, the prophet."

"I don't know why——"

"He wants to put his seed in you, that's why. And he'll get his way because he's the goddamn prophet."

Rachel sucked in hiccups of air. "Please . . ."

He took a step closer to her. She felt like there was ice in her stomach, yet the heat in the small shed threatened to suffocate her. Her feet shuffled backward. He inched closer until his chest grazed her breasts. She burned in shame.

"What do you do to these men? It's like you're a witch castin' your spell and making men want you. Are you a witch?" He backed her into a corner where those nameless forms were hiding. "Answer me, girl." His palms were pressed against both sides of the walls. His breath was so hot it felt like it scalded her face.

"No . . . no . . ." She could feel something crawl up her back, but she would have to lunge into her father's bulk to squirm away from it, so she allowed the bug to run up her spine. She screamed in her head, until she felt the vibrations in her ears.

"It's not right what you do to them. You prance around, like you're God's gift, swinging your hips, and looking at these men with those eyes like you want it. Now you've tricked the prophet into thinkin' you're some pure vessel. You'll be away from here in a few weeks, and you won't even look back at your own father. Oh no, you'll be too good for us. It's time you learned some humility," he said, but he made no move to take off his belt.

The thing was on the back of her neck, worming its way into her braid.

"Please . . ." she said, shaking her head and stifling the rising tide of screams. "There's something in my hair . . . please." Her hands flailed at her braid. She stumbled toward him. He caught her, crushing her shoulders into his chest.

She'd never been this close to him before. He held her so hard she couldn't move. He didn't say a word. He just stood there with his iron forearms locked around her. She could feel his heart racing as if he had just finished sprinting. His shirt was damp, and she could smell his sweat. Heat came off of him like it radiated up from a blacktop highway in the peak of summer. She would rather be beaten right now than held this close to him.

"Let me look at you." His voice was husky as he loosened his hold.

Her heart thundered, and her mind clouded in confusion.

His eyes blazed as he raised his hand. She winced, preparing to be slapped. Placing the tips of his fingers at the top of her neck, he slid them down between her breasts. Her heart thundered, but she didn't dare move. He pushed the palm of his hand across the swell of her chest.

Her throat thickened in revulsion. "No!" The room began to spin. Looping his arm around her waist, he pulled her into his hips. "Please stop!"

"Shush, girl."

His free hand moved back up the front of her dress. Biting back a scream, she convulsed in fear, slamming her back into the wall. She felt feverish with humiliation.

"Don't you ever move away from me like that again."

Blood rushed to her head, giving her temples a sharp stab that cut through the revulsion. "I can't . . . please leave me alone."

"Sara's next, you know."

Rachel's cowering body snapped to attention.

"If you tell anyone what's happened here tonight," he said through clenched teeth, "or you don't come to me when I need you . . . I *will* go to her." Moving his mouth next to her left ear, he said, "And that baby sister of yours, she will ripen into a real beauty someday."

Her ear was misted with steam from his ragged breath. She gulped down the bile that had crawled up her throat.

"Do you understand me?"

Rachel swallowed a mouthful of acrid air. Her head fell in defeat.

A knock and then a rattle on the doorknob. Mother Jane's thin voice seeped in. "Abraham, are you in there?"

"What the—" His forehead swam in sweat. "What is it, Jane?"

A tidal wave of relief washed over Rachel.

"Aaron. He woke up vomiting, and he won't stop."

"Damnit, woman!"

He released her, and Rachel's arms flew up, crossing her chest. Yanking the horse from under the handle, he threw it into the corner.

Glaring at her, he put his index finger to his mouth. She nodded.

Jane's eyes widened in confusion when she saw Rachel follow her father out of the shed. "Oh, I didn't know Rachel was with . . ." Her voice trailed off.

Rachel forced her chin up to meet her questioning gaze. She hoped Mother Jane could hear the soundless plea banging against the inside of her mouth. *Keep Alice away from her father.*

EIGHTEEN

Morning came as a relief. Sara rose shaky and slightly sick from the nightmares and yesterday's anxious events.

"Are you going to tell Luke about the announcement?" Rachel rose with exaggerated slowness.

Sara's heart leapt with joy. She was thinking of Luke. That was a good start. "I think he needs to know. Don't you?"

"I don't understand . . . how the prophet could just ignore our testimonies," Rachel said.

Hope beat a new rhythm in her chest. Still, she held herself in check and waited for Rachel to steer the conversation. "Uh-huh. Doesn't make much sense, does it?"

"You need to leave here."

A surge of euphoria propelled Sara off the bed. "Yes! Oh yes . . . Rachel . . . I'm so glad . . . okay . . . when do you want to leave?"

"I can't leave. But you need to go."

"What! You want me to leave without you? Why?"

"I can't leave, *but you have to*. I'll be okay."

"But . . . Luke loves you, Rachel. You were meant to be together. God wants that."

"I don't know what God's will is anymore. All I know is that I can't leave."

"*What?* You know the prophet's wrong. He made a mistake."

"You have to leave, Sara."

She couldn't believe her sister was begging her to leave the

Principle. Rachel had to doubt the veracity of the Principle or else she wouldn't ask her to leave. "This makes no sense."

"Look, even if you're right . . . about everything. I can't leave Alice. She needs me." Rachel turned her back to Sara. The hairbrush dangled limply in her hand.

"*Baby Alice?* What about Luke and me? We need you. I need you."

"No, you don't. You're strong and smart. You don't belong here."

"What about Luke?"

Rachel turned back to face Sara. Her bottom lip trembled. Sara's guilt pricked at her conscience.

"I want to be with him." Rachel's face was lined in anguish. "But it's not about what I want. It's about what Alice needs."

"Why are you so worried about Alice? She's years away from the shed."

Rachel refused to make eye contact as she lifted the hairbrush and pulled it through tangled waves. "She needs protection."

"If you stay, I stay and then we're both damned!"

"No! Please, I'm begging you . . . you don't understand."

"No, I don't. If we stay, I marry Walter and have his children, and you marry Silver and give birth to . . . *the messiah.*"

SINCE the announcement of Rachel's marriage, Abraham made no attempt to mask his rage. His fist and hands were a constant source of fury and loss. He had smacked Jane across the face when she overcooked his eggs. That behavior was normally reserved for his children. Within a few days, Sammy stuttered and four-year-old Adam defecated in his underwear, hiding his accidents around the house like treats from the Easter bunny.

Sara had witnessed his behavior and intercepted all of his poop packages. She searched behind the sofa, in the bread box or under the couch for them. Without telling a soul, she cleaned his pants off with the garden house and dish soap. Sara couldn't bear the thought of his punishment should he be caught. Something was going on in Adam's head, but no one cared enough to get to that something.

Her mothers were in the basement dealing with the laundry when Sara went past her father's bedroom. Her mind snapped to attention. That's where the birth certificates would be hidden. Her knees shook as she pushed open the door. The bed was massive. Thick wooden posts elevated the mattress like a throne fit for a king. Her stomach did a slow somersault.

She moved to the bureau. Opening the drawers, she scanned the contents. Socks. Underwear. Sacred undergarments. A stack of scratchy button-down shirts. Work pants. No documents. She heard the shriek of a small child travel upward from the basement. Moving to the bed, she dropped to her knees. A metal lock box was centered against the wall. The pounding of her heartbeat drowned all sound. If she were caught, she had no doubt her father would bury her for good this time. She snaked an arm out, grabbing the box. A flimsy lock secured the contents inside.

Almost without thinking, she was on her feet again, heading back downstairs and into the kitchen. She had seconds to do this. Fear wafted from her stomach, burning her cheeks until they puckered. As she yanked open the drawer, the cutlery clanked so loudly it could have roused the dead in the cemetery in downtown Centennial. She held her breath. No voices rose from the bowels of the basement. She seized the most ferocious kitchen knife they possessed and returned to the room. Wedging, pushing and twisting, the tiny lock snapped. She pressed the broken lock in her pocket and lifted the lid. Official-looking documents lined the interior.

She lifted out a stack and unfolded the first one, titled: Certificate of Live Birth. Rachel Shaw. Mother: Marylee Shaw. Father: Abraham Shaw. She slipped it into her pocket. Her hands shook so hard, she almost couldn't unfold the second one. Sara Marx. Mother: Anna Marx. Father: Unknown. In the eyes of the state of Utah, she had no father.

And that was just fine with her.

A CAR arrived early the next morning, whisking Rachel away for her marriage preparations. In her absence Abe raged louder. At night,

Sara tried to engage Rachel in conversation. She had a plan to deconstruct the brainwashing but no opportunity to implement it. Panic fluttered in her belly as the days rushed forward.

When Abe left on Saturday afternoon, Sara took her opportunity and raced to the woods for her rendezvous with Irvin. He sat on the boulder near the creek. As she approached, he smiled.

She climbed onto the rock. "Listen, I have something to tell you. We're meeting a friend today. Luke? I told you about him?"

Sara spoke as rapidly as possible, explaining everything that had happened. When she finished, he handed her his notebook.

I THINK YOU'RE IN JUST AS MUCH DANGER AS RACHEL. YOU NEED TO LEAVE.

"Well—" Tears clogged her words. "There's something else I have to tell you. I've been *placed*, or engaged if you want to call it that, to my uncle. If Rachel goes through with this and marries the prophet, I'm next."

"I'm next," Irvin repeated. He scribbled furiously in his book. THAT'S SICK! YOU HAVE TO LEAVE. EVEN IF IT MEANS GOING WITHOUT YOUR SISTER.

Sara shook her head. "I can't do that."

He repeated her remark without writing a word down. Instead, he stood up and walked to the edge of the rock.

"I'm afraid if I leave her, she'll die inside. It'll be bad enough for her to live without Luke. I don't really think that she'll come through that okay."

WHAT ABOUT YOU? YOU WON'T COME THROUGH MARRYING YOUR UNCLE OKAY. I WON'T COME THROUGH THAT OKAY.

"What do you mean?"

Before he had a chance to write his reply, she heard her name. Looking up, she spotted Luke. He was jogging toward her.

She scurried down the rock and ran to him. His hair was greasy, and dark circles ringed his eyes. He wore a red flannel shirt and filthy jeans. Only his smile was bright. They hugged.

"You look like you've been through hell."

He ran a hand through his hair. "Being homeless does wonders for your hygiene."

"Are you okay?"

Luke's tentative smile faltered as he stared up at Irvin. "Who's that?"

Sara turned. The sight of Irvin standing on the rock made her heart ache. He was so handsome and so completely unsure of himself. "Don't worry that he's black."

Luke expelled air. "Why would I care?"

"Well . . . um . . . his name's Irvin."

"I really need to talk to you privately."

"I know," Sara whispered. "But I've already told him everything. Actually, he knows even more than you do since it's been a month since I've seen you. He has this problem though. He repeats things. He can't really talk unless it's to echo what you just said. We communicate by writing, which—"

"I'm sure he's a really nice guy and everything." Luke stopped whispering as Irvin closed the gap.

He handed Luke his notebook and gestured for both of them to read it. She scanned the contents quickly. IT'S OKAY. I'LL GO.

"No!" Sara said. "You don't have to go. I don't want you to. Please stay."

"Please stay," Irvin repeated.

Something passed across Luke's face. The hitch in his breath told her he was okay with it. "I'm sorry, man. I . . . it's been . . . I guess I wasn't expecting anyone else here. If Sara trusts you, so do I. I'm Luke." He held out his hand.

"I'm Luke." Irvin shook it.

"Um, we talk by writing things down," Sara said.

"Writing things down."

"Come sit down." Sara looped an arm through Luke's and pulled him toward their rock. "I'm so glad you're here. You've got to tell me *everything*. Like where have you been? We've been going crazy not knowing how you were doing."

"How you were doing," Irvin repeated.

"Oh. Just so you know. If you talk really fast and don't pause, he won't repeat until you're done."

"Until you're done."

"See?" Sara grabbed Irvin's hand, hoping that he didn't feel so weird about this whole thing.

Irvin repeated, "See."

"Not a problem. Before I start," Luke rushed. "Is Rachel okay?"

"Is Rachel okay?" Irvin said as he began writing in his notebook.

Sara swallowed hard. "You first."

"You first." Irvin handed her the notebook. SINCE I'VE HEARD THIS ALREADY, I'M GOING TO GO TO THE CREEK WHILE YOU CATCH UP. IT'S COOL. I'M NOT LEAVING.

"Irvin, it's fine. You don't have to leave," Luke said.

He echoed while shaking his head and walking off.

"Don't go far," Sara said. He waved without looking back.

"He seems like a good guy."

"He's amazing. He's been through a lot too. Tell me everything, like how you've been surviving for starters."

Luke settled on the slab, his legs dangling off the rock.

"Is Rachel . . . feeling better?"

"Yes. But I'm not saying another word until you tell me what's been going on." Sara jumped on the rock and sat next to him. "We've been really worried about you."

Luke eased onto his back, resting his head on a crooked arm. "The first few days were hell. I had nowhere to go. I slept in the prophet's new house."

She slid her back onto the slab. "Ha! I hope you peed on a wall or something."

Luke laughed. "Of course. I had to leave at dawn before the workers showed up. I basically staked out my mother's house. My father didn't leave her alone for a second. I ate out of our trash can for a few days."

"All this because you love my sister."

Turning his head away from her, he looked up to the sky. "He must have figured I'd left town by the fourth day 'cause he finally left her alone. When my mother saw me, she couldn't stop crying. She fed me, gave me clothes, all the money she had in the world, which was a little over a hundred bucks. I hiked to Lufkin, bought a cheap bike, a pup tent, some camping stuff and a sleeping bag."

"Oh, Luke—"

"It's okay. I'm doing construction at a bank in Lufkin. I sleep in my tent, eat food straight from the can and save every dime. Tell me about Rachel."

The craggy branch overhead looked like skeletal figures clawing at the sky. She did not meet his gaze. "She's not doing well."

As she told him about William's death and Esther's suicide, his face darkened with each new revelation. She wondered how he would ever be able to handle the rest of it.

"There's something else you're not telling me."

She needed to tell him. It was now or never. "The prophet thinks Rachel's the one chosen to bear the *one mighty and strong*."

Luke bolted to his feet.

Sara sat up. "She's supposed to be sealed to him."

Luke staggered. He kicked a tree trunk and paced like a caged animal. "I can't believe this!"

"The few times we've actually talked, she vacillates between thinking the prophet is wrong and worrying that she's going to be an apostate if she leaves."

"I can deal with that. I just need a chance to talk to her."

"I can't even talk to her. She's developed this irrational fear that our father is going to hurt Alice. I don't understand."

He picked up a fist-sized rock and hurled it at a spruce tree. A squirrel tore down its trunk and hid behind a moss-ringed cedar. "I need to see her. Right now."

"You can't just go to my house, knock on the door and go in. We need to figure this out."

He stopped, resting a hand on the trunk of a tall pine.

Sara gave him time to consider her words before speaking. "This isn't about you. She's brainwashed."

"I thought I'd be enough to overcome that." He smacked the tree with an open palm before turning back to face her. "I thought she knew how much I love her."

"It's not enough."

For a moment his features sagged in defeat. "Don't say that. I just need to get her alone."

"I don't think—"

"It doesn't matter." The fire had returned to his eyes. "If I have to carry her kicking and screaming out of here, I'll do it."

She knew he was right. Rachel would forgive them later, once she was in her right mind. They had no other choice but to get her out of here. "Okay, we'll do that, but we need a plan."

"When's the wedding?" His voice was strained as if his vocal cords were bruised.

"In two weeks. On March twenty-second."

"Two weeks?" He clenched and unclenched his fists. "Shit! We have to get her back here next Saturday."

"I don't know. They're watching her like a hawk. If Abe is at work, Marylee has her working right next to her. Plus, she's always gone."

"Gone? Where does she go?"

Sara realized her mistake too late. She didn't need him angrier. She needed him focused.

"Where does she go?" he repeated.

"Um. With the . . . to marriage preparation."

He exhaled violently. "Okay. I'll come by tomorrow around midnight. Have her ready."

"We can't leave at night anymore."

"Why not?"

"Abe put a lock on our door. Someone lets us out in the morning."

"I should have known." Bitterness choked his words.

"It has to be next Saturday."

A twig snapped and Sara looked up. Irvin stood upstream, framed by the sour yellow of the fading sun. Alienation must have haunted him everywhere. Even here, where someone cared for him, he removed himself. Sadness twisted inside. She waved him over. "It'll still be hard, but I'll figure out a way to get her here."

"If you can't make it during the day, I'll come to you that night. I'll get a ladder and we'll take her out the window. Whatever it takes."

"Okay," Sara said, keeping her eyes on Irvin's approach. "Hey, Irvin."

"Hey, Irvin," he repeated.

"I have an idea. Why don't you two exchange numbers?" Sara said. Irvin nodded while repeating the last part of the question.

"I don't exactly have access to a phone, but I'll give you my mom's number. In an emergency," Luke said.

"If you need to get a message to us, call Irvin," Sara said to Luke. "He obviously won't be able to talk back, but he'll make sure I get it."

"Make sure I get it." Irvin removed his notepad and dug around for his pen. Luke recited his number. Irvin wrote it down.

"I have something for Rachel." Luke reached into the rear pocket of his jeans, removing an envelope. "Maybe this will help change her mind before Saturday."

Irvin echoed the remark while they all stood there feeling awkward.

"Listen, I'm going to push off now. Next Saturday, I'll be here. *All day.* So, when you see an opening, take it. And be prepared."

"I will."

They watched as he climbed onto his bike and rode away. At the sound of an approaching vehicle, Irvin grabbed her hand and pulled her into the cover of the trees just as the vehicle shot past them.

They sat in the brush looking at each other. She wanted desperately for him to kiss her. Instead Irvin removed his notebook, flipped to a page, stared at it and pointed to the phone number scratched there. Sara peered at it. "Oh no. We forgot to give it to Luke."

Irvin's brows furrowed.

"Don't worry. I don't think he'll need it anyway."

He echoed the last remark while writing. Finally, he handed it to her. I WENT BY YOUR HOUSE THE OTHER DAY AND SAW A MAN STANDING BY A PICKUP TRUCK. I FIGURED THE GUY WAS YOUR FATHER. HE WAS YELLING AT THIS BEAUTIFUL GIRL WITH BROWN HAIR. WAS THAT ONE OF HIS WIVES?

Sara read it, feeling her heart lurch at the word "beautiful." "No. That would be Rachel."

"Would be Rachel," he said. WHY WAS HE YELLING?

"Why does the sun rise?"

A melancholy wind followed Sara home. Trepidation curdled her stomach, tossing acidic juices with each step she took. She crossed the threshold into the house, removed her coat and hitched it on the peg. Sara listened hard for any signs of danger. A rumble of small steps trampled overhead. The lights were off in the kitchen and no dinner simmered on the stovetops. The lack of activity in the room put her further on edge.

She entered the room, taking small, quiet steps. She could only see half the kitchen table. The other half was hidden behind a wall. Moving as close to the sinks as possible, she entered diagonally to avoid the blind spot. A chair scraped. Shoes scuffed on linoleum. Sara cut hard to the left while a fist whizzed past her ear. As she put the island between her and her father, her eyes fell on his face: an anvil of hammered rage.

He held up a finger, turned it upside down so it was pointing to his feet. "*Right here. Right now.*" His voice splintered with fury. "Get over here you filthy, nigger-loving whore."

Her bladder shuddered, squirting fear into her underpants. "*Please, I can explain.*"

"Get over here right now before you get it even worse." He started to unbuckle his belt. "I saw you with that *nigger*. Did he touch you? Hmm?" Seizing the strap, he released the belt from the buckle and slid it through the loops of his pants.

"It's not like what you think."

"*What do I think?*" His face twitched, the corner of his lip snarling upward. The belt looked impossibly long, like miles of boundless pain. He gathered it in both hands. "Did you let that nigger put his filthy black—"

Rachel screeched into the kitchen. Her feet were clad only in stockings, and she slid dangerously close to Abraham. Her eyes were bouncing around in their whites, and her breath came in chopping squalls. "*Wait!* This is not Sara's fault. That boy is my friend. I asked her to meet with him today."

"What the hell are you talking about?" He folded the strap in half.

"To give him a message. He was my friend. From our old school."

"That's not true!"

He spun around to Sara with teeth snapping. "Shut up!"

"I asked her to tell him . . . that I'm to be married soon," Rachel said through compressed lips.

He pivoted back toward Rachel. "*You let that nigger touch you, didn't you?*" The belt swung menacingly from his hand. He cocked his arm back as though he intended to use it across Rachel's face.

"He's not her friend," Sara screamed. "*He's mine!*"

"I got me two girls fighting over a nigger boy?" He shook his head.

"Sara had nothing to do with him. He's my friend!"

Sara shook her head, panic blinding her. What was Rachel doing? "No! She's lying!"

Rachel moved toward him. "I promise you, Father, Sara's an innocent in all this."

He snatched Rachel's arm. "A nigger boy touched you?"

"No!" Sara rushed around the table, launching herself at him.

He swung around to grab her fists before they reached his face. Shoving her backward, he jerked the basement door open and pushed her in.

Sara flew back, stumbling down several stairs before catching herself on the railing. She used it to propel herself up, but the door slammed closed. Reaching for the knob, she twisted and pushed. He had thrown the lock put there to keep the babies from tumbling down the stairs. She slammed her palms against it, smacking with all her might. "No! Rachel's lying! She's got nothing to do with this!"

Screaming, pounding and kicking the door, Sara repeated the mantra over and over. She knew it was too late. Abe had already taken Rachel outside. Crazed out of her mind, she collapsed on the top step, crying hysterically, until her voice lost pitch, settling into a gravelly whimper. "She had nothing to do with him."

NINETEEN

The clink of flatware and murmur of conversations alerted Sara that the mothers were in the kitchen. Virtually no light penetrated her prison last night. Now only a weak sliver slipped beneath the gap. Stretching stiff limbs, Sara lifted herself off the ratty couch where she'd spent the night. Her eyes felt as though someone had held them open and dropped shards of glass into them. With a throat raw from crying and stinging palms from hours of banging, Sara knew the cost of her discomfort was much less than Rachel's suffering.

She climbed the steps and pressed an ear against the door. Jane chortled about something Anna said. Baby Alice banged cooking lids together. She detected the presence of only the three mothers and the baby. Did they even remember her? Sara worked her nerve up to knock on the door. All conversations halted with only Alice still contributing to the noise. They weren't going to let her out. Not unless *he* allowed it.

Sara touched her pocket, feeling the outline of Luke's letter. If she failed to get Rachel to the woods, they were doomed. After waiting several minutes at her perch, she drifted back down the stairs. Wrapping herself in the clean sheet she'd filched from a laundry line last night, Sara settled back on the couch, mentally listing the things she would pack in her bag.

Her bladder woke her up much later. Disoriented and confused, Sara struggled to sit up. Fragments of conversations drifted down the stairs. Scrambling to her feet, Sara doubled over at the pain in her bladder. She managed to climb the stairs and twisted the knob. It was still locked. Her nostrils flared and stomach rumbled at the assault of baked chicken. They were preparing for Sunday dinner. Usually they made it between three and four in the afternoon. They must plan on starving her to death.

Balling up her fist to knock, she stopped herself midair when she heard the roupy tones of her father. Leaden rage churned her gut. Sara backed down several steps, her lips curling in disgust at the sound of him.

Fine, if they weren't going to let her out to go to the bathroom and eat, she'd just pee on his clothes. Relishing the idea, but knowing she would never have the guts to do something like that, Sara pulled out a pail from under the utility sink, peed and then poured it all down the drain. Filling her stomach with mouthfuls of water, she hoped to distract it from the clawing hunger.

THE air was softening with the new warmth of spring, but Rachel shivered from the cold despair swelling in her chest. Father had decided to take her into town for the afternoon. He told her mothers that he wanted to buy a gift for her and to have lunch in Lufkin with his daughter before she was married. Soon the mothers were handing him lists of items, scribbled on shreds of paper, for him to pick up from the Wal-Mart, if he wouldn't mind, of course. His face had puckered in annoyance, but he took the lists, shoving them in his pocket.

Rachel's body was stiff with unease as the landscape sped past them. She tried to relax. After all, what could he possibly do to her out in public? Just pretend he was like other girls' fathers. Just pretend that he was proud of her and wanted to take her to lunch to let her know how much he respected and admired her for trying to be such a good girl.

A sign announced the Lufkin city limits. Rachel noticed plumes of smoke swirling out of the funnel of an oncoming locomotive. For a split second she feared that her father would try to beat the train.

The lights at the crossing were flashing their frantic red warning, as her father pressed his foot on the accelerator. The wooden arms fell from the sky, slicing the distance between their truck and the tracks. Her father stomped on the brakes to keep from hitting the barriers.

Rachel bounced so high, her head nearly hit the cab's ceiling.

"What are you so jumpy about? You afraid of me?"

She could feel the heat from his gaze travel down the length of her dress. She welded her knees together.

"No, sir." *Please God, let the train pass. Hurry, hurry.*

"My Lord, you are a pretty little thing."

Rachel's throat thickened with fear. *Please stop looking at me!* She couldn't think of anything worse than to be considered pretty by her father.

"If God expected good men to be able to control their God-given urges around you, He shouldn't have made you so pretty."

He put his hand high on her left leg. She recoiled from his touch as if he had poured boiling water on her thigh. A shadow of anger passed over his face.

"You haven't forgotten our little talk already, have you?"

She shook her head, her throat held captive by anxiety.

"I don't care who you're with or where you are, I'll find you. If you're not there when I want you, I'll go to Sara. And if you two get any ideas about leaving me . . ."

"I'm sorry," she blurted out.

"You better be." He didn't move his hand.

The caboose rounded the corner, entering her line of vision. His fingers crept up her thigh. *Please hurry!* The train's whistle trilled just as loud and high as the scream filling her head. The gates rose up toward the sky as if they were giving glory to God.

"It's about damn time." He removed his moist hand, leaving a wet indentation on her dress. He didn't say another word to her until they reached Wal-Mart. "Stay here."

She watched his lanky frame nearing the entrance to the store, all angles and bones with a layer of lean muscle stretched taut over his skin. She couldn't decide if she hated him or not. All she knew was that she had to come up with a solution, and fast, because she could no longer think clearly when he was near.

Thoughts sizzled in her mind. *Here's the plan.* Sara leaves town with Luke. Rachel would have to tell her what happened with their father. Otherwise Sara wouldn't understand why she must stay to protect Alice. Rachel would do whatever he wanted. If Sara stayed, she'd end up with Uncle Walter, a deformed baby, and their father's hands all over her when Rachel couldn't get back to him in time.

For the time being at least, Sara was safe in the basement. But Rachel was worried that her mothers hadn't fed her. She had tried all day yesterday to sneak food to her sister, but she was watched constantly. If they didn't let Sara out tonight, she'd have to do something drastic.

Then there was the issue of her father and his authority. He was not a good man right now, she thought. It's okay not to obey the family priesthood holder when he is committing sins that violate God's laws. A father should not touch his daughter like that. It was just wrong, no matter what he said.

But if her father didn't have authority over her, and the prophet was likely a false one, or at the very least, a misled revelator, then she couldn't marry the prophet! She had to marry Luke or they would be violating what God had intended. She had to run away with Luke and Sara. But what about Alice? A dull pressure formed behind her eyes. Her head continued to buzz with ideas. If she could just make up her mind about what to do. . . . Her stomach gurgled in hunger, and she was shocked by its betrayal and irritated by its need to be filled. How could she even think about food after what she and Sara had been through?

She had just begun to seriously consider taking Alice again when her father emerged. He carried a bag of diapers and a cold drink in one arm and in the other, four filled plastic bags with their handles looped along his forearm.

He threw the bags in the back of the truck, riffled through one of them and pulled out a box of donuts that he brought into the cab with him. He glanced at his watch again and said, "No time for lunch." He ate three jelly donuts in quick succession, stuffing them into his mouth, chewing loudly then gulping them down with a carbonated drink. Rachel suspected it had caffeine in it. He no longer seemed to follow any of the rules of the Church.

Pushing the open box toward her, he said, "Eat." Trapped in the tiny cab with him, she had immediately lost her appetite. But he was staring at her, waiting for her to take one.

She pulled her chin off her chest and turned toward him. "Yes, sir."

"That's better." A glob of purple jelly was perched on his chin, and it quivered whenever he opened his mouth to speak. He licked his lips and waited expectantly.

He apparently wasn't going to leave the parking lot until she ate. She pulled a sticky donut out of the box and took a nibble at the corner, safely away from the gooey jelly inside.

"We don't have all day," he said. But he wouldn't start the car.

She took a larger bite this time, and she could feel the jelly ooze onto the left side of her mouth.

"Here, let me get that," he said, moving his hand to her face.

She flinched, assuming he was going to slap her, but instead he rubbed the jelly off with his thumb. Why was he treating her so kindly? Was this his way of apologizing?

"See, we can have a nice time together, can't we?"

"Yes," she said, telling an easy lie.

"COME on, get up." Marylee's voice sounded like it snaked through a tunnel to reach her. Disoriented, Sara struggled to sit up. She'd fallen asleep again. What was wrong with her?

"You'd better wash that sheet later today, young lady," Marylee added. Her arms were folded over ample breasts as she straddled two stairs to glare down at her. "Now, get on up here and get something to eat. And hurry up. It's starting to storm, and I need you to get some of the laundry off the lines outside."

Sara stood up. Her legs quivered. She felt confused. What had Marylee just told her? Her stomach issued mournful cries. How long had she been down here? Looking at her hands, she realized that she was supposed to do something with the sheet. She started to fold it.

"I said you need to wash that sheet, not reuse it. You'll have plenty of laundry chores to do later. Move it. Your meal's getting cold!"

It was cold, but it was the best bowl of stew Sara had ever eaten. She sat alone at the table, frantically shoveling spoonfuls of soggy carrots, potatoes and beef into her mouth, barely chewing before each swallow.

Rachel wasn't in the bedroom when she went up. Crossing the room, she pulled back the towel and peered outside. Black clouds piled like giant stones, blotting out the mountains. The wind raked the ground, swirling leaves and dirt in a haphazard fashion. Abe's truck was gone. Normally, that sight relieved her, but with Rachel's absence that only contributed to her sense of unease. At least he couldn't get to her if she was at marriage preparation. Oddly enough, she was safer with the psycho prophet than her own father.

Removing Luke's letter, Sara pulled her backpack out from under the bed and placed it inside. Adding several changes of underwear for both of them and some toiletries, Sara zipped up the pack and stuffed it under the bed. She didn't even know what day it was.

A SPASM of rain veiled the windshield. Before the wipers could sweep it off, the glass was pummeled with pellets of hail, coming down with enough velocity to shatter it to pieces. Father kept driving. His nose was nearly pressed to the glass. He opened the window a crack to clear the windshield that was thick with the steam of conversation and the simple act of breathing.

With the rain so blinding, Rachel was unaware that her father had taken a detour, until they pulled under a huge awning of the Traveler's Nest, an aging stucco motel directly across the road from her old school. Her father threw the car into park and said, "I thought we'd sit out the rain a little and have our chat." He leaned into the seat, stretching his arms over his head. She could smell a stale perspiration on him.

Her right hip was sealed to the passenger door, while her hands rested in her lap with fingers laced together so tightly her knuckles whitened.

"Uh . . . the rain is letting up, Father." The words were out of her mouth before she had time to censor them.

He opened his eyes. "With a sky that gray we'll be headed for trouble if we get back on the road right now." His words pulled an alarm in her head. They were just a few minutes away. He had already driven here from Lufkin with no regard to their safety.

He opened the driver's door and stepped out. "I'll be right back," he said, smiling and relaxed. He closed the door, and then, as if he could read the doubts littering her mind, he opened the door back up and said, "Besides, I've got that gift special for you. I want to give it to you when it's just the two of us."

What was her father doing? Ever since he got out of Wal-Mart he had been a different person. He told jokes. He asked her if she would miss school after she was sealed. And in the strangest part of the conversation, he inquired about whether or not her mothers treated her well.

She was afraid of this new father, even though he had become exactly the type of father she had wanted just an hour earlier. She had come to trust her fear of him, rely on it. She knew how to act around him because of it. Now the rules were changing, and her foundation of fear was cracking and shifting under the weight of his gentleness.

She watched him talk to the young man at the desk. He smiled and laughed with him as if they were best friends. She hadn't seen her charming father since—she couldn't remember, but it must have been years. Maybe he felt like he had made a mistake touching her. Maybe he would fall down on his knees and beg her forgiveness. Of course, he needed to do that in private. And she would do the right thing. She would forgive him, like God forgave her every time she sinned.

She watched him sign the paper that the man had slid across the counter at him, pocketing his keys on the way out. He walked like he had springs underneath the soles of his shoes. She couldn't help but smile. This was the father whom she knew when she was younger: sweet, boyish and happy. He loved her when she was a little girl. She had just forgotten.

When he got back in the truck, he was whistling. Maybe her prayers had been answered; God must have touched his heart.

He looked at his watch and said, "We got some time to kill, so how 'bout we go to a room, and then I can give my special girl her gift."

Special girl . . . That's what he used to call her when she was little, and he did make her feel special . . . like she was his best girl, and that he was so proud of her. Her eyes welled up from his tender words.

"Now, don't you go cryin' on me," he said, but in that gentle way, as he brushed away the tears dribbling down her cheeks. This time she didn't flinch. Clearing his throat, he started the car, pulling around the lobby as the wind tumbled across the hood of their truck.

The rain returned, hard and fast again, as they pulled up to a parking spot in the deserted lot. "I forgot to put a tarp over them groceries. Let me do that, and I'll come around and get you."

"Okay," she said. She watched in the rearview mirror as he got drenched while she sat in the cab staying dry. She couldn't recall the last time he had been courteous to his children, though, come to think of it, he could be quite thoughtful with his wives.

When he reached her side, he pulled off his coat and opened the door. "Put this on top of your head. I don't want you gettin' a chill."

"Thank you," she said, completely amazed by his kindness.

BLACK clouds, like knotted fists, glowered at the tall man, following him down the road like a bad omen. Sara pulled the soaked carpets off the outside laundry line while keeping an eye on the man's progress. The sky had opened again, releasing a burst of rain. The man pulled the bill of his baseball hat down. His urgent stride made her uneasy. Thunder rumbled and the sky crackled with electricity. Her sodden dress clung miserably to her skin, weighting her arms down as she tried frantically to finish her job before the storm got any worse.

Oh God . . . it's Irvin!

He crested the last hill and sprinted in her direction. Her heart hammered with fear as he approached the garage.

"Irvin, what are you doing here?" Sara could feel her eyes bulging with rising panic. "You know you're not supposed to come here." She cast her eyes at the house. Her stomach plummeted as she saw the curtain in the kitchen rustle. *Oh dear God, somebody saw me talking to him!*

"Not supposed to come here," Irvin repeated.

"You need to go. *Right now.* Please!" Sara stepped away from him, placing more distance between them. "Please!"

He shook his head furiously.

"What . . . what happened?"

He mimed writing on an imaginary pad.

"I don't have one. Look, I'm going to be in huge trouble for this." Sara could barely speak. Fear strummed the frenzied cords of her nervous system. She didn't know whether to turn and run or vomit. "You need to go now, please . . ."

He shook his head emphatically while repeating Sara's words. Balling his fists together, he opened his mouth. A strange gargling sound passed through his lips. Sara realized he was trying to speak. "What is it?"

He shook his head and mimed writing again, pointing to the house.

"I can't just go in there and get a pen and paper. Where's your backpack? Why aren't you in school? You're scaring me."

Irvin kicked the side of the garage. He was effectively mute without his notepad. Should she risk going inside for a pen? No. Impossible. Her eyes darted toward the house. The curtain was cocked back for better viewing. The mothers might as well string her up right this minute because she was as good as dead when Abe returned from town.

He pursed his lips together, attempting to speak. "RRRRR."

"Rrr . . . you've run away?"

He shook his head while repeating her words. Smacking his head with the palm of his hands, he released a groan of frustration.

"Oh Irvin, I can't guess . . . is it about me?"

"About me?" His words were more swallowed misery than actual recitation. Again, he slammed his hands against his head.

Sara grabbed them and steadied her eyes at him. "Stop hurting yourself. I don't understand what you're trying to say." Something clicked in her mind. She rushed her question before he had a chance to echo words back to her. "Does it have anything to do with Rachel?"

"Anything to do with Rachel?" He pushed away from her and nodded vigorously.

"And my father?" He nodded while echoing her question.

Darkness threatened, but Irvin's arms steadied her. Peals of lightning forked across the sky. "There's been an accident. A car wreck?"

"A car wreck." He shook his head no and made that strangling sound again before crumpling against the shed and sliding down to a kneeling position on the ground. Holding his head between his hands, he continued shaking it no.

"Oh God, Irvin, you've got to tell me."

"You've got to tell me."

Suddenly, he yanked his head out of his hands. His eyes jumped around her until he found what he wanted. He snatched a stick off the ground and began engraving words into the soft earth. Sara stood next to him, as the letters H O T E L were formed. Almost immediately the letters started to blur together.

For a moment, all she heard was the howling of the wind.

"A hotel?"

Irvin nodded furiously as he repeated her.

"What in the world would they be doing there?" Fear stampeded the spindly exterior of her back as the realization dawned. "Oh my God. Where?"

S C H O O L. He wrote then dug an arrow between it and the fading word H O T E L.

"The hotel across from Centennial High?"

He rammed his thumb into the air.

"I'm going to kill him!" Sara screamed.

"Kill him," Irvin echoed.

For a few seconds, she contemplated her readiness to take her father's life. But her anger fueled her onward, burning up any hesitation.

She turned toward the direction of town, and then, spinning around, she faced the house. The backpack. It had her life inside, and more importantly, the letter from Luke. That might be her only weapon to get her sister out of here. "Irvin, I have to leave. I won't be coming back ever—"

"Coming back ever." He grabbed her arm and leveled his eyes at hers. He jammed his index finger at his chest and then pushed it back at her. Grabbing her hand, he raised their entwined fists to eye level.

Did he want to help her? Leave with her?

"But it's forever. I'm not coming back."

He nodded. "Not coming back."

"What about your mother?"

He dropped her hand and wrote O K in the ground.

A flash of grief threatened to douse her anger. "Are you sure?"

"Are you sure?" he repeated, nodding, scribbling a dollar sign into the mud.

"You have money?"

"Have money," he said, nodding.

"With you?"

He shook his head.

"Can you get it?"

He nodded.

"Meet me at the hotel. Hurry." He turned and bolted down the road.

Sara raced for the house. Leaping straight up onto the top landing of the side porch, Sara flung the door open. The drying plastic bags clipped to laundry wire caught the wind and gaped open in a silent scream.

"Sara!" screeched Marylee. "Get over here, right now!"

Sara shot past her, taking the stairs two at a time. She heard the commotion start as she banked the corner and hoofed it to the attic. Keep moving, keep the mothers off balance. It was the only way to prevent them from trapping her.

Quaking with adrenaline, Sara dropped to her knees and jerked the backpack out from underneath the bed. Stumbling, she crawled spiderlike to the top of the stairs before gathering her feet beneath her. Footsteps pounded down the hall, getting closer to the door. Sara launched herself into the air and leapt down the final eight or nine steps. Somehow, she landed on her feet just as Marylee snatched the door and was slinging it closed. Sara lunged with all her might, managing just in time to wedge her arm and shoulder into the opening.

"Anna, Jane . . . come help!" Marylee screeched.

The full weight of her anger pressed on Sara. With two more bodies applying pressure, Sara stood zero chance of escaping. It was now or never. Possessed with unnatural strength, Sara shoved as hard as she could. "Nooo!"

The door gave a few more inches, just enough for Sara to squeeze her body through. Marylee's meaty hand shot out and gripped her neck. Sara gasped, clawing at the hand choking her. She kicked and thrashed, desperate to breathe.

"I saw you with that nigger boy!" Marylee screamed. "You little slut!"

A wheezing, empty sound warbled from her mouth. There was no air. From the corner of her eye, she saw her mother charging down the hall, and for a brief second, she thought Anna would help her. Still fighting the death grip around her neck, Sara heard the whoosh and felt the bite of strap slicing across her backside. She needed air. Another whistle from the belt as Anna struck her again. Air and pain all cobbled together as need and avoidance. Darkness inked the corners of her vision.

Frenzied for breath, Sara reached blindly for Marylee's face, her fingers connecting with an eye. She shoved her finger in with whatever strength she had left. Marylee screamed, releasing her choke hold. Sara sucked air, huge mouthfuls of delicious air, as the belt whizzed down on her back. Another slash of fiery pain engulfed her backside, then another. Her mother wouldn't stop beating her until she collapsed. In a hoarse, choked voice interspersed with Marylee's whimpers, Sara wheezed, "Mama . . . no. Let me go!"

Anna brought the belt down on her back again. The injustice of it all suddenly steeled her will and Sara shoved, but Marylee charged with the full weight of her body, pushing Sara into the corner. With one eye clenched tightly shut, Marylee screamed, spraying spittle all over her face. "You're not leaving this house!"

Sara's hand tightened on the backpack, which suddenly felt arm-breakingly heavy from the weight of her fear. "Get out of my way."

"You little bitch!" Marylee's breath was hot and rancid with hate. "Get back in the attic."

Anna chucked the belt, no longer having a target. She stepped closer to help Marylee subdue her. Sara hoisted her backpack, leveling it as though it were a battering ram and careened into Marylee. The hit knocked Marylee off her feet. She left the ground with an *oompf*. Anna lifted feeble arms to stop the fall as her mouth widened into an "O." They both tumbled to the floor. Sara pushed past, knowing this would be the last time she would lay eyes on her mother.

Lurching down the hall, Jane bolted from the children's room where she had corralled the kids. Reaching out, she ensnared a fistful of hair. Sara flailed her free arm toward Jane's head. Her hand latched on to Jane's hair and she jerked. Jane immediately dropped her grip on Sara's hair to do battle with her handhold. Sara whipped the backpack around and hit her square in the knees. Jane doubled over just as Anna and Marylee scrambled to their feet.

She charged toward the stairs as Marylee screamed after her, "You're dead, you little bitch! You hear me, dead!" The words were twisted with such rage that they powered Sara's legs, sailing her down the stairs. Baby Alice screamed from her bedroom. Shouldering her backpack, she ripped through the kitchen and out the side door.

Adrenaline powered her thighs and blinded her to the rain that pelted the earth. She sucked in great, moist mouthfuls of wet air through her bruised windpipe and returned it hot and frantic.

Lightning flared repeatedly, illuminating the path. Ghostly faces swarmed in the shadows of the trees, peering at her as though to mock her courage. It drove her harder. She thought about how she would gain entrance to the hotel room. She needed the element of surprise on her side, which meant she couldn't knock on the door. No. She had to finagle a key from the front desk. Then what? She certainly was no physical match against Abe. Her only advantage was surprise and wits.

And then she remembered.

It would set her back several minutes, but it was her only chance at overpowering Abe. She'd have to sacrifice the time. She had no other choice.

RACHEL had never been inside a motel before. She assumed they were only for rich people. As they climbed up the steep flight of stairs, she worried about how her father could afford this room, especially after he bought a gift for her too.

The room was small and dark, with a musty odor hanging in the air. The stench of old cigarette smoke clung to the lime green walls. It had a thick lawn of burnt orange carpet, and the white chenille bedspread wore a mysterious coffee-colored stain in the shape of a tree.

He looked around as they entered the room. "Very nice."

"Yes. It's very nice." She was becoming quite a skilled liar, but maybe it was okay. She just wanted him to know how much she appreciated all his efforts today.

He beamed, wiping his hands on the front of his pants. "Look here, we got us a TV." He pointed to a spool-shaped table. "This here's quality," he said, knocking on the tabletop. Pulling out a slender white box from the pocket of his pants, he handed it to her. "Open it."

She removed a long silver chain with two small interlocking hearts dangling from it.

"That's to remind you that I was the first man you ever loved."

She felt uncomfortable with his remark. She must have looked confused because he pointed to the hearts and said, "This here's mine, and the other one is yours. They're bound together. You like it, don't you?"

"Oh . . . yes . . . thank you."

"Let me put it on you."

She turned around, sliding her braid to expose the back of her neck. It was then that she remembered the chain she had borrowed from Sara, so that she could wear her ring near her heart.

"What's this?"

He fished the chain with Luke's ring on it out of the safe harbor of her collar. He arced around her body so his eyes reached her face, still clutching the chain hanging from her neck.

"Who gave you this?" His eyes bulged so far out of his skull that she thought they would never recede back into their sockets again. "Did Silver give you this?"

"No," she said weakly. Maybe she should have said yes. After all, he knew they were betrothed. But lately, he seemed to have an intense dislike for the prophet.

"Tell me. Now!"

"Uh . . . it . . . Luke . . . it was Luke."

The skin on her neck stung as he yanked the chain off with one sharp tug. The heel of his hand slammed into her cheek. She felt her teeth scrape across the soft gummy flesh inside her mouth. Her knees began dissolving underneath her weight. He dug his thumbs under each of her armpits, popping her back onto her feet. The room continued to spin, taking her along for the ride. Her knees sagged again, while her torso began crumpling.

"Oh no you don't," he said, in the familiar clipped voice of the angry father.

He grabbed the backs of her upper arms, encircling them with his hands, and with one short pull, he forced her body into an upright position. Adrenaline ripped through her, helping lock her knees into place. Once she regained her footing, she stood quaking from the aftershock of his rage.

He rested his scratchy chin in the curve of her collarbone. He let go of her right arm, using his free hand to creep up her breast. She screamed and lunged forward. He grabbed her elbow and yanked it harshly, flipping her around to face him. Her elbow ached with a deep in-the-bone pain. It no longer felt like it could fit in its original place in the crook of her arm.

"You let that rich boy put his hands on you, but your own daddy isn't good enough for you, is that it?"

"No . . . it's not like that . . . I love him . . ."

"Love him! Is that your excuse for acting like a whore?" He inched closer to her. She kept shuffling backward until the protruding edge of the mattress stopped her progress.

"I bet you let that nigger boy touch you too."

"No . . . no . . ."

"Are you tellin' me, I'm not as good as your nigger boy?"

His breath smelled like cough medicine, and combined with the gamy odor of his greasy hair, they twisted her intestines until her lower abdomen pulsated with cramps.

"Why shouldn't I touch you if you've already whored around with every other male in this town? Even Farley had a taste of you, and I've kept my hands off of you for years now, just to keep you pure. A lot of good that's done."

A sliver of hope opened in her chest. He didn't think she was still a virgin. That's why he thought it was okay to touch her.

She forced herself to return his gaze. "I . . . promise . . . I . . . I'm . . . a . . ." She couldn't get the word out. She was so ashamed.

"Spit it out." His eyes had lost their flecks of gold and the ring of green around the irises. They were darker than she had ever seen them.

"A virgin."

His soft mouth had thinned into a sardonic grin. "Well, I'll just have to see about that, won't I?"

Rachel squeezed her eyes shut and prayed for God's mercy.

TWENTY

A game of dodgeball was in full swing when Sara opened the door to the school gym. There was no way to be subtle about her entry when she was soaked to the skin and wearing a prairie dress. Her ugly shoes squawked and slapped, the echo of her presence reverberating off the walls. Even the twitter of laughter and the smack of the ball against flesh couldn't diminish the sound of her passage. All eyes focused on her, exactly what she hoped wouldn't happen. She smiled, shrugged her shoulders like she was one of them and then hustled toward the dressing room.

The supply locker was located inside the cheerleading coach's office. It was separated by a tiny hall catty-corner to the dressing room. She prayed the coach was off coaching somewhere, but she wasn't. Sara dropped to a squat in front of the small window and uttered a silent curse. The coach spoke with a cheerleader, and the chirp of the girl's perky voice set Sara's teeth on edge. She squat-walked into the dressing room, grabbing the first towel she saw to mop off her face and body.

An abundance of normal, everyday clothes were strewn on benches throughout the locker room, giving Sara an idea. She peeled off her soaking dress and her stockings. Her hands shook as she removed the sacred undergarments. Without them she was not protected from the evils of the outside world, but in reality, they hadn't protected her from the evils within. The shield had failed them. She let the garment fall to the ground.

She settled on a pair of blue jeans that looked longer than most.

They were baggy and short, but they felt perfect. With panicky in-
takes of breath, she pulled on a soft blue sweatshirt with the word
"GAP" written on it. She snagged a similar outfit for Rachel and
stuffed it into her bulging backpack.

Sara returned to her post to listen. They were still talking. She decided she couldn't waste another minute. If they didn't leave by the
time she counted to one hundred, she would have to do something
drastic. On forty-nine, the door opened. The chirpy girl laughed before prancing back to the gymnasium. Only one set of feet had exited,
which meant the coach was still in her office. Without gaining access
to the supply room, she stood no chance of overpowering Abe. She
needed to act now.

She darted out of the locker room and reached for the fire alarm
directly next to the coach's office. Sara pulled it.

The sound was deafening. She shot back into the locker room
and waited a few seconds to ensure that the coach had exited her office. She pushed her way inside, crossed the room in four steps and
grabbed the handle to the supply closet. It was locked. Her eyes
scoped the desk for keys. Nothing.

She jerked open the first drawer, shuffling around. Nothing remotely resembling a key was in it. Then her eyes fell upon a neck
band bearing an old photo ID of Coach Clarkson. She snagged it,
grateful for her detective-novel education, and wedged the card between the doorjamb and lock. Immediately the knob turned.

Sara selected the thickest baseball bat and smacked it against the
palm of her hand to verify its strength.

Satisfied, she pulled the top of her pants away from her stomach
and slid the bat along her right leg. Arranging the sweatshirt over
her waistband, she moved stiff-legged out of the small room.

Moving in step with the swell of kids gathering at the emergency-
exit doors, Sara hobbled to the nearest exit. Students bunched there,
not wanting to go outside with torrents of rain pummeling the
earth. No one took the alarm seriously, and they didn't want to get
drenched for a "fire drill." Someone did a cartwheel, while another

girl shot off a handspring. Fire trucks clanged in the distance. Sara struggled to squeeze past, but the students weren't budging.

Terrified some girl would recognize her clothes, or notice the odd cylindrical object pressed inside her pant leg, Sara screeched, "Move it! There's a huge fire in the locker room."

Some boy said, "Cool."

Another student screamed, starting the stampede. The momentum propelled her forward until she burst through the doorway. Kids were running. Some were screaming. Sara moved in the opposite direction. With one hand still clasping the top of the bat down her pant leg, and the other clenching the strap of her backpack, she hustled awkwardly to the road.

Rain needled her face and chilled her skin. She hobbled and shivered to the highway. Her vision was partially obscured by the relentless drops.

The Traveler's Nest was an old hotel with a weathered, mission-style façade painted mustard yellow with burnt orange trimming. She stepped beneath the portico and removed the bat from her pant leg, stashing it behind one of the ceramic pots that framed the entranceway. She opened the door and swiped her feet on the interior mat.

The clerk was slouched on a stool, hands wrapped around an electronic game. He was flour-faced and bored looking with an angry rash of acne that skirted his cheeks. Sara prayed that his age would work to her advantage. Thank God she'd stolen normal clothes or she would never be able to pull this off.

"Dang, get a little wet out there?"

Sara laughed like it was the funniest thing she'd ever heard in her life. "I'll be glad to get in the room and dry off."

"We don't get rain like this much."

"That so?" Sara approached the counter and gave him her warmest smile.

"Uh-huh. Plenty of snow, though. If you're around here in the winter."

"I hear the skiing's pretty good in Utah."

"Oh yeah, we got some great resorts, just none here."

"That's too bad." Technically, she knew how to flirt from her paperback education, but the reality was much more difficult.

"So what are you doing out in this weather?"

"I thought I'd check out the town before I got caught in the rain. My dad said he'd leave me a key."

He frowned. "I didn't get a key, and I've been here all day."

"Could you check?"

"Sure. What room?"

"Room . . . oh . . . what room was it that he told me? That rain soaked more than my clothes."

A look went across his face. She'd seen that same look in men's eyes when they noticed Rachel. Seizing the opportunity, Sara swallowed her revulsion and said, "I'll be glad to get these off."

His eyes dropped south before flicking up with the realization that she was looking at him. "What room was it again?"

"I don't know. You tell me."

"Name?"

Her fleeting cool exterior crumbled. Sara panicked. What if her father had used a fake name? "I'm Sara . . . Shaw."

He clicked on the keyboard. "There's an Abraham Shaw in two-fourteen."

She sighed audibly. "That's him. That's my father." She could tell that she was losing him, and she still needed the key. "So, what's your name?"

"Dale Walters."

"What time do you get off?"

His eyes widened and a smile crimped his mouth. "Around six. You want to hang or something?"

"Why don't you get me the key, and I'll get cleaned up and come down around six." She sounded like a character in one of her stolen novels.

He licked the corners of his mouth then reached below the counter to extract a key. "Sounds good. I'll see you at six, Sara."

"Okay, Dale. See you then."

Sara took the key and tucked it quickly into her pocket, hoping to stabilize the shaking that had crept into her fingers.

Her eyes immediately found Abe's weathered truck, and the reality of seeing it punched her in the gut. She gasped, nearly doubling over before regaining her composure. Spinning around, she scanned the parking lot for Irvin. Where was he? A bright maroon Buick parked near the second stairwell was the only other car. A blade of fear flayed her resolve. Tears hit her cheeks, surprising her with their force. How would she pull this off?

The drapes were closed tightly on room 214. A rectangle of wet paper with a welcome message was plastered against the railing. Dread dug spurs into her chest as Sara slipped the key into the hole and pushed in. The door slammed closed behind her.

Everything seemed to disappear in the room except for the sight of her father. His skinny muscles bunched along his back and shoulders as he lifted himself off her sister. His limbs uncoiled as he raised his arms to ward off the blow. She shot across the room like an unleashed rubber band and brought the bat down on him, listening to the splinter of bones.

He let out a sick howl and cradled his broken arm. This changed to a yell of surprise as she lifted the bat to finish the job. Toppling backward off the bed to avoid the blow, he landed in a crouch.

"Sara, no!"

Sara heard Rachel's words and lost her nerve. Abraham darted away from her aborted swing; his legs caught on a jumble of bedding. He reached out to catch himself as he fell. His broken arm took the brunt of the fall. Jagged bone ripped through the flesh of his forearm. He crumpled to the floor and didn't move.

"You killed him," Rachel said flatly.

His chest rose and fell. "No, he just fainted." Sara couldn't look at her sister, at her nakedness. "Quick. Go clean up. We have to get out of here."

Rachel didn't move. "Oh my God, you killed him."

"No. Look, he's breathing." Sara panted, pointing with the tip of her bat at the rise and fall of his chest. "We have to leave."

Rachel said nothing. Even after what he did to her, Sara didn't know if Rachel would go. Finally Rachel leaned toward the floor, reaching for her torn shield.

Sara hadn't noticed the undergarments before. Even she was shocked. He must have gone crazy. It was forbidden to remove the shields except for bathing. Even to consummate a marriage, the garments must remain on.

"No, Rachel. If he defiled the sacred undergarments, he doesn't believe. Leave them." Sara transferred the bat to one hand and slipped her pack off. She removed the small bundle of clothes. "Put these on."

Rachel didn't move. She pressed her ripped garments to her chest.

"Put these on." Her pitch teetered on hysterical.

Rachel's eyes glided back and forth in their sockets.

"Rachel!" She didn't seem to hear. Trying not to panic completely, Sara nudged her sister with the bundle. Rachel blinked. When she looked at Sara, her gaze was steady. Sara gently loosened Rachel's grip and slid the garments from her fingers. She pressed the clothes into her hands. "Put these on instead. Okay?"

Rachel reached for the clothes and slipped into the bathroom, closing the door behind her with a soft click.

Sara expelled her breath. She couldn't worry about what she'd just seen, not yet anyway. Reshouldering her backpack, Sara continued to watch her father, the man she'd nearly killed.

Darting her eyes about the room, Sara noticed his pants partially obscured beneath the bed. She hooked them with her left foot without taking her eyes off his body. Bending her leg, she forked them up into her right hand and wedged them against the bat. She fished in his pockets. The front right pocket held his car keys. Looping a finger around them, she continued searching the other one. She removed a Swiss Army knife and nestled both keys and knife into her left hand to slip them into her own back pocket.

Abraham still had not moved. The diameter of the bloodstain was widening. She pushed the thought that he might bleed to death from her mind as her finger crawled around to his back pocket. Slipping his wallet out, Sara let the pants drop to the floor. It was a Velcro wallet and when she pulled it open, the ripping sound sent a shock wave to her already skittish nervous system. Guilt suffused her as she lifted the bills from it. Three crisp twenties were inside. She thought about putting the cash back, for the sake of the little ones, but she couldn't. Surely, the cost of her sister's innocence was worth more than this. These twenties were probably the bills that he intended to use to pay for this room once he was finished raping her.

Rachel emerged from the bathroom, holding her arms away from her body as though dripping wet. "Where did you get these?"

"A friend from school. It's okay, Rachel, they're just clothes." Her arms and face were a fiery red. It looked as though she had scrubbed the top layer of skin off. "You okay?" Sara flushed at the profoundly stupid question.

Rachel shrugged before settling her eyes on Abraham.

"He's beginning to stir a bit. We need to go."

Abraham moaned. She snatched up the bat and wielded it over his form. His eyelids were fluttering. "Go." Sara motioned toward the door with her head.

Rachel was deathly white. "Don't hurt him anymore."

"I'm not going to." Sara stepped away from him and backed toward the door. Rachel opened it. Sara charged past her, poking her head out to look both ways. It was clear. She closed the door on their father.

Rushing down the stairwell with Rachel close behind, Sara ducked her head as they stepped into the downpour. Sara led Rachel to the truck.

"We can't take his truck."

Sara unlocked the door. "We have no choice. We don't have enough money for bus tickets." Sara sloshed onto the seat, tossed the bat behind the seat and rammed her backpack onto the floor of the passenger's side. "Get in."

Rachel stood beside the driver's door, not moving. "You don't drive."

"I've watched."

"He'll call the police."

"No, he won't. Get in." Sara slid the key into the ignition.

Rachel walked around to the passenger side and opened the door. "Yes, he will."

Sara leaned over to look at her. "He won't because if we get caught, we'll tell the police what he did. He's not stupid."

"What if they don't believe us?"

"They will."

Rachel snuffled. "I can't leave." She was wringing her hands and biting her bottom lip. Rain dripped off her bangs, sending tears of water down her face. "Not without Luke. And Alice."

"Get in. We'll go find Luke right now."

"What about Alice?"

"We'll come back for her. I promise."

"But . . . what if we don't get back in time?"

"Rachel, did Abe hurt you when you were a little girl?"

Rachel shook her head slowly.

"Then he won't hurt Alice." Sara resisted the urge to shove Rachel into the truck. She glanced up at room 214. No signs of life. She cringed from the thought that she might have killed him. Or hadn't. Which was worse?

Rachel's eyes rolled up again, watching the show on her forehead. Sara raced around the car and gently guided her sister into the seat. She buckled the seat belt, closed the door and returned to the driver's side.

"You're safe with Luke and me. Let's go get him."

At the mention of his name, Rachel's eyes cleared. "You know where he is?"

"He's in Lufkin. I'll tell you all about it later. We just have to get out of here first."

Turning the key, she jerked in surprise when the engine responded. Examining the dash, she found the icon for the wipers and pressed them on. Thankfully, the rain wasn't quite as ferocious as it had been when she arrived. Spinning around to peer out the rear window, she scanned the lot for Irvin. If he didn't arrive in the next minute or two, she would have no choice but to leave.

Her heart twisted at the thought of never seeing Irvin again. If Abe regained consciousness, who knows what he would do. He could call the prophet for help. That terrified her.

Putting the car in reverse, she eased her foot off the brake and onto the accelerator. The car jerked backward, startling her so badly that she slammed the brakes. The engine died. "It's okay. I just need to get a feel for it."

Restarting the car, Sara crawled a few feet backward before shifting into drive. The car jerked and sputtered. They surged forward as she maneuvered out of the parking lot. She wondered if Irvin had changed his mind. She blinked a few tears away and turned around to face the road. Sara merged onto the highway, gripping the wheel as though she intended to wrestle it to the ground. Her fingers ached. Cars whizzed by them.

Nudging her foot down a bit on the accelerator, she brought the speed up to a whopping thirty-five miles per hour. A semi bore down on them. It switched lanes and shot past them with a long, annoyed blast from his horn. Sara pushed on the pedal and held her breath as the speedometer rose to fifty-five. "There. I'm not going any faster."

"Do you swear about Alice?"

"I swear." It sickened her to lie to Rachel. She thought of baby Alice and her soft, pudgy cheeks and gummy smile. Her eyes filled with tears. Maybe they could do something for Alice. "Listen, Rachel, the mothers are going to be extra careful in protecting the kids now that we've left. Whatever Abe tells them, they won't believe him. Not completely. They'll know deep in their hearts that he did something to drive us away." More lies. She knew his wives would never question whatever worm-infested garbage crawled out of his mouth.

"You think so?"

"I know so. I think the kids' lives will dramatically improve." *Please God, let that be true.*

"Maybe." Rachel curled against the window and began ripping a cuticle.

She had a bad feeling in the pit of her stomach as they drove to Lufkin. She didn't want to think about *them* or worry about *them*, but now it was too late. Rachel had planted the idea in Sara's narrow, self-interested brain. She would be forced to acknowledge their loss. "Look, I'll figure something out. Maybe when we get settled, we'll come get them all."

Rachel said nothing for several minutes, choosing to look out the window instead.

"How did you know Father had taken me to the hotel?" she asked in a voice barely above a whisper.

"A dream. I saw it in a dream." The lie rolled from her lips. Sara didn't understand what motivated her to say that.

"A dream?"

"Well, more like a vision. I think your guardian angel sent me."

As Sara turned onto the exit for Lufkin, her anxiety notched up. Why hadn't she asked Luke where he was staying? Now, it would be nothing short of a miracle finding him. And though the day had been filled with strange miracles and awful realities, Sara's confidence began to flag. She paused at the end of the exit ramp, trying to decide which direction she should turn.

Rachel watched her hesitation. "You do know where he is? Don't you?" Her voice rose slightly.

"Um . . . well, not the *exact* location. But he's camping out at some construction site in town. We'll go to every site and ask. Somebody's got to know him. Don't worry."

The rain tapered to a lazy drizzle, making driving slightly less nerve-wracking. Sara turned right at the first intersection. Cresting a hill, she saw tiny unpainted homes with clay-colored trims that seemed to tilt depressingly, as though they hadn't the heart to keep standing straight.

The quality of the stores changed from pawnshops and a small used-car dealership to drug stores, photography studios and a florist ringed by a quartet of furry pines. By the time they arrived at Wal-Mart, Sara hadn't seen a single business under construction. She drove through the center of town with a sinking heart. Swiveling her neck back and forth, she looked for a road that held promise, when she noticed a framed building with a sign reading FUTURE HOME OF LUFKIN SAVINGS AND LOAN.

"That's it!" Sara signaled a turn. The light changed. Sara pulled the truck into the parking lot. *Thank God.*

"I'll run in and ask if he's here," Sara said. "Are you going to be okay?"

Rachel nodded, studying her hands that lay on her lap like they belonged on a corpse.

"Okay then," Sara said after a few seconds of waiting for a reply. "I'll be right back." She climbed out, rushed to the trailer and knocked once.

"Door's open," a male voice said.

Sara entered. A large folding table held a slew of papers, some rolled and held together with rubber bands, others spread flat. The man sat behind the table, with his feet up and a portable computer perched on his lap. He squinted at her through eyes that were wind-weathered and permanently bruised from the blinding glare of working outside. "Can I help you with something?"

"I'm looking for a friend who works construction. His name is Luke Wilkinson, and I was wondering—"

"I know him all right. I hired him just to put a thorn in his daddy's side. Nice enough kid though."

"Is he coming in today?"

"Took off this morning. Said he was splitting town."

Sara felt the wind leave her body.

Spinning on her heel, she rushed to the door. The man's warbled voice followed behind. Her hands shook so badly that she could barely turn the key in the ignition. Sara pulled blindly out into the road. A horn blasted behind her as the car cut a sharp left to avoid hitting them.

Sara gripped the wheel with both hands and slowed to a crawl. Fear glued her tongue to the roof of her mouth. Numbness dissolved her lips.

"Did you find Luke?"

"Wait. I need to concentrate," Sara managed to say. She turned at the intersection and headed toward Main. They drove in silence until she ramped onto the highway. "He's gone, Rachel. I have no idea where he is. He's just gone."

A scream ripped through the car, shaking Sara from her guilty stupor.

"Nooo!"

The word was filled with such soul-grinding pain that Sara's teeth snapped together. She nearly doubled over onto the steering wheel. "I'm so sorry."

"Please. I can't go without him."

"I know . . . just let me think. Irvin will help." Sara glanced at her sister. She held her head in her hands and rocked back and forth, keening her grief.

"You've got to listen to me. I promise we'll find him. I gave Luke Irvin's number—" As soon as she said that, she realized her mistake. "Oh no!"

"What?" Rachel sniffled.

"We wrote the number down, but forgot to give it to Luke."

"I can't leave Luke behind, Sara. I just can't."

"It's way too dangerous to stay here. Abe will tell Silver that you

ran away. He'll search every corner of hell to find you. I'll call Irvin
and tell him to go to the woods on Saturday. He'll tell Luke where
we are."

"Let's do it now before we leave. Just to be sure."

Sara realized with a sinking heart that she didn't have Irvin's
phone number either. A sign flashed on the highway indicating the
exit for Centennial. She had unknowingly returned. Maybe fate
guided her here for a reason. Risk everything by driving within
a mile of home or drive past the exit and never return?

The exit ramp was only a few hundred feet ahead. Sara took the
exit. Absolutely nothing she did today was sane or rational, so why
start now? "We'll have to go to his house. I don't have his number
either."

Rachel dropped her gaze to her hands. "Thank you."

A knot shimmied up her throat. She owed at least that much to
her sister and to Irvin, even though he must have changed his mind
about leaving with them.

There was no influx of emergency vehicles outside that repulsive
hotel. She didn't see their van indicating a wife was there either.
Gripping the wheel tightly and breathing slowly through her
mouth, she kept her eyes locked straight ahead and willed Rachel
to keep her own down. Thankfully, she did.

After passing the hotel, she took the first right turn. Sara's heart
crawled into her throat. This was their road. Any second one of her
mothers could come barreling down it at breakneck speed and dis-
cover them in his car. Marylee would kill them. It wouldn't matter
that her husband had just raped her daughter.

Sara noticed a figure walking up ahead on the side of the road
with a camping pack on his back and two sleeping bags under each
arm. Sara used both feet to jump on the brake and the result was an
abrupt halt.

Irvin spun around with a look of fear across his face. Shielding his
eyes, he peered into the cab. "That's Irvin!" Sara said. She waved,
watching as his face lit up with recognition.

"He's coming toward us." Rachel backed into the seat as though she wanted to crawl into it.

Sara put her hand on Rachel to steady her. "He's going to help us, remember?"

The truck thumped as Irvin unloaded his packs into the rear of the cab. He came around to the passenger side.

Rachel scrambled over the seat, plastering herself against Sara. Sara felt the quiver of fear pulsing through her sister's body.

"It's okay. I trust Irvin. Don't be scared," Sara whispered to the back of her sister's head.

The door opened and Irvin climbed in. He pulled it closed behind him and turned to face them.

"I'm sorry, Irvin. We couldn't wait."

"Couldn't wait," he repeated. His face was taut with anxiety. He pulled out a pad of paper and a pen from his coat pocket, scribbling his explanation. Reaching across Rachel, he shoved it under Sara's nose. His mother had come home early from work because she had a dental appointment. He had to sneak out when she got a phone call.

Sara suddenly remembered the lie she'd told her sister about the guardian angel leading her to Rachel. And here was Irvin with his bags packed and ready to go. She swallowed hard, regretting that she hadn't had the courage to tell Rachel the truth in the first place. She'd have to let Irvin discreetly know what was going on. Clearing her throat, Sara began. "Rachel, this is Irvin. And Irvin, this is Rachel."

"This is Rachel," Irvin repeated, smiling.

At least she'd had the foresight to tell Rachel about his echoing problem. She continued. "Irvin had the same vision I did . . . and we met up on the road. He wanted to leave with us."

Irvin's smile dulled a notch as he processed her words.

Sara winked and nodded at him since Rachel kept her chin glued to her collar. Sara jerked the wheel around. The truck issued a grating, high-pitched squall as she hopped on the highway, intending to tell Irvin about the change in plans before dropping him off at the next available exit.

"Okay, here's the situation. Irvin, we have a huge problem." Sara rushed her words so that he wouldn't have to parrot everything back. "As you know, Luke was planning on meeting us on Saturday in the woods. Obviously, plans have been changed, and we have to leave right this minute. I know you want to leave with us . . ."

Something caught her eye in the rearview mirror: a flash of chrome, the plastic-encased revolving lights. Sara's heart punched her chest as though it were a pair of fists. "Don't turn around, but there's a cop car behind us."

"Cop car behind us," Irvin repeated.

Rachel quaked as she pressed her body tightly against Sara. Glancing at the speedometer, she accelerated to fifty-five, not wanting to attract attention by driving too slowly.

They passed several exits before entering Lufkin's city limits in silence. The northbound traffic went teeming past them, while the southbound traffic slowed in pace with the cruiser. Sara's hands cramped from her death grip on the wheel. Rivulets of sweat coursed her forehead, dropping in her ears with stinging regularity.

The cop car stayed directly behind them. She kept waiting for the lights to rotate, the sirens to scream. The highway in front of them emptied of traffic, but the cars and trucks stacked behind them like a funeral procession. No one had the courage to pass the trooper. Sara set the pace at fifty-five. They couldn't return now. Once again, fate dictated the direction of their future. Perhaps the police car behind her was a sign not to return. She had no choice but to keep going.

TWENTY-ONE

Rachel avoided thinking about her father, her mind carefully skating around the shame. The truck chugged along the highway, through the red-rocked canyons crisscrossed with streams swollen from spring runoff. Everything around Rachel represented rebirth, and yet all she felt was loss: of her way of life, of her purity, of her true love and even the loss of her sister's lone devotion, now shared with this dark boy.

But it was nearly impossible to escape thinking about the Negro sitting next to her. He had just pulled a medium-sized spiral notebook out of his coat pocket. In the half-hour or so that they had been driving with him, he hadn't moved until now.

For the past several minutes she had managed to inspect his body without slanting her head in his direction. Long tapered fingers belonged to hands that were not actually black, but more the color of wheat bread. Still, his skin was darker than anyone's she had ever seen in person. There were people in the community who had skin that browned in the sun, but it was that golden color that rests lightly on the surface. His color was deep underneath the shell of his skin, the blackness running in his blood.

And the longer she sat next to him, the more she realized he was more man than boy. His shoulders were broad, their width taking up a disproportionate amount of space in the cab. His hands were large, in addition to being dark. Big enough to require only one hand around the neck to squeeze the life out of her. He scribbled something on the pad and placed it in Rachel's lap. His hand brushed hers, and she convulsed in a spasm of shock at having been touched by the black boy.

She needed him now, to help communicate with Luke, but she couldn't wait to get him out of the truck. When were they going to turn around and drop him back off?

His index finger tapped the pad in her lap. She jerked again.

"Rachel, read it to me."

The boy repeated what she said.

Sara's eyes were busy traveling between the road directly in front of them and the rearview mirror where the police car followed at a snug distance.

"He said that we need to get to a big city." The boy repeated what Rachel had just spoken, and she found it incredibly distracting.

"But first we have to drop him back in Centennial," Rachel reminded them.

"Back in Centennial."

"Or maybe just Lufkin. It's not a huge walk home for him," she continued.

"Walk home for him."

"We can't stop anywhere yet. I need to make a decision after this next exit whether to head west or east." Fresh worry lines etched across Sara's forehead, making her look much older than fifteen.

"But we're getting too far away . . . from Luke," Rachel said. Had her sister forgotten about him already?

"From Luke," the black boy said.

Rachel shivered.

"I don't know what to do. Should we go to Denver? It's closer than some of the other cities," Sara said.

The boy scrawled letters all over the surface of the notepad.

"He says he thinks we should head west," Rachel said. "But why don't we just decide that later, after we drop . . . uh . . . Irwin off."

"Irwin off."

"It's Irvin," her sister said.

He repeated Sara's words this time, and Rachel was getting confused. What was his name? "But he said his name was Irwin."

"Name was Irwin."

"See," Rachel said.

"He just repeated what you said. His name is Irvin."

"Name is Irvin," the boy said.

"What should I do? Denver's not too far, and we could get out of the state faster," Sara said.

The boy handed Rachel his notepad. It read LAS VEGAS.

"Not Denver. We need to go to Wyoming. Just turn around now and head north. Then we could drop Irwin off on the way. And besides, it won't be that far for Luke to travel to get to us on Saturday," Rachel said.

"It's Irvin, Rachel!" This time Sara shouted.

"It's Irvin, Rachel."

"Okay," Rachel said, hurt. Why had her sister yelled at her?

The boy tapped his finger on the pad impatiently.

"Oh great, now I am going west," Sara said as the highway split, offering two competing directions.

"Going west," the boy said.

"The cop is still following us," Sara said. Her voice had a shrill edge to it.

Irvin had snatched his notepad off Rachel's lap and was back to his scribbling.

Rachel felt a quiver of desperation rock her stomach. "The policeman probably wouldn't follow us if we turned around, and even if he did, he'll stop at the Utah state line."

Irvin dropped the notepad in her lap.

"What is Irvin saying?" Sara asked.

Rachel picked it up. "He says we should head to Las Vegas. It's big, and there are lots of jobs there for teenagers. He also says—"

"He also says," Irvin repeated.

"What?"

"He says we can't turn back with the cop following us."

"He's right, Rachel."

"No . . . no way! We have to turn back."

"I'm going to keep driving southwest until we lose the cop. Then we'll make a decision." Turning her head, Sara gave Irvin a glance. He nodded.

Rachel's heart sagged.

She couldn't believe that Sara was taking his side over hers. Her sister really liked this boy. He seemed to like her too, maybe even as a girlfriend. They talked without saying anything, which was a good thing considering his speech problems. Wait! What was she thinking? It wasn't a good thing for Sara to have anything to do with a Negro. Their relationship was immoral and unnatural. But her sister didn't seem to care about that. Sara would leave her and marry the black man and be mother to his black children, and she would be an aunt to those black children, and they would all be part of Satan's extended family.

Anxiety kinked her stomach, while Rachel squirmed in her seat, the vinyl crackling underneath her. "What about Luke?" The cop might follow them for hours, and they were getting farther and farther away from him.

"I have his . . . I mean his parents' phone number," Sara said.

"You do?"

"Yes. It's in my backpack. I could call his mom and she'll get a message to Luke. Oh, I almost forgot, I have a letter from him too."

"You have a letter from Luke?" Her heart jumped in her chest.

"Letter from Luke."

Stop it! Every time the black man repeated Luke's name, Rachel felt like he had desecrated it.

Sara was right; Sister Elaina loved her son. She could probably get a message to him. "So, when can we call?"

"When we get to our final destination, we'll call. First thing."

"First thing," the black man said.

Panic teased Rachel's stomach. "I don't know. I really want us to just drop Irvin back off, so he can talk to Luke himself on Saturday. Besides, if we travel to a big city out west, we may be too far away for Luke to follow us."

"Luke to follow us." The black man jotted something down, then, shaking his head, he handed Rachel his notepad.

"What does it say?"

"He told me not to worry . . ." She read the rest of the message silently, blinking back threatening tears.

"What else?" Sara asked.

"He said Luke would follow me to the ends of the earth." How could this man/boy from a race of people that originated from Satan himself be so kind to her? Rachel bit down on her lip hard enough to draw blood.

"That's for sure," Sara said.

"So Irvin is coming with us?" Rachel finally said, defeated, sick with worry and more unnerved by Irvin's kindness than she would have been if he had acted like the typical child of Satan.

"Coming with us."

"It's okay, Rachel. Irvin is my friend . . . our friend."

AFTER the decision had been made to take Irvin with them, the three of them fell into an uncomfortable silence, punctuated only by the truck sputtering to climb the steep inclines that the narrow road snaked around. Occasionally, Sara would comment about the cop and speculate as to what he might want with them or do to them if he actually pulled the truck over. Sara dismissed Rachel's request to make a bathroom stop, and the pressure in her kidneys became a distraction.

During the entire drive, she stayed busy monitoring the width between her body and Irvin's, while examining the tiny curls coiled around the back of his neck when he looked out the window.

She also stole glances at his doodling, which he did on and off for hours. Page after page, he drew everything that fell into his line of vision: the police car behind them, horses grazing in a valley, a family eating at a picnic table outside a rest stop and finally, the sun sinking behind the mountains. She was amazed at how artistic he was. His sketches bordered on genius, but it would be impossible for someone from an inferior race to produce such beauty. How could a child of Satan be given such an extraordinary gift from God?

Maybe she should pray about it. But what had been as effortless as breathing yesterday was monumentally difficult today. For the first time in her life, she wondered if God had abandoned her.

THE city shimmered. Even the welcome sign to Las Vegas was larger than life and jeweled with neon lights that flashed in every direction. Irvin had suggested that they head toward what he called "The Strip" to find a place to stay for the night. He and Sara went back and forth debating whether to rent a room for the night. Writing furiously, Irvin told them that the hotels were inexpensive because they wanted to encourage their occupants to stay as long as possible to gamble in the casinos. Irvin explained that if they got a room, they would be able to shower and look for jobs the very next day. There were numerous places to work and make tips so that they would have money in their pockets immediately, instead of waiting weeks for a paycheck.

Sara's voice was giddy, her speech rapid-fire, as she pointed out one amazing structure after another. Rachel had never been out of Utah. In fact, Lufkin, with its population of 10,600, was the largest city she had ever visited in her entire life. Now she felt like she was traveling to several different countries, all within walking distance of one another.

"Look, there's an Egyptian sphinx. Oh my gosh, it's the Eiffel Tower!" Sara's head swung pendulumlike from one side of the street to the other. Although her fingers were locked around the steering wheel, Rachel noticed the truck inching over the white line and into the next lane.

"Uh, Sara—" Rachel said.

"Did you see that? Over on the left. A Caribbean island with a pirate ship." Sara kept up her frenzied speech.

"A pirate ship," Irvin repeated. His eyes were as wide as banjoes. He tapped the passenger window as they passed what looked like a Roman coliseum. When Sara turned to look out his window, the truck moved with her, edging back into its original lane. Someone honked behind them.

Sara sucked her breath in. "A circus!" She took her right hand off the steering wheel and shook it spasmodically in the direction of an approaching casino.

A nerve was pinched in the crook of Rachel's collarbone, and she felt a tremor forming underneath her right eye. But for Sara's sake, she would try to keep an open mind and accept this place as her new home. At least she was away from her father.

They parked the car on a side road, deciding to check out the various hotel prices before settling on one for the night. Irvin scribbled on his pad that they needed to take the supplies out of the back of the truck and put them into the cab to lock up. Rachel felt off balance getting out of the truck. They never even locked their homes at night, much less a car. Her resolve was shaken by the thought of some stranger taking the few things they possessed.

Giraffe-necked palm trees lined the wide sidewalks, and caravans of people bustled in and out of the casinos. A man with a cowboy hat sat on a stool playing some kind of song on his guitar. Rachel wasn't familiar with any music other than church hymns. He had his case open. People placed coins and dollar bills inside it. He started to sing something about lost love, and it was like a switch had turned on her tear ducts.

Sara squeezed her elbow and said, "Look at that guy over there. He's juggling." Rachel eagerly turned her head away from the musician to watch the man with a top hat and a red rubber nose juggle four balls in the air at once. She was stunned at how many talented people there were on just one city street. How could she possibly get a job when she had absolutely no talent in anything?

Out of nowhere, a fountain of water, lit from behind in white lights, erupted from a pond that had, just moments before, absorbed the black night into its recesses. Rachel had walked ahead several steps before she realized that Sara and Irvin had dropped behind her. They stood on the sidewalk, transfixed by the dancing water. Leaning her head onto Irvin's left shoulder, Sara locked her elbow around his. He kept his hands in his pockets, but he was smiling. Rachel felt like she was watching some stranger, not her own sister.

The man that approached her was probably her height and in his mid-twenties, wearing at least five gold necklaces around a spindly neck. "You look lost," he said. Her spine snapped to attention. He scanned her face as if he were choosing a piece of produce at the grocery store. His eyes were lashless and as beady as a snake's. They rested on her bruised cheek, and she fought the urge to sling her hand over it.

"No."

"Maybe I can help."

She couldn't figure out why he was so odd looking until she realized he had no eyebrows, and he was bald underneath his baseball cap.

"I don't think so." Her heart fluttered in her chest. She craned her neck around his head to locate Sara. Clumps of people had gathered near the fountain, and she could no longer see either of them.

"I'll tell you what . . ." He leaned close to her ear, while her eyes darted up and down the sidewalk. "I'll give you twenty-five bucks to party."

"What?"

"And if you're any good, I can help you get a real steady business going."

She took a step back, wondering where she should run. *Toward the fountain.* She sidestepped him, but he lunged at her, vising her wrist with a clammy hand. "Come on. Let's have a little fun."

Should she scream? It might get the attention of the police, and they would be sent back home, and their father would kill both of them. She could feel the bulk of someone against her back, and for a split second she thought it was Luke. The person behind her thrust a sinewy arm out, and a tawny-colored hand smacked the bald man's forearm. Surprise doubled the width of his beady eyes as he dropped Rachel's arm and took a shaky side step away from her. He put both his hands up in the air as if he were going to be arrested.

"Hey man, I didn't know this was your girl," he said, looking over her shoulder. He zigzagged backward and was absorbed into the crowd.

"This was your girl."

Rachel spun around to see Irvin, his face taut with worry. She was stunned by his concern. His tenderness reminded her so much of Luke that she thought she would dissolve into tears. "Thank you," she managed to tell him.

"Thank you."

Sara ran up to them panting and flushed with exertion, asking Rachel if she was okay. Rachel nodded, no longer trusting her ability to speak.

"What happened?" Sara said.

"What happened," Irvin repeated.

Rachel shook her head.

"All right, let's just find a place to stay for the night," Sara said.

They walked for a few more blocks to where the crowd thinned out. Leaning his backside against a palm tree, with his head between his legs, a man vomited into a large clay pot of cacti.

"I think he needs help," Rachel said.

Irvin repeated her, took one cursory look in his direction and then shook his head. He scribbled, HE'S DRUNK. JUST IGNORE HIM.

Sara looped her arm into Rachel's and whispered, "He'll be okay."

A girl in her late teens approached Irvin. Licorice-stick thin, with a bob of stringy black hair, she was tottering on spiked heels that elongated her feet so much, she appeared to be standing on the tips of her toes. A dish-towel-length skirt, made of a shiny pink material, hugged her hips. Handing him a brochure, she winked and said, "Let's party sometime." Then she rotated on her heels, hobbling off as if she were a beginner on roller skates.

"Let's party sometime," Irvin repeated in a strained voice that sounded like he was trying to pull the words back into his mouth.

"What is it?" Sara asked as Irvin flipped open the brochure. It was filled with grainy pictures of women in various stages of undress. Irvin dropped the booklet as if it were on fire, burning his hands.

"Why did she give that to you?" Sara said, her eyes darting to Rachel.

Rachel's cheeks felt hot. She was immediately uncomfortable around Irvin again.

"Give that to you?" he parroted, and then fished his pad and pen out of his pocket. He scrawled the words, holding it out in front of him for both of them to read together when he was done. IT WAS A CATALOG OF WOMEN SELLING THEIR BODIES.

Sara gasped. "How can they just pass out these catalogs selling . . ."

"These catalogs selling."

Irvin wrote, THEY'RE SELLING SEX, AND IT'S LEGAL IN NEVADA.

"But that girl was so young," Sara protested.

"So young."

MOST OF THEM ARE RUNAWAYS. THEY THINK THEY HAVE NO OTHER WAY OF MAKING MONEY.

Rachel's mouth filled up with saliva. "I want to leave. I don't want to stay here another minute."

"But Rachel, where will we go?"

"Where will we go."

"I don't care, as long as it's away from this place."

"It's just one bad apple," Sara said.

Rachel couldn't believe that her sister wanted to stay in this den of sin. "He wanted to pay me to do something for him," she said, ignoring her earlier impulse not to tell them about what the bald man said to her.

"Something for him."

"What?" Sara seemed confused.

"That man back there. He wanted to pay me . . . to party. Just like these girls." She pointed to the catalog rustling in the wind.

"Like these girls," Irvin said.

Sara grew pensive. Rachel felt a twinge of guilt for demanding that they leave, but she didn't want to stay another minute in this updated Sodom and Gomorrah.

Rachel noticed Sara's eyes flicker with an idea. She shot out of the starting gate with a rush of words. "He only approached you because you look like a runaway. We have to look like we aren't homeless. Like we're normal teenagers. Let's get to a hotel, and you can take a hot shower. Maybe we'll buy a couple of new shirts—"

"I'm not staying here."

"Staying here."

Irvin held up his index finger, gesturing for them to wait until he finished writing.

I THINK LAS VEGAS MIGHT NOT BE THE RIGHT PLACE. HOW ABOUT L.A.? IT'S NEAR THE OCEAN, AND THE MOUNTAINS AREN'T THAT FAR EITHER.

"I think it would be better there," Rachel said.

"Better there."

Sara bit her thumbnail while looking wistfully at the city lights. "Okay. Let's do it."

Thank you, Irvin. He had come to her rescue twice tonight. It was getting more and more difficult to accept the notion that he was part of some evil race of people.

IRVIN insisted on driving. As they moved farther from the city, the familiar stars from home appeared, glittering like diamonds against the velvet black sky. She picked out the Milky Way and the Big Dipper. It was as comforting as a warm blanket to know that no matter how far she traveled from Luke, they still shared that same night sky.

After a few hours, Sara had nodded off. Rachel noticed Irvin rubbing his eyes.

"We should stop soon. We can just camp out under the stars."

"Under the stars," he said, flashing a set of straight ivory teeth. Her lips curled on their own accord to return the smile.

Irvin eased off the smooth highway and onto a road pitted with potholes. Maneuvering around the scarred street woke Sara up. After driving for several minutes, Irvin found a gravel road to pull the truck onto. Irvin stopped the truck, apparently satisfied that they would be safely tucked away from view.

Rachel assured them that she would be fine sleeping alone in the cab, while the two of them hunkered down in the rear with Irvin's sleeping bags. They said their good nights, but Irvin returned to the cab just moments later. Pulling the flashlight out of his pocket, he clicked it on, motioning for her to hold it while he wrote. YOU'LL NEED THIS TONIGHT SO YOU CAN READ YOUR LETTER.

His kindness overwhelmed her. "Thank you so much. For thinking of me."

"Thinking of me."

Rachel slid the letter that Sara had given her out of her pocket when stillness came from the back of the truck. She smoothed it over her lap. He had printed it, in small blocky letters, big with meaning. He wrote with a poet's lyricism about the depths of his love for her, how she made him feel, how he wanted to grow old with her and finally, how he would never stop loving her . . . no matter what happened between them.

She was about to fold the letter back into the envelope, when she realized there was a picture tucked inside. It was a snapshot of him outside a lighthouse that was perched atop a moss-covered cliff towering above a frothy sea. She remembered him telling her about a family trip he had taken to the ocean a year or so ago. He was wearing a white short-sleeved shirt, and his skin was bronzed and his eyes were bluer than the ocean waves tumbling behind him. But in spite of his soft, bow-shaped mouth, his expression was one of unyielding despair.

Her teeth rattled inside her stiff jaw as she ran her index finger over the photograph, tracing the lines of a face that was immortalized in sadness. She slid the letter and picture back into the envelope. Not wanting to wrinkle it, she placed it in the glove box, yet she eyed its new home warily, afraid to have it too far out of her reach. Every muscle in her body was cramping and shaky from fatigue, but Rachel was terrified to close her eyes.

Curling herself up into the tightest ball she could, she wrapped the coat around her. Rubbing the webs that dipped between the fingers of her left hand, she reassured herself that the ring was still anchored securely with no room to slip off. She was grateful that when her father had snapped her necklace, the ring had landed harmlessly in plain sight. She would just rest for a few minutes, just enough to get through the next few days. Until she could be with Luke again.

Her father's eyes, lewd and penetrating, pulled her out of her sleep with the quickness of a whip snapping. A guttural scream pushed itself through clenched lips. Fat sobs began clogging her throat, cries so wretched and despairing, she didn't recognize them as her own. Her lungs heaved until they pushed against the bars of her rib cage in a panicked flight.

Sara and Irvin appeared at her side. She sat, crumpled and shaky in between them, while they attached themselves to either side of her. Resting her head in the cradle of Sara's shoulder, she tried to rein in the sobs. She felt Irvin's hand, steady and sure, on her back.

Even in the throes of icy grief, Rachel's brain sizzled with thoughts. She was stained in the ugliest possible way. How could she live with the shame? How could Luke love her anymore? How could he be anything other than repulsed by her?

"Sssshhh. It's okay," Sara soothed.

"It's okay," Irvin repeated.

"Luke will never want me . . . not like this." She was shocked that she had given voice to her deepest fear. She sucked a panicked breath in, trying to steal back the words still hanging in the air.

"Oh, Rachel, he will never stop loving you. You will always be the most beautiful person in the world to him . . . to all of us."

"To all of us," Irvin said.

She started trembling again, her thread of control snapping. "Why did he do this to me? Why? Oh, God, why?"

Irvin put his hand on her forearm. He whimpered like an animal with its leg caught in the steely teeth of a trap. Rachel turned to face him. His lips moved slowly, stretching in exaggerated wideness.

"It . . . it . . . was . . . not . . . not . . . your . . . fau . . . fault."

Rachel gaped at him.

"Irvin?" Sara said. She reached across Rachel's lap, the tips of her fingers finding the hand that remained draped over Rachel's arm. "Oh my God, Irvin, you're speaking."

His eyes were closed. Sara started to say something else, but after watching his face, she fell silent. Several moments passed until he pushed open his eyelids, so carefully, so tentatively, as if he were given sight for the first time. His lips were trembling, too weak for the act of forming words and stringing sentences together.

Pulling his notepad out, he wrote slowly, stopping to scratch out words and then rewriting entire sentences. His face was contorted with effort. When he was finished, he gently placed it on Rachel's lap.

I'VE NEVER TOLD ANYONE THIS BEFORE TONIGHT. MY STEPFATHER RAPED ME WHEN I WAS FIVE YEARS OLD. Rachel dropped the pad.

"Oh my God," Sara said. "Oh . . . my . . . God . . ." Sara's voice trailed off, finding her tears.

"Oh, no . . . no. Irvin . . ." Rachel took his hand in hers. Shedding her self-pity, she said, "I am so sorry."

He picked up the notepad and wrote one last sentence. I NEVER SAID ANOTHER WORD ON MY OWN AFTER THAT.

Rachel's heart stretched like elastic from the shock, then the surge of empathy, and finally, the emergence of profound sadness, a swelling in her chest so great, it might just break her heart in two.

She squeezed his hand until it spasmed from the contraction. "I'm so sorry for your pain. So sorry . . ." she managed to say before the current of sorrow swept her words away.

A lump bobbed up and down in his throat. It was then that she realized he hadn't repeated her. Not one repetition since his revelation. A single tear, a perfectly formed drop of sadness, quivered down his cheek. Raising her hand to touch his face, she took it away, placing it with all the other tears dampening her own hand.

"Th . . . th . . . thank . . . yyy . . . you."

His words were halting and jumbled, but they were his own.

Chapter

TWENTY-TWO

Sara stood at the ocean, allowing the tide to rush over her feet. The water felt so refreshing after the long drive from Las Vegas. She could taste the sea, salty on her lips. It was a taste she hadn't realized she'd been craving all her life. Deafened by the power of the waves, Sara was filled with quiet urgency for this city. This was where they belonged.

Irvin came over and took her hand.

"I'm free," Sara said. "Right now, at this very moment, I don't have to worry about anything."

"T-thank you for e-e-everything."

"Thank *me* for taking you away from a warm bed and roof over your head?" She said it playfully, but the look on his face was serious.

"I'm s-standing at the edge of the ocean with this a-amazing girl, having a c-conversation. You have no idea w-what a gift that is."

Sara hid her eyes so he couldn't see how much impact his words had on her. "You're the one who should be thanked."

"I feel like I can d-do anything right now. Absolutely anything."

"Is the compulsion completely gone?"

Irvin grinned. "It's gone. I c-can't explain it. Before I had the b-breakthrough . . . the impulse to r-repeat was s-stronger than breathing." Irvin nosed the sand with his toe. "I m-must have been eight or nine years old. My m-mother couldn't s-stand my repeating . . . she s-snapped. She s-started slapping me, ch-chasing me around the house, s-screaming at me to 'shut up, shut up.' Of course,

I w-was screaming right back at her 'sh-shut up, shut up.' She f-finally got tired and fell on the ground, s-sobbing. She t-told me she hated me. I echoed that right b-back at her. We b-both were crying. It was p-pretty awful."

"Do you wish you could tell her that you no longer repeat?"

"You m-mean tell her that I can finally sh-shut up?"

Sara nodded.

"No." He took both her hands and leveled his eyes at hers. "I h-have you."

She wanted to cry.

"I th-think you're . . ." Hesitating, he dropped her hands. He reached into a wave and pulled out a pebble. He flicked it over the water's surface. It hopped and skipped and seemed to mesmerize him.

"What?"

"Amazing. In every w-way."

She flushed with happiness. "So are you."

They jumped back as a large wave crashed against them, soaking the bottoms of their bunched-up jeans.

"Do you think Rachel will be okay?" Sara nodded her head at Rachel, who studied something in her hand.

A painful quiet held the air between them. Irvin cleared his throat. "I-I think so."

Sara dared not look at his face. She didn't want to see the lie. "What did you find?" Sara yelled, but the wind knocked her words away. Rachel didn't look up until they were right next to her.

Rachel held a small conch shell, turning it over and over in her hands. "Isn't this beautiful?"

"Put it to your ear. You can hear the ocean."

"I can hear the ocean now. It's everywhere." A dewy tenderness ringed Rachel's eyes, a flirtation with the gentle soul that had been hiding behind the grief of the last few days.

Sara smiled so wide her cheeks hurt. "Yes, but when you're away from the water you can still hear the ocean if you press the shell to your ear."

Rachel returned the smile. The first one Sara had seen in days or perhaps it was weeks. "How did you know that?"

"Books. They've taught me everything I know."

THE afternoon melted into evening. They sat on the beach watching the light play on the water, inking it with purple and gold as the sun drooped down the horizon.

"This place is mesmerizing," Sara finally said. "It's like I don't ever want to leave. I just want to sit here forever."

"I saw a phone booth at the corner." Rachel screwed the cap off a water bottle and took a sip. "I think we need to call before it gets too late."

A cantaloupe orange streetlight illuminated the phone booth as Sara deposited money and dialed Luke's mother's number. Handing the phone to Rachel, she held her breath while Rachel pressed the receiver to her ear.

"I think you dialed it wrong." Rachel returned the phone to her. Sara listened with a sinking heart to the electronic voice telling her the number was disconnected. She hadn't made a mistake with the number. Still, she repeated the procedure two more times and called information only to be told the new number was unpublished. Sara's heart sank. Of course, Luke's father would have changed their phone number after he kicked his son out. Sara shook her head. "I'm sorry."

Rachel bit her lip, trying to hold in her tears. "We've got to go back there before Saturday," Rachel said. "We just have to."

Sara's stomach heaved. "Oh, Rachel, I'm so sorry, but you know we can't do that. Silver has probably mobilized an army to find you. Let me think." Sara rubbed her cheeks. "Irvin, do you know anybody we could call to have them go to the woods on Saturday?"

He shook his head.

Rachel cried on their return to the beach. She didn't make a sound, but fluid streamed from her eyes. No matter what Sara said or did, Rachel continued the eerily silent cry.

THE shriek of gulls woke Sara at dawn. Her face felt salted and moist. As she opened her eyes, a flock of herons passed overhead with long legs that trailed behind them. Inching her head farther out of the bag, she noticed that Irvin was gone, leaving a nest of sandy, squashed clothes. Irvin sat near the shore watching enormous breakers pound the sand. Sara wiggled out of the sleeping bag, careful not to wake Rachel. Wrapping her arms around herself for warmth, she navigated the cold sand.

Sara and Irvin sat silently, letting the approach of light dilute the uncertainty of their future. "W-we need to f-find a library and g-get on the Internet to find help for r-runaways."

"I guess we can't stay here forever."

Rachel came and sat quietly beside them.

A couple jogged in front of them. Sara envied their casual strides and comfortable existence. She wanted that so desperately that it hurt. Turning to Rachel, she said, "Maybe not next week, but we *will* go back there and find Luke. I *promise*. He'll wait for you. I know he will. And when we're strong enough and safe enough, we'll go get him. Do you believe me?"

Rachel sighed, closing her eyes. "I think so."

"We're not leaving this beach until you say that *you know so*."

Rachel's lashes fluttered open. She peered at Sara with such a bone-weary gaze that Sara couldn't find room in her chest for a breath.

"I know so."

Returning to their bags, Irvin repacked his backpack with the clothes and Sara rolled the sleeping bags. Taking shampoo, soap, brushes and a clean change of underwear, Sara had to prod Rachel to accompany her to the public restroom. They were homeless and jobless, and had very little money. Yet she was less stressed than when there was a roof over her head and food in her belly.

After cleaning up in the restroom, they began the hike back to the truck. Arriving at the street, a small blue Honda was parked where the truck had been. "Oh my God, where'd it go?" Sara said.

Irvin shrugged off his heavy pack and sat on the curb. He dropped his head in his hands. "It's been s-stolen."

TEEN Haven occupied half a block on a street just north of Hollywood Boulevard. The exterior was starchy white interrupted by two slender posts that were painted a rich mahogany. These columns framed the front door, which had been left hanging open. They entered, passing young faces with eyes painted black and lips the color of blood.

A black woman, with rows of beaded braids and a clunky silver crucifix that jostled between her breasts, approached them. She was tall, at least six feet, with bones heavy like a man's. When she smiled, it plumped her cheeks and crinkled her eyes, giving her a merry look. "Is this your first time to Teen Haven?"

Sara cleared her throat. "Yes, ma'am."

"We're glad to have you. Why don't you come this way, and I'll show you how things work around here." She motioned for them to follow. Irvin met Sara's eyes and she nodded.

She took them into an office hosting an array of inspirational posters. Taking a seat behind a battered desk, she motioned for them to do the same. A computer monitor was pushed to one side, and several Styrofoam coffee cups, tattooed with cinnamon-colored lipstick, were clustered in the right corner of the desk. A homemade ceramic mug, pocked with little finger indentations, held an assortment of pens.

Sara glanced at Rachel out of the corner of her eye, noticing that she kept her head down, staring at hands folded complacently in her lap.

"My name is Ernadine Johnson, and I'm the director. The first thing I want you to know is you're safe here. Ain't nobody gonna make you call your mamas and daddies unless you want to. Ain't nobody gonna call the police just 'cause you're living on the streets. We're here to help. Okay?"

Sara nodded, feeling the tightness in her body loosen just a notch.

"We provide breakfast and lunch, hot showers and lockers. We can also help you find shelter for the night, and we got lots of donated clothing if you need some. Additionally, we provide AIDS testing and substance abuse counseling. Also, if you need to see the doctor, we have one in from eight A.M. 'til four P.M. every other Thursday. Our mission is to provide healthy alternatives to street life and get you independent and self-sufficient. So, why don't you tell me what we can do to help?"

Rushing tears surprised Sara. She batted them back. "We need to get some work, and we're hungry."

"We'll be serving lunch here in less than an hour. As for work, is it okay if I ask you some personal questions?"

Sara realized pretty quickly that lying about who they were was not only unnecessary but counterproductive. Ernadine asked their names and ages. Glancing quickly at Irvin and hoping he didn't mind, Sara told her the truth about their identities.

Ernadine shifted her weight, causing the chair to creak. "Do you have any ID at all? Birth certificates? Social Security cards?"

"I h-have both."

"We only have our birth certificates," Sara said.

"Well, the good news is that with Irvin already having a Social Security card and being sixteen years old, we should be able to fix him up with something pretty quick." Ernadine folded her arms across her breasts, resting them there like they were lying on a fluffy cushion. "Sara, since you're the only one here who is still fifteen, it'll be harder to find someone who will hire you. Not impossible though. Also, I'm going to have to send you girls to the Social Security office to apply for cards. Those will take a few weeks to get. 'Cause nobody's gonna hire you without one."

"But w-we don't have an a-address," Irvin said.

Ernadine nodded. "You can use this one. When you apply for work, you give them a number that we have set up for that as well. With me so far?"

Sara nodded, as Ernadine continued to give them information about Teen Haven's services. She had naively assumed she could just walk into a place and get hired. Mentally kicking herself, she wondered what else she had overlooked about living independently.

TWENTY-THREE

Slices of lemony sunlight slipped through the edge of the heavy plaid curtains that decorated the cheap hotel they had rented with money from their new jobs. With eyes still partially closed, Rachel rolled away from the window and fingered the fresh indentation left by Sara's absence. She shot up in bed, her heart beating inside her like a stampede of wild horses. *Oh my God, where's Sara?* With clenched teeth, she bit off a rising scream. Thrashing out of the tangled sheets, she reached for the lamp on the nightstand. The force of her jerky hand rattled a glass of water, causing it to hit the lamp, shattering it to pieces.

"What h-happened?" a male voice hurled his accusation at her. *A man is in their room!*

The fleshy part of her palm picked up shards of glass like Velcro. Making contact with the switch, she pushed a shaky thumb into it. The room burst into view. *It's just Irvin.* He was kneeling on his sleeping bag on the floor. His face was troubled.

"Sara's gone!"

"She's in the sh-shower."

She exhaled with a shudder. "Oh." It was all she could think of to say.

She shrugged off her jumbled fear, trying not to dwell on its source too much. The fuzzy hands on the wall clock across the room sharpened under her squint. It was 7:00 A.M., and Sara was already taking a shower, getting ready for her first day at the library: her dream job. It was also the first day that Rachel would be doing their paper route alone.

Irvin watched her closely. She barely remembered the fear and revulsion she'd felt when she first met him. He was like a brother now. The best possible brother. He no longer repeated sentences. She hardly noticed his stuttering. She had no doubt that he would go back to school and accomplish amazing things with his life. Just like Sara. The two of them were so capable, their gifts so astounding.

He turned his attention to the broken glass. "L-let me get this cleaned up. Why don't you r-rest for a few minutes? You look very p-pale."

"Thank you," she said, swallowing rising nausea. She really didn't feel well. Laying her head back on the pillow, she listened to the hum of the hair dryer coming through the door of the bathroom. She closed her eyes. If she could just drift off to sleep for a little longer, maybe the noisy thoughts murmuring in her brain would also rest.

They had been in L.A. over a month now. She had learned more about life than she ever cared to. The ugly, dark part of life. Where children went to bed cold and hungry. Where teenagers were forced to sell their bodies for food or even the drugs that their bodies needed as much as the food. The world was a dangerous place, filled with people who were not to be trusted. Especially men. She could never be too careful.

And not a second went by without Rachel mourning over Luke. She often asked Sara when they would get back there to look for him and was always told it wasn't the right time. Sara was undeniably happy with her life just the way it was. Now that her sister had her dream job, they weren't going anywhere. Rachel was sure of that.

Rachel didn't know how she could live without him. The last day they were together he said he would die without her. Would he? Had he already? The thought rocked her stomach. Her heart started fluttering again. *Stop. He's not dead.* Several times over the past few weeks, she felt like it would be much easier to die than to

go about creating a new life for herself here. It was only that sliver
of hope that she would see him again that kept her heart beating re-
liably every day. Sara really didn't need her anymore, and if Luke
was gone, what was the point of her existence?

Irvin had just left for work when Sara asked her, again, if she
would be all right doing the paper route alone. Guilt lined her face
as if she were abandoning her firstborn child.

"Sara, I want you to do this. It's where you belong."

"I just feel so bad leaving you."

"I'm fine. I really am."

"But—"

"Get going. You'll be late on your first day if you don't hurry."

Sara gnawed on her bottom lip. "I don't know."

"I'm the one who's going to feel bad if you don't go today."

Sara gave her an unsteady smile. "Okay. You know the number,
if you need to get ahold of me."

Rachel nodded. "Go."

It wasn't until the door had clicked closed behind Sara that
Rachel let the tears flow. She curled up, soaking the bedspread with
her unhappiness. Eventually she stopped crying, her body too tired
to manufacture any more tears.

She forced herself off the bed. She had to deliver those papers today. The monthly room rate expired tomorrow. Lately, it seemed
that Rachel was more of a hindrance to her sister than anything
else. And an expense. If it wasn't for the fact that she was scared of
the people at the homeless shelter, they could be saving hundreds of
dollars a month in rent. If she didn't do both routes today, they
would be short on cash and be forced to rent by the week at a much
higher rate. It would take her twice as long to deliver the papers
without Sara, but she still would be done with her day three or four
hours before Sara was finished at the library. Irvin had been working double shifts all week at the restaurant, so she would be spending a lot of time alone.

Pulling her ponytail through the opening of the back of her L.A.

Dodgers baseball cap, she made sure to shove far up into the hat any disobedient waves trying to cascade around her face. She chose a black T-shirt, extra large, from Irvin's drawer. It hung limply, too much material to catch the curve of her breasts, and just the right amount of material to cover the swell of her hips. She looked safely angular.

AN icy gray sky had stolen the brassy morning light, restless and twisting. Trees shivered from the strengthening wind, and she tried to gauge how long she would have before the storm. She still hadn't started Sara's side of the street. Because Rachel was unnerved by change, she insisted that she do the west side of the street each time. Sara didn't care. Today she was forced to do the east side too, city blocks filled with strangers. New threats lurked behind every storefront and inside every apartment lobby where she would have to deliver the fliers. She sucked in handfuls of air, expelling them in short, open-mouthed breaths.

She stepped into an alley, trying to calm herself down. Stroking the band of her ring, she leaned against the wall of a brick building. The stench from the garbage Dumpsters assailed her nostrils. She swallowed the rushing current of saliva again and again until it ebbed. Needing reassurance, she pulled her envelope out of the backpack. There was Luke. *He's dead.* The voice was back. She ate the air again, gulping and then swallowing, her hands trembling violently as she dropped his picture in a muddy puddle. "Oh no!" Snatching it up, she blotted it on the front of her shirt. One of his eyes had a smudge of purple over it. The rest of the picture was covered with water stains that drained his face of color. Corpselike. *You killed him when you left him there.*

The rustle of tumbling paper pricked her ear. Luke's letter! She lunged toward it. As she stumbled over an empty beer can, the load in her canvas bag pulled her toward the ground. She landed hands first on the alley's grease-clogged street, and her palms were scraped and embedded with pebbles and debris. She didn't care. She just wanted that letter. It was dancing in the wind, soaring up and then spiraling down in the breeze, a corner of it picking up a smudge of mud, weighting it down like quicksand, drawing half of it into a puddle.

She pinched the dry tip of the letter between her index finger and thumb, while coaxing the submerged end out of the water. The ink had collapsed on itself, the water erasing words and chopping sentences in half. *Just get it back home. You can resuscitate it then.*

A doe-eyed baby girl, with wispy butterscotch hair, waved a chubby fist at her. "Alice!" Rachel cried out. The woman who had braced Alice on one hip looked at her strangely, then covered the baby's head with a cow-print blanket and crossed the street hurriedly. *You're so stupid.* Alice wouldn't be here. *Just think for once in your life.* She just looked like Alice, that's all.

She couldn't do it. She just couldn't. Not today. She would be much better tomorrow. It was just that it was her first day without Sara. Of course she was nervous. She would take back Sara's papers and tell them she was too sick to deliver them today. The buzzing in her head was getting too loud, and it was causing her to be so careless that she may have ruined two of her three most valuable possessions in a matter of minutes. *Don't think about that right now.* At least she would get paid for her route. That would leave her ten dollars short, minus another ten or so after she went to the pharmacy.

Her limbs were shaky and unreliable as she made her way back to the office where she had started her route. She returned the undelivered fliers, feeling terrible about it, but her new supervisor just shrugged it off.

"Don't worry about it," Todd said, his acne-pitted face flushing as she explained the situation. He wasn't much older than she was. "Just get better."

His kindness made the tears threaten again. She hurried off. Todd may have excused her for today, but she had no excuse to give Sara and Irvin for not doing her part. The money situation left her no choice. She knew what she had to do.

The man had slaty eyes and a leering mouth with spidery purple veins mapped across the bridge of his nose and the apples of his cheeks. Little black hairs sprouted out of his cauliflower ears. She could now recognize the metallic smell of alcohol coming from his parted mouth. "You are just a pretty little thing aren't you?" His voice was tinny and sounded very far away, but he was mouthing the words just inches from her face. *Pretty, pretty, pretty.*

"How much for this?" she asked, sliding the ring across the counter.

He looked at it and laughed. "You're kidding, right?"

"How much?"

"Well, let me get my microscope out and take a look at this beaut." His meaty laugh returned and intensified. He slapped the counter in amusement. Rachel jumped.

"Five bucks."

"What!"

"Maybe we can work out a little something on the side. Make it worth my while."

You do something to men. She grabbed the ring and turned to leave.

"Wait, little lady." He exhaled tiredly. "How much do you need?"

"Twenty. I need twenty dollars."

"And you're coming back for this?"

"Of course! Next week. The first chance I get."

He slid a twenty across the counter. She plucked it off before he could change his mind. "I'll be waiting," he said as she swung open the door, not looking back.

She walked onto the street feeling naked without her ring. *Pretty, pretty, pretty . . .*

The bold red lettering of the drugstore swam to the shore of her vision.

Remember to hold your head up.

Walking into the store, she casually perused the aisles. Finding her intended location, she backed away from it to take a quick detour through the magazine aisle, feigning intense interest in an article on makeup tips. She glanced up to see a stern gray-haired man observing her reflection in the mirror that ran along the back wall of the store. She put the magazine back on the shelf. She inched her way over to the correct aisle, and in spite of herself, she looked up at the mirror again. He was still staring, this time with his arms crossed, while saying something to the girl behind the checkout counter.

She was alone in the aisle, except for his wandering eyes that had followed her across the store. *Do it!* She took the box off the shelf, cradling it in the crook of her arm, where he could see that she wasn't trying to steal it, but he couldn't see what she was carrying to the counter.

"Benson, line two . . . Mr. Benson, pick up line two," the intercom announced. Rachel wanted to cry in relief as the wandering eyes disappeared behind a side door next to the photo lab.

She placed her shameful purchase on top of the counter. The girl smacked her gum, and her bored expression remained as she rang up the scandalous item. She popped a bubble and said, "That'll be nine forty-five."

While Rachel pushed her hand into the front pocket of her jeans for the twenty, the girl mercifully dropped the box into the plastic bag behind the counter. Rachel grabbed the bag from the girl's outstretched hands a little too quickly, mumbled a faded "thank you" and backed away from the counter, turning to flee.

"Young lady . . ." His voice was formal and scolding, hinting of a British accent. She forced herself to turn back around. Wandering Eyes had returned, now standing behind the bubble-popping girl. "You forgot your change," he announced.

She was so stupid and careless. She couldn't afford to leave ten dollars behind. Not after all the trouble she'd gone to for that money in the first place. "Oh . . ." She glanced at the clerk. A net of wrinkles covered his face. Deep-set, iron-rimmed eyes took in her every gesture. He had a slash for a mouth with a slender moustache quivering above it.

"Thank you," she said to the harmless, kind old man.

"Why do you hide your beautiful face under that cap?"

"What?" she said, taking the ten-dollar bill and loose change from his hand.

"And your hair . . . it's lovely. You should wear it down."

You do something to men. To good, kind old men.

She dove into a cresting wave of panic. "What do you want from me?" she snapped back.

His eyes widened. "My dear, it was just an observation, a compliment, if you will. I'm sorry if you took offense."

She backed out of the store, pushing the door open with her backside and clutching the plastic bag to her stomach. She ran for the next two blocks until her lungs seared, her heart pumping too fast for her breathing to catch up. The hair. It was her hair that inspired lust in the hearts of good men. It must be. The hair must go.

Nearing the hotel, she sniffed sewage in the air mingled with marijuana. She passed the neighborhood bars with their neon beer signs, eyeing the dancing colors in the windows. She threw her loose change into the Styrofoam cup held out to her by a withered woman with gnarled fingers growing out of a liver-spotted hand. "God bless you," the woman said.

God doesn't bless me. Not anymore.

Climbing the stairs, she stopped at the top of the musty hallway, stale with the smell of cigarettes and greasy food. She dug her room key out of the backpack, went in and threw her bags in a heap in the corner. First things first. If she organized her time, she could get everything done today. She pulled the letter out of her pack, and spread each page on the bed. She would see how it looked when it dried completely. The sight of her naked ring finger on her left hand startled her. For a quarter second, she panicked, wondering if it had slipped off her finger. Then she remembered, with troubled relief, that the ring was on loan. Just for a week.

She laid Luke's picture on top of the pillow she had used the night before. It was already dry and curling around the edges. Next step. She opened the night table drawer. Sara kept the pocketknife in there. Just in case. Irvin had told them an intruder could unlock their room with the swipe of a credit card. But they were ready, especially during those times when Irvin didn't arrive at the hotel until late into the night.

The blade felt cold under her fingers. She stood in front of the mirror. Her eyes were bulging and glassy and gray. *Fish eyes. Dead eyes.* Whose eyes were they? Was someone hiding inside her? *Stop it.* She raised the knife to a crinkly handful of hair and sawed it off, watching it fall as softly as a gentle snow. She felt euphoric. *That's better.* She grabbed the next clump, sawed, and the next. Faster and faster until a caramel rug covered the entire bathroom floor. She would clean it up later. She placed the knife next to the sink.

Next, she retrieved her bag, and opened the box. Reading the instructions with one hand, she held the plastic stick between her legs with the other hand. Shivering on the toilet seat, she tried not to think about the significance of this moment. She willed herself to purge her mind of any thought other than getting herself to pee onto the stick. Finally, she squeezed a few drops out, and just as she relaxed from her success, a rain shower of warm urine released, pouring over the stick and soaking the sleeve of her shirt. *Plenty.*

After washing her hands, she popped her head around the corner to check the time. Irvin would be gone until late tonight, and Sara was safely occupied at the library for several more hours. All she needed, according to the instructions, was five minutes. She went to lie on the bed. 3:05 P.M.

Folding her hands on top of her chest as if in prayer, she had a brief vision of herself in a coffin. Strangely reassuring. She could finally rest. They would rearrange her hands exactly that way: prim and saintly. *Please, God, please help me.* She would do anything. Go back to the Church, maybe not go back home, but maybe join another community. She would even become a plural wife. 3:06 P.M. *Don't look at the clock. It takes longer.* She may have to give up Luke. Maybe not. If she worked at being more devout, maybe she could keep Luke. *He doesn't want you, you dirty girl. No man will ever want you after I'm through with you.* 3:07 P.M. She picked up Luke's letter.

The line where he had written, "I'll always love you," had been violated by the water. It now said simply, "I'll always . . ." It was left for her to fill in the blanks. "I'll always hate you for leaving me."

Had it said that? Maybe she just imagined the old words, read just what she wanted to read. The letter scared her now. 3:08 P.M. She picked up the picture of his blurry face. She was destroying him, the picture was proof: his life was being blurred out until he faded into nothing. She can't be with Luke. *You were mine first.* She's destroying him. *Slut, whore.* When he discovers her dirty secret, he will cease to exist. 3:09 P.M. *Please God, have mercy. Lord have mercy. Merciful God.* It was the same useless prayer she had said right before her father had violated her. 3:10 P.M. *Judgment day.*

She reached the bathroom on shuddering legs. The plus sign was there, bloodred, announcing how far she had fallen.

She retched over and over into the toilet, the vomit, mixed with her pregnant urine, splashing up into her face. *Daddy's baby.*

TWENTY-FOUR

The streets were filmy from the rain Sara had just missed. The cars hissed along the streets, their headlights painting the asphalt in streaky blurs. Over the course of the month, Rachel had not improved. Time hadn't applied its healing balm like she'd hoped. If anything, she'd deteriorated. Her body twitched in her sleep, riddled with nightmares. When they talked, she seemed to look right through Sara. Pushing all those thoughts from her mind, Sara refused to let her fears taint the first day of work.

Moving along the clean, glittery parts of Hollywood into the seedier area, Sara turned onto a side street where abandoned shopping carts and overflowing trash cans flourished. She didn't mind the peeling paint of their hotel-home, or the salty grease of the windows that belonged to each unit. Sara decided to only notice the beautiful things about her life. At least today she would.

One of the regular hookers who used the hotel on an hourly basis was unlocking the door to a room while her john stood behind her, darting glimpses at her behind as though it were a rump roast he was getting ready to carve up. The girl's eyes flickered with recognition as Sara approached. Her mouth, smeared with lipstick the color of a fading bruise, twitched with what could be construed as a smile. They were probably the same age. Sara smiled back.

Removing her own key, Sara hoped she wouldn't startle Rachel too much. She always jumped when Irvin came home. The slightest noise unsettled her. That was doubly unfortunate due to the neighbors and their drunken brawls, the working hazard of creaking beds at all hours, and the moans and groans of men as they did their business.

Irvin worked a double tonight, so she wasn't surprised that he was gone. Still, Rachel's absence alarmed her. "Hello? I'm home."

Kicking off her shoes, she knocked on the closed bathroom door. "Rachel? You in there?"

Silence answered her. Knocking more forcefully, she raised her voice. "Rachel?" Twisting the knob, she was met with resistance. Blood rushed past her ears as she pushed hard against the door. "Open up. You're really scaring me!" Stepping backward until her back pressed against the sliding doors of the closet, Sara charged forward. Her shoulder slammed against the door. It held fast. She banged. "Open this door right now!" Kicking with all her might, she regretted removing her shoes. Running back to the bed, she slipped her feet into them. Coiling her right leg against her chest, she struck hard. The door flung open with such force that it rammed the wall and ricocheted back at her as she moved inside. Hitting it open with both hands, Sara rushed toward the tub. Images seared her brain: the hair everywhere, red water, a Swiss Army knife on the floor, Rachel's lifeless body.

"NOOO!"

Rachel's head was curled on her chest, not completely submerged but bobbing dangerously close to the water. Sara reached for her.

Pulling, lifting Rachel out of the tub, onto the floor . . . *towels, need towels, stop the bleeding . . . Oh God . . . my fault . . . so sorry . . . don't leave me!* Rachel's arms flayed open from her wrist toward the elbow, spilling her life. Despair driving Sara's hands: winding the towels around and around her wrists, pulling, cinching tight at the upper arms to stop the flow. "Don't leave me, don't you dare leave me!" Sara pressed her head against her sister's chest. Can't hear Rachel's breath, too noisy . . . someone's screaming. Touch her neck, feel a tiny, insignificant flutter like a moth beating against a glass. *Help, help* . . . She's back on her feet, stumbling across a floor of hair, propelled outside, screaming at the top of her lungs for help.

AT the police station, Sara huddled under a blanket unable to get warm. "Please, just let me see Rachel. Please."

Harold Stein, the detective who first questioned her at the hotel, leaned forward in his chair. "Sara, the doctors have assured me that your sister has been stabilized. Right now we need to sort out what happened. Then I'll take you to see her."

Sara slumped into her shoulders. She had given him only the most basic information at the hotel. Obviously, it was not enough. "If I tell you, do you promise not to send us back?"

"Where?"

He didn't promise. Closing her eyes, she shook her head slowly.

"Was someone threatening her?"

She opened her eyes. "No, no one."

The detective held up a picture of Luke. It was water-stained, causing his face to blur in different directions. "Can you tell me who this is?"

Fresh tears shot down her cheeks. "Where'd you find that?"

"On the bed, along with a note of some sort . . . it's illegible. Can you tell me who this person is?"

"It's Luke. She loves him, but he's gone."

"Gone?"

"We left him behind in—" *If Rachel dies, it's all my fault.*

"Where?"

Sara's memory sizzled with Rachel's gentle pleas to return to Utah for Luke. Not only had she let her sister down, but she'd turned her back on Luke. And he was her friend. He trusted her, just like Rachel had. But she was a cowardly human being . . . and now she'd ruined everyone's life.

"Utah," she finally said, her voice scratchy with grief.

"All right. Would Luke want to hurt her?"

"No! God, no! He loves her! We had to leave so fast."

"Why'd you have to leave?"

Sara shuddered. "Please, I need to see if Rachel's okay."

"The only thing you can do right now to help your sister is to answer my questions." His eyes were a warm brown color, crow's feet flying upward from them. He was a man who smiled often. Why couldn't he have been their father? "She's in good hands, and you can see her as soon as we're through here." His face was etched in concern. "Now tell me, why did you have to leave Utah?"

Resignation seeped into her bones. Their secrets had nearly killed her sister. It wasn't worth it. Sara knew she would be arrested when she told them what she did to her father. But that didn't matter either. All that mattered was getting Rachel better.

She gulped several shuddery breaths. "Rachel was being forced to marry the prophet."

"The prophet?"

"Yeah. He's really old and—"

"How old?"

"Like seventy."

His eyes flared in surprise. "Okay." He cleared his throat. "Why did she have to marry this man?"

"Because he had a celestial testimony saying she was to be joined with him for time and all eternity. And even though other men had the same testimonies, the prophet speaks for God."

The detective wore the same shock on his face that Irvin had when she first explained their lifestyle to him.

"I *used* to think he did. Speak for God, I mean."

"What did your parents think about all of this?"

"My father seemed mad, but mostly at Rachel. And it didn't matter what he thought about it anyway . . . he still had to obey the prophet. But the mothers were happy about it, since the prophet is such an important man."

"How many mothers do you have?"

"I have my birth mother. She has three sister-wives counting Rachel's birth mother." She felt a dull thud in her chest as she remembered that Esther was no longer there.

His eyes lit with understanding. "So your father is a polyga-mist?"

"We, I mean they, believe in plural marriage."

He rested his palms on the table and let out a long, stretchy sigh. "Sara, what you've told me is very disturbing. I know you want to see your sister, but we have a lot more questions . . ." He looked at his watch. "I'll tell you what, I'm going to get us some-thing to drink, so just sit tight for a little longer."

"Okay."

"Would you like a soda?"

"Yes, thank you."

As the door closed behind him, she exhaled explosively. Oh God! She had just told on everyone. She had been taught from day one never to tell any outsider about their lifestyle, especially not the law! She began to mentally measure how much more she should say. Had she already said too much?

Her head jerked up as a young man, with a mop of brown hair, opened the door. Detective Stein followed behind him with a soda in each hand. "Sara, this is Jake Braedon. He's from the district attorney's office."

"Hi, Sara," he said, smiling. "It's nice to meet you."

"I'd like you to talk with him too. He'll be coordinating with the local D.A.'s office where you lived in Utah so that we can put together a case against your father and possibly the entire sect. Bigamy, plural marriages, whatever you call it . . . it's against the law, in all fifty states."

A case against her father. "Okay," she said, a knot of fear moving to her throat.

Thoughts of the family she left behind swirled in her head. And Irvin . . . what would happen to him? Would they send him back? He must hate her too. "I need to talk to Irvin." She spoke aloud be-fore thinking. "Someone has to tell him about Rachel . . . he'll be so worried."

"Who's Irvin?" Detective Stein asked.

"A friend. He came with us from Utah. He works at the Astro on Sunset."

"Is he your friend or Rachel's friend?"

"What do you mean? He's friends with both of us."

Reaching into a box at his feet, the detective pulled out a clear plastic bag, with the word EVIDENCE marked across it. A thin wand displaying a plus sign was inside. "Then maybe you can tell me whose positive pregnancy test this is?"

"What? I've never seen that before." Her words were marbled: a grisly piece of meat that wouldn't go down. "Where did you find that?"

"In the bathroom of your hotel room."

"*What?*"

"It was on the sink."

Nausea rolled like a pail of slop in her stomach. Horrific images flashed across her brain: their father hunched over Rachel, the bat crashing against his forearm, her sister huddling in the corner with her ripped sacred garments. "I'm gonna be sick."

Detective Stein jumped out of his chair, yanking a trash can out of the corner of the room and thrusting it toward her. She dropped her head between her knees and vomited until there was nothing left but acid coating her tongue. After the last explosive heave of bile, a savage rage detonated in her brain.

She stood up on shuddering legs. "I should have killed that bastard when I had the chance! Oh my God . . . he's a monster!"

"Sara . . ." Stein's voice was soft and smooth. Capping her elbow, he eased her back into the chair. "You have to tell me who did this to Rachel."

For once in your life, help your poor sister.

"Abraham did this to her."

"Who's Abraham?"

"He's our father. And he raped my sister."

AT the hospital, Detective Stein spoke to a nurse outside the ICU. When he returned, he led Sara into the small conference room that was an offshoot of the unit's waiting area. A few minutes later a nurse, with earrings that looked like petrified worms caught on a fisherman's hooks, introduced herself. She rubbed a finger under her nose. Sara found her attention locked on the bloodless cracks on the skin of the nurse's hands. "Did your sister ever mention wanting to kill herself?" she asked.

"No, never."

The identification clipped on her lapel said: DINA WOHLMUTH, R.N., B.S.N. "Did she ever exhibit signs of delusional behaviors before today?"

A smolder of fear began burning inside her. "Delusional?"

"Did she hear voices or exhibit odd behaviors that weren't normal?"

"No. I mean she was jumpy, scared a lot of the time. She had been getting more withdrawn over the past couple of weeks, but I didn't think she would ever try to . . . kill herself. She's very religious, and her biggest fear was going to hell."

Dina's earrings shook as she made notes on the chart. "Your sister has lost a lot of blood. When you go in to see her, she won't know you're there, but it's good to talk to her anyway."

"Is she in a coma?"

"No. She was quite distressed in the emergency room once we had her stabilized. We had to give her a psychotropic drug and a sedative. The combination of the two will knock her out for a good long time. I'm telling you all this so you'll know what to expect, okay?"

Sara nodded. *Psychotropic?*

"You can see her for a few minutes. Just go up to the front desk when you're ready," the nurse added, capping a pen and leaving the room.

"You okay?" Stein asked.

Her head felt as though it was splitting open, allowing the darkness to pour in. She clutched it, squeezing with all her might. "I don't know . . . yes."

"You sure?"

Dropping her hands, Sara stood up. "Yes, I just want to see Rachel."

Stein pulled out his card. "I can be reached at these numbers. Call me if you need anything before I come see you again."

Sara took the card. "I didn't know . . . I didn't know people like you did things like this for people like me."

"People like me?" he asked.

Sara wrestled down the knot in her throat. "Yeah. We were taught . . . not to trust the authorities. They were evil."

"Sounds like they told you many lies. You up for serving them some justice?"

"More than you'll ever know," Sara said. He gave her shoulder a quick squeeze of reassurance and left.

Through eyes dissociated with shock, she took in Rachel's condition piecemeal as if she were in parts rather than a whole: the IV in her neck, a sheet white face, the tiny narrow body of her sister and how still it looked under the sheets. Then the shock flittered away and horror swept in. Sara approached the bed with every nerve in her body shivering. Grief seized her throat while air sawed its way through the narrowed passage. Her heart ratcheted as she took in the sight. This couldn't be Rachel. But when she held her hand, reality slammed her in the heart. This was Rachel, and she wanted to be dead.

"I'm so sorry, so sorry . . ." Sara repeated those words a thousand times, dripping snot and wet sorrow onto her sheet. "I told them everything. They're going to help us. Just get better. Please, I can't live without you."

The nurse with the earrings came in and touched her shoulder gently, saying, "It's time to go, Sara."

Sara leaned down to kiss her sister. "Let me stay, please."

"Go back to the waiting room," Dina said. "We'll come get you later."

"What are you going to do to her?" Sara asked.

"Just routine stuff. Besides, the best thing you could do right now is let her rest."

Sara mopped her nose with her sleeve. "You'll come get me?"

"I promise. Now go on out."

Irvin sat in a chair, his head bent over a magazine, flipping the pages without really looking at them. When his eyes fell on hers, he chucked the magazine on the chair next to him and went to Sara. They fell into each other's arms, rocking with pain.

Sara gulped back her sobs, whispering, "I'm sorry. These tears . . . ugh. I hate them!" What she really hated was herself. "Oh, the police . . . they're going to . . ."

"I've already talked w-with them. I called Er-Ernadine. She's c-coming here as s-s-soon as she can. I even called m-my mother." Irvin's eyes filled with tears. "Sh-she wasn't angry. She c-couldn't believe I was *talking* to h-her. She w-wants me to come h-home. I told her I w-was home."

Sara turned around in her chair and picked up his hands. "This might be good for you. You could go to college. You're far too talented to bus tables for the rest of your life."

"N-not without y-you and Rachel."

"Irvin . . ."

"N-no way. You j-just don't get it. You and R-Rachel are my family now. I will n-never leave you two to f-fend for yourselves."

A weariness seeped into her limbs. "But this is no life for you."

"It's the best I've ever h-had." Sara pressed her face against his shoulder and just held on.

THEY spent a sleepless night in the waiting room. Sara's grief had wrung her dry. The smell of coffee filled the room as the morning swung into action.

Irvin had just left for work when Ernadine walked in with the clacking of plastic beads that swished in rhythm to her steps. She settled onto the chair next to Sara. At first, she said nothing, tucking an arm around Sara's shoulder and squeezing. Watching the carpet as her tears struck the tight maroon weave, Sara couldn't seem to speak. Ernadine's compassion made Sara cry harder.

Brushing the hair from her face, Ernadine said, "Listen to me, 'cause I know you didn't hear word one of what I just said."

Sara ticked her shoe side to side like a metronome before finally straightening her shoulders and turning to look at the warmth of Ernadine's face.

"Rachel is going to get through this okay. And you know why?"

Sara shook her head, wondering at the certainty that was present in her face.

" 'Cause she's got Irvin, you, me and lots of people with important degrees looking after her. Now, let's go to the cafeteria and straighten some things out over breakfast 'cause this diet makes my mouth taste like soap bubbles, and all I can think about is eating something to get rid of that taste."

Ernadine took Sara's hand. She let her body be led, as pliable as a rubber band. Resistance was for strong people only.

The cafeteria was packed so they took their trays outside on the patio. Ernadine kept up a steady prattle, lifting the plastic lid off Sara's steaming water and dropping the tea bag inside. A spider toiled between the metal slats of the patio railing, its web pearled with mist. "I should have known."

"What? Somebody give you a crystal ball? 'Cause if you got one, I wanna take a look."

"She was pregnant with our father's child. How can anyone live with that?"

Ernadine snuffled. "Did you know this before?"

"No."

"The detective told me you had quite a story. You gonna tell it to me?"

Sara dunked the tea bag a few times. At first, her words were halting, as unfamiliar to her as a foreign language. As she continued, the telling became easier.

Ernadine shook her head and clucked her tongue. "It sounds to me like you got a job ahead of you."

"A job?"

"More like an obligation. See, something terrible happened to me a long time ago. And I had two choices. I could let it destroy me or let it make me stronger. There was nothing I could do to change the past, but the rest of my life could be dedicated to changing the future. Not just for me, mind you, but for others like me."

"What do you mean?"

"I mean you got an obligation to those girls that don't have a voice. What these folks are doing up there is against the laws of this country, and you can't get nobody to change nothing if you don't start making noise. It's Utah's dirty little secret, and they want to keep it that way."

"But how can I do anything about it?"

"Sister, you are living in a city that loves a good story. You got to get out there and tell yours. If you don't, then you just turned your back on all those women and girls back there. And the only way Rachel's gonna get better is to right a wrong that's been done."

"I will do anything for Rachel. Anything."

"Don't forget about *you* in all this."

Sara sipped her tea. "Will you help me?"

"It would be my honor," said Ernadine. "And pleasure. Now, let's talk about what we can do for Rachel and how all of you are going to come live with me once she gets better."

And with those words the sun bled through the fog overhead, striking the ground in rails of light. Maybe it was okay to hope.

TWENTY-FIVE

Rachel's head felt thick and cloudy. She remembered being desperately sad, but she couldn't imagine leaving Sara and Irvin behind. The hazy hours accumulated into tired days, where Rachel's physical strength was so sapped it kept her from being able to sort out what had gotten her to the point where she was bent on self-destruction.

When Rachel first caught a glimpse of herself in the mirror, she screamed hysterically for her lost hair. She thought someone had stolen it in her sleep. Dr. Miranda Hamilton, her psychiatrist at the hospital, finally convinced her that she had cut it on her own. A flash of a memory, as quick and bright as a strobe light, formed a picture in her brain of a girl with darting eyes, knife in hand, sawing off thick clumps of hair.

"But why don't I remember?" she asked, wondering what else she didn't remember about that day.

"The stress on you was so great that it made you forget you had cut your own hair." Dr. Hamilton's voice crackled with logic, but the warmth underneath softened its precision.

"I don't even know why I got so upset. It's just hair," she said, suddenly embarrassed.

"You thought someone had violated you. Taken something that belonged to you . . . again. It's a normal reaction given the trauma you've been through."

The doctor arranged for someone to come in and trim and shape her hair that very day. Rachel was so grateful. She wasn't sure if she could ever look at her hair in that condition again, without seeing that glassy-eyed crazy girl staring back at her.

DR. HAMILTON never pushed, always allowing Rachel to take the lead. Over the next week, Rachel found herself offering more and more painful memories to her psychiatrist. Sometimes the doctor held them for her when they were too heavy to carry on her own. Other times she helped Rachel sort through the memories, analyzing the impact they had on both sisters. But the entire day she tried to kill herself was like a foggy day in the Utah valley: on a day like that, she could never see the mountains, but they were still there, just waiting for the fog to lift.

Rachel jolted awake one morning. She couldn't stop screaming. "No, oh my God, no!" She took the test. It was positive. Did she dream it? Was she pregnant?

Maggie, her night-shift nurse, rushed to her bedside. "You had another bad dream. Let me get you some more water," she said, reaching for the plastic pitcher.

Rachel placed a weighted hand on Maggie's wrist. "Wait . . . I need to know . . . is there a baby?" She tried shaking the panic out of her voice.

The woman would not look at her.

"Is there a baby!" She screamed so loudly, her vocal cords vibrated.

"Let me get Dr. Hamilton. She's on duty tonight."

The doctor hurried into the room, followed by Maggie, who carried a syringe filled with that mind-numbing solution that made her quiet and forgetful.

"Oh my God. I remember . . . I remember now. I'm pregnant . . . my father's . . . oh my God. I can't do this."

"It's okay. Remember what I told you. You don't have to do this alone." Dr. Hamilton's satiny voice tried to reassure her.

She gripped the rails of her bed, squeezing until her hands tingled from the loss of sensation. Her father, plunging into her, seared through her memory. And then the image dissolved.

"You were pregnant." Dr. Hamilton's face was bathed in compassion. "But you miscarried."

Rachel tumbled into a dark place.

"Are you ready to talk about this?"

"No."

RACHEL was released from the hospital after three weeks. Ms. Caine, their social worker, had picked her up on that late spring day, chatting nonstop about how beautifully Sara and Irvin were settling into their life with Ernadine and her little boy. Mentioning that Ernadine had a master's degree in counseling, she told Rachel that she would be a "wonderful confidante" if Rachel needed someone to talk to. She went on to explain that Ernadine's adopted eight-year-old son, Jamal, was born to a drug-addicted mother. He had some learning disabilities and a mild case of cerebral palsy, but he was a charming little boy.

The sun-bleached clapboard home had salmon-colored bougainvillea pouring over the iron-latticed fence. As she walked up the sandstone path to the house, the front door flung open. Sara's mouth was as wide with a smile as her arms were spread apart in welcome.

"I'm so glad you're here." She enveloped her with a strength that should have been reserved for the older sister. Shiny eyes that once skipped through life with curiosity now sought Rachel's face to gauge her level of contentment. Rachel pulled back the tears. She was the cause of all of this worry.

"Me too."

Irvin stood patiently behind Sara. When he wrapped his arms around her, she felt such a fierce love for him that she realized their bond was at least as strong as any made by shared blood.

Ernadine embraced her as if she were her long-lost daughter. Her own mother had never hugged her with that much emotion. She pulled back to look at Rachel, her grin wide and disarming. Her eyes were as rich and brown as milk chocolate. "Honey, I want you to know that this is *your* home now."

"Thank you." Rachel knew that those two words were entirely inadequate to convey the gratitude she felt toward this woman.

Ernadine corralled everyone into the airy kitchen, where she had iced tea and cookies for "Rachel's homecoming."

"And this is Jamal," Erandine said, pointing to the little boy with walnut eyes, sitting at the table expectantly. Giving her a lopsided smile, he slipped off his chair and walked toward her with a pronounced unevenness, as if one leg was much shorter than the other.

"Nice to meet you," he said in a slushy voice. He held out a hand that trembled slightly.

Rachel was moved by his sweet earnestness. "I'm so glad to meet you too."

He cupped his hand into hers, pulling her to the table. "Are you going to be my new sister?"

"Jamal, she just got here," Ernadine scolded.

She thought of all her little brothers. Rowan was exactly Jamal's age. The passage of time didn't make it any easier to do without them. Her throat felt swollen. "I would love to be your big sister."

SARA showed Rachel where they would be sleeping. It was a small room crammed with books and a simple desk-and-chair set pushed into a corner. Sara pulled her backpack out of the coat closet. "I have something that belongs to you," she said, unzipping her pack. Handing her a large cream-colored envelope, Sara brushed away tears that rimmed her lashes.

In it were Luke's picture and letter. Rachel could now look at them without feeling like their deterioration somehow mirrored Luke's physical condition. She had dropped them in a puddle. It was nothing more than that. Dr. Hamilton would be proud of her ability to think through this. She hugged her sister tightly then placed her treasures on the windowsill next to her sleeping bag.

"Wait, this belongs to you too." Sara cupped her outstretched hand. "Take it."

She dropped Luke's ring into Rachel's open palm.

Her voice caught in her throat. "How did you get this?"

"The pawnshop claim ticket was found in the room. Ernadine took me to get it."

"I thought I would never get it back. You have no idea how much . . ."

"Yes, I do."

Pulling air into her lungs, Rachel exhaled slowly, restoring her control. She wasn't ready to put the ring back on yet. Not until they found Luke. Not until she knew how he felt about her.

"My biggest regret in all of this was that I didn't allow us to go back for Luke. I'm so sorry," Sara said, her face bitten with grief.

"Don't, Sara. Please don't. I can't . . . I'm not ready to talk about that right now."

Rachel had become afraid of her love for him. Its intensity seared in her heart and burned her flesh.

Holding Sara's hand, she said, "I'm the one who should apologize for everything I've put you through. It was so selfish of me . . . to leave you."

They both sat cross-legged on the floor, clinging to each other. Rachel swallowed fat sobs. Always skirting the edge of her consciousness was the possibility that if she let go too much, she would plunge back into the abyss. There might be no salvation next time.

ERNADINE'S presence was felt everywhere at Teen Haven: a hand on a shoulder, a smile so jubilant it was contagious, a face wrapped in concern for a troubled teen, a way of making everyone around her feel that they could accomplish anything, the refusal to give up on anyone, ever. But perhaps the most striking thing about Ernadine was the way she seemed to exude gratitude, as if it was her privilege to help others.

Ernadine kept Rachel busy, filling her hours and denying her too much time for reflection or self-pity. At Teen Haven, Rachel became an adept short-order cook and found a strange satisfaction in scrubbing the filth off piles of dishes. Every evening after immersing herself in the flow of activity, she would glance up in surprise to find that the day was nearing a close. In the absence of her father's unpredictable outbursts, a rhythm to her life emerged, and she swayed to its music.

SUMMER roared in like the Santa Ana winds. One Saturday, Ernadine suggested to Rachel that they take Jamal to the beach. The air was salty enough to taste. Islands of tall grass dotted the ocean of sand. The sun sprinkled gold dust above the shimmering water. A ridged cliff, lined with fluted palm trees, cut into the sea. The base of the cliff had been sandpapered smooth by the fingers of the waves. Slipping her feet out of her tennis shoes, Rachel wiggled her toes in the sand. Something resembling joy flickered in her heart, trying to light.

Jamal dragged his body toward the shoreline. Rachel watched his sunken chest heave with exertion. She cringed as he stood at the edge of the vast ocean, a sliver of a boy, wearing a fire-engine-red bathing suit with elastic sagging around his concave waist. Watching his wounded body, she felt her heart swell with protectiveness. He began erecting a massive sand castle using a dozen or so pails of varying sizes and shapes.

"Jamal," Ernadine yelled into the wind, "don't make it too close to the surf."

"Okay, Mama."

"That boy's going to be singing the blues when the tide rises." Patting Rachel's knee, she said, "I'm glad we have time for a talk." She glanced back at Jamal, patiently dragging overfilled pails of water to his newly dug moat encircling his castle. Rachel watched Ernadine's crucifix swing lazily on its chain. "I just want to tell you that I know all about hurt. So if you need to talk to someone who speaks that language, I'm here for you."

Rachel couldn't imagine how this strong, intelligent, self-confident woman could ever know how sad and vulnerable she felt.

"Why did you take us in? You didn't know us. We could have been bad people."

Ernadine laughed: a rich, infectious laugh that never failed to make Rachel smile. "Sugar, I also got a long history with bad. I know what it looks like, smells like . . . and no matter how it's disguised, I know bad when I see it. The trick with recognizing bad is that you can't let it build up so high that you stop seeing the good in others. With the three of you, I knew what side of bad you were on."

"I did a very selfish thing."

"You did a very desperate thing." Ernadine fingered her crucifix. "I've been there . . . in that dark place."

"You? I can't imagine you ever wanting to end your life. You embrace it more than anyone I know."

"When I was your age, I was homeless and pregnant."

Rachel sat on the blanket stunned into silence. Ernadine said it with no apology in her voice, no shame to pull her steady gaze down.

"You seem surprised."

"It's just . . . I can't picture you . . . you're just so strong."

"I wasn't strong enough to raise my baby."

"I wasn't strong enough to have my baby." Each word cut like a blade across Rachel's throat.

"You didn't earn this guilt. It was offered to you. But you sure did take it, gobbling it up like it was the gourmet type. And now you don't have a taste for anything else. Girl, if you want to talk about guilt, talk to someone who earned every bite of it through the choices *she made*, not ones that were made for her."

"But you never hurt anyone. Not like me."

"Oh, I get it now. You want to play *Who's the Bigger Sinner?* I can tell you right now . . . girl, you are out of your league. I gave up my baby when I was sixteen. A baby born addicted to crack cocaine, courtesy of his mother, who didn't care enough to stop using for nine months. Oh, did I mention that I had no idea who fathered this baby? I was turning tricks to survive on the streets, and I didn't want a kid. I couldn't deal with his needs, not when it was getting in the way of my need for the drugs."

"But at least you didn't try to get rid of him. You gave him life."

Ernadine didn't seem to hear Rachel's last comment. "He was sick when he was born, no surprise there, and they couldn't find a family for him. No one wanted a sick black baby. So . . . they put him in foster care."

"Where is he now?"

Her spacious eyes were far away. She cupped her elbows in each upturned hand, rocking slightly as if soothing a fussy infant. The gesture had such an air of sorrow about it that Rachel felt her own heart fragment.

Closing her eyes, she set her jaw and said, "He's dead."

"Oh my God." Rachel placed her arm around the slope of her shoulder. Ernadine's soft body swayed under Rachel's steady hand. "I'm so sorry."

They sat for several minutes, watching the gulls dipping toward the sea, skimming the surface with their white bellies and then swerving up into the clouds, their mournful calls following behind them. Water licked the shore, the foaming surf washing up tangled seaweed. Rachel picked up several smooth gray stones. They rested lightly in her palm.

"My baby," Ernadine began again, revving up like an engine on a cold night, "was taken to the hospital one night, barely breathing. And you know what his foster mama—" She shook her head violently. "No, she wasn't his mama. Do you know what that woman said to the police?"

Rachel couldn't find her tongue. All she could do was shake her head.

Ernadine sagged on the blanket. "She said, 'He just wouldn't stop crying so I shook him.' That was her excuse." Her voice was limp. "He wouldn't stop crying."

"Oh no." Rachel patted Ernadine's hand. "I am so, so sorry."

"Oh Lordy." Her fingers fluttered in front of her face. "Well, I sure didn't expect to unload on you like that. It's just that you have such a tender spirit, such a loving, gentle way . . ." She absently tapped a crimson nail against the bottom of her chin. She turned her gaze on Rachel. "I know what it is . . . it's the way you look at people; you take their pain away, with the love you hold in your eyes. It's a rare gift."

The wind twisted into the curving dunes, kicking up funnels of sand.

"Do you think I was responsible for my baby's death?" Ernadine said. The quivering regret was gone from her voice. It sounded reinforced, strong again.

"Of course not. You didn't know he was going to be hurt. How could you know?"

"True enough." Ernadine's voice was steady on a course. "So if you don't think I caused my son's death, why are you blaming yourself for the loss of a baby you never intentionally hurt?"

"Well . . . I tried to take my own life—"

"You don't even remember that. And don't go confusin' not wanting to have your baby with wishing that baby harm. I used to feel exactly the way you do. That everything was my fault, including, well . . . especially, the death of my baby."

"But you were stronger than me because you didn't take the coward's way out."

Ernadine grabbed her hand. "First of all, you were psychotic. There was no conscious intent to hurt anyone, not yourself or your baby."

Rubbing the cold stones in her free hand calmed her. A glimmer of understanding flashed in her head. "I guess . . . maybe you're right." *Please be right.*

But even if Rachel's grief could explain her actions, maybe even justify it, that didn't change the fact that it happened . . . all of it. She still didn't know how to live with the facts of her past. She opened her palm and let the stones travel down the length of her hand, her fingers bridging their way into the sand. Yet Ernadine did it. She lived in spite of the pain, carving her way through it and then triumphing over it.

"How did you do it? Release the guilt?"

"Starting the Haven helped . . . you know . . . it took me out of myself. But that little boy over there . . ."

Rachel followed her wagging finger ringed in turquoise. Jamal was busy patting his sand towers into shape with his fragile bird-like arms.

". . . he's my redemption. His mama was one of my girls at the Haven. She was on crack, just like I was when I gave birth." She paused, her eyes darkening in memory. "She was determined to take care of that baby and clean her life up. She and her boyfriend got an apartment together." She looked in Jamal's direction, staring absently over his head, her eyes reaching into the sea.

"He had a bad start. It's hard for these tiny babies to come off those drugs. One day the girl comes in all frantic and tells me her boyfriend shook him so hard he stopped breathing. She had rushed him to the hospital, and he was still alive, but she told me she just couldn't do it anymore. The next day, I petitioned the court to adopt him."

Jamal tore his eyes away from his masterpiece and smiled. "Look!" he shouted.

Ernadine shot her thumb high into the air. "You rock!" she told him. "Best decision I ever made," she said, turning back to Rachel.

"That's for sure."

"Rachel, I've told you this before. You got a way with children. The way you interact with Jamal, playing with him every night. He just loves you. Your way makes people trust you and open up to you, and there are some children who are really hurting. A friend of mine called me from a shelter, asking if I knew anyone that could help out over there. They are just so shorthanded. These are kids who have been abused . . . and they don't trust anyone . . ."

"You don't have to say any more. I'll be there."

"You know, sugar, you gave me something today."

"Me?"

Ernadine clucked, shaking her head ferociously. "You gave me the gift of understanding, of empathy. You felt my pain, my regret and most of all, my loss. And I want to thank you for that."

Rachel was stunned by her appreciation: after all Ernadine had done for her, for all of them. She decided to learn everything she could from this woman who built such a soaring life from the ashes of tragedy and hardship. She was the woman Rachel wanted to become. And she was black.

The irony was not lost on Rachel.

TWENTY-SIX

Ernadine put Dana Hopkins, the D.A. for Lufkin County, Utah, on the speakerphone. She'd called to discuss the progress of the case. "Well, we've had a bit of a setback. I've been unable to get the judge to approve the subpoena to force your father to submit to a blood test to test his DNA—"

"What!" Ernadine said, grabbing Rachel's hand.

The blood test to compare her father's DNA with the DNA of the baby she miscarried was the most upsetting part of all of this for Rachel. The lawyers had told them that it was absolutely necessary in order to have the physical evidence of the rape. Otherwise, they just had the testimony of Rachel and Sara, and it might not be enough to put him behind bars. "The judge had been born into a polygamist family, and although he doesn't practice it himself, he's obviously biased. I've already requested that he recuse himself," Dana said.

"Recuse?" Sara asked.

"To take himself off the case because of a possible conflict of interest."

"Well, what did he say?" Ernadine pushed, her eyes flashing with anger.

"He refused."

"Damnit," Ernadine said.

"We're working on it. Rachel, you will have to testify. I know you've been afraid to face your father in court, but that's all we have right now. And Sara, the same goes for you."

Rachel's mind churned with anxiety. How could she ever get up in front of all those people and tell everyone what happened to her? Especially with her father looking right at her.

"Are you still there?"

"Yes. Dana. We're here. It's just hard on the girls."

"I know. That's why I hate to ask you for anything else . . ."

Rachel found her voice. "Dana, what else can we do to help?"

"At the D.A.'s office, we've been trying for years to get enough evidence for law enforcement to file bigamy and child abuse charges against some of the Blood of the Lamb members. We've been stymied every step of the way. When the polygamists cry religious freedom, everyone just looks the other way."

She continued, "The whole town of Centennial is owned and controlled by the Blood of the Lamb. No one will talk to us, and if they aren't actual Blood of the Lamb, they're most likely related to someone who is."

Ernadine asked, "So you want the girls to testify about all of it?"

"Exactly. The plural wives, the underage brides, the prophet, the entire lifestyle. It could really help us break this case wide open. Just think about it."

"Okay," Sara said miserably.

After they finished the call, Rachel fought back tears. "How are we going to do this?"

"Sugar, all I can tell you is that I'll be there for you. Every step of the way," Ernadine said.

Rachel just wasn't sure if that was enough.

RACHEL walked slowly from the bus stop, shoring up her courage to enter Children's Alliance, the shelter for abused kids who were in between foster homes or hadn't yet been placed. Pulling open the door, she smiled at the young woman sitting behind the front desk.

The Alliance was not a particularly cheerful place with its sterile gray walls and metal bunk beds housing slim mattresses. Ernadine had warned her that they raised just enough money to open their doors. "It's strictly no-frills," she had said.

Open for only two weeks, they were already filled to capacity. Ahandi, the director, was apologetic. "We just don't have enough funding to do what we want to for these kids," she explained to Rachel.

Rachel spent the rest of the afternoon passing out snacks and playing games with the kids. Ahandi told her that they were too young to be out on the streets but too old for most people to want to adopt them. The foster care system was overburdened and simply didn't have enough homes to place all of them.

One little girl, Nina, stood out. She watched Rachel with large almond-shaped eyes, taking in every gesture Rachel made with the other kids. But she would not join in any of the games. She was very young, seven at the most, but her eyes were much older. After an hour of playtime, Rachel was supposed to help the children get started on their summer-school studies before dinner. She passed out books from a meager stack, for the kids who finished early. Most of the children groaned, but she coaxed them into starting their work. Nina continued to watch her but made no move to open her books.

When Rachel came over to the table in the back of the room where the girl sat stoically, she asked her if she could sit with her. When Nina nodded, Rachel folded herself onto the small plastic chair and said to the child, "You are a very smart girl. I can see that about you from your eyes. Tell me why such a smart girl wouldn't want to learn new things or have some fun with the other kids."

The little girl gnawed on her bottom lip. "I'm just too sad."

Rachel strained to hear her. "You know, for a long time I was too sad to have any fun either."

"You were?"

"Yep. Hey, I have an idea. What if I came in every afternoon and spent time with you? We could talk or read together or play a game . . . just you and me. Would that make you feel better?"

The little girl nodded again. For once in her life, Rachel thought maybe she could really make a difference. She had been given so much, and it was time to give a little back to a damaged child. She left the shelter that evening with lightness in her heart and a startling sense of accomplishment.

Between the Haven in the morning, therapy sessions over lunch and afternoons at the shelter, Rachel's days were packed full. She realized her schedule provided a convenient excuse not to prepare for the trial and to put off discussing the case with the D.A.'s office. It was so hard to think about it much less to talk about it, especially with strangers. But her avoidance was shattered when Nina opened up to her on her third week at the shelter.

They were sitting at their usual table in the back of the room playing with Barbie, Ken and their baby twins. Playing with dolls was Nina's favorite thing to do. Rachel had never had any dolls as a girl, so she also enjoyed playing with this perfect little doll family. Rachel liked to pretend Ken was the best father ever, super nice to the twins.

Nina put the twins down on the table and announced, "I don't like this game anymore."

"Oh, honey, what's wrong?"

She picked Ken up and put him back in the toy bin. "My stepdaddy was a bad man."

"What did he do to you?" She dreaded hearing the answer.

"He hurt me down there." She pointed down while dropping her chin.

Rachel swallowed the wave of nausea, the panic of her past, and looked into Nina's eyes, which were gauzed in tears. "I know all about that. And you and I are going to get rid of this pain together."

WHEN she went into her session the next day she wanted to get right to it. She looked at Dr. Hamilton full in the face and said, "I can do this now."

"What can you do?"

"I can talk about what he did . . . and talk about . . . the baby too."

"You're a strong girl."

"No, I'm not . . . at all. But I am ready to move on."

THAT night, after Jamal was asleep, Ernadine announced they were having a "family meeting." Rachel loved to hear her call them a family.

Rachel had made everyone hot chocolate. As she placed the mugs on the table, Ernadine started waving a piece of paper in the air before tossing it on the table in front of Sara. She stood with her hands balled up high on her puffy hips, waiting for a reaction.

"What is it?" Rachel asked.

Sara's eyes widened as she scanned the paper.

"Should I tell them or should you?" Ernadine said, shrugging ropy hair off her shoulders.

"You," Sara said, glancing at Irvin, the color creeping into her cheeks.

"Our Miss Sara has scored in the *highly gifted* category on *every* test that she took for placement next fall. In fact, when I called the counselor at Fairview High, she said that Sara scored off the charts in several areas. You're a certified genius, little girl."

Rachel rushed to hug her. She was so happy that Sara now knew what Rachel had been convinced of all along.

Irvin's fingers grazed Sara's cheek with a fluidity that graced every gesture he made with his artist's hands. "You astound m-me."

Sara gave Rachel and Ernadine a shy smile, avoiding Irvin's admiring gaze.

"Okay, Sara, here's the plan. Actually, Rachel and Irvin are part of it too." Ernadine's voice was crisp with authority. "We're a family, and we all support each other. So the first thing we need is to have Sara go to the library every day. No need to come to the Haven anymore . . . you'll be too busy."

"But—"

"No buts. I have Rachel and Irvin to help out for the time being. You can work some more hours at the library if you want to, but I want you to spend most of your time studying. You'll have computers there and all the books you need. You need to play catch-up because come fall we are signing you up for the most rigorous classes they offer and putting you in the gifted program."

"But Rachel—"

"We'll get to Rachel in a minute. With your brain, you can do anything. But right now you're doing nothing to prepare yourself for the coming school year. That goes for you too, Rachel. Which means our television nights together are numbered."

"I'm just not sure, you know . . . about whether I want to go back to school in the fall. I mean, Rachel hasn't decided if she's going back, and I thought I would wait until the two of us could go together . . . when she's ready."

"Whatever Rachel decides shouldn't affect what you want to do."

"Sara . . ." Rachel exhaled, trying to keep from crying. "You can't spend your life worrying about me. I'm okay now. Actually, I'm better than okay. Irvin and I are getting what we want. It's your turn for some happiness," Rachel said.

"Irvin is going to art school, but Rachel, you don't have anything but me."

"Oh, Sara . . ." The lump in Rachel's throat was so large she couldn't squeeze any words around it. "Don't you see . . . you're the reason I'm still here. I never doubted your love, and it never left me."

"But I took you away from Luke."

"Stop it! I had to get away from that place . . . from our father . . ." Rachel held out her hand for Sara to see the ring she had slipped back on her finger.

Her sister looked up at her with confusion and caution darkening her eyes.

"I put the ring back on because I believe in Luke's love, just like I believe in yours. And I also believe that if we are supposed to be together, we'll find our way back to each other. So no more regrets. Okay?"

Sara's bottom lip trembled violently.

"I was planning on telling all of you tonight. I'm going back to Utah to testify against Father. I won't hide from him anymore. And he's never going to hurt one of his children again," Rachel said.

Sara sat in stunned silence.

"It's time," said Ernadine.

"Yes, it is. And Sara . . ." She held her sister's gaze. "Please, please, let go of the guilt. You have done nothing but good things for me, and every decision you made for us has been out of love. You were a victim, just like me." Rachel's eyes blurred with tears. "And I will never . . . ever be able to thank you enough for that."

Rachel hugged Sara, feeling her sister's spine straighten as if the weight of worry finally eased.

"I have something else. I'm going back to school in the fall with Sara. I'm going to study like crazy, and I want to go to college. I want to become a counselor, like you, Ernadine. I want to help abused kids."

Sara's face lit up. "Oh, I'm so happy! And college . . . I can't believe it!"

"Oh, I just couldn't get any prouder of you girls," Ernadine said, shaking out a folded napkin. She blotted her eyes dry.

"Well, I've been thinking a lot about the child abuse that goes on . . . everywhere . . . it seems," Sara said. "And Dana was right. We can't just stop the abuse in our own family. I want to stop the abuse that's covered up in all the polygamist houses. I need to do this."

"Me too," said Rachel, her fear mixed with a certainty that it must be done, and an excitement that Sara had the courage to speak about it first.

"I've been hoping and praying you girls would be ready to really take a stand on this issue."

"But what can we do?" Rachel asked.

"You can tell your story and be the voice for all the girls and women that have none. You can expose all of it. Now, it's not going to be easy. But you girls are stronger than all of those people who tried to control you in that *cult*. I am so proud of both of you."

THE house was empty when Rachel went into the garage to look for some of Ernadine's psychology textbooks that she said were boxed up. Rachel wanted to learn everything she could about human behavior. It fascinated her. As she opened up box after box of books a flash of color on the edge of one of Irvin's canvases caught her eye. A jumbo-sized beach towel covered up all but the corner of the painting. She told herself she would just take a quick peek while she was draping the towel back over the corner. What she saw took her breath away. She had no choice but to pull the towel completely off the painting to get a better look.

Sara's beauty was transcendent. Irvin had captured every shade of her flaxen hair: the honey tones underneath and the platinum streaks at the crown. His brush had found each jewel of color in her warm amber eyes, sprinkling flecks of gold and emerald into them. Her lips looked so soft, the upper lip slightly fuller than the lower one and upturned over the bottom lip: the exact curve of Sara's mouth. Even the light dusting of freckles across her nose was evident. She looked like an angel: as beautiful on the outside as she was on the inside.

He must have studied every inch of her face over a long period of time to replicate it so perfectly from the image in his mind. She had never seen her sister look quite this way before. Through Irvin's eyes, her sister had become the most beautiful girl Rachel had ever seen. Only someone who was in love with Sara could have pulled all of her beauty and all of her goodness to the surface in such a stunning way.

The next morning, Rachel took the first moment they were alone together at Teen Haven to ask Irvin about the painting.

"I saw it."

"What?" he said, continuing to scrub the floors without glancing up.

"Your painting of Sara."

He stopped mopping, looking at her while his eyebrows shot up in surprise.

"I'm sorry. I was looking for something in the garage, and it was uncovered."

"Uncovered?" he said, his head tilted slightly.

"Well, not completely. Anyway, I was just amazed. It is so beautiful."

"Sh-she is," he said, nodding.

Ah-ha! Just as she suspected. That was a *Freudian slip,* as she learned last night from Ernadine's book. He was thinking about how beautiful she was, and it slipped out.

"I think you're in love with Sara," Rachel said. With her newly honed powers of observation, she watched as his face softened ever so slightly at the mention of her name.

"I think you're j-jumping to c-conclusions."

"What are you afraid of?"

"Look, Rachel. Even if I did l-like her in that w-way, and I'm not saying I do, I have n-nothing to offer her."

"That's just ridiculous. You can give her everything she wants and needs. You're in love with her, and you're holding back because you don't think you're good enough for her."

"What's the c-cliché: isn't that the p-pot calling the kettle—"

"Yeah, in my pre-enlightened days, it would have been. But I'm trying to get over those self-defeating thoughts, and you should too. My sister loves you. I'm certain of that. All you have to do is accept her love. It's that simple."

"Love is never that s-simple."

"Well, I guess that's true or Luke and I would be together right now." She wagged her ring finger in front of him, tapping the ring for emphasis. "But at least I'm going to try to fix things, even though I have no idea what Luke will think about me . . . about us, until I see him again. You *know* how Sara feels about you."

"No. I d-don't. How does she f-feel?"

Rachel assumed he already knew. Oh well, for the greater good she had to betray Sara's confidence. Besides, love conquers all.

"She loves you, and not in the same way that I do, just so we're clear. She's like madly in love with you, but she thinks you only love her like a sister."

"You really think she could be happy with me?"

"I have no doubt about it. And she'll make you very happy too. If you let her."

He seemed to be considering her words. "I'll make you a d-deal. You find Luke and get b-back with him, I'll tell Sara h-how I feel about her."

"What will you tell her?"

"This is a t-trick question."

She noticed a sliver of a gap between otherwise perfect white teeth that lit up his coppery skin as he slid into a smile.

"You're too smart for your own good. Irvin, I know you're scared. But don't you think the two of us have already left enough unsaid to the people we love just because we've been scared? And if you can't tell me how you feel, how are you going to tell her?"

Irvin picked up the dishrag and wiped the stove top over and over. Finally he looked up at Rachel. "I would tell her how beautiful she is. How I can't imagine my life without her. How I just want to be with her . . . all the time . . . and . . . I would tell her that from the first moment I saw her, I knew I loved her, and I will never, ever stop loving her."

Tears dribbled down Rachel's cheeks. His words, and the way he spoke them so eloquently and with no hesitation, made her heart soar. "Promise me . . . promise me you'll tell her . . . just like that."

"When the t-time is right."

ERNADINE called a local news reporter named Natalie Swanson, who came by the house and interviewed both Sara and Rachel. She had a small mouth, set primly, and a button nose. She wore thick black cat glasses, leaving an overall impression of intelligent seriousness. With a fresh degree in journalism, she was an enthusiastic listener, sufficiently shocked at the lifestyle the girls were brought up in. Now that Rachel and Sara were so far removed from their old life, when they talked about the prophet, the Law of Placing, the Principle and all the other ordinary aspects of their past, it sounded bizarre and perverted to Rachel's ears.

Natalie told them that the article would be in the paper in a few days, and she would call them and let them know what kind of response she received. At the end of the interview, Natalie asked the girls if they had any questions for her. Sara asked her all sorts of things about her schooling, journalism and how she landed her job.

As Natalie was preparing to leave, Sara said, "I have a favor to ask."

"Sure. What is it?"

"There's someone we need to get a message to at Blood of the Lamb. Can you help us?"

"Sara!" Rachel said.

"I'll see what I can do. I'm contacting the local paper there to see if they want to cover the case. What's the name?" she said, pulling out her BlackBerry again.

"Her name is Elaina Wilkinson."

A week later, Natalie stopped by to update them. She said she had been inundated with e-mails and calls. People were outraged that the judge in the case wouldn't step down and that forced marriages of teenage girls go on in the United States. Readers wanted to know how they could help. Natalie said that she had contacted the local paper in Centennial, and they weren't interested in working on the story at that end. In fact, they seemed almost hostile when she started asking questions. But she had found a reporter out in Lufkin who was interested. He said he would keep the story in the paper as much as possible, and he had already tried to interview several Blood of the Lamb members.

"He wasn't having much luck, but he did find out one piece of information," Natalie said. She pecked at her BlackBerry. "Elaina

Wilkinson no longer lives at the address you gave me. A woman named Beulah lives there with her husband, Robert. This woman, Beulah, apparently has no idea where Elaina is currently living."

Rachel's stomach pulled in on itself. It never once occurred to her that Elaina wouldn't be there. Virtually no women from Blood of the Lamb left their husbands. Now, her one connection to Luke was gone. She felt the tears spring to the corners of her eyes.

"We'll find him," Sara said, looking alarmed.

"It'll be okay," Rachel said. She had already decided that if they were meant to be together they would be. Now she needed to act like she believed that.

THE next several months passed by quickly. In the fall, Rachel and Sara started attending the local high school. Rachel found that when she focused, she could do well in even her most difficult classes, like Algebra II. Sara had talked her into taking it, and every night she sat patiently with Rachel, showing her how to solve the more complicated problems. Rachel loved her psychology class, and Ernadine was so proud of her for having the highest average in the class.

Whenever a guy at school came up to Rachel and talked to her, she no longer had that panicky feeling in her stomach. Sara told her to tell these guys she had a boyfriend, if they bothered her.

"But I don't!"

"Yes, you do! What is that?" Sara grabbed her hand and held up her ring finger.

"I still don't know if he wants to be my boyfriend."

Sara rolled her eyes and sighed.

"Okay. Okay. He's my boyfriend."

"*Thank you.* At least that's settled."

SARA had already taken her college boards, and she had made a perfect score. Ernadine told her she needed to "dream high." Not only could she get into a top college, but she might even get a scholarship to pay for it. Sara got more excited about her studies every day, and she dove back into her writing with an intensity Rachel had never seen before. She wrote about her childhood, from her earliest memories through the day they ran away.

At Ernadine's urging, Sara sent parts of her journal entries to Natalie, who then showed them to her editor. The editor was so moved by her story and impressed with her talent as a writer that she decided to print it in parts over several weeks. Letters poured in from readers all over Los Angeles, responding to the series, "Growing Up in Polygamy." The phone began ringing regularly for Sara to do interviews with various media outlets, and the more she talked about her ordeal, the more her confidence soared.

THE case was going to trial. With the local Utah media pushing hard, the judge had finally recused himself. The new judge ordered the DNA test and had set a court date. He also consolidated the bigamy charges with the rape and incest charges, so the girls would testify about plural marriage as well. In spite of the blood tests conclusively showing that Abraham Shaw was the father of his own daughter's baby, he refused to plea bargain. He denied everything, including the fact that he was a polygamist.

"ARE you ready to face your father?" Dr. Hamilton asked Rachel in what was to be their last session together.

"Yes."

"You're a strong girl."

"I know."

TWENTY-SEVEN

An icy white dusting of snow sprinkled across the sky as they stepped off the small plane that had taken them from their short layover in Salt Lake City to Lufkin. Snow piled up in drifts around the runway. They maneuvered around the mounds. Leaves, crisp with frost, crunched under their feet. It was the familiar Utah winter of her youth, but it no longer felt like home.

The courthouse was a one-story modest building sandwiched between the county jail and the local police department. On the morning of the trial, the parking lot was packed. Cars lined the nearby streets for blocks. Reporters guarded the entrance, making sure that Rachel and Sara didn't slip by them unnoticed.

Rachel fought the urge to turn around and flee back to their rental car. She silently berated herself for wearing the royal blue coat that Ernadine had bought her for Christmas. She was too easy to spot: already two reporters had left their post and were weaving between cars to get to them. Bracing herself for the onslaught, her breath caught in her throat when she noticed her mother's face just a few yards away and staring right at her. She grabbed Sara's hand, as if the gesture could make her disappear. Ernadine and Irvin had moved ahead of them, trying to intercept the reporters before they reached Sara and Rachel.

Jostling her way around a knot of people, Marylee lumbered toward them. Anna and Jane followed obediently behind her. Marylee had gained weight, the added flesh making her deceptively unthreatening in the face. Her long tapered fingers had always been her last concession to slimness. Now, they were padded with fat and resembled sausage links. Her wedding ring remained defiantly on her finger: the only one of their father's wives who had the legal right to wear it.

"I can't believe what you've done to this family," Marylee said icily.

Rachel almost gushed an "I'm sorry," instead swallowing the words and waiting for the slap to arrive. It never did.

"You are no longer my daughter." She spat the words in Rachel's face.

"I'm not Abraham's daughter either. Not after what he did to me."

Marylee had already turned her back on Rachel, leaving Jane, with her face crumpled, standing in Marylee's shadow. Jane had lost her youth. Chubby cheeks were eaten away by worry, leaving sharp angles under a crossed brow. Her thin flesh was already etched with fine lines that skirted her eyes and mouth.

"Please protect Alice from her father," Rachel blurted out.

Jane's face clouded. Cupping her elbow, Anna ushered her away without a word.

THE district attorney, Dana Hopkins, was in her mid-forties, with a wide mouth built for an easy smile. Pacing back and forth behind the prosecutor's table, her body coiled with energy. She had a man's close-cropped haircut, a naked face, and hair so silver, it looked like it had lost the color of youth a decade too early. "Remember, Mr. Brandt will come after you. Hard. But you've got the truth on your side."

Rachel's stomach quivered with fear at the mention of her father's attorney.

"Are you girls ready?"

They had spent the past two days in Dana's office going over all the testimony. Dana had one of the assistant D.A.s play the role of the defense attorney until Rachel no longer broke down under their practice cross-examinations.

Rachel stole a glance at Sara, gauging her opinion. They both nodded solemnly.

The bailiff led their father into the packed courtroom. His face was gaunt, his eyes filmy. The full head of hair that he had been so proud of had thinned and was threaded with gray.

"Are you scared?" Rachel whispered.

"No. He looks broken," Sara said.

When Rachel was called to the stand, she walked up on shaky limbs. Acid roiled in her stomach just as it had that day Prophet Silver had called her up to announce that she would be his bride. She told herself that this time she would be strong. This time she knew the truth. This was the right thing to do.

After Rachel was sworn in and asked some preliminary questions, Dana began her direct examination. "Ms. Shaw, what does it mean to be placed in a celestial marriage?"

Rachel closed her eyes for a brief moment to gather her resolve. She thought of all the girls still trapped here. The lies so deeply ingrained in their hearts and souls. She opened her eyes and spoke. "In the Blood of the Lamb community, a girl is assigned to be sealed for time and all eternity in a celestial marriage. That is called placing."

"When were you and your sister first told that you would be placed in marriage?"

"We were both fifteen at the time."

"Fifteen seems awfully young, isn't it?"

"Objection."

"Sustained."

"Let me rephrase the question. Is fifteen the average age the girls in Blood of the Lamb were placed in a spiritual marriage?"

"No. Prophet Silver had set the age of preparedness at thirteen."

"What is the age of preparedness?"

"That's the age when a girl can be married."

"So there were some girls who were married at thirteen?"

"Most are thirteen or fourteen. Sara and I were considered old. Especially me, because I was almost sixteen."

"Can you give me any examples of girls you knew who were *under sixteen* being forced to marry older men?"

Mr. Brandt shot out of his seat. "Objection, Your Honor!"

"Overruled," the judge said. "You may answer the question, Ms. Shaw."

Rachel nodded. "My best friend from grade school had to marry when she finished sixth grade."

"And how old was she at the time of her marriage?"

"Twelve."

"How old was her husband at the time they were married?"

"Fifty-four, I think."

"Were they related by blood?"

"Yes. They were first cousins."

"Is it common to marry a blood relative?"

"Yes."

"Who was your sister assigned to marry?"

She felt the heat of anger move into her cheeks. "Our uncle, Walter. My father's half-brother."

"What does it mean to live the Principle?"

"Objection, Your Honor, she's not a theology expert."

"Counselors, approach the bench."

The two attorneys went up to the judge's box.

The judge covered his microphone as Dana said, "Your Honor, she is permitted to talk about her own personal experiences and what was expected of her as a girl growing up in that religion."

Rachel could hear everything they were saying. She risked a look up at the gathered attorneys.

"Ms. Hopkins has a point," the judge said.

Mr. Brandt sighed. "Well, it's irrelevant, anyway."

"It goes to the bigamy charges, Your Honor."

The judge shooed them back to their tables. "I'll allow it."

Dana smiled at Rachel and nodded. "Can you answer the question?"

Rachel took a deep breath and began again. "Living the Principle means to live in a plural marriage, where a man has more than one wife."

"And why do they choose to live the Principle?"

"In order to get to the Celestial Kingdom, a man must take at least three wives."

"What is the Celestial Kingdom?"

"The highest level of heaven that one can reach."

"So if the men must take at least three wives to reach the Celestial Kingdom, how do women reach it?"

"They must be pulled through the gates of the kingdom by their husbands, or if the girl is unmarried, then by her father."

"What happens to girls who refuse to marry the man who has been assigned to them?"

"They'll go to hell."

"What I mean is what happens to them within the community?"

"All of us were taught that if we don't live in a plural marriage, we'll be condemned to hell for all eternity. Most of us agree to our placement, even if we don't want to marry the man."

"So they can say no if they are assigned to marry a man they don't like?"

"Yes, but only if we want to go to hell."

"Objection. That's one child's opinion."

"Hmm. Child?"

"Be very careful here, Ms. Hopkins." The judge leaned back in his chair and steepled his hands over his abdomen. "Very careful."

Brandt thrust an arm out to Dana. "Your Honor, I'd like the *witness's* response stricken from the record."

"Your Honor," Dana said. "This is not an opinion; this is their dogma that they've been taught all their lives."

"Objection!"

"Counselors, approach."

Dana launched right into her explanation. "Your Honor, this is not," she used her fingers in a quotation gesture, "one child's opinion. These were the facts of her religion."

"I'm going to allow it."

Dana returned to her place catty-corner to the box where Rachel sat. "What role does the prophet play in the spiritual marriages of these young girls?"

"The prophet receives divine revelations. When a man comes to him and tells him that he has received a testimony in marriage for a particular girl, the prophet will consider that girl for placement in a celestial marriage."

"How many testimonies of marriage did Prophet Silver receive for you?"

"Seventeen."

"Seventeen?"

"Eighteen if you count his own."

"Who were you ultimately assigned to marry?"

"The prophet."

"Did you want to?"

"No."

"Did you feel you had to?"

"Yes. Every girl in the community is expected to obey the priest-hood holder of her family—that's her father or husband—but obey-ing the prophet comes first. Even over the priesthood holder."

"Why is that?"

"The prophet talks directly to God. So if you disobey the prophet, you disobey God."

"Where are all the young men?"

Rachel's heart tightened in her chest. The loss of Luke was still too great.

"Lots of them are forced to leave unless they're important some-how."

"Who is considered important?"

"Someone with money or power"—Rachel dropped her gaze to her hands—"or lots of daughters."

When she got to the part in her testimony where her father raped her, her throat knotted. She looked between Sara, Ernadine and Irvin. They steadied her with their encouraging smiles and love-filled faces.

Give him the shame. Dr. Hamilton's words rang in her ears.

"Is the man who raped you in this courtroom?" Dana asked.

"Yes." She pulled her chin up and locked her eyes on him. "He did." She pointed her finger at him. "My father."

He stared back at her, his eyes defiant. His skin looked creased and puckered. Prison did not agree with him. A flicker of guilt threatened to light inside her, but the utter lack of remorse that he held in his eyes doused her lingering regret.

Securing her gaze on his face, she was more determined than ever to show him and everyone in that courtroom that she would not back down from the truth. The room was hushed as they continued to stare at each other. His head shook slowly back and forth, suggesting she was not credible. Rachel felt a torrent of anger rise in her chest.

"You took everything from me. You should be ashamed—"

"Objection."

"Sustained."

"How could you rape your own daughter?" She realized again that she had spoken aloud, barely recognizing her own voice. It was so strong.

"Objection!"

"Miss Shaw, please don't address the defendant directly," the judge said.

"Yes, sir." Even though the judge was correcting her, she felt euphoric. Her words were clear with no hesitation. Her eyes never once left her father's face. Abraham winced and began squirming in his seat. His eye contact faltered under a spasm of blinks. Finally he lowered his head.

"Your witness," Dana said, the crevices in her cheeks holding a private smile.

Rachel braced herself for the assault. At the defense table, the attorney and his assistants huddled around her father, murmuring in hushed tones.

After a few minutes, the judge let out a sigh and said, "Your witness, Mr. Brandt."

The attorney stood up, smoothing his tie. He smiled at her with bloodred lips that housed teeth the size of corn kernels. Disappointment seemed to pass in his eyes, but he held the smile. "No cross-examination of this witness, Your Honor."

Rachel wilted with relief as she was led back down to her seat.

Marylee was called as a defense witness. She was sworn in and then proceeded to tell the court how she was Abraham's first and only wife. When asked about the other women living with her, she said they were friends who needed help.

"These poor women and their fatherless children . . ." She sniffled. "They had nowhere else to go."

"Your husband, Abraham, helped many people over the years, didn't he?" Mr. Brandt beamed at her.

"Yes. He's a good man." Her voice caught. "He was a loving father to Rachel," she added, removing a wrinkled hanky from her lap and blowing her nose.

Rachel's stomach began to twist in on itself. What if the jury believed her mother?

After several more minutes of Marylee praising Abraham, Mr. Brandt finally turned to Dana and said, "Your witness."

Dana approached the witness stand for her cross-examination. Marylee straightened her spine and tilted her chin upward.

"Mrs. Shaw, you testified under direct examination that you are Abraham Shaw's only wife."

"Yes."

"You also testified that you lived with Anna Marx and Jane Sooner. You called them 'friends' of the family. Are they your sister-wives?"

"Absolutely not. I am Abraham's only wife. Under the laws of Utah."

"But what about under the laws of God?"

"Under God's law, I was his first wife and his only wife. Nothing else matters."

"Don't you mean no one else matters?"

"Objection!" Mr. Brandt flew out of his seat.

"Withdrawn, Your Honor."

Rachel glanced over to the row directly behind the defense table. Anna's lips compressed to a slash of red on a parchment face. Jane's spine bent like a sickle. Her head was bowed with hair veiling her face.

Dana paced back and forth. "So who is Sara Marx's biological father?"

"I have no idea."

"You testified that you lived with this girl and her mother, Anna Marx, for over fifteen years, and you don't know who her father is?"

"No."

"What about Sara's other siblings, Seth and Sammy. Who is their biological father?"

"I don't know."

"And Jane's children. Who is their father?"

"I don't know."

"Is the defendant, Abraham Shaw, Sara Marx's biological father?"

"No."

"Are you aware that you are under oath, Mrs. Shaw?"

"Of course."

"Do you know what perjury is?"

"Objection, Your Honor."

"Withdrawn.

"Mrs. Shaw, you testified that the defendant was a 'loving father' to Rachel."

Mother Marylee nodded vigorously. "Yes."

"Does a 'loving father' rape his own daughter?"

Rachel's stomach plunged as she watched her mother's face harden.

"Mrs. Shaw?"

Marylee leveled her eyes at Dana. "No. My husband never laid a hand on that girl."

Rachel fought back the tears from her mother's final betrayal.

As she swallowed the lump clogging her throat, she caught Jane wiping her eyes.

HER father did not take the stand, nor did any other Blood of the Lamb members. There were a few "experts," including a legal scholar who threw out First Amendment language that Rachel really didn't understand, as well as a scientist discussing the DNA evidence. Rachel tried to ignore the anxiety worming its way back into her stomach.

Mr. Brandt's chair groaned as he pushed it away from the table. "The defense rests, Your Honor."

After the jury was instructed and court was adjourned, Dana told them that the defense attorney didn't cross-examine because Rachel's testimony was so compelling it wouldn't have helped their case to cross, and it could have very well hurt them. "You were extraordinary," she said. Glancing at a text message on her phone, Dana's mouth ovaled in surprise.

Moving them to a vacant corner of the courtroom, she said, "You're not going to believe this! We just got the warrant signed by the judge, and CPS is going in, as we speak, to take the children out of the community."

Rachel was dizzy with joy. "Oh, Dana, thank you so much!" Her siblings, and all the other children, would finally be safe.

"No. You girls did it. You had the courage to change everything."

The lawyers said it could be hours or even days before a verdict was reached, but none of them wanted to go back to the hotel. Ernadine sent Irvin across the street to get some sandwiches and drinks. She told the girls to take a bathroom break. The judge had allowed them to use the back restroom reserved for court personnel so that they wouldn't have to deal with questions from the media.

Once in the privacy of the bathroom, they hugged each other.

"I'm so proud of you," Sara told Rachel.

"We did it together."

"Now they all know what he did. What the entire community

did to us and to the other girls just like us," Sara said, moving into the stall.

Rachel glanced in the mirror. It startled her to see a tall young woman with clear confident eyes looking back at her. She was no longer that small scared girl. She smiled tentatively at the woman she had become.

Jane opened the door, looking into the mirror at Rachel. "I believe you."

Rachel was stunned. She turned to face her.

"And I'm sorry . . . for what he did to you . . . and to Sara. And I'm not going to let him hurt my girls."

Girls?

"I'm leaving him. Taking the kids, and I'm gone. I had me another baby just last month. A little girl. I know it's not going to be easy, but I can't . . . I won't let him near my girls."

Sara rushed over to where they were standing. It was obvious that she had heard everything.

The three of them stood there awkwardly. Rachel never realized before how painfully young Jane was: only twenty-three. With four children.

Rachel could almost hear her sister's mind crackling with an idea. "We can help," Sara said, thrusting a business card into Jane's hand. "There's a group in Salt Lake devoted solely toward helping women in your situation."

"We're going there anyway for a few days. Maybe we could take you and the kids with us," Rachel said. A thread of grief, sewn into her heart by Alice's absence, loosened ever so slightly. She missed her so much . . . she missed all of the children.

"Let me think about it. It's all happening so fast. Are you going to Salt Lake to see that boy of yours?"

Rachel's mouth went dry. "Luke? You know where he is?"

Jane's eyes softened with realization. "He helped his mama leave the community one night when Brother Robert was staying at Beulah's house. Rumor has it that they're living in Salt Lake."

Sara grabbed Rachel's hand. "I told you," she said in a squeaky voice.

The thought that they could find Luke there, that they would be in the same city together in just a few days, made Rachel's stomach churn with hope. Dizziness swept over her as her palm found the cool porcelain sink. It was really happening. Maybe, just maybe, they would find him.

"Thank you . . . so much," Rachel managed to say in a guttural whisper.

"I'm glad I could do something to help. I should have done something long before now," Jane said.

The bathroom had stopped spinning. "It wasn't your fault," Rachel said. She recognized the doubt Jane held so closely in her face. It used to be her own. "And it's going to be okay." She took her pen out of her purse and scribbled Ernadine's cell phone number down. "The woman we're with—"

"The black woman?"

"Yes. She's so good to us . . . like a mother." Rachel's eyes swam in tears. "She would love to help you."

Jane took each of their hands. "I'm glad you got someone good to you."

"You will too," Rachel said, the tears now streaming down her face.

"What's the baby's name?" Sara asked, sniffling.

"Hope," Jane said.

"That's beautiful," said Rachel. She was amazed that Jane had had the courage to go against the naming rules Abraham had put in place.

"He was sitting in a jail cell so I named her myself. I want something better for her. For all of them."

"It's the perfect name," Sara said.

THE jury deliberated for less than an hour to reach its verdict. Abraham Joseph Shaw was found guilty on all of the charges. Rachel felt reborn.

As she came out of the building and into the weak winter light, her heart was buoyant. Saying a quick prayer of gratitude, she sucked in the smell of pine and earth, savoring the beauty around her. Snow had fallen during the trial, scouring everything clean with its whiteness.

There he was, under a towering evergreen, waiting.

She lost her breath, unable to move as time stood still. The crowd around her blurred, and she saw only him: black hair tumbling around his face, tie slung around his neck, blue eyes fastened on her, the curve of his lips in the faintest of smiles. Her joints unlocked and she sprang toward him, hurtling past the fullness of the crowd. Chasing her was Sara's voice, clear and pleading, rising above the sea of people, asking the reporters to *give them some time alone.*

His smile spread and his arms opened to catch her. Swinging her around, his body shielded her from view. He crushed her to him. Sweeping his hand through her hair, he cradled her upturned head. His mouth was open, his breath soft and moist and mingled with hers. When he pressed his lips, so slowly, so tenderly onto her mouth, she knew nothing that had happened before mattered to him now.

They stood locked in their embrace, neither of them moving, not daring to end the moment. She felt his heart beating, so certain and true, just like his love. This time it wasn't a dream.

The rest of the world, the place where Sara and her other loved ones existed, beckoned. She looked over Luke's shoulder, and the crowd snapped back into focus. She found her family. Ernadine was flapping her hands, trying to dry her tears. Irvin stood behind Sara, looping his arms around her waist and pressing his lips to her ear. He spoke into it. Just like he had promised.

Sara's cheeks were pink and her hair was spun silk, framing a face that was mantled in joy.